WHAT LIES BENEATH

The Laura Chambers Mysteries

Last Girl Gone

WHAT LIES BENEATH

A LAURA CHAMBERS MYSTERY

J. G. HETHERTON

NEW YORK

This is a work of fiction. All of the names, characters, organizations, places and events portrayed in this novel are either products of the author's imagination or are used fictitiously. Any resemblance to real or actual events, locales, or persons, living or dead, is entirely coincidental.

Published in the United States by Crooked Lane Books, an imprint of The Quick Brown Fox & Company LLC.

Crooked Lane Books and its logo are trademarks of The Quick Brown Fox & Company LLC.

Library of Congress Catalog-in-Publication data available upon request.

ISBN (hardcover): 978-1-64385-020-7
ISBN (ebook): 978-1-64385-021-4

Cover design by Melanie Sun

Printed in the United States.

www.crookedlanebooks.com

Crooked Lane Books
34 West 27th St., 10th Floor
New York, NY 10001

First Edition: July 2022

10 9 8 7 6 5 4 3 2 1

For my parents

PROLOGUE

Sunset spread like a fresh bruise across the western sky, raised pink welts ripening toward purple. Insects chittered and wailed among the trees, lost children crying out, pleading to be found in the thickening dark. Old pines marked the border of the field, a shadowed place where the collective whine guttered and throbbed, a current through the gloom.

But the girl could not hear them.

Her cheap cotton dress had been white once, now worn continuously without washing until it had turned a translucent gray. The left shoulder strap had torn free two days earlier in her haste to hide herself, ripped asunder as she pressed her body down on the grimy rear floorboards of a stolen Cutlass Supreme. She'd managed to mend the strap with a safety pin, but in her present circumstances, not much could be done about the filth.

In the distance, a light flicked on outside a weather-beaten barn.

Her footfalls were silent across the last stretch of pine needles before crunching into raw earth. The field lay fallow, but still she stepped carefully, avoiding sharp rocks and sandspurs, barefoot in the dirt.

* * *

The work light cast down a yellow pool of light, and in its center lay the truck's engine. Bob Merritt swiped a hairy forearm across his face, truncating the little beads of sweat cascading down across his brow. He tried once more to reach, forcing his meaty fingers around the curve of the fan belt before prodding left and right, feeling for the missing part.

He'd been examining the various components underneath the hood for the past two hours. Linda had asked him to drive into town for a gallon of milk and he'd obliged her: kissing her on the cheek, plucking his keys off the coatrack, and climbing into his truck. The driver's seat had borne his weight for more hours and miles than he cared to remember, and just this past year stuffing had begun to erupt out the seams. So it was with care that he'd settled himself down on the faux vinyl, inserted the key in the ignition, and turned it.

Nothing had happened.

There hadn't been even a peep in response, and now, finally, he had it figured. The starter relay had gone missing. Somehow it had worked itself loose and dropped down into the engine compartment.

Bob Merritt puzzled over the various possibilities. He had never seen it happen before, not once in the twenty-five years he'd been repairing trucks and farm equipment. Which bothered him. Something about the way the relay had just up and vanished made his scalp crawl, as if a spider had decided to scuttle its way across his bald spot. But no matter how many times he turned it over in his mind, Bob couldn't quite manage to articulate the source of his unease.

It's nothing, he decided finally.

A missing starter relay was one of those simple, everyday mysteries where an explanation would not be forthcoming. Where did all those socks missing from his laundry end up? When he dropped a screw in an empty room and still couldn't find it, had it slipped into some kind of vortex? Or what about his grandfather? Little ten-year-old Bob had been alone with him when he passed, the papery skin of his fingertips clinging to Bob's hand, their grip tightening like a vise as he slipped into the great beyond. Just before he died, the old man had fixed his gaze on an empty chair in the corner and then pulled Bob close, muttering a few sentences in his ear. All Bob had been able to make out was a single phrase, repeated over and over: *They're here.*

Who was?

Bob had never gotten the chance to ask. The old man had gasped one more time, puckered his lips, and then gone still. Little Bob had been left alone to spend the next few minutes prying his hand free of Grandpop's rapidly cooling grasp.

Now what possible explanation could there be for something like that?

Bob grimaced at the memory, rubbing the back of his neck. It was like his grandfather had always said: "There are stranger things in heaven and earth than we can imagine."

It has to be nothing.

He decided to make one last go of it and pushed up onto his tiptoes, lifting his gut clear of the grille and stretching toward the back of the engine. His fingers forced their way down into the truck's metal bowels, his hand flexed, and this time he felt something, his skin catching on a rough, serrated edge. On instinct he yanked back, quicker than he'd intended, and something sliced through the fleshy pad of his thumb.

He tilted his head back and pressed his eyes shut, not wanting to look at it, knowing he must, forcing himself to open his eyes. A ragged strip of skin hung free; beside that he could see nothing but blood. Red bloomed out of him, coming fast now, as if the stuff had always secretly resented being trapped inside his body, as though it had been waiting patiently for an opportunity to escape.

"Goddamn it," he said, jammed the thumb into his mouth, and turned around.

A girl stepped into the pool of light, and Bob Merritt spit blood all over his shirt.

* * *

They sat at the round kitchen table. Her husband Bob had crafted it himself in the shop out back, sanding the planks and burning an intricate compass rose into the wood surface before lacquering it smooth again. He sat at the south position, like always. Linda was opposite him, his true north—a joke he made before most dinners and one that never failed to earn him a groan followed by a smile. Emily had been stationed to the east since she was in a high chair, and the western chair was always empty.

Almost always.

Emily used a box of crayons to color a picture while Bob and Linda Merritt looked the other girl up and down: unkempt blond hair, dirty in color and in condition; clear, pale eyes in the center of a face smudged dark with dirt; filthy bare feet. She maintained an oddly erect posture, almost formal, with her shoulders back and her feet crossed at the ankles.

Linda reached out and took the girl's hand. "Tell me your name, honey."

The girl just shook her head. She still hadn't uttered a word.

"Tell me your name, and we'll call your parents to come get you."

The girl gazed back at her without moving.

Something was wrong with her, Linda realized. Maybe some kind of learning disability. She spoke slowly, sounding out the words. "What's your name?"

Nothing.

"How. Old. Are. You?"

The girl cocked her head to one side, raised eight fingers.

The same age as Emily.

"What's your name?"

The girl pinched her thumb and forefinger together and traced a squiggly line through the air, like she was calling for the check in a restaurant.

Behind Linda, Emily scratched away on the paper.

"Let me borrow that, sweetheart," Linda said, and slid the paper from east to west. Depicted on the front were a house and a tree and a horse, the creature a passable likeness despite the uneven lengths of its legs. Linda flipped the paper over and placed a black crayon down next to it.

The girl picked it up and began to write. Her scrawl trembled across the page as if formed on an Etch a Sketch, thin wisps of letters that took great effort to form.

I AM DEAF

Linda touched her ear, shook her head.

The girl nodded.

Linda held two fingers up to her eyes, touched her mouth. *Do you read lips?*

The girl shrugged and took the paper back, and they waited for her next message.

I AM LOST

"I know, honey," Linda said, then caught herself, realizing she'd answered out loud again. With an exaggerated nod of understanding, she asked, "Your name?"

The girl just stared back at her.

Linda took the paper and formed some of her own neat block letters in the corner, turned it back again.

NAME?

The girl didn't answer. Her face remained smooth and expressionless, without any hint of understanding.

Linda turned to her husband. "Call the sheriff."

Outside the kitchen window, lightning danced and flickered on the horizon. Distant thunderclaps echoed like gunshots across the empty fields. Bob picked up the phone and held it to his ear for a moment before replacing it in the cradle. "Line's dead."

Linda frowned.

"Must be the storm," he said.

* * *

Emily Merritt was excited to have a roommate. Her parents had been promising her a sibling for most of her life, but somehow one had never appeared. Her momma didn't mention it much anymore, and Emily understood perfectly—some promises had to be broken. She had been alive for eight years, plenty long enough to know that things didn't always work out the way you planned.

The girl sat cross-legged on the floor of Emily's bedroom in a pair of last year's animal-print pajamas, the cuffs riding up across her forearms and calves. She pawed her way through Emily's toy box, pulling out the plastic horses and unicorns, the stuffed animals, the blond-haired dolls, arraying them like soldiers in formation.

"You want to play dolls?"

The girl nodded emphatically.

Emily reached out and ran her fingers through the hair of the nearest doll before glancing back at the girl. "Is that what we should call you? Doll?"

The girl's lips pulled back from her teeth to form a silent snarl, and she jerked her head back and forth, her greasy locks bouncing from side to side.

No!

Emily understood that just fine, no sign language necessary.

Over the girl's shoulder, Momma's head poked around the edge of the doorframe. "You girls doing okay?"

"We're playing dolls," Emily said. She caught the girl's eye and pointed toward the door.

Linda Merritt spoke in the same overpunctuated cadence, inventing her own crude sign language on the fly. "You stay here tonight. Tomorrow we'll be able to call your parents or just drive you home." At the appropriate moments she pointed to the ground, tapped an imaginary watch, held her pinkie and thumb up to her mouth and ear respectively, and pulled back and forth on an imaginary steering wheel.

The girl studied her for a moment, then shrugged and nodded once again.

"You can use the bottom bunk. Emily, take her with you to the bathroom before bed, okay?"

"Yes, Momma," Emily said.

Her mother let the door half close behind her, but her last words drifted in from the hallway: "Sweet dreams."

Together they ordered the stuffed animals into rank and file, dressed the dolls for war, rode the horses hard. At a quarter to nine Emily Merritt stifled a yawn and led them to the bathroom—her guest brushed her teeth with her finger—then pushed the girl into bed and drew the pink covers up under her chin. The girl gazed up at Emily, her pale, colorless eyes unblinking, a laser-like stare that felt charged with meaning. Electric, as if she were trying with all her might to beam a message directly into Emily's head.

Emily's toes tingled; the crown of her head started to buzz. She felt the weight of the girl's eyes on her, but no matter how hard she concentrated, she couldn't discern their meaning.

"What is it?" she whispered, reaching out and touching the girl's cheek.

But the girl didn't even blink.

The moment faded, and Emily's certainty faded with it, eroding away until it was nothing at all. There had never been any message, no hidden meaning behind that flat and glassy stare. She blushed and turned away, embarrassed to have misread things so badly. "Good night," she said, then scampered up the ladder and laid her head on the pillow, listening. Beneath her the girl rolled side to side, adjusted the sheets, and finally went still. Ragged inhales and exhales turned to slow, even breaths.

Emily sighed and tried to close her eyes. It was all very strange, she thought. When her mother asked the girl questions—her name, her address, her phone number—the girl couldn't seem to understand. But playing together, the two of them hadn't had any trouble communicating.

None at all.

* * *

It was the girl's father who'd taught her the trick of pretending to be asleep.

She curled up on her side, careful to avoid any focus on her breathing. The more she thought about her breaths, she knew, the less they would adhere to the smooth exhalations of actual slumber. Some of the techniques made sense only if she were being watched (a slackening of the facial muscles, the lazy drooping of her eyelids), but she couldn't excise these parts of her performance from the whole. All were of a piece, a bit of method acting that allowed her body to achieve total relaxation despite the paper-thin mattress. She summoned her patience, fighting the urge to scratch or otherwise adjust herself, and in time she sensed her new friend on the top bunk lapse into unconsciousness.

What kind of person could allow themselves to fall asleep all alone with a stranger? What kind of family would let a fox into their henhouse?

The girl had been underestimated may times before. Usually at this moment she would be struggling to parse the cause as overconfidence or naïveté, but with the Merritts, she knew it was the latter. She'd seen them take in her bony knees and her dirty dress, and instantly they'd written her off as nothing more than a lost little deaf girl. They looked at her and saw only a wounded lamb.

Mistakes like that were cause for punishment. The girl was only eight years old, but it was a lesson she had learned many times over.

Still she did not move, and her hush worked a spell on the house, a potion made of patience and quiet in just the right measure. She waited, waited until the storm passed, until the only sounds were the persistent chirping of the crickets and the occasional creak of joists settling in the cool night air. With care, the girl rolled out from under the covers and dropped onto all fours, distributing her weight, and scuttled across the room into the hall. Outside the door to the master bedroom, she sat back on her heels and listened.

From inside came arrhythmic snoring, the occasional rustle.

She nodded to herself and moved on, down the stairs and through the parlor. She stopped and removed a photo album from its place on the bookshelf, stood next to the front door, and thumbed through the pages. The pictures confirmed her suspicion: the Merritts were happy in a way she would never manage.

The door had an unusual number of locks. She stretched on her tiptoes to remove the chain at the top, then flipped open the two dead bolts. Despite not wearing a watch, she was certain it must be the appointed hour. She cupped one hand around her ear and pressed it against the door, straining to hear.

Outside, nothing but night sounds.

The girl reached out, caressed the antique brass doorknob, and hesitated for a moment before rapping her knuckles once on the dark-stained wood, a knock so insubstantial it almost didn't exist.

Then she waited.

And soon, from the darkness, came a knock in return.

PART ONE

NORTH CAROLINA TO RESUME EXECUTIONS;
SHOTGUN SLAYER BARROW SCHEDULED TO DIE

By Laura Chambers

Sept. 13, 2019

RALEIGH, N.C. — Convicted murderer Simon Barrow has been scheduled for execution in October, according to a spokesperson for the North Carolina Department of Public Safety. Barrow will be the first prisoner put to death since 2006, when executions were stayed by a federal court case that began the state's de facto moratorium on capital punishment.

Two previous governors have declined to take the legal action necessary to resolve the impasse and allow the state to once again administer lethal injection. According to sources in the North Carolina Department of Justice, however, a new pro–death penalty policy has been in effect since the resignation of Governor Greg Teasdale last year. Between that and a favorable ruling by the Fourth Circuit Court of Appeals in Richmond, and with the Supreme Court declining to hear the case, the current administration now has a clear path to reinstituting capital punishment.

"A thirteen-year delay in sentences handed down by juries is an unconscionable arrest of justice," said North Carolina Senate Majority Leader Ronnie Jayne. "Victims' families have been in limbo for more than a decade, denied the closure they so surely deserve. Simon Barrow is the poster boy for the death penalty."

Barrow, the so-called Shotgun Slayer, was convicted of the murder of Robert and Linda Merritt in Hillsborough, NC, after entering their home and then shooting them during the early morning hours of August 22, 1996. Because there was no evidence of breaking or entering, he is believed to have gained access via an unlocked door earlier that day and then concealed himself, a "lying in wait" scenario deemed especially heinous. Barrow refused to testify on his own behalf at trial and has never confessed to or even commented on the crime.

"The brutality of these murders resonated through the community," said Orange County Sheriff Michael Fuller, then an assistant district attorney and part of the team that prosecuted Barrow. "The Merritts were ordinary, hardworking people, victims in the truest sense of the word. Working this case is what turned my career into my calling."

Lt. David Whitley, today a part of the Orange County Sheriff's Office Investigations Division, was the first deputy on the scene in 1996. "This is one offender who absolutely deserves the maximum punishment," he said. "Just imagine the sort of person who would hide himself in your house, wait for you to go to sleep, and then do his worst. To this day, the Merritt home is the most affecting crime scene of my career. I'm just sorry the daughter had to see it."

The victims' daughter, Emily Merritt, was the sole survivor of the attack. Eight years old at the time, she was discovered more than twenty-four hours later in a cluster of nearby woods, reportedly so devastated by her experience that police could never get a clear statement.

The execution will be carried out by lethal injection at Raleigh's Central Prison. An exact date has not yet been announced.

CHAPTER

1

ADDICTION RAN THROUGH the Chambers family tree like an invasive species, a creeping vine that choked off the individual branches as surely as hands around a throat.

For her father it had been booze—liquor, brown, straight, room temperature, anytime, all the time, the sword and shield he made sure never to be without. If alcohol could be considered a weapon, then her father had been well armed. His own childhood had been less than idyllic, but more than that she could not say. Only after his death had she learned her paternal grandparents were called Agnes and Rupert; in all her life, he never spoke their names.

Her mother's poison was twofold: food, and attention at any cost, the kind of desperate need to be seen that makes people want to look away. Diane Chambers lived on a diet of empty calories washed down with gossip. She thrived on news of others' misfortune, always certain she'd just moved up one notch in a zero-sum game.

Diane said, "Your article this morning nearly gave Fran McInery a coronary."

"I don't know her," Laura replied.

Diane laughed, but her cackle quickly became a cough. She held up a finger, pressed the clear plastic oxygen mask to her face, and sucked down a breath before continuing.

"Didn't think you would. She barely goes outside these days, just to church. And to the Food Lion when she thinks no one will be around to see her load up on snack cakes. Did you know she was best friends with Linda Merritt growing up? The two of them always together, co-captains of the cheerleading squad. Beautiful. Popular. Of course, back then she had a metabolism like a hummingbird. Hard to picture her getting tossed in the air these days, isn't it?"

"Were you a cheerleader too?" Laura asked.

Diane gave a heavy-lidded blink. "Don't change the subject. You almost sent her over the edge, I heard. I bet her heart looks like a goddamn head cheese."

Laura's mother was clinically obese, somewhere north of three hundred pounds, but Laura was careful to avoid pointing out the hypocrisy. "I'm sorry to hear she's not well."

"Don't be. She never wanted to be seen with me back when she was queen of Orange County High. Why should I treat her any different now? Still, I'll never understand why Bass Herman prints this tripe."

"He's the one who asked me to write it."

"Better to leave the past in the past, I always say."

"If something's newsworthy, I write about it."

"People like to hear about nice things too, you know," her mother said.

"Not many folks would consider an old friend's heart attack nice, but you seem to be enjoying yourself just the same."

Her mother sniffed. "She's the one who quit returning my calls."

Thunder crackled in the distance. The farmhouse where Laura had grown up stood in the center of a hundred acres cleared of any trees, a roughly square area about four-tenths of a mile on each side. Sight lines in every direction were long, so Laura just pulled open the woolen curtains on the nearest window.

Row after row of field corn marched all the way to the tree line. Each stalk stood nearly eight feet high in the late-summer heat. Above them, clouds clawed their way over the horizon, one piling on top of another, rising and thickening into an anvil shape ten thousand feet high. Purple thunderheads, pulsing with internal lightning, roiled at the base.

Severe weather is common in central North Carolina, especially thunderstorms during the summer months. Humid air hunkers near ground level while cool wind pours over the top of the Appalachians in the west. The hot air wants to rise, and rise it does, enormous swords of cloud thrust upward through the atmosphere. The distant trees hissed in anticipation, leaves rubbing like sandpaper, presaging what was possible during a storm like this: barrages of lightning strikes, hail, downbursts powerful enough to rip away the roof of an exposed house.

A faint whiff of ozone clung in Laura's nostrils. She knew that smell.

"I have to close the windows."

Her mother frowned. "For this little drizzle? I thought I raised you to have a few ounces of guts."

Laura ignored the jab and climbed the narrow stairs two at a time. The farmhouse was almost 150 years old, built in the era before air conditioning or central heating, and no real improvements had been made since Laura was a child. Her father, drunk, had tottered his way up a ladder to the roof and installed a new television antenna. She'd been in kindergarten then, excited for improved reception on her cartoons, appalled that she might have to watch her father break his neck in order to get it.

For cooling, they had always relied on the house's original design. The deep, shadowy front porch had been built as a refuge from the hottest hours of the day, and for the interior they depended on cross-breezes threading between opposite windows. For as long as she could remember, all the windows had been left open between May and October each year.

The door to her old room squealed on its hinges.

Inside she found her scarred wooden bed, its bare mattress still covered with the same Minnie Mouse bedspread of her youth. Shoes with cracked soles, pairs she'd last worn in high school, waited in a neat row on the floor of her closet. The corner of the room featured a fireplace bricked up sometime around the turn of the century. A rough wooden mantel ran above it, home to pictures and trinkets she had collected from elementary school onward.

Laura scanned the items, her eyes landing on the only photograph that featured her mother. She wiped dust away from the frame.

Her mother had always been a stout woman, but twenty years ago she had possessed a kind of raw athleticism. In the picture she had the same dark, beady eyes, but muscular legs poked out of her olive hiking shorts and her skin had the high, windburned color of someone who lived their life outside.

It was a person Laura couldn't remember.

She'd left her hometown immediately after high school and only come back two years ago when she had no place else to go. She'd found her room looking exactly like it did now, a time capsule filled with memories she'd never wanted to preserve. For almost a year she'd lived back at home, but the relationship between her and her mother had eventually bubbled over, just like it always did. She'd found herself a cheap apartment, and her mother, it seemed, had put things back the way she liked them.

She ran a finger across the top of the dresser. Dust clung to the surfaces. Spiderwebs hung like cotton off the window screens and in the corners.

"How long since you've been up here?" she called down the stairs.

Her mother said something she couldn't hear, then dissolved into a fit of coughs.

The window seemed welded to its jamb, but on the third pull it rattled down to the sill. She twisted the brass latch shut and made her way through the other upstairs rooms, closing the house up tight. In her mother's room, the master bedroom, she found the same thin layer of grime on everything. The room smelled dank, stale, as if the air had been undisturbed for some time.

Back downstairs, Diane Chambers was fiddling with the valve on her oxygen tank. "Damn thing won't come open."

Laura pushed her mother's hand aside and twisted it experimentally. "It's all the way open already."

"Then it's spent."

"How many have you used so far?"

Diane glowered up at her, not answering.

"I'll just check the closet. I know how to subtract."

Her mother paused. "Seven," she said finally.

Laura let herself sink down into a musty armchair in a corner of the living room. "That's almost all of them. You don't get your delivery until, what? Tuesday?"

"I'll be fine."

"You must be using it more often than not. The doctor said if—"

Her mother reached up and, with a savage yank, ripped the plastic tubing out of her nose. "I'm fine, damn you. And I'm not going to sit here under my own roof and listen to my daughter give a lecture."

"Seems like sitting is just about the only thing you do. You're sleeping downstairs now?"

"My easy chair is just more comfortable."

"But you could climb the stairs if you wanted?"

"If I wanted," her mother agreed.

Laura was about to tell her to prove it when the lamp next to Diane began to glow more brightly. A high-pitched electric whine filled the air, the lightbulb popped, and the room plunged into darkness.

CHAPTER

2

LAURA SHUFFLED TO the wall and felt for the light switch, working it back and forth a few times with no result.

"Power's out."

"You don't say," her mother drawled.

She checked her phone. "No bars either. Must have knocked out the cell tower too."

"Remember where we keep the light?"

In the pantry Laura found a cheap plastic flashlight hanging from a nail. It threw a weak beam, the batteries nearly dead, but it was better than nothing. She put a finger on the nail. It had been her father who hammered it into the wood. For as long as she could remember, this nail had been the location of the emergency light. Power outages had always been frequent on the Chambers farm, and they'd needed a light where it could be scooped up quick. Back when her father was around, the emergency flashlight had been substantial, the heavy metal kind that swallowed D-cells one after another. This current dollar-store iteration had her mother's name all over it, Laura thought. But she'd never once seen Diane swing a hammer. The nail was her father's handiwork. She hadn't watched him put it there, but she knew it just the same.

She lifted the plastic light in one hand and cast the beam around. It landed on dirty dishes in the sink and on the roaches skittering back under the garbage can.

She made her way back to the living room, and the two of them sat across from each other without speaking for a while, with only the patter of rain on the roof and the whistle of wind under the eaves to break the silence. Laura wondered for the thousandth time why she even bothered with these weekly visits. *Because one day soon, she'll be gone,* her inner voice reminded her. Moments like these would become, if not exactly good memories, then at least valuable by virtue of their scarcity. A time was fast approaching when the phone line connecting them would go dead permanently and any chance to fix things would be lost forever.

Her hand rested on the arm of the chair, and the flashlight shone on the previous Friday's edition of the *Hillsborough Gazette* resting on the coffee table. Her article about Simon Barrow's pending execution was above the fold, laid in next to an awkward picture of Sheriff Fuller and Lieutenant Whitley she had taken herself.

Neither Fuller nor Whitley had been enthusiastic about talking to her for the piece, which hadn't surprised her—her relationship with local law enforcement could charitably be described as frosty. But the Merritt murders had a special place in local legend. Simon Barrow had never spoken a word to the police or anyone else, as far as Laura knew, and the mystery surrounding his motives was fertile ground for speculation. She'd heard variously that the killings were the work of drug addicts, Satanists, and Democrats who'd committed the crime as part of a plot to dismantle the Second Amendment. Even after twenty years, Hillsborough was a place where "Shotgun Slayer" was a popular choice of Halloween costume.

The execution of Simon Barrow was sure to make waves in such a small town, and both Fuller and Whitley were seasoned enough to understand the importance of public relations. A simple "no comment" would only fuel the rumor mill.

That hadn't meant Laura rated a real meeting, however. She'd had to corner them on the courthouse steps with a camera in hand. They'd allowed her to snap the photo, but then Whitley had turned and walked into the courthouse without another word. Fuller had spoken with her less than five minutes before making an excuse to leave.

From the coffee table, she pulled the paper into her lap and shined the sickly beam of light down on the front page.

The two men stared up at her. Fuller made her think of a politician in his dark-colored chalk-stripe suit, a red tie knotted across his throat in a thick double Windsor. Whitley looked like he'd rolled out of bed in yesterday's clothes: a rumpled dress shirt, wrinkled slacks, unkempt hair clinging to the side of his head. Neither man had bothered to smile for the camera.

"Still the same old Laura."

She glanced up at her mother, now just a murky shadow on the other side of the room. "Excuse me?"

"Even as a child you used to spend hours looking at yourself in the mirror."

"It's a newspaper, Diane, not a mirror."

"A paper with your name up there at the top, and you with that just-same slobbering look on your face. Pride's a sin, no matter how you commit it."

Laura remembered the cheap plastic mirror she'd pasted to the wall, the glass baby-food jar of hair ties and barrettes, the broken-handled brush fished out of the trash. "I was just a kid. I think Jesus would have wanted me to look nice."

"Or maybe it was envy," her mother said. "You were copying Emily Merritt, as I recall. The two of you were thick as thieves back then."

Laura glanced down to the article and then back to her mother. "Is that what this is about?"

"She was the leader, and you were the sidekick. You'd have drunk up her backwash if she asked."

"She was my best friend."

"Oh, it was more than that, I suspect."

Laura felt the words slip out before she could stop them. "I wanted to *be* her, do you understand? She liked herself. Her daddy wasn't a drunk. Her momma used to take her to the beauty parlor to get her hair done."

Diane scoffed. "Everyone thought they were the perfect little family, even you—that's the thing I could never stand. The Chambers farm and the Merritt farm have almost the same acreage. They're backed right up against each other, separated by nothing but the railroad tracks and a bit of woods. On paper we should have had the same station in life. But everyone loved the Merritts. And us? We were no-good trash. Couldn't you at least have the decency to hate them for the unfairness of it?"

"Hate them," Laura repeated, turning the words over in her mouth. "I never did. Maybe in time I'd have grown into it. Maybe when I got to be your age."

"Yes, I suppose you never had the chance." Diane leaned forward and tapped the newspaper in her daughter's lap with one bloated, sausage finger. "Because the world went ahead and evened itself out, didn't it?"

Laura didn't answer. They sat in silence again, and together waited out the worst of the storm. After an hour the wind faded and the rain slowed. The lights flickered once before coming back strong, and the phone in Laura's pocket buzzed with a series of notifications.

"I always figured you must have hated her but kept it to yourself," Diane said.

"Who? Emily?"

"Thought that's why you wrote the story, taking your opportunity to smear them the way they deserve to be smeared."

"I barely mentioned her."

"Not in this one. More to come, I'm sure, between now and when they slip him the needle."

Laura stood and headed for the door. Through the window she could see her car parked at the bottom of the porch stairs, waiting to carry her away. All she had to do was climb inside, turn the key, and go. Just leave, she told herself, and don't look back.

Her mother reached up and turned off the lamp, its light too bright after so long an absence.

"The Merritts were never perfect," she said. "Remember that."

* * *

The car was a 1969 Dodge Dart GT convertible, the 273 V-8 model with a three-speed manual transmission. It had come off the manufacturing line in B5 blue, a silvery metallic azure, but decades of exposure to the elements had diluted its paint toward gray. It had a hard brake pedal and a stiff clutch, and the rear-wheel drive setup meant it tended to skid around corners in wet conditions or at high speeds. The tires would slip their way across asphalt and set a person's heart to hammering in their chest.

The Dart was more than a few years past its prime, in other words.

But Laura loved it just the same. The key turned smoothly; the exhaust burbled to life. Rain still rustled against the Dart's canvas soft-top as she fiddled with the mirror until it displayed a view of the backyard. The sound reminded her of wet nights spent in a military-surplus pup tent erected behind the house. She would set it up on Friday afternoons and stay outside until Sunday, coming inside only to use the bathroom. Her mother never bothered to check on her, and that had been fine by Laura—avoiding Diane was exactly the point—but from time to time her father would poke his head in the flaps.

"Rain coming," he would say.

Her father had been a man of few words, and usually that would be the end of their conversation. Sometimes he would stay with her, though, and she would sit cross-legged in the light of the lantern and listen to his stories.

That was one of her good memories.

Laura shifted the mirror back into position, fished her phone out of her hip pocket, and hit the unlock button.

The screen populated with a series of missed calls, all from the same number. It had a 252 area code, which covered the northeast quadrant of the state and ran all the way to the Outer Banks, far from Hillsborough's location in the central Piedmont. Whoever was on the other end, they had called her four times in quick succession, one call right after the other.

Whenever she'd had reason to call someone back to back, Laura thought, it had always been out of desperation. Calls that close together were a message in and of themselves. If she looked hard enough at the screen, Laura could almost read it.

S.O.S.
Emergency
Pick up now!

The caller had also left a voice mail. She thumbed through to listen, then almost dropped the phone when it started to vibrate.

It was the same number, calling her again.

"Hello?"

"To whom am I speaking?" The voice belonged to a man.

"This is Laura Chambers."

A pause on the other end of the line. There was a low voice murmuring in the background and what might have been the back-and-forth swish of windshield wiper blades trailing across glass, but it was all very faint.

She checked the screen to see if the call was still connected before pressing the phone back to her ear. "Are you still there?"

"Yes, Ms. Chambers, I'm still here. This is Lieutenant Whitley from the Sheriff's Office."

"I see. I must have taken down your number wrong."

"No, I'm sure you didn't. We need to meet."

"Tomorrow in your office?" she asked.

"No, it has to be now." He paused. "Do you have a rain jacket?"

CHAPTER

3

THE RAIN DIDN'T fall so much as hang in the air, a hazy mist that pulled the world slightly out of focus. The crisp red rectangles of brake lights mutated into rose blooms bleeding at their edges, hundreds of them marching one by one down the solitary open lane of I-40.

A state trooper directed traffic, and she wore a plastic bag cinched over the broad brim of her campaign hat. Rivulets of water shuttled down its creases, streamed across her neon reflective jacket, and soaked the seams of her beige uniform pants. She kept her arm moving in a circular motion, urging the cars along.

Laura stood twenty feet back, waiting for the trooper to notice her, clad in an old squall jacket she had rescued from her mother's front closet after Whitley's phone call. It was zipped up under her chin, but the hood had ripped years ago and subsequently been trimmed away. The jacket worked as intended in all other ways, however, and in the Chambers family, waste was a sin as great as pride.

Water plastered her thick hair down onto her head and up against the back of her neck, adding what felt like ten pounds of weight.

She pulled out her phone and opened up a messaging app called Signal, popular among journalists as a way to communicate with sources. It had end-to-end encryption for texts and calls, a level of security that no one—not the government or even the nonprofit foundation that offered the service—had the ability to crack. Initially it required a phone number to register, but there were ways to sever even that last thin thread connected to a real identity.

Heard anything about an accident on the interstate?

She didn't expect a quick response, but the answer came almost immediately.

Something serious, it's all over the police band. Why?

Whitley called me, asked for meet at accident site.

A pause, then: *Why bring you in? Doesn't make sense.*

Hence my message. Any guesses?

No. He doesn't like you, Laura.

An understatement, she thought, and signed off.

Road flares sputtered and hissed at regular intervals, painting the trooper's face in fleeting glare and shadow. Laura gave a vigorous wave, and the trooper finally noticed her. She held up a hand, stopping the traffic for a moment, and Laura hurried across to the other side.

Whitley had given her directions on how to reach the accident site without getting stuck in the congestion. She'd parked her car on the shoulder of Orange Grove Road just before it crossed above the interstate, cut through a backyard, and then walked down the concrete embankment onto the shoulder. Now it was easy, just a quarter-mile hike in the rain with every passing vehicle spraying her with puddles and gravel.

Up ahead, two highway patrol cruisers crouched like lighthouses in a dark sea, their turning reds and blues reflecting down the black mirror of the pavement. She passed a second trooper, who popped the top off a five-gallon bucket and swung it toward a gap in the oncoming traffic. Sand spilled out across the roadway, covering a darkened strip fifty feet long and blending into a merlot-colored slurry. A car rolled over top of it, the tires crunching like boots in fresh snow.

For a moment, Laura didn't understand what she was looking at. Then realization dawned, and her eyes went wide.

The trooper caught the look on her face. "That right there is why we've got to cover it up," he said. "Lookie-loos always slowing down the traffic. We call this a two-bucket job. Yes ma'am, not too many of those."

She moved past him to an unmarked car parked to the side and knocked on the window.

The electric motor whirred, and it opened an inch. "Mind getting in the back? It's unlocked."

Laura opened the door and slid in, the wipeable vinyl seating crinkling under her weight. She hesitated for moment, then pulled it shut behind her. Doors in the back seats of cop cars only opened from the outside—now she was trapped back here until someone decided to let her out.

"Better this way," a second voice said.

The interior light clicked on and the man in the driver's seat turned around. Even with his face partially obscured by the honeycomb cage between them, Laura recognized Whitley.

He was perhaps forty-five, with close-cropped red hair. The part down the side was straight as a ruler, every strand held in place by stiff hair gel. His complexion was unnaturally smooth and freckled, almost boyish. He wore shirtsleeves rolled up to the elbows, a muted tie, and an expression of menace that lived in a permanent sneer at the corner of his mouth. The overall effect was off-putting, like that of an aging, angry cherub with a gun dangling under its arm.

His jaw worked, lips smacking, as he chewed a gray-looking piece of gum. "This is Captain Bynum," he said, and pointed with his thumb toward the passenger seat.

Bynum bothered to turn only halfway around, but Laura guessed he was more than a decade older than his partner, past the age at which he could retire with a full pension. He was already dressed for it, in a loose khaki fishing vest and bucket hat, and he sported thick-framed black glasses with Coke-bottle lenses.

Without a word, he passed her his card through the divider.

"Sorry to call you down here in the rain," Whitley said.

He didn't sound sorry.

Laura tried for a winning smile. "All part of the job."

He scratched at his chin. "You report on a lot of accidents like this?"

"Depends. What makes this one special?"

"Fatality," Whitley said. "Plus we're having some trouble identifying the body. No identification on her person and no car, which means no glove box to root around in for a registration."

Laura frowned. "I don't understand."

"This wasn't a two-vehicle collision. The victim was on foot, and she was hit by a Chevy Silverado. The four-door, extended-cab variety. Metal versus flesh. When push comes to shove, metal always wins."

She said nothing.

"Can you tell us who it is?" he asked.

"How would I know?"

Whitley just watched with his beady black eyes, studying her reaction.

Laura swallowed hard. Her eyes darted toward the window, to the roadway with its paltry mound of sand concealing the carnage beneath. The implication of his question washed over her.

Her throat tightened, threatening to close up. "This is someone I know," she managed.

Whitley nodded.

"Who?"

"Haven't the foggiest. Knock, knock—anybody home? Are you listening to what I'm saying, Chambers?"

She turned her focus back to Whitley and noticed for the first time the look of supreme satisfaction on his face. There were at least a hundred and one better ways to make a death notification, but the lieutenant had chosen this method specifically because he would get the chance to watch her squirm.

"She's a smear on the pavement," he continued. "We got no idea who it is. That's what *you* need to tell *us*."

In that moment, Whitley's arrogant sadism was a kind of gift. She had always been prone to stubbornness in the face of mindless authority, and now that same reflex refocused fear into anger. She batted down the sliver of rising panic in her chest and forced herself to think straight.

There was an inherent contradiction to these questions. How could they be certain the victim was someone Laura knew and yet simultaneously not know her name? Whitley was leaving something unsaid. What was he holding back?

"Quit playing Columbo," she said. "Skip to the end and just ask me what you want to ask me."

He turned to Bynum. "I heard she had a mouth on her. You think that's the kind of thing Frank Stuart likes?"

Bynum said nothing; he didn't bother to look at either of them.

"Oh, that's right, I forgot—he doesn't like or dislike anything anymore, does he?"

Bynum shrugged.

"'Cause he's dead. He got gutted like a fish. People don't have opinions with a head full of worms and whatever the fuck else eats people up under the dirt."

"Dave," Bynum said quietly.

"Maybe the big juicy one that got his brain has some of Frank's personality rattling around inside him. Maybe it likes 'em mouthy too now. Maybe you can fuck it instead, Chambers. Just like old times."

Bynum reached out and put a hand on his shoulder. "Let it go."

Whitley shook off the hand. "I will fucking not," he said, and got out of the car. He ripped open the rear door, came in beside Laura, and pulled the door shut behind him until she heard the latch go click.

Laura tried to slide across to the far side. Before she could, he caught her by the wrist and yanked her close. The human quality was gone from his eyes. Cords bulged in his neck. His chest was heaving under his shirt, and a V-shaped stain had formed down its center. She could smell the sweat on him, musky, like the cage of an animal.

A cage she had been locked inside.

"You don't get to do that," she said, and was pleased to hear the steel in her voice.

He glanced behind him. "No one around. Who's going to stop me?"

She tried to pull away, and he tightened his grip. The small bones connecting her hand and arm began to compress, flexing inward, pain radiating all the way up to her elbow. Whitley's forearm looked like it were made of stone, thickly muscled, the blue veins standing out in relief as if they'd been carved by a sculptor.

She said, "You're hurting me."

His bloodless lips set themselves into a hard, white line, and for a moment she thought he would add one last ounce of pressure, shattering her wrist. Instead, he glanced down and saw the way his fingers were digging into her flesh. The gleam in his eyes died, and he let go of her arm. But he stayed where he was, too close for comfort, and he never stopped staring at her. His expression was defiant, challenging her to be the first to move away.

She kept still.

"Tell me the name," he said.

"I can't tell you what I don't know."

"You're a little liar." He practically spit the last word, and flecks of his saliva spritzed her on the cheek.

"When I want to be," she replied. She rubbed the spot where he'd grabbed her; the purplish marks left by his fingers were perfectly legible. "But it won't be a lie when I file a complaint."

Whitley's face was a slab of marbled beef.

"And I'd bet good money it won't be your first complaint about this type of thing."

He opened his mouth, closed it again.

"No," she continued. "It never seems to be the first time, does it?"

For a moment he gritted his teeth so hard, Laura expected to hear a molar crack. Then, finally, he seemed to deflate. "Open the door," he said to Bynum, who exited the car and did as he asked. Whitley pushed past him and stormed up the highway shoulder, seemingly without regard for the rain or the passing traffic. Bynum stayed, continuing to hold the door open in an almost courtly fashion. He waited patiently for Laura to climb out.

Once she had, he said, "Stuart . . . he and Whitley knew each other quite a while."

"Is that supposed to be an apology?"

Behind the thick lenses, his eyes appeared magnified. He blinked twice before looking down at his shoes. "We still need you to take a look. A young woman is dead, and I'm asking for your help. Please."

She gave a quick nod, then followed him up the shoulder.

The place where Whitley had touched her felt greasy, and on every other square inch of her skin was a sensation of grime. She'd never been more grateful for the rain. It trickled through her hair and across her hands. She turned up her head and let it run over her face, into her mouth, washing away the sensation that she had been corrupted by something unclean. She had never felt water as cold or as pure, and she savored it all the way to their destination.

CHAPTER

4

THE WIND TORE at their jackets, finally releasing its grip when they reached the back of an ambulance. The rear doors stood open. She was hesitant to enter another enclosed space, but almost as if he had anticipated her objection, Whitley had crammed himself all the way forward on the opposite bench. Bynum hoisted himself inside, and Laura sat next to him, perched on the very edge of the seat, ready to slip back through the doors at a moment's notice.

In the space between them was a gurney covered with a white plastic sheet.

Neither Whitley nor Bynum spoke, and the silence began to grow uncomfortable, working its way into her like bamboo shards under her fingernails. In the realm of interrogation techniques, this was a simple one, but as her editor Bass Herman liked to say, "If it's stupid and it works, then it's not stupid." Moment by moment, it grew more difficult for Laura to bite her tongue.

Mostly because a single question had printed itself on the surface of her mind. Whitley seemed convinced that she was personally familiar with the victim, but if Laura had been forced to make a list of people close to her, she could've counted them on one hand. She imagined this was what it felt like for most folks when the phone rang in the deepest, darkest hours of the night, when the voice on the other end said, "There's been an accident," the overwhelming powerlessness of a moment in which there was nothing to do but wait for the next words to be spoken, words that would answer an unspoken question, a question birthed the moment the bell inside the telephone had begun to titter and wail.

Who?

That was always the question when the police came knocking.

Who's hurt?

Who's dead?

Or in her case, *When they pull back this sheet, who am I going to see?*

It was Bynum who finally broke the silence. He doffed his hat, revealing a horseshoe of gray hair. "We're sorry to do this to you."

"What my esteemed colleague here is trying to say is, there's not much left to see. Doesn't matter. Ready to take a peek?" Whitley gave a half-hearted sneer, aiming to recapture his air of superiority, but all the arrogance and ego had drained out of his voice. A smidgen of dread crept onto his face.

At that moment, Laura knew it was going to be bad.

"Do it," she said.

He and Bynum lifted the sheet by opposite corners and folded it down, exposing the gruesome result of some terrible experiment. What happens when a human being is hit by two and a half tons of automobile? Metal wins, Whitley had said.

About that much, he was right.

The woman's head lay turned to the wall, and the side of her face pressed to the gurney had been pulverized beyond any recognition. Someone had wiped the other part of her face clean of blood, leaving a startling juxtaposition between the two hemispheres, a horror-show version of before-and-after pictures. The mouth had locked in a ghastly twist of fear; the eyes, round and blank, were the eyes of a dead fish. Only hours ago, this face had belonged to a person. It had been malleable, the conduit of expression, the window on her inner life.

Now it was nothing more than a rubber Halloween mask.

Laura braced herself, then took a good, long look. Mask or not, she didn't get even the barest flash of recognition.

"Know her?" Whitley asked.

Laura just shook her head.

The woman wore only a soaking-wet slip. Her feet were bare, the bottoms scraped and cut. The side of her chest looked caved in, and both knees were bent in the wrong direction.

Laura pointed questioningly toward the shattered legs.

"She's tall," Whitley said. "Was tall. People don't curl up into a ball when they see a truck coming, they stand up even straighter than normal. It's a moment of shock before they get ready to dive one way or the other."

"Which way did she dive?"

"Neither, she ran out of time. And because she's tall, she didn't get pulled underneath. They think the truck caught her half-turned, and she rolled up and over the hood until the driver's side pillar stopped her."

The woman's final moments played like a movie in Laura's head, making her stomach churn. She took a breath and reminded herself it would all be over soon. This was just a moment in her life, a brief slice of time where she was trapped in a coffin-like box with two men, one of whom disliked her very existence, and a woman who would never dislike anything again. This moment would pass like all the others.

"Tell us who she is," Whitley demanded.

"I don't know. She wasn't carrying anything with her?"

Whitley and Bynum exchanged a look.

"Where are the rest of her clothes? Her shoes?"

He shrugged. "What you see is what you get. What about this?"

She watched as he used the end of his pen to lift the slip's fabric away from her upper torso. The undamaged side of her rib cage featured a tattoo, abstract at first glance: filled-in circles the size of dimes, each surrounded by a zigzag pattern and connected to the others by dotted lines.

"Recognize that?"

"No, I'm sorry," she said.

The blood seemed suddenly redder than before, and her head started to swim. She shoved up against the door, eager to leave.

Whitley clapped his hands together once, the report echoing in the enclosed space. "Look again," he said softly.

She glared at him, her breath whistling in and out her nose, but he met the anger in her eyes and reflected it right back. She wanted out and away, out of the back of this ambulance, away from Whitley and Bynum, away from the corpse pressed between them, and far away from the choking sensation the torn and savaged body had deposited in the back of her throat. If one more glance was what it took—

Laura gritted her teeth and looked.

"You know her. Don't lie to me."

She turned to Bynum. "I've done my civic duty. I've been more than accommodating—walked through a storm, tolerated his insults, endured his cryptic questions. No more. You think I know this person? Fine, tell me how. I think I'm entitled to hear it. I'm owed an explanation."

"You're owed. You're *owed*?" A red flush mottled Whitley's face again. "What a world-class—"

"Enough," Bynum said sharply. "She's right. Tell her."

Whitley glanced at his partner, and when he looked back at Laura, the tiny hook in the corner of his mouth had returned. He looked like the cat who ate the canary, which made her nervous. She'd been waiting for the other shoe to drop.

So when her phone started to buzz, she nearly jumped out of her seat. She tugged it free from the hip pocket of her jeans and looked.

The same number that had called her before lit up the screen.

"Important call? Go ahead, take it."

She swiped to decline. "I thought I said no bullshit."

"Who called you?"

"You know what? I am going to file that complaint. Tomorrow morning I'm going to march down to—"

"Who just called you, Laura?"

Her name sounded mealy in his mouth, and it brought her up short. "You did," she answered. "Before, when you called me . . ."

But he was already shaking his head. His tongue made a *tsk-tsk* sound against his slug-white lips. "No, no, no, not so fast."

"Christ," said Bynum.

Whitley just gave a closed-lip grin.

"Quit it. Just tell her already." The older man sounded tired.

"Tell her what she's won, Johnny!" Whitley intoned. He reached between his legs and held something up.

A plastic evidence bag twisted back and forth under the dome light. Inside hung a cell phone, spider-webbed cracks radiating across the screen, and on the back side, a reddish-brown stain that looked like two overlapping fingerprints.

Through the plastic, he slid his thumb across the screen, but nothing happened.

"I don't—"

Whitley held up a finger. "Quiet now."

Her phone vibrated again in her hand.

"Earlier you asked me why I called you. To answer your question, Laura, I didn't call *you*. All I did was hit redial."

The rain picked up again, fat drops thrumming on the ambulance's roof. Laura didn't speak.

"When you picked up, you were surprised it was me," Whitley continued. "You were expecting someone else."

"It was just a random number."

"No one here seriously believes that. Give me the name of the person who owns this phone, and things won't get more serious for you than they already are."

She bristled at the threat. "You're the one with the evidence in your hand—am I a saved contact? Do you see a history of us talking?"

"The history was erased. Your number is the only one in the call log. Four calls, as a matter of fact. Doesn't seem very random to me. Can you understand why we're having trouble taking your story at face value?"

"I don't have the information you're looking for," she said.

"Convince me."

"You're asking me to prove a negative." She let out a sigh of frustration. "I never spoke to this person. There was a power outage earlier; it took out the cell tower too. You can confirm that yourself."

Whitley frowned.

"I missed the calls. I didn't speak with anyone this evening."

"You spoke with me," Whitley said.

Laura corrected herself. "I never spoke with anyone up until you."

"It's possible you communicated another way. She could have erased messages, whole apps if she wanted to. Maybe she planned to do the same with the call log and just never got the chance."

"That's not what happened."

Whitley reached out his hand, palm up. "Mind if we take a look at your phone, put our minds at ease?"

"Absolutely not."

"Problem?"

"Big problem," she said. "It wouldn't be ethical."

Whitley seemed surprised. "Ethics," he said. "Heard those weren't your strong suit."

Now it was Laura who felt a flush cross her face. "I work with confidential sources. I can't let you look at my phone."

"We could get a warrant," Whitley said.

"Be my guest. I'll be happy to comply."

"You're sure you want to refuse?" Now Whitley showed her all his yellow teeth. "I can make life very difficult for you."

She set her jaw, nodded.

Bynum spoke from his corner. "That's enough."

"Captain, this is at least obstruction—"

Bynum waved him off. He turned to Laura. "He's right, you know. This is a major inquiry, you understand?"

"It's a traffic accident."

"No, it's a homicide."

Whitley cut in, surprised at his partner's candor. "There's no reason to give her that!"

Bynum waved him off again. "It's a homicide investigation, which means we need to proceed along the lines of motive. Without knowing who she is, that will be exponentially more difficult for us. You want me to get a signature from a judge? I'm here to tell you that when I get done describing the circumstances out here tonight, the judge is going to sign."

"If I knew her name, I would tell you, Captain."

Bynum blew out a breath. "I'm sorry to say it, but Whitley is right. Under these circumstances, no one's ever gonna believe those calls were just a coincidence."

His caterpillar-like eyebrows climbed his forehead in an expression of concern.

"Four separate calls, from a few minutes to just a few seconds before the accident," he continued. "In fact, between the call log and the witness statements, we're pretty sure calling *you* is the absolute last thing this woman ever did."

CHAPTER

5

When it came to her love life, Laura Chambers had never had much luck. For most people that would have meant a string of bad dates over worse food. Their relationships ended in breakups, not funerals.

If only things were that simple, Laura thought.

Frank Stuart had lived in Hillsborough all his life, and his neighbors had watched him grow up to be handsome, well intentioned, and trustworthy, the sort of man who became a cop for the right reason: because he liked helping people and wanted to make a career of it. Folks around these parts still believed in quaint truisms like right and wrong, or good triumphing over evil, so the loss of someone like Frank Stuart went beyond injustice. It represented a fundamental imbalance in the scales of the universe, a terrible karmic mistake.

Someone had to be responsible.

Someone must be held to account.

Laura had liked him as much as anyone, and guilt over his death still lingered in all the quiet moments of her life. She and Frank had both been early risers, and together they would drink coffee and watch the low-hanging mists burn away under the morning sun. Now she drank her coffee alone, the empty chair on the other side of her table stiff with accusation. Occasionally she managed to forget, but someone like Whitley would always be sure to remind her. Hillsborough was a place where everybody knew everyone else, so it wasn't unusual to turn around at the supermarket or the dry cleaner and find herself face-to-face with one of Frank's old high school buddies or a sheriff's deputy he'd worked with for years.

Reactions varied. Most just glared from a distance, but a few had given her a piece of their mind. She sensed they were aiming to get a specific response from her, as though they had rehearsed the confrontation over and over in their minds and now that it was here, they needed Laura to play her part too. Whether she'd been cast as a defiant, mustache-twirling villain or a sniveling apologist begging for forgiveness, she was never sure.

It didn't matter. She never gave them anything, never even made a face. Just walked past them like they didn't exist.

Back in her car, she massaged the place where Whitley had caught her around the wrist. There would be an ugly bruise, and for a moment she considered whether to make good on her threat to file a complaint. No, she decided, the optics would be terrible. There would be blowback, and it was easy to imagine how it would play out during early-morning conversations in the diners and late-night conversations in the bars.

Laura Chambers is as far from supporting the police as a person can get. She hates the Orange County Sheriff's Office. Hell, she got one of 'em killed, now she's trying to get another one fired.

And just like that, whatever goodwill she had left in Hillsborough would evaporate. Folks would no longer consent to be interviewed; sources would dry up. A complaint would compromise her effectiveness as a reporter. Whitley knew it too, she was sure. He knew he could get away with hurting her because no one would bother to listen. She might as well cry wolf.

Well, she wouldn't give him the satisfaction, Laura decided. She would keep her mouth shut and play the hand she'd been dealt.

On the passenger seat, her phone still displayed the voice mail icon: a message, just waiting for her attention.

The absolute last thing this woman ever did.

Those had been Bynum's words before she'd shoved her way out the back of the ambulance. He and Whitley had known about the missed calls, but the one call that had connected had somehow escaped their notice.

Laura hadn't lied exactly, at least not directly. She was certain Whitley would count lies of omission as bad as all the rest, but Laura thought that if a person wanted answers, it was their responsibility to ask the right questions, and as a person in the professional question-asking business, she could summon little sympathy for a career police officer who couldn't do it well.

She could have volunteered the voice mail, of course, but under no circumstances would she listen to it for the first time in the presence of the police. Laura would never admit it to Whitley's face, but he had a point: so many calls in a row, right up until the moment of this woman's death, must mean something. Whatever information was on the message, however, had been intended for her ears alone.

The lieutenant's jab about ethics had hit home because he was right. In the past, Laura had bent the rules when it suited her ends. The confidentially of sources, however, was one rule she took very seriously indeed.

Alone at last in her car, Laura held her finger over the button that would start the recording. At the last second, she moved her finger down, opened Signal, and returned to the encrypted message thread from earlier.

Can you meet?

Sunday night, busy.

Important.

A pause. Then: *The office, half an hour.*

She signed off.

Alone in her car once again, she called up the voice mail.

She pressed play and held the phone to her ear.

* * *

The *Hillsborough Gazette*'s office was empty. She let herself in through the front door, made sure to lock it again behind her, and took the stairs two at a time to the second floor, where the modest newsroom was located.

Bass had a habit of abandoning his office precisely at five, and no one on staff bothered to stay much longer once the boss was gone. By now he was doubtless balanced on a stool at one of the local watering holes, holding court with a martini in his hand.

She flipped on a few overhead lights.

A row of darkened desks led to a single pebbled glass door. It hung open, left ajar in his end-of-day exodus. No one besides the editor in chief rated an office at the *Gazette*. Bass had traditional ideas about the nature of a workplace pecking order, but Laura had almost managed to wrangle an exception to that rule.

In the very back of the main floor, she pushed open a door under an emergency exit light. She emerged onto the top of a cement staircase. Just on the other side of the landing, another door led to what might have been intended as a small storage room or perhaps a roomy broom closet. It had cinder block walls, with a small slit of a window up at the top, and just enough room for one desk, one chair, and one filing cabinet. Technically it was a private office—two different doors separated her from the main newsroom—but she had never heard Bass or anyone else complain about her using it.

Maybe it had something to do with the lack of air conditioning.

Even during a storm, the air in Laura's office hugged her like a blanket. She sat, wiped away the film of sweat developing on her forehead, then plugged her phone into her computer and dumped the voice mail onto her hard drive. She put a copy on a small flash drive, slipped it in her pocket, and went back through the doors.

She stopped, confused.

All the lights were out again.

The first electric flashes of an imminent thunderstorm shimmered through the skylight, painting the newsroom in black and white. The two rows of desks looked like stone sarcophagi, the room itself a mausoleum.

The first boom of thunder shook the windows in their panes.

A hand gripped her shoulder.

She spun around, heart pumping, and found herself staring into the rheumy eyes of Bass Herman.

"Keep the damn lights off," he said. "I've already got the air conditioner running twenty-four seven in this infernal heat, and now the lights too? You were the last person I expected to catch wasting electricity, Ms. Chambers."

"You scared me, Bass."

He frowned. "Are you listening to me? By the end of the summer our power bill will be so high, I'll be able to jump off the top of it and put an end to my misery."

He was in his late sixties, overweight, and owing to the banker's shirt under suspenders he wore as his daily uniform, the cigars he favored, and the great shock of white hair he kept swept straight back from his face, a person could be forgiven for mistaking Bass Herman for a British diplomat just so long as he kept his mouth shut. He was North Carolina born and bred and proud of it, and it showed in his accent. Whenever he spoke, he displayed his pronunciations like a badge of honor.

"Ms. Chambers," he said. He drew out the title, making it sound as if it ended in a *z*—*Mizz Chambers*. "To what do I owe the pleasure?"

She described her call from Whitley and gave a brief sketch of the accident.

"And you thought that sufficient reason to pull me away from pressing matters—"

"That's what we're calling sitting at the bar, telling the same story for the tenth time now?"

"Sitting with the *mayor*, I'll have you know."

"Oh. He pass you any interesting tidbits?"

"Lord no, the man is a certified moron."

A ghost of a grin sneaked onto his face, the first chink in his armor. He liked to wear the costume of a hard-charging, take-no-prisoners newsman, but after two years working for him, Laura understood her boss well enough to know that his shell was brittle and underneath was a soft interior. Practically mushy.

"And so you contacted me via your ridiculous special software?"

Bass wasn't a complete Luddite, but it was Laura who had explained the basics of public-key cryptography and the way it would allow them to pass secure messages. The need for such measures at a small-town newspaper was limited, but Bass—who as a boy had written his journals in a code of his own invention and as an adult had immensely enjoyed the works of John le Carré—delighted in his newfound digital prowess.

She remembered explaining how to keep their messages private: buy a SIM card with cash, make sure to avoid any cameras, download the app, and afterward smash the new card with a hammer. Bass had lit up like a kid on Christmas morning.

"You're the one who insists we talk that way. You love it."

He scowled. "I hate that you know that about me. Yes, fine, it makes me feel like a spy. Or a Boy Scout with a walkie-talkie."

They repaired to his office, where he turned on the desk lamp and waved his nicotine-stained fingers in her direction, gesturing for her to sit down. "Tell me the rest, then."

She was careful to steer clear of the gorier details. Bass had been in the profession long before Laura was even born, but he was also the product of a career spent in small towns dotted across the South, places where a canceled bake sale or a lost dog rated a first-page story. Laura, on the other hand, had cut her teeth as a crime reporter for a few major dailies, most notably the *Boston Globe*, and she'd seen more than her fair share of violence.

No one ever got used to watching people tear each other apart, but the experience forced you to cultivate certain coping strategies. Either that or be torn apart yourself.

She'd been present when Bass Herman had gotten a firsthand glimpse of the underbelly of the human experience last year, and it had not been pretty. She remembered a sickly paleness in his face, the way he'd clutched at the wall as if he were about to vomit.

So Laura stuck to the facts.

At the end, Bass tented his fingers, thoughtful. "And you have no idea who she is?"

"None whatsoever."

"Interesting." He tapped a fingernail against his front tooth. "Let's have that flash drive now."

He plugged it into his computer and turned the volume up to the maximum.

At first it sounded like the static of a bad connection, but then Laura picked out the pattering of raindrops. Not white noise at all but rather the swirl and whoosh of wind at the height of tonight's storm. Another sound cut through the background noise: the heavy, labored breathing of someone under immense physical strain.

Then came footsteps slapping on the ground, and a sudden crash that could have been a person running through underbrush.

Another moment of tense breathing . . . then silence.

They listened to it again, and a third time.

"Doesn't help much," Laura observed.

"Strange the caller never speaks. Why bother?"

Laura didn't know.

"Did she leave the message on the first call or the last one or somewhere in between?" Bass asked.

"The last one."

He leaned back in his chair. "No reason not to pass it along to the sheriff's office. Lieutenant Whitley and Captain . . ."

"Bynum."

"Yes, I know Bynum. He's the head of records."

"Not investigations?"

"Job's been empty for a few months now, probably he's just filling in. Don't let him fool you, though—they picked him as substitute teacher because he knows what he's doing. He ran investigations until, oh, maybe three or four years before you moved back. Then he kept threatening to retire, so they shifted him over."

"Fine, I'll give it to Bynum."

She stood to leave.

"Sit down, Ms. Chambers." When she was back in the opposing chair, he continued. "You've done plenty of good work for me over the last eighteen months. Plenty."

She waited.

"You have done every assignment I put on your desk and done them well. That was the only reason I hesitated to hire you—I suspected you'd find the sort of stories we do here to be small potatoes compared to the ones you used to work on."

"Do you hear me complaining?"

"Not once."

"Is this your weird way of telling me I'm getting a raise?"

He ignored her attempt at levity. "Not a peep. You come in on time, you sit at your desk, you do your job. You never push back. Most of the time you're as quiet as the person who recorded that message for you."

"Still can't tell if this is a commendation or a tongue-lashing."

He gave a great sigh. "You're capable of more, and we both know it."

"Oh, and this is my big chance." She didn't bother to conceal her sarcasm.

Bass threw up his hands. "Who knows? Who ever knows until they try?"

"Whitley is never going to talk to me, he's—"

"Whitley's a vulgar ape, but he's not the real problem."

"—never going to take my calls. Even if I come bearing gifts and just hand over the recording, it's worthless. It's less than worthless. He'll know I didn't give it to him until I'd listened to it myself, which will set him off again."

She held up her bruised arm.

A shadow passed over her editor's face. "He did that to you? He ought to be locked up."

"Well, you can't have it both ways," she threw back at him. "I'd sooner get blood from a stone than get Sheriff Fuller to give him more than a slap on the wrist. And then you can kiss my career as a crime reporter in these parts good-bye. Would you ever give up the work just to extract some small measure of personal justice?"

Bass Herman studied his own lap. When he spoke again, the fire had gone out of his voice. "You're right, of course."

Again Laura stood to leave, and this time he didn't try to stop her.

She made it to the top of the stairs before she heard him call her name. When she turned, he was leaned over some other reporter's desk, yellowy hands flat on the surface supporting his bulk, and in the dim, abstract dark of the outer office, he reminded her of nothing so much as a bear in a cave, older than it had any right to be but still sure-footed on its own turf.

"Forget Whitley then," he growled. "What about that woman?"

"Good night, Bass."

"She *chose* you, Ms. Chambers. Of all the people she could have called in those last few moments of her life, you were the one. Now tell me why."

"Could be she was crazy, out of her mind."

He didn't bother to comment on that explanation; it sounded weak even to her own ears.

"Could have been a wrong number."

"Four calls, Laura." He never used her first name. "Four times isn't happenstance; it's desperation. As far as I'm concerned, she begged for your help. Won't you bother to find out why? Don't you at least owe her that much?"

She didn't speak, but her silence was an answer of a kind. Leastwise there must have been a quality to her quiet that satisfied him, because he located a scrap of paper on the desk, jotted down a few words, and held it out to her.

"I've got a cousin with the medical examiner. Let's set up a meeting, just to see if there's anything worth writing about. I'll make sure he's expecting you."

CHAPTER

6

LAURA HAD EXPECTED to drive to Raleigh, to the Office of the Chief Medical Examiner. The OCME was responsible for investigating "unexpected death"—a broad category. Jurisdiction ranged from those in otherwise good health unlucky enough to die alone, so-called unattended deaths, all the way up to suspected homicides. The institution had satellite offices in other corners of North Carolina, but here in the central part of the state, the remains of all those who met violent ends ended up in a boxy office building tucked away in a nondescript corner of the capital. Laura had been there once before. Afterward, she had walked to the art museum in less than fifteen minutes.

But to her surprise, the meeting place had been set for a funeral home right here in Hillsborough. Laura pushed through the front door into a musty viewing room filled with church pews. At the front was a squat pedestal, gray and unadorned. It could have been metal or concrete or natural stone. It looked sturdy enough to support the weight of a coffin, empty or otherwise. Right now it held nothing but air.

The lights were off, the windows curtained.

"Anybody here?" she called out.

"This way."

The voice was muffled, but it seemed to come from the back of the room. She skirted the pedestal, pulled aside a heavy velvet drape, and found a door.

The hallway beyond reminded her of a hospital, and here the odor of wood polish and mildew gave way to a smell of bleach so strong it seemed to burn the fine hairs in her nostrils. A second door at the end of the hallway stood half-open.

Laura paused for only a moment before going inside.

"Pittman," the man in the room said, and he shook her hand. He was about thirty, tall and stick thin. Tufts of jet-black hair jutted up from his skull, but he was otherwise so pale as to be colorless. Even his eyes were a shade of dirty water. He tried on a smile, but it seemed too big for his face, a rictus grin.

She pulled back her hand.

Pittman must have sensed her discomfort. "Don't get much interaction with the public," he said. "Didn't mean to scare you."

"Not your fault," Laura replied. "I'm out of practice myself. Two wrongs don't make a right, my mother used to say."

"Mine too," he said, and that seemed to put him at ease. She took in the rest of the room. The medical examination setup at the OCME had included an overhead light, an adjustable table, trays, implements, and drawers, all in the same stainless-steel finish. Here were components of identical purpose, but it was as if she'd been transported a century back in time. Both the fixtures along the wall and the table in the room's center were made of a bone-colored porcelain, and under her feet was hand-laid mosaic tile.

The floor sloped slightly, at its center a drain. The tiles surrounding it were stained a deep maroon, like the mouth of a child who has eaten too many black currants.

Pittman noticed her expression. "Retro, don't you think?"

"Practically Victorian. Nothing like in Raleigh."

"You'd be surprised at the overlap. Not that much has changed when it comes to poking around inside a person. It's all still scales for taking weights, and tweezers, and things with sharp edges, of course." He pointed to an expensive-looking camera on the end of a flexible tube that was angled straight down at the tabletop, then to a monitor that displayed the feed. "Optics are better. And the biggest difference is probably the chemistry. Most of the square footage back at the office is devoted to lab space."

"So why have you work out of a funeral home?"

"It's hot."

Laura furrowed her brow.

"The weather," he explained. "When it gets this hot, more people die."

"Older folks without air conditioning, you mean."

He nodded rapidly, his shoulders following behind his head in a kind of shimmy. "Sure, some of that. But there's more violent death too. More accidents, more homicides. And if it's humid, forget about it. Things get even worse. The coolers fill up, so they start asking places like this to store the bodies. And if it's possible to do the autopsy on-site, they send me out."

"Dr. Pittman—"

"Just Pittman," he cut in quickly, the kind of reflex that comes from repeat experience. "I'm not a doctor, just a tech. An autopsy tech."

"Did you do the autopsy on the Jane Doe from the interstate?"

"I did."

"Here?"

Again he nodded.

On the wall behind him loomed rows of drawers stacked on top of each other. A sheen of condensation clung to their metal surfaces.

"Is she in one of those?"

"Yes," he said, and paused. "Would you like to see her?"

Laura was careful not to look at the drawers again. She kept her gaze fixed on Pittman. She was very still. "No, thank you. Would you be willing to answer some questions, though? About your findings?"

Pittman sucked his teeth and stared at the tips of his sneakers.

"Problem?"

"I just don't know if I can," Pittman said.

Bass had arranged the exact time and place of the interview, and his last message had made it seem like a done deal. Now that appeared to have been wishful thinking. Laura was disappointed by Pittman's reticence but not surprised. Agreeing to talk to a reporter in theory was one thing. In practice, with the red blinking light of a recorder in one's face and the prospect of having one's exact words preserved in print for everyone to read, second thoughts were common.

The good news was that Pittman hadn't outright told her to go to hell. His hesitation was an obstacle, to be sure, but more the stumbling-block variety as opposed to the razor-wire-fence type. Laura had seen it before, and she had finessed this very situation more times than she could count. Instead of pressing him for answers directly, she slid the conversation sideways into less fraught territory.

Keep the conversation alive—that was the name of the game.

"Smoke?" she asked.

He accepted her cigarette and led her out a back door into an alley. Stepping outside felt like walking into a greenhouse, and her shirt stuck to her back within seconds. They leaned against the brick wall of the mortuary in silence for a while.

"My girlfriend wants me to quit," he said after a bit. "She says it stinks."

"You should listen to her."

"But I just—"

"What?"

"It's a stupid reason. I like smelling like smoke better than I like smelling like dead people."

"It's that bad?"

"They don't send us the good ones." He held the cigarette in his mouth and scratched away at the top of his head with both hands like a mole snuffling in the dirt. "Soap doesn't get rid of it. It gets on my clothes, even the ones I didn't wear to work. Smoke covers it up, though."

Laura said, "The lesser of two evils."

"Can you believe she doesn't even want me telling people what I do? But I get it. The next question is always, 'What's the worst thing you've seen?' And then off we go, down the rabbit hole. Not good dinner party conversation."

"Well, that depends on the dinner guests, doesn't it?" She pivoted again. "Bass said you're his cousin."

Pittman smiled, not the obsequious overstretched monstrosity from earlier but his real smile. It was mostly sad, Laura thought.

"What do you think?" he asked.

"I think Bass is the sort who has a cousin in the ME's office, and a brother-in-law who works for the sheriff, and a niece who works for the mayor, and probably his godson's barber knows a guy at the courthouse. A real big family, in other words."

That earned her a chuckle. "Yeah, we've got the same uncle. Name of Franklin, first name Ben."

"What a coincidence—that's my uncle too."

Pittman displayed the last quarter-inch of cigarette between his fingers. "You treated me half human at least, so we'll call it even. But you can't use my name, all right? You can't even say where you got this stuff. I could lose my job."

"Deal," Laura said, and they shook again.

Back in the room with the drawers, he cleared space on a desk in the corner and spread out a modest collection of printouts and photographs. The pictures were close-ups. The shocking destruction of the body was on full display, but only in bits and pieces. Unfocus your eyes a bit, Laura thought, and it was possible to forget they'd ever been parts of a person in the first place.

She started the recorder on her phone and set it down between them, one eyebrow raised in Pittman's direction.

He nodded his assent and pointed to a stack of papers clipped together. "I made you a copy of the report."

"Summarize it."

"All right," he said, and scratched the top of his head again. "The truck killed her."

"I think everybody figured that much."

"But if the truck hadn't hit her, she probably would have died anyway. She'd been shot."

Laura was quick to shake her head. "No, that's not right. I saw her in the ambulance. I'm here about the Jane Doe from the freeway, remember?"

He riffled through the photographs as efficiently as a blackjack dealer and found the one he wanted. To Laura it looked like all the others: patches of undamaged skin juxtaposed with horribly abraded flesh, and places where the wounds went deeper still. She couldn't tell what she was looking at and said as much.

Pittman circled a particular spot with his finger. "Doesn't stand out to you, I'm sure, but it's actually pretty obvious if you've done more than a thousand autopsies. This is a gunshot wound. The bullet went in here"—he flipped through the pictures again, retrieved a second—"and came out here. Through and though. The injuries from the truck are extensive and conceal it at first glance, but the damage from the bullet is significant on its own. It's a large-caliber bullet, from a rifle. Probably a three-oh-eight or thirty-aught-six."

"A hunting round," Laura said, a note of skepticism in her voice.

He glanced at her. "There's no mistaking it. I can even make an educated guess that she was shot from a distance. There's no stippling and no residue on the skin or the garment she was wearing, so close range is out of the question. Additionally, though, we can trace a line from the exit wound back to the entrance wound and estimate the projectile's angle of impact. I'd put it at nearly ten degrees off the horizontal plane. Some of that is probably attributable to the parabolic flight path, but the more likely explanation is terrain: the shooter and the victim were at somewhat different heights when the trigger was pulled."

"So the shooter could have been standing within speaking range on a slight rise. That's no great distance."

"It's possible," Pittman allowed. "As I said, an educated guess based on experience. They'll make room for her at OCME now, and a pathologist will retrace my steps, someone with a degree who can testify in court if it ever gets that far. But I promise they'd tell you the same thing. Look, take a gander here."

He showed her a photograph of the bottom of Jane Doe's feet, pale and wrinkled like they'd been in the bath too long. At the bottom, it was possible to discern the porcelain table currently sitting just behind them.

"You can see the soles are cut and scraped like the rest of the body, right?"

Laura nodded.

Pittman shook his head. "Not right at all. The level of coagulation signals these wounds occurred antemortem. Also, I extracted foreign material from a few different locations. On the torso, on the exposed sections of the limbs, that material is consistent with road rash. Bits of asphalt, gravel, things like that. In the feet, though, the composition is totally different. I found soil, very small rock shards, even a bit of pine needle."

"From the woods, in other words."

"All consistent with the scene as I understand it," Pittman said. "There were no shoes found, so presumably she was barefoot. The information I have is that no one saw her walking on the shoulder, and there's no other access to the interstate at that spot. What's surprising is the extent of these injuries to the soles. Combined with the gunshot wound and the slides I took of some of her blood vessels—"

He stopped speaking.

"What is it? Please, go on."

"I shouldn't speculate. That's not what we do here. Fitting the evidence together into a narrative isn't my job."

"Speak for yourself," Laura said.

He fixed her with a look. It was more than hesitation; an expression of worry flitted across his face.

"You knew those rifle rounds. Do you hunt?"

"Not since I was a girl."

"What did you hunt?"

"Deer, mostly."

His eyes darted sideways, and when Laura followed his gaze, she realized he was looking directly at one of the metal drawers.

"The energy of a round like that is immense. It caught her in the shoulder—that's the only reason she survived as long as she did. But by the time the truck hit her, most of her blood had already drained away."

"She was still on her feet," Laura countered.

"Running for her life through those woods, it seems to me." Pittman turned back in her direction and blinked rapidly, as if a mote of dust had caught in his eye. "Like a deer, when the first shot fails to kill. Like she was being hunted."

Laura collected her copy of the autopsy report and thanked him for his time. He spoke again just as she reached the door.

"You must be real special, you know."

"How do you mean?"

"I've been feeding tips to Bass for years, but never once did he send any of his other reporters to meet me."

CHAPTER

7

"SHIT, DON'T YOU wear a watch?" Don Rodgers's voice grated like sandpaper, and he pulled the phone away from his mouth to let out a sharp hack of a cough.

"It's barely nine o'clock."

"We're asleep over here, goddamn it. Call back at a decent hour."

"Weren't you just spouting off about your love of late-night drinking?"

"Yeah, but this is different."

"How?"

"This is Monday. I save the hard stuff for the weekend—I'm a civilized man, after all." In the background, Cooper barked once. "Easy boy, easy. That's right, it's your very best friend in the world."

Laura asked, "You think dogs understand sarcasm?"

"Oh hell, did you call me up to criticize Cooper's sense of irony, or was there some other pressing matter about which you wished to speak?"

"If you're not busy," she said.

"It's the middle of the goddamn night, Laura. Spit it out."

* * *

She located the rutted track he called a driveway and bumped the Dart down to the front of a shabby, single-story house with a wrap-around porch. The scrubland here had once been farmed, for what crop she could not imagine. To dig and find clay soil was no surprise in Hillsborough or the surrounding areas, but this place had gotten the lion's share.

She teased him about it from time to time, like the previous year when he'd invested countless hours trying to grow vegetables and earned back nothing but a handful of cherry tomatoes—and then a single strawberry he'd presented as dessert at one of the dinners he cooked for her every few weeks. He'd cut it in half, popped his part into his mouth, and winced—it was sour as a lemon.

With a serious face, she'd advised, "You should have tried pottery instead."

The house stood dark. A quick knock rattled the door in its frame, but there was no answer.

Don Rodgers had been the elected sheriff of Orange County, North Carolina, during Laura's high school years. By the time she'd moved back to her hometown, however, he'd long since retired. But it was Rodgers alone who had been willing to hear her out once Frank Stuart was killed, and it was Rodgers and his dog who had pulled her out of the blaze that had nearly ended her life.

Standing now on his front porch, she reverberated with a memory. Snow had been falling. It had been late December. The air had been very cold, and she recalled her own detached surprise at the sudden shift between fire and ice when man and dog had managed to drag her to safety. His ugly, slobbering face had been just about the best Christmas present a girl could ask for—and the dog wasn't much to look at either, if she was being honest.

This evening she found Don Rodgers in the canted red barn at the back of his property. He was elbow deep in a tractor engine, and it was Cooper the bloodhound who insisted on greeting her. He came bounding around the edge of an old hay bale, floppy ears ricocheting off the side of his head, and when he smelled her identity, he lifted his snout toward the roof and let a great bay escape his throat.

She knelt and scratched the spot he liked, right between his eyes, and he took off out the door, wet nose pressed to the ground, hot on the trail.

"He don't do that for me," Rodgers said, and wiped his hands on an oily rag.

"Sorry to drop in like this," Laura said. "Thought I'd find you in your robe or some such."

"That's one of the things they don't tell you about getting old: sleep is elusive. All the conditions have to be just right. The temperature, the mattress. Gotta get your back aches down to a low simmer."

"Cooper seems to nap more than he doesn't."

Rodgers frowned, perplexed. "You're right, now that you mention it. He's older than me in dog years, but he sleeps like the dead. It's a genuine mystery."

"Maybe he just has an incredible ability to ignore ringing telephones," Laura suggested.

"I should unplug it at night. But I am now officially up and about, so let's have it."

He wore ratty jeans and cowboy boots, and a Stetson that might once have been white crammed down over stringy blond-gray hair. He leaned against the unfinished wood wall of the barn, chewing tobacco and occasionally spitting into an empty beer can while he listened.

She filled him in: the accident, Whitley redialing her number from the victim's phone, the voice mail from the same number just before the woman died. When she told him about the gunshot wound and floated the notion that someone had stalked this woman like a deer, Rodgers gave a low whistle.

"You haven't heard anything?" Laura knew he still had plenty of friends in the Orange County Sheriff's Office.

"Naw, nobody tells me nothing. They find the bullet?"

Laura shook her head.

"And the message was blank," he repeated.

"It was like someone dialed the number and then just left the line open. No one spoke. I don't even think she hung up; the recording just timed out."

"You're sure you didn't recognize her?" Rodgers asked.

"Why does everyone keep asking me that?"

Rodgers spit into the can, which made a twang like a metallic guitar string. "'Cause it's the only thing that makes a lick of sense." He saw the look on her face and held up his hands in surrender. "Don't get pissed at me, Laura. Think—I'm asking you to think is all. I'm not that asshole Whitley, making an accusation of dishonesty. Run it through your mind is what I mean. You saw things you didn't know you saw. I know you did, because that's always the case. Now you've got to sift through it again."

From anyone else it would have sounded patronizing. But Rodgers was a keen investigator, she had seen as much firsthand, and he had just shared an insight about his method.

Laura did her best to play back the image of the woman's face. Her expectations were low, because dead people were always strangers to her. The subtraction of life changed them somehow, the transformation from person to object making them unrecognizable. She so often thought of a person's face as the sum of its features, but then she witnessed the dead and realized their true aspect had always been in the furrow of an eyebrow or the stretch of a smile; they hid in the spaces between parts. A person's face could not be separated from its animation, and when it turned static for the last time, it also became foreign to her.

"She was dead," Laura said, "and half her face was crushed, but no, I don't think I knew her."

"Tell me what else you saw."

She took a breath. "Everything was wrong. None of it made sense."

Rodgers grunted. "Go on."

"First of all, the phone was a burner, one of the cheap ones you can buy at a mall kiosk or gas station. When people call a reporter with a phone like that, it's because they want to keep it a secret. They're doing something they shouldn't be, or someone they know is, and they don't want it traced back to them."

"Or they've just got bad credit," Rodgers said, settling comfortably into his role as devil's advocate.

"She wasn't wearing a jacket, just a very short, thin dress. It might have been a slip. Do you know what a slip is?"

"I was married for many years, Laura."

"That was all she had on, not even underwear. And she was barefoot."

"Maybe she got knocked out of her shoes. That really happens, you know."

She shared the rest of the forensic evidence gleaned from the medical examiner's office and described the location of the accident. Rodgers knew the spot she was talking about, where the freeway approached an interchange and the two directions of travel split before joining again.

Laura procured a pad and pen from her back pocket and drew a crude sketch. "According to Pittman, the forensic evidence says she was running through the woods just before. The accident happened in the westbound left lane, so she must have climbed up from here—"

"Embankment's awful steep there," Rodgers observed.

"—or she could have come from the other direction, but it's unreachable, completely boxed in and surrounded by the interstate on all sides. She would have had to cross the eastbound lanes first, then gone through the wooded area in between, then tried to cross the other direction of traffic."

"Maybe she got lucky the first time."

"And not so lucky the second."

"One way to reach that spot may be more difficult," Rodgers said, "but it doesn't seem to me its relative ease should play much part in our calculation. You're describing someone in a panic, someone who had already been shot. It was probably a surprise to her when she ran up against the interstate, and then she tried to cross from whichever direction."

"If she climbed the embankment, she could have come off Occoneechee Mountain." Laura indicated the spot on her crude map where a state natural area abutted the highway.

"Or she crossed almost the whole damn thing and came from the southwest. There's nothing out that way for miles except fields and trees," Rodgers countered. "On the other hand, maybe the difficulty reaching that spot was the whole point. If there's someone after you and you see a chance to slip onto that island, you might just take it. There are worse hiding spots."

"Then how'd she end up in the left lane?"

"There are better hiding spots too." Rodgers paused. "Maybe hers turned out not to be good enough."

"You were in the Army," Laura said. It wasn't a question.

Rodgers gave her a suspicious look. "Who told you that?"

"My father. Back when you used to write me underage drinking tickets, he told me to show you some respect. Said you were in Vietnam like he was. Said you won a few medals."

"We're the same generation, me and your dad. We didn't serve together or anything like that, but we both grew up around here, so I knew him just to say hello to before the war."

"And after?"

"By the time we got home, your old man didn't much like to say hello to anyone, as I recall."

"What did you do in the Army?"

"Infantry."

Laura pressed him. "Specifically, though."

He spit again, into the dirt this time. "I don't talk about that stuff."

"He was the same way."

"Sounds like he blabbed to you plenty about ol' Don Rodgers."

She held up her hands, the same way he had earlier. "No need to raise your voice."

"Well, it wasn't his story to tell. Sounds like you already know what I did."

"You were a sniper," she said carefully.

He crushed the beer can in his hand and lobbed it into an open garbage can. "And what's that got to do with this poor girl?"

Laura collected her thoughts for a moment, and when she was ready, she said, "If we went out there together, you and me, to the accident site . . . could you figure where she was shot from?"

Rodgers glared at her. "Ah, the other shoe drops—you didn't pick me out of a hat, did you? That's why you're really here, to see if me and Cooper are game to go trooping through the woods looking for God knows what tiny iota of evidence. You know me well enough not to ask, Laura. I don't do that stuff no more."

"*Could* you do it, I'm asking."

He looked off into the middle distance. A moment later he said, "I'm not saying I will, you understand?"

"But you could," she finished for him. He was a talented detective; apparently he had been a very capable solider. This was the answer she had expected.

"Maybe," he allowed. "Sure as shit had enough practice at that sort of thing back in the day."

"It would help, I think. Be nice to put a name to this woman and be able to tell her people what happened to her."

Rodgers said nothing.

"Maybe even catch the bastard who shot her."

"Goddamn you, Laura," he said, but she understood what he really meant.

Yes, I'll do it.

"You sure do need the help," he continued. "Because there are other obvious avenues to exhaust before you go get bit up by mosquitoes."

"Such as?"

"If we knew which direction she came from, that would narrow the search by half. So how's about we talk to the one and only witness."

"The driver of the truck?" Laura was incredulous. "Whitley will never give me his name, and it won't be public record until someone sues him in civil court a year from now. It's a nonstarter."

Rodgers gave her a grin. "Oh, would it interest you to know they arrested the driver, and he's sitting in jail right now?"

Laura stepped back and crossed her arms. "Don Rodgers . . . and you said people don't tell you anything."

He shrugged. "I fibbed a bit. One caveat, though: if you're going to talk to him, first you're going to have to figure some way to get on the approved-visitors list."

CHAPTER

8

"His name's Kevin Romano," she said. "Owns and operates a small general contracting business."

"I don't understand how you managed to get it that fast."

"I've got my methods. The clerks at the courthouse all go out together on Monday nights. Lucky for us, Monday is one of the nights Bass Herman likes to indulge as well. He filled me in this morning."

It was the next morning, and Laura and Rodgers were speaking on the phone.

"Every night's one for indulgence if you're Bass Herman," Rodgers said.

"He knows the places they like to go, and he's been buying their first round for years." She read off the address Bass had given her, which she had jotted down in her notebook.

"Are they still holding him? Has he been charged with anything?"

"Nothing more than the name and address, I'm afraid," she said. "None of it is supposed to be public yet, and it's not exactly legal for a clerk to pass information to the press. Bass says he received the information scrawled across a napkin, crumpled up and pressed into his hand, and that even these tiny morsels required all of his considerable charm."

Rodgers just snorted.

While facts about the current legal situation of the man in question might be scarce, the internet had a bit more to say about Mr. Kevin Romano. A quick search had revealed him to be forty-two years old, a general contractor by trade. He had a wife, one child, and a criminal record: a four-year-old conviction for aggravated DUI.

The address was only a little more than an hour's drive away, part of a freshly built neighborhood just outside Greensboro. The house Laura parked in front of stood in the center of a cul-de-sac of identical houses, like the keystone in an arch.

Its forest-green shutters were closed up tight, and the house was so new that grass had just barely begun to take root in the fresh-turned dirt of the front yard. The only sign of life was a persimmon tree heavy with apricot-colored orbs. As she stood on the front step, Laura thought she could smell fresh paint.

"Can I help you?"

A woman stood behind the screen door with a baby balanced on one hip, her T-shirt soiled. Fresh spit-up shone wetly in the noon sunlight. The baby was crying.

"Kevin Romano?"

"Shh," she soothed the baby. To Laura: "I thought you all were finished with him."

"Not quite."

"Well, I am. Keep him for all I care."

The baby's plaintive wail ratcheted up to a scream, and Mrs. Romano shut the door in Laura's face.

She knocked again.

The woman swung the door open and pressed her face close to the screen. "What? What could possibly be so important you all need to come over here and question me again? I want you off my property. Is it even legal to keep harassing me like this?"

"You must be Kevin's wife. Sara, am I right?"

The woman glowered at her from behind the screen. The baby cried.

"Can I call you Sara?"

"It's my name, isn't it?"

"Sara, I'm not with the police."

"Who then? Child services."

"I don't work for the government."

"Then I don't have to talk to you."

"No, you don't," Laura said.

An obvious question hung in the air between them, unasked by Sara Romano and unanswered by the stranger on her doorstep but begged by the presence of someone who, without any official connection to the government, seemed to know so much about the Romano family and their troubles. Laura stood silently and waited, certain she would not be outlasted. She'd caught plenty of flies with both honey and vinegar, but for her money, curiosity beat them all.

Sara broke first.

"So who are you?"

"I'm a reporter."

"And you're here about Kevin."

"About the accident, yes."

"Well, that's just swell. That's just what we need, our dirty laundry aired in the most public way possible."

"So tell me about it. Maybe we can clean it up a little bit."

She scoffed. "Why would I help you?"

"Because it's coming out whether you talk to me or not. Right now, all I have is a copy of the police report and some interviews with the cops. They're telling the story, and Kevin doesn't come out looking too good."

The baby had quieted down some, and Sara just patted it on its back, rocking her hips back and forth.

"Unless there's another side to things," Laura said.

"You're not coming in my house."

"That's fine."

"You can go around the back."

Laura followed a flagstone path down the side of the house. The house was set into a hillside, the grade creating a walk-out basement. Here a well-maintained lawn sloped down to a firepit surrounded by folding chairs.

Five minutes later Sara Romano came out the back of the house without her baby, locked the door behind her, and picked her way across the lawn. She sat down next to Laura and fiddled with a knob on a baby monitor, adjusting the volume until it emitted a constant hiss of white noise. Satisfied, she placed it in her lap. Her eyes, red and puffy, stared down into the wet pile of ash. "You know what this is going to do to us? It's going to ruin us."

"He was drunk," Laura said. She had no direct evidence that Kevin Romano had been driving under the influence, but if the police were still holding him, not many other conclusions could be drawn.

"He promised me it would never happen again."

"It happened before?"

Despite the heat, Sara wound a sweater around her body, drawing it tight. "Years ago. We were younger, it was easier to bounce back. We didn't have a bloated mortgage payment. We didn't have a baby."

"You bounced back once. You can do it again."

She laughed a laugh that set Laura's teeth on edge, the sound of someone teetering on the edge. "He didn't kill anyone last time, though, did he?"

Laura reached out and tried to take her hand. "I'm sorry."

She snatched her hand away. "Don't pretend."

"Because of the prior conviction, they're going to charge your husband with aggravated felony death by vehicle."

Sara bit down on her lip.

"The sentence runs more than ten years."

She started to cry.

Now Laura threw out a lifeline. "But I'm here because I don't believe Kevin is totally at fault. I have evidence to suggest someone was chasing after the victim. That might explain how she ended up in front of Kevin's truck."

Sara looked at her. "That would help, right?"

"I can say with certainty that it would. Kevin is going to spend some time in jail, but if we can prove extenuating circumstances, maybe the DA drops the charge down to the misdemeanor death by vehicle charge. That's six months at the most."

Sara narrowed her puffy eyes. "And you're helping us for nothing."

"No, I need your help in return. I need you to tell me anything you know about the accident, and I need you to get your husband to put me on his approved-visitors list at the jail."

"And if I do it?"

"I'll hold off on printing Kevin's name in the paper, and anything helpful I find gets passed along to your lawyer. I promise."

Sara bit her lip again, and the lip, already bruised from abuse, threatened to bleed. "I just don't know," she said.

From her lap, from the baby monitor, came a tiny wail.

Laura reached out as if to take Sara's hand again, but instead she tugged the monitor away and twisted the volume knob. The baby's cry shrank, winnowing away to nothing, and then the volume knob clicked into the off position.

"Hey! Give—"

"How old is your baby?"

"Give it back."

"Stop grabbing for it and answer me. How old is your baby?"

"Eleven months."

"Boy or girl?"

"Girl."

"She won't remember."

"Please, I—"

"A couple years and all this will blow over. All of this can just pass you by, and that's when she'll start making real memories, the kind that last. All you have to do is listen to me."

After that, it was easy.

CHAPTER

9

SHE TOLD LAURA everything she knew, which wasn't much. She agreed to get Laura in to see her husband at the Orange County Jail. She agreed to pass along any new information received by her lawyer. And there was one more thing.

"He had a dash cam on the truck. It's a work truck, and it made the insurance company happy."

"The police took the camera along with the truck, right?"

She nodded. "But to get a break on the premium, we had to buy the nice one. It uploads the footage to the account automatically."

Laura waited outside while she tended to the child, and then Sara returned and led her back up the yard and through a low door into the basement. The room inside had been set up as a home office or a den, with wood paneling and secondhand club chairs, and on the far wall a computer. Sara sat in front of it and started swirling the mouse in circles.

"Here it is."

The recording was crisp. Most of the screen showed a forward-facing perspective, but there was also picture-in-picture in the lower corner that featured a synchronized rear view from a second camera.

The feed had audio as well. Rain lashed the truck's windshield, and the wipers squelched endlessly left and right across the camera's field of view. Soft music played in cab, some kind of jazz, featuring a saxophone. There was another small sound, and at first Laura couldn't make it out. When she leaned closer, Laura realized it was Kevin Romano—he was humming.

He traveled along at a constant rate, and based on dead reckoning, Laura thought the speed couldn't be more than a few miles per hour over the limit. The truck stayed solidly in the center of the left lane.

Sara clicked the mouse, and the recording stopped.

"This is the right one, isn't it?" Laura asked.

"This is the one." Her voice had acquired a rasp. "I've already seen it once. Once was enough."

"I can finish by myself if you prefer. Can I get a copy as well?"

"Kevin left the computer logged in, but you need to enter the account password again to copy or delete files. I don't know it."

With that, she exited the room through the same low door into the backyard and closed it firmly behind her.

Laura pressed play.

The video started up again, and her overwhelming impression was one of normalcy. There was nothing to portend the coming doom. Kevin Romano had apparently failed a sobriety test, but there wasn't anything obvious to suggest that he was drunk.

Laura waited for the inevitable impact, a tightness in her chest growing by the second. At any unexpected sound, she startled. It reminded her of turning the handle on a jack-in-the-box: she knew what must come next, but the anticipation was awful to endure.

The lanes started to split, and oncoming traffic—

A flash of movement from the left, a tumble of beige near the driver's side, and it was over.

"Shit." Kevin's voice from inside the cab. "Oh shit. Oh no. No, no, no, no."

He braked hard, pulled to the left, and punched a button on the dash. Both the front and rear cameras displayed expanses of empty asphalt. Only the sound held her attention now. The telltale *click-clunk, click-clunk* of hazard lights, the door opening, the slap of boot soles on wet pavement, wind and rain blowing past the door he'd left open in his haste. The truck started dinging, a warning that the keys were still in the ignition. The rear camera captured a brief moment of a hooded figure running back down the shoulder until it disappeared from view. Kevin Romano, making good time toward a futile attempt to fix what he'd broken. Some things can't be fixed, and this was one of them, but of course he didn't know it yet.

Through it all, the soft music never stopped playing.

* * *

The nature of her job often meant meeting people on the worst days of their lives, but Laura had never quite gotten used to it.

Good journalism is a public service, but when it comes to crime reporting, that service comes at the cost of its subjects. The vast majority of people are reported *to*, but for the very tiny fraction who are reported *on*, there is virtually no upside. Victims' stories are exploited. And worse, when there is even the slightest whiff of guilt, a scarlet letter is applied. It was a fundamental tension of her profession, the trolley problem writ large: the paradoxical, inescapable requirement that in order to help the many, you must hurt the few.

Laura Chambers was a necessary evil.

And now Kevin Romano had been selected for sacrifice. He knew it, too. She could see it in the unfocused cast of his pupils, the circles under his eyes the color of spoiling beef. He was imagining all the ways his life would change. The way his friends and neighbors would look at him once they knew. The way his marriage would collapse under the weight of all those stares.

"How did you get my name?"

"Does it matter?"

"It was an accident. They weren't supposed to release my name."

"You're right, it's not public record," she said. "Not yet. Not like DUI convictions."

"Oh Jesus," he said. "I was in the Marines. Did you know that?"

She shook her head.

"Ten years. I did four tours, and I never killed anybody." He held his hands out in front of his body, stared at them like they were contaminated. "My wife is never going to let me touch her again. We have a little girl. How will I be able to pick her up?"

"Give it time," Laura said. "It's only been a few days."

He wiped at the corners of his eyes. "It was an accident."

"Pretty late to be out drinking on a Sunday night."

"It was raining hard."

"I know."

"It was dark."

"Was it you behind the wheel or someone else?"

His shoulders hunched. "I'm not a bad person."

"Why were you out there?"

"I had a job in Durham. We were behind, so I worked all Sunday. Afterward I took the guys out for a few."

"And got drunk."

"I thought I was fine. I blew over the limit. What do you want me to say?"

"The woman you hit called me a few minutes before the accident."

"Jesus," he said again.

"She left a—"

"You knew her? I didn't know you knew her."

"I didn't know her. I don't think I knew her."

"What do you mean, you don't think you knew her?"

Laura paused. "They're having some trouble identifying the body."

He pressed his thumbs into his eyes, like it was a bad dream he couldn't wake up from.

"I can be a friend, Kevin."

"You're a fucking vulture here to pick my carcass clean."

"Sometimes I am," she answered.

After a moment he pulled his hands away from his face. "My wife said you can help me."

She gave him the broad strokes. At the end, she said, "Anything you can do to point me in the right direction would be appreciated. And in return, I don't see any special reason your name needs to be in the paper."

"Whatever you want," he said.

"Tell me everything you can remember, anything that struck you as out of the ordinary."

It didn't amount to much, and when he was finished, Laura closed her notebook.

"Look," he continued, "on the one hand, I had a few and it was raining. But on the other hand, that truck has xenon headlights, the tires are less than a year old, the wiper blades are new. None of that mattered. I could have been driving at noon on a sunny day, hands at ten and two, staring straight ahead, and I still would have hit her. She came out of nowhere."

"I saw the tape."

"Sara showed it to you?"

"I tried to make a copy, but you need the log-in credentials."

"The username is my work email, the one on the website."

"And the password?"

"Promise me you're going to help," he said. There was a high-pitched note of despair in his voice, the vocal cords stretched like violin strings, the pegs overturned.

The jail uniform fit him poorly, the pants huge and baggy, the shirt a size too small. Its neckline grabbed around his throat, and he pulled at it like he couldn't get enough air. Jail sounds—metal on metal, men shouting—bubbled out the doorway behind him. Soon he would be drawn back through it, boxed up, severed from the life he had known.

She stood to go, and watched any remaining defiance melt out of his face until only fear remained.

"Promise me."

"You ought to be ashamed of yourself."

"Don't you think I am?"

"You can't bring that woman back to life, but you can still do right by her. Tell me the password."

He looked down at the dented and scarred tabletop. "It's almost her birthday," he said. "She's going to be one."

Then he gave it to her.

"It's all the little things that had to line up, you know? I spent a minute searching for a charge cord in my glove box before I pulled out; someone cut me off at the entrance ramp. A thousand moments, and I only had to choose to do a single one differently. I've got to live with that."

"Yes," Laura said. "You do."

C H A P T E R

10

SHE DROVE.

It had begun to rain again. Almost forty-eight hours had passed, and before long even the barest hint that an accident had taken place would be erased by weather and traffic and time. Laura was determined to take one last look.

Orange Grove Road passed over I-40, and her view from the bridge was of taillights still twinkling in the westbound lanes, beginning to pick up speed. She made two rights and ended up on Old NC 86, a piece of two-lane blacktop that hooked back to an entrance ramp. The Dart dropped down onto the freeway, and she twisted in her seat, looking for a landmark she remembered. The squad cars, the flares, the ambulance—all were gone. Each section of highway tends to look like all the others, and for a moment she thought she wouldn't be able to pick out the spot where it had happened.

Then her tires slipped, crunching over a gritty surface. Sand rattled down the length of the undercarriage.

Laura suppressed a shudder.

Microscopic specks of the woman's remains had just sprayed across the bottom of the gas tank, the differential, the oil drain plug. Usually she changed her own oil. She imagined pushing herself underneath the car, the openings of her mouth and nose exposed to any debris falling from above, and the thought nauseated her.

Her foot came off the gas as she looked back and forth, taking in the larger context: the height of the concrete barriers, the terrain, the woods on either side. This spot lay more than a mile from the entrance ramp Laura had used, and it was miles still to the next exit. Off the right shoulder, the embankment was almost too steep to climb. It was difficult to believe someone could approach from that direction.

Yet in some ways, the alternative seemed just as unlikely.

Here the eastbound and westbound lanes had split apart and were separated by dense woods. Laura couldn't make out the vehicles traveling in the opposite direction. In fact, all she could see on either side of the road was trees. She glanced at the map on her phone. It was easy to pick out the freeway, and it was easy to see where the two halves separated and then came back together again. Between was an area trapped, a no-man's-land shaped like an elongated triangle and bounded on all sides by interstate. It was perhaps a thousand feet long and almost as wide, thickly forested with trees and covered with impenetrable undergrowth, and it was totally inaccessible, an island floating in a sea of asphalt.

Laura took the next exit and circled back, this time threading her way through a neighborhood of depressing houses. Finally, she reached an otherwise empty section of road running beneath an overpass. She pulled over out of the rain and turned off the car, listening to the *tick-tick-tick* of the engine, hot metal contracting in the cool, wet air.

She waited.

Soon headlights shone in the rearview mirror, and an F-150 of 1990s vintage pulled in behind her. It was low-slung compared to the modern iteration, a boxy red truck that had collected more than its share of skinned knees over the years. The windows were rolled down, and a floppy-eared dog stuck out his head. He bayed, the deep baritone echoing off the concrete walls.

Laura got out and scratched him behind the ear, and he nuzzled her in appreciation.

"Good boy, Cooper," she said, then slid into the passenger seat next to him.

Don Rodgers shook his head in disgust. "Damn dog likes you more than he likes me."

"Can't fault his taste."

"Hell, I feed him. You think that would count for something." He leaned forward and spit tobacco juice into a Styrofoam cup.

"You told me you were going to quit," Laura said.

"I did quit." He spit into the cup again. "Smoking."

Cooper yowled.

"Can't believe you asked me to meet you under an overpass," he said. "I hate all this cloak-and-dagger shit."

"Don't try that line on me," Laura said.

It was hard to see in the dim light, but he might have smiled. "You want to have a secret meeting? Fine, but let's make with the secrets already. I got places to be."

"It's not even five yet."

"Whiskey don't know how to read a clock."

Quickly, Laura explained what she had in mind. Rodgers shrugged into a raincoat and leashed his dog, and the three of them clambered up the concrete ramp of the overpass. At the top, they climbed over the guardrail onto I-40 and started up the right-hand shoulder.

Passing cars kicked up a dirty haze, and Rodgers was careful to keep Cooper close against his outside leg. In about ten minutes they reached the accident site. Laura did her best to locate the precise spot where the woman had been struck. A strip of sand still nestled against the concrete barrier.

From across both lanes of traffic, she pointed. "There, I think. In the left lane."

They examined the embankment behind them, on the right side of the highway. It was loose rock, like scree on the side of a mountain. The slope was extreme.

Rodgers said, "Hard to imagine climbing that in the rain."

"Barefoot," Laura added.

"If she didn't come up the embankment, she must have come from that way." He pointed. "From the southwest. Across the eastbound lanes off in that direction, through the woods in the middle, and then when she popped out into the left lane there . . ." He trailed off.

"All the while she's trying to call me," Laura said. "She's wearing nothing but the sort of thing I sleep in, and she has no shoes on her feet. Put it all together, what do you get?"

Rodgers didn't bother to answer.

He checked behind them and, when there was a gap in traffic, jogged across the lanes with Cooper by his side. He spared a quick glance for the bit of sand, then bent and hooked his dog under the legs. In one smooth motion he picked him up and then deposited him on the outside of the guardrail, then climbed over himself. Laura followed.

After a moment Rodgers's eyes picked out what looked like a lightly used game trail. "This way," he said, and followed it.

Laura hesitated; she peered into the trees, but her gaze penetrated only a few yards into the murky forest beyond.

"Come on now," he said, and she fell into step behind him.

Even here, on an island in the middle of the interstate, there was evidence of squirrels and rabbits, bigger animals too. Leaves were eaten away from the brush as high up as Laura's head.

"How do they make it? I thought it would be only birds."

"Same way we did, I expect." Rodgers shook the water off the crown of his cowboy hat. "We got plenty of calls about hit deer around here during my time. Doubt that's changed much."

They walked on. Occasionally he would crouch down to study a broken twig or some overturned patch of dirt. Laura didn't ask questions, just let him work. The whizzing sound of traffic grew fainter, then stronger again. Eventually they reached another guardrail, and beyond it two more lanes of interstate headed in the opposite direction.

"Don't need to do any more jaywalking," Rodgers said. "If you want to see the woods on the other side, we can drive around. But I've been in those woods, and I'm not sure we're going to see anything over there we can't find over here."

"So it's a bust."

He crossed his arms. "How certain was your man at the medical examiner? Might be he was trying to impress you with a scary story."

"He wanted to impress me, but not that way. I got the sense he had more skill than the job required, and knew it. He wanted to show off, you know? All the samples were bagged, his identifications seemed certain. I believe him when he says she came out of here."

Rodgers just shook his head and handed her the leash, then started back the way they'd come.

Halfway across the island, Cooper started to sniff hard to the left. He pulled and let out a bark.

"What is it, boy?"

The dog tugged her along, leading her off the barely discernible game trail and into thicker brush. Water droplets rained down from the leaves above, but Laura didn't feel the wet. She slipped once and went down on one knee before springing back to her feet. Her knee was scraped up, and there would be a ferocious bruise in the morning, but the pain retreated to a distant corner of her mind. For now there was only her hand and the leash and the dog, all of them hurtling through a dark tunnel made of trees.

Cooper stopped. He pawed at the ground. Above them spread the branches of a great white oak, at least a hundred years old, with a trunk so wide it would take three or four people to join hands around its circumference. The rain was far lighter under its canopy.

"Mighty big tree." Rodgers, from behind her. "The kind of place a person might think to hide. Pull that dog back."

She did, and with enormous caution Rodgers circled the oak, studying the ground from all angles, careful to step in his own footsteps on the second and third pass.

"Here," he said at last, and showed her.

The tree was partly hollow. Near its base a huge knot had caved inward. The space wasn't large enough to hide a person, not really. But there was a concavity, a place less exposed than others. There, pressed into loamy soil, was the ghost of a footprint. A heel. Five toes.

Laura took a picture.

"And here," Rodgers said. He crouched down, pointed with a pen. "Not as complete, but that's her other foot. Those are the toes right there."

The feet were pointed outward.

"She had her back to the tree," Laura said.

Rodgers stood up.

"Wouldn't you?" he asked.

* * *

They climbed back into the cab. Rodgers had a clean towel. He let Laura use it first, then used it on himself, and last did his best to dry off the dog. "Cooper, you're stinking up my trunk."

"I don't mind," Laura said, scratching him behind the ear.

"You were hoping I could tell you where she'd been shot from, that about right? Work out a likely place the shooter might've posted up?"

"That's what you did in the Army, isn't it?"

He gave a quick nod. "I didn't see anyplace like that, but I can tell you the opposite. I can tell you about all the places we saw where a person *couldn't* have shot her. If we assume that rifle was getting used for its general purpose, which is to say shooting at targets, oh, more than ten yards away, then that brush pile we just hiked through makes a piss-poor place to do it. Trees are mature, undergrowth all in the way. Sight lines are next to nil. I'd guess she got shot before she ever made it to those woods."

"Someone chased her in there."

"She was shot. She ran. But from who?"

Laura's mouth pulled tight. "Wrong question. What I want to know is, from *where*?"

She held up a finger, retrieved her phone from a pocket, and called up a map of the area. Math had never been her strong suit, but she still remembered basic geometry. Two points make a line, and a line can be extended in either direction. She traced a path southwestward on the map, from the accident site to the oak tree, across the eastbound lanes of the interstate and beyond.

Her finger crossed a single road, Dimmocks Mill, and then there was nothing. She switched to a satellite view, and the tops of trees and a creek sprang into view. She zoomed out and caught occasional houses spread out from one another on large pieces of property.

One of the houses, however, seemed too near a road. It had an odd shape. From above, it looked like a half circle.

A half-formed idea tumbled into Laura's head. If Whitley hadn't been able to identify the victim, that meant no one else in town had recognized her either. She hadn't fit the description of any missing person, so it seemed a fair assumption that she wasn't local. If so, where would she have stayed?

Laura's finger twitched as it crossed over the U-shaped building.

There was the possibility the woman hadn't been staying anywhere, of course. She could have been homeless, or perhaps had just chosen to sleep rough during her travels. No, Laura said to herself. None of that comported with the dead woman being barefoot in only a nightgown. She had looked for all the world like a person who'd been in bed, someone who had undressed, lain down, pulled the covers up over themselves, and fallen asleep, only to be startled awake by—

"Is that what I think it is?" she said, and showed Rodgers the map.

He grimaced. "With a bullet hole in her? It's too far."

"But possible. Any other ideas?"

He grunted.

"Well, that settles it," Laura said. "Looks like possible's the best we've got."

CHAPTER

11

THE PARKING LOT'S single light pole listed to one side as if threatening to tip over, and the bent metal cone at its top cast a ragged blade of light across the asphalt that seemed to point toward the front door. Up on the roof, a neon sign blinked its letters in vertical sequence: M–O–T–E–L. The last thing to light up was a curved arrow pointing downward, beckoning to sleepy travelers. Laura knew from experience that only the top two letters were visible from the interstate.

Rodgers backed his truck into the lot's far corner and cut the engine. "How far you reckon we drove?"

"Two or three miles," Laura said. "But we had to quarter south and west to make it over here. As the crow flies, it's probably only a bit more than a mile."

"Still a hell of a long way to run in her condition."

"If you're scared enough, it doesn't really matter how many times you've been shot, does it?"

If the woman had been caught by surprise, as the evidence suggested, and if this was the direction from which she'd come—two very big ifs, Laura reminded herself—then the motel was the only possible point of origin. A horseshoe-shaped curve of rooms, it had been owned by Elias Quant for as long as she could remember. He was an old man, well into his eighties, with old-fashioned wire-frame glasses and a hearing problem that seemed to come and go. When she was in high school, kids would buy a case of cheap beer and then try to rent a room. Quant, an immigrant from the Netherlands, would cup a hand around his ear and shout at them in his Dutch accent. "What? What did you say?" He would repeat it over and over, and eventually her classmates would decide to do their drinking in someone's basement or at the quarry.

With Laura, on the other hand, he never seemed to have any trouble understanding what she was saying.

"Quant will answer my questions," she said.

Rodgers shook his head. "Don't think so."

"I know he's old-school and that he takes customer privacy very seriously. But there's a body involved, so he'll bend the rules. Besides, he likes me."

"Liked you."

"What, I'm on the outs with him too?"

"You could put it that way, I guess," Rodgers said. "He died this past winter."

Laura's mouth hung open. She tried to imagine old age finally coming for the jovial motel owner in his sleep, but as hard as she tried, the image wouldn't resolve itself. Quant had been white haired and potbellied for as long as she'd known him, old the way a statue is old, permanent and unchangeable.

"What happened?"

"Heard he fell off a ladder."

She screwed up her face. "I didn't know."

"It was around the time you decided to get out of town for a while."

She paused, processing. "But the place is still open."

"Yep," Rodgers said. He pushed his hat back on his head and rolled the chaw from one cheek to the other. "Benny Morno bought it at auction."

* * *

His name was Benito Mornopopolis, but everyone called him Benny Morno. They called him that because anything was better than the mess of letters on his birth certificate, but also because every good gangster needs a nickname. In truth, no one in Hillsborough, North Carolina, population six thousand and change, could be called a gangster with a straight face. Benny Morno just happened to be as close as it got.

Laura knew him only by reputation and from the police blotter. He'd dabbled in selling marijuana and running basement card games before finding his real passion in prostitution. These days he ran protection for a small group of sex workers in town and, if the rumors were true, into parts farther east. Durham. Raleigh, even. It wasn't organized crime exactly—that would imply an organization, and Morno was a solo operator—but rather a small-time thug with a jailhouse juris doctor and just enough experience to skirt the law.

Laura gave a low whistle. "Benny Morno, *hotelier*. Never thought I'd see that."

Rodgers snorted. "I heard if a person wants a room for the night, he charges for twelve hours."

"Think you can persuade him to help us?"

"Us? There is no us. I'm a civilian now, I can't go around bracing witnesses and corrupting an ongoing investigation."

Laura gave him a look. "But I can?"

"Well, that's different, you being a reporter and all. Besides, Benny was never all that cooperative with law enforcement. I arrested him more than once back in the day, so he'd recognize me the second I walked through the door."

"Cooper's more help than you are," Laura said, "and he's a damn dog."

"I'm driving you around, aren't I?" Rodgers glanced over his shoulder. "Speaking of which, we'll circle the neighborhood until you're done."

"In case the real cops are hot on our tail?"

He pulled down the brim of his hat until it shielded his eyes. "I'll do my best to blend in."

* * *

The same bell jangled when she pushed the door open, and she recognized the wingback chair behind the front desk from when Quant had been the owner. In fact, the only difference was Benny Morno. He sat with his feet up on the glass countertop, reading a magazine. On his feet were boots with black crud clinging to the bottoms. The dingy white tank top that had pasted itself to his torso glistened with sweat.

He didn't bother to glance up.

"I'm looking for someone," Laura said.

He stuck out his tongue and licked the tip of his finger, then turned the page of his magazine.

"What is that, *The Economist*?"

"Yeah," he said.

"Not a lot of pictures in that one."

He turned his head to stare at her. "Jesus, you've got some mouth on you."

"Want me to help you sound out the big words?"

"Have mercy." He closed the magazine and put it down. "The mouth's going to be a problem, but it's not a deal breaker. I've got experience with fixer-uppers. We'll get you whipped into shape in no time."

"I'm not here for a job."

He looked her up and down. His eyes traced a slow path over the slick front of her rain jacket before moving down across her legs and lingering on her feet. "You sure?"

"My face is up here, Benny. Do you know it?"

He studied her for a moment, frowning, but after a moment she could see recognition dawn. "You're that reporter broad."

"Now you've got it."

"The one who found that missing kid a couple years ago."

"That's the one."

"Whatta you doing in my place?" He paused, calculating. "We don't have a lot of the regular amenities. You might be happier at one of the chain hotels closer to the highway."

"Not interested in a room. I'm here because of a tip."

"A tip?"

"Yeah, it's like when someone gives me information."

"There's that mouth again." He put both hands flat on the countertop and stood. "I bet I could make you close it. I bet I could make it so you open it only on command."

A shiver of disgust gave Laura gooseflesh. She wasn't afraid of Benny Morno, but then, nothing was stopping her from turning around and walking out the door. Basic economics hadn't conspired to make Morno the most viable option for putting a roof over her head. She felt certain, though, that at least one of the women staying in this motel tonight couldn't say the same, had ended up in his orbit by virtue of abuse or addiction or plain old bad luck. To Benny Morno, those weren't problems to be pitied but rather assets to be leveraged.

The balance of power between a criminal and a reporter was far different than between a pimp and a working girl, but Benny Morno hadn't seemed to realize that fact. He kept challenging her with his oily eyes, the tip of his tongue perched on his lower lip.

Laura wanted to put a knife in him and twist.

"A newspaper is a bully pulpit," she said.

"What's a pull-pit?"

"Christ," she muttered.

"What's he got to do with it?"

Laura just shook her head. "I meant that it's pretty interesting, you owning a motel, especially with your very specific list of priors. It would be fascinating to a lot of people, I think. This is a small town. Folks around here love to get to know their neighbors."

He squinted at her. "Nothing illegal going on."

"That so?"

"Nothing you can prove."

She shrugged. "I'm not a cop; this isn't a court. I don't need proof to write an article about your convictions over the last few years, or the drug-dealing ones before that, or your new address in a motel at the edge of town, and anyone who reads it can draw their own conclusions."

The eyes suddenly started shifting back and forth as if looking for an exit. He raised his hands, palms out. "Hey, I never wanted any trouble."

"You didn't? That's not what it sounded like to me."

"No, ma'am," he said. "Must have been a misunderstanding. You were looking for someone?"

"A woman, about my age, slender build, dirty-blond hair."

He tapped a fingernail against his teeth. "A female guest? That does narrow it down some."

"I figured it might. Any cops come around asking about her?"

"Cops don't have any reason to visit. We're real quiet."

"Did you have someone like that staying here the last few nights? She would have been here on Sunday night for sure."

Without breaking eye contact, he said, "I'm trying to remember, but it's kinda hazy."

Morno's new business venture had been under way for almost a year, and Laura hadn't heard a peep about it before tonight. Clearly he had put a lot of time and energy into discretion, so she'd been certain the threat of exposure would be enough to knock him into line. Why the sudden delay?

"You're not trying what I think you're trying," she said.

He let a sly smile play across his lips.

"Cash?" she asked, incredulous.

"Couldn't hurt."

She checked over her shoulder. Rodgers was right: no reason an enterprising young sheriff's deputy couldn't make the same assumptions, trace the same path, and end up in this very motel office. They could be pulling into the parking lot right now. The idea of financing even an iota of Benny Morno's lifestyle made her want to retch, and yet—

"I don't have time for this." She dug into her bag and came out with a twenty.

Morno plucked it from her fingers, looked at it, and sighed.

"Don't test me," she said.

"Fine, fine. She's in room seven."

"She looks like I described?"

"To a T. She came on Sunday, like you said, and paid up through tomorrow morning."

"You have a key?"

"Just knock."

"I'm pretty sure she's not going to answer," Laura said.

He raised one slimy eyebrow, then pushed aside the magazine and retrieved a tarnished brass key from beneath the desk. Outside, halfway down the walk, Laura turned to him. "Do you really read *The Economist*?"

Benny Morno tugged down on his sweat-stained tank top as if he were adjusting a waistcoat. "Of course," he said. "I'm very smart."

CHAPTER

12

THE ROOM WAS dark inside.

"Light switch?"

"To your left," Morno said, and then he was gone, the sound of his retreating footsteps fading into the distance.

For the first time, Laura considered the possibility of danger lurking somewhere beyond this door. In her enthusiasm, she'd forgotten that Jane Doe had ended up dead for a reason. Someone had menaced her severely enough to send her on a mad dart through the woods and across the freeway, pursued to the very end of her life. Whoever her killer was, they could have been lying low inside the motel room since the accident. They could be hiding inside even still.

The prudent thing would be to go inside only if accompanied.

But there wasn't time.

Laura took a step inside and paused, listening. The air seemed stagnant, and the only thing she could hear was the raindrops spending themselves on the thin roof.

Two quick steps and she was at the switch. The overhead lights snapped on and there it was, a dingy but otherwise unremarkable motel room. The patterned commercial carpet was worn from hundreds of passing feet and the paint on the walls was leached of color, but everything seems grayer in the rain. In the room's center was a queen bed with a brown floral bedspread. One side lay turned down, the extra pillow tossed away, as if someone had been sleeping and then gotten up to go to the bathroom.

As if they might come back at any moment.

Laura quickly checked inside the closet and then went into the bathroom, looking behind the shower curtain. No one was hiding in the room, and at first glance she saw nothing out of the ordinary. The closet held a single blue dress on a flimsy hanger, and in the bathroom there was only a small travel toothbrush resting on the sill of the sink.

If someone had been staying here, where was their luggage? Their personal items?

Above the sink hung a mirrored medicine cabinet, and it swung open at her touch, already unlatched. She peered inside but found it empty. Back in the bedroom she opened one dresser drawer after another and saw nothing but their scarred pine interiors. The last one, at the bottom, was empty like all the others.

She pushed it closed, and as the bottom drawer moved back into place, her eye was drawn to a small rectangle of carpet just in front of the dresser. It was a different shade than the rest, brighter in color, cleaner. She got down on all fours and ran her fingertips over the pile, feeling the embossed troughs on the rectangle's edges.

The dresser had been moved.

She stood up straight and looked again at the room, seeing it with new eyes, and sniffed at the air. Just at the edge of her perception, as light as gauze in the air, she caught the very last trace of an odor. It was sharp and clean against the backdrop of damp mildew: the scent of a cheap aftershave.

Someone had already been here; the room had already been searched.

Laura went back to the bathroom to look again, and this time a slight current of air tugged at her hair. Above the toilet, a small transom window made of pebbled glass hung downward from its hinge, the lock open. She gave it an experimental push, and it swung outward without resistance.

She hurried back to the office and stuck her head in the door. "Did you get a name for the woman in room seven?"

Benny Morno shook his head. "We don't keep a register."

"Credit card?"

"She paid cash," he said. "We didn't even speak to each other. She laid the money on the counter, I gave her a key."

Outside, the parking lot was empty. No sign of Rodgers or anyone else. Laura made her way back to the room and propped the door open so she would be able to hear if any vehicle approached, then went over the space inch by inch. Whoever had already searched the room presumably had just finished chasing a young woman to her death. They must have been shaken, or at least in a hurry.

Maybe they had missed something.

Just as she was about to give up, the sickly yellow glow of the overhead fixture caught on something metal. It glittered, drawing her attention. She reached down and dug between the carpet fibers, bringing it out into the light. A screw.

Her eyes moved upward. Where the wall met the ceiling lay a small heating grate made to look like ornamental wrought iron. She stood on a desk chair and saw screw holes in each corner.

One of them was empty.

From her pocket she produced a dime. The edge just managed to fit the slot in the first screw head, and she twisted until her fingers began to ache. Slowly, the screw began to turn, loosening, finally coming free in her hand. The second one was easier. She started on the third and heard sound from behind her: the squeal of tires on blacktop.

Color splashed across the wall next to her, the turning lights of a police cruiser.

Her breath hitched in her chest as if a giant fishhook had just threaded itself between her lungs. She glanced behind her, but there was nothing to see. The squad car itself was farther down the line of rooms, closer to the parking lot entrance. She thought she heard the faint jangle of the motel office door, and she could picture them—two cops speaking with Morno. In less than a minute he would be leading them down the covered walkway to room seven.

She twisted the dime hard, and it slipped.

As it dropped toward the ground, she stuck her hand out without thinking. It bounced once on her palm, and then she closed her fingers over it. *Take it easy*, she told herself, pressed it back into place, and began to turn. Her fingertips turned white from the pressure, the nerves crying out for her to stop.

Another jangle from the office door.

Laura gave one last twist and the screw came free, this one bouncing off into a dark corner. The grate swung open.

She thrust her arm into the opening. Her hand scrabbled left and right across dusty metal, reaching deeper, and finally her fingers landed on coarse fabric. She gripped the object and pulled it out.

It was a photo album, bound in what looked like canvas.

A small picture was pasted to the front, but Laura didn't bother to look at it right now. She had only enough time to make one quick and important decision.

There was no absolute proof this was Jane Doe's room, but the evidence was mounting rapidly. An extension of the woman's trajectory had drawn Laura to this place; Morno had recognized her description; and now law enforcement had arrived at the motel as well. All the twisty threads of possibility seemed to have converged beneath her feet.

Laura weighed her options. She could walk out the door right now. If someone from the Orange County Sheriff's Office caught her snooping around a motel room that later turned out to belong to a murder victim, the worst that could happen was a harsh tongue-lashing. On the other hand, if they could ever prove she'd stolen evidence and impeded a homicide investigation, her punishment could be up to a year in prison.

In the end, it was Bass Herman's plea that tipped the scales.

Don't you at least owe her that much?

She shoved the album into her bag, rushed into the bathroom, stood on the toilet lid, and pushed her way through the transom window.

On the other side, the rear wall was flat and unadorned. There was nothing to grab hold of. She would have to jump to the ground below. It was only five or six feet down, but if she went out the window headfirst, she would have to break the fall with her hands.

She reversed course back into the small bathroom, gripped the sides of the toilet tank, and started to lever herself through the window feetfirst. One leg went through the opening.

In the room, the doorknob began to rattle.

Her second leg followed. Laura pushed off the tank lid, expecting to drop through the window, but instead she stuck in place. It took her a moment to locate the culprit: her bag. With its bulky cargo, it had wedged her firmly into the window casing.

Years ago, at the *Boston Globe*, she'd written a fluff piece about a row of antiques stores on Charles Street in Beacon Hill. One of the proprietors had looked like an antique himself, with the salt-weathered face of an old fisherman, and she'd run his photograph next to the story. He'd been delighted to see himself in print, and as a thank-you, he'd sent her the old leather camera bag he'd caught her admiring on more than one occasion. The waxed exterior was like armor, and it had been capable of handling anything she threw at it over the years.

Most important now was the strap. It was made of quarter-inch-thick cowhide held in place with brass rivets so big they could have bolted together a battleship. It was indestructible. Laura wore it crosswise across her body, and it had now effectively tied her in place.

She thrashed side to side.

A low murmur of voices, then the scrape of a key in the lock.

The tips of her shoes clawed at the outside wall, searching for purchase. Her feet might only be a few inches above the ground, she realized, but as tightly as she was wedged, six inches might as well be a mile.

The doorknob twisted.

She managed to get the top of the bag open, reach inside, and pull the photo album free. Then three things happened almost simultaneously. Time stretched like taffy, and she registered each in turn.

She heard the door to the motel room swing open.

She became unwedged and started to slip through the window, pulling the photo album along behind her.

But also, a small rectangle of paper slipped out from inside the album's cover. It drifted toward the window, but some random air current made a last-minute change to its flight plan, and it fluttered back into the bathroom.

Just before time seemed to accelerate again, Laura noticed that the window was a tight squeeze, and that if she'd been any heavier or broader in the shoulders, passage would have been impossible. Then she was twisting and falling, landing with a thud on the packed brown earth next to a whirring air conditioner.

The window was only five and half feet off the ground, as it turned out, and Laura risked peering inside. The scrap of paper had landed faceup on the top of the tank lid. She could see now that it was a business card.

Male voices came from just around the corner, well inside the motel room. Another moment and they would see her.

She reached her arm through the window and stretched until the beveled wood cut into her bicep but only managed to brush the card's edge with the tip of her middle finger.

"Anyone in here?" a voice called.

She thought it might be Whitley, but Laura didn't stick around to find out. She ducked down, slid the album back into her bag, and then headed away from the motel's rear wall into the nearby underbrush. Down at the end of the building, the silent reds and blues of the light bar twirled out among the trees.

She looked left and right. A feeling of unease scratched at the back of her neck. It was the creeping impression that she was walking in someone else's footsteps—or across their grave.

A sense of history repeating itself overcame her, an icy certainty that all this had happened before.

She fled through the woods, not the first to travel this path, acutely aware of where it had ended the last time.

CHAPTER

13

SHE CUT HER way north through undergrowth and rain, finally stumbling across a deserted-looking stretch of highway. Rodgers knew the spot when she described it to him on the phone, and within a few minutes she spotted a pair of headlights cresting the far rise. Laura waited until she could make out the distinctive red hue of his truck, then pushed her hood back and stepped out from the trees, one hand held high.

"Was it her room?" Rodgers asked, once she was inside.

"Benny recognized her."

"You gave him a description?"

Laura paused. "The woman they showed me . . . there wasn't any information left to glean except what's on a driver's license. Race, hair, weight, height, that kind of thing. That's what I gave him, and that was enough."

"Did they see you?"

"Don't think so."

Rodgers drove in silence for a minute, then said, "I don't like this one bit. Running? Running, Laura? We ought to go back there right now."

"You could have headed them off in the parking lot, if you think announcing ourselves was the right way to go."

"I would have done exactly that," he said seriously.

"But you weren't there. You left me high and dry, and I was alone."

"What's the difference?"

"The difference is you're Don Rodgers, member of the good ol' boys club, professor emeritus of investigations. They would have treated you with kid gloves, asked a few questions, then told you to have a good night. Tell me I'm wrong."

Rodgers kept his eyes forward.

"Do you really believe I would have gotten the same treatment?"

He grunted. "Just tell me what you found."

He was already angry she had put him in this position, but if she told him about taking a piece of evidence, he would be enraged. One sharp corner of the photo album pressed against her hip, and it felt like an accusation. Laura ignored it and instead filled him in on the strange emptiness of the motel room and her notion that it had already been searched. By whom, she didn't know. "But it wasn't the cops. Morno said they hadn't been there."

"The killer, then."

"So when they showed up, I went out the window. She went the same way, Don."

"How do you know?"

She didn't know, but she felt it in her bones. Jane Doe was a picture out of focus. Fact by layered fact, however, the image of her was sharpening in Laura's mind. Separated by only forty-eight hours, they had shared the same room, breathed some of the same air. The mystery woman seemed closer than before.

She put on the heater. Cooper pushed up from his sleeping position between the two of them, nuzzled Laura's arm, then curled up next to her with his nose tucked underneath his tail and let out a sigh of satisfaction. Summer or no summer, the last few hours of rain had chilled Laura to the bone, and the warm air felt pleasant on her skin. Her eyelids grew heavy and she closed them, just for a moment. She tipped over into the dark well of sleep and at its bottom found a bright flash of memory. The moment was frozen, like a scene inside a snow globe that had been pushed to the back of a high shelf, invisible and untouched for years.

The truck came to a stop and her eyes popped open again, taking in the overpass with her car parked beneath it. Jerked from her reverie, she clutched at the last scrap of an evaporating idea.

"She had a tattoo," Laura said.

Rodgers looked at her. "What kind?"

She grabbed her bag and turned it, making sure Rodgers wouldn't be able to see inside, before pulling out a notebook and pen. Working quickly, she sketched the dotted lines and jagged circles that had decorated the woman's ribs, then held up her drawing.

Rodgers studied it, his white mustache drooping over the downturned corners of his mouth.

"I thought it was abstract," Laura said. She added a few more lines to represent a torso and arms and traced her fingers down the lines, nodding. "It's not just a zigzag, see? It's a big W shape. And these dots with the flares surrounding them—I think those are supposed to be stars."

Rodgers said something in response, but Laura had stopped listening.

Childhood memories rose, unbidden, to the surface of her mind. On cold winter nights, when the sky was free of clouds and the air was as clear and fragile as crystal, her father would wake her. He would shuttle her down the stairs, pack her into her coat and boots, and carry her out across the dark and fallow fields, far from any light. As they lay back, heads pressed together, the stars would spread above them, thick and fine as dust. Her father knew them all by name, and it had seemed to her then a mysterious and arcane knowledge to possess, the territory of wizards and magic. She'd asked to be taught and he had agreed, passing down to her constellations named in ancient tongues.

"It's Cassiopeia," Laura said, interrupting Rodgers.

She could picture it clearly: five stars in a W shape cascading down the northern sky. It floated alongside the Ursa Major, the Big Dipper, and together they were essential to celestial navigation. A line drawn through the outside of the Big Dipper's cup and a line drawn through the second and third star of Cassiopeia would converge on a single star hanging between them. The star was otherwise unremarkable, not especially bright, but everyone knew its name: Polaris.

"Don't see what else it could be," Rodgers said.

"Only it's not pointing to the North Star," Laura said. "Go ahead, trace the line. It's pointing to her heart."

* * *

One quick scratch behind Cooper's ears and they were gone, leaving Laura to drive alone back to her apartment, the dingy top floor of a carriage house north of town. In the summer it had roaches, and in the winter an ancient heater huffed and puffed, struggling to keep the space warm. But the price was right, and the empty mile between her place and downtown meant quiet. In a professional life filled with shouting, heightened emotions, and more than its fair share of human misery, the cramped apartment was her shrine to silence and solitude.

She climbed the exterior stairway and unlocked the door. Inside, she shucked her raincoat and boots, shed her clothes, and took a hot shower before putting on sweats and sitting at the small kitchen table.

Her notebook already lay open to the correct page: a name and part of a phone number, written in Laura's idiopathic all-capital scrawl.

BETH BANCROFT
DAVIS + PRITCHARD

Laura hadn't been able to reach the business card that had dropped from the album . . . but she had been able to read some of it.

A quick search returned the law firm of Davis and Pritchard, in Raleigh. Laura found the legalese on the website difficult to parse, but it seemed they were corporate lawyers specializing in litigation. It was almost midnight and they were sure to be closed, but she called the number anyway. A robotic voice asked her if she knew the name of the person she was trying to reach.

"Beth Bancroft."

Two clicks, then a human said, "You've reached the office of Beth Bancroft at Davis and Pritchard. Please leave a message, and she'll return your call as soon as possible."

The machine beeped.

"My name is Laura Chambers, I'm a reporter with the Hillsborough Gazette. I'm trying to reach Ms. Bancroft for comment on a story. It's time sensitive, so a quick call back would be greatly appreciated."

She gave all her contact information before hanging up.

From her bag, she extracted the photo album.

In the truck, just for a moment, she thought Rodgers had spotted it. His eyes had narrowed just a few millimeters, but the effect had been startling: the hard, unflinching stare she remembered from his days as sheriff. But she must have been mistaken, because if Rodgers had realized the contents of her bag, Laura felt certain she would not still have it in her possession. A career in law enforcement left people with very concrete ideas about right and wrong, and Rodgers had spent the better part of his life in a profession where morality was codified and quantified—every situation covered by its rule, every crime balanced by a complementary punishment.

Which wasn't to say retirement had left Rodgers unchanged. He was terribly bored, unmoored by his lack of function, and some of the old rules had started to bend. Investigative jaunts with a reporter would never have been considered back when he was sheriff, but desperate times called for desperate measures. Their work together, Laura knew, offered a sense of purpose to fill his otherwise empty days.

Other rules, though, were ironclad as ever—no tampering with evidence, for example. To Rodgers, having a look around and talking to people was all well within the bounds of the law and her role as a reporter; concealing evidence germane to a homicide investigation was another matter entirely.

The hell of it was, most of the time Laura would agree with him.

But something about the mysterious woman from the freeway had spooked her. For a moment, however brief, Whitley had convinced her the former human being now spread across asphalt like jam on toast belonged to her, was one of her people. That had been a lie, and yet a sense of responsibility had nested in the back of Laura's head. The woman had made one final cry for help in the moments before she died. She could have called anyone—a loved one, the police—but had chosen Laura instead.

And Laura hadn't answered.

In that moment, an unspoken agreement had been struck between them. A debt was owed, and despite Laura's best attempts at indifference, she found herself determined to pay it back.

She ran her hands over the photo album's canvas cover, its coarse fabric rough under her fingertips. A faint odor of old paper emanated from the pages. The small, square photograph pasted to the front was faded, nearly white, as if it had been left out in the light for many years. Three figures were visible, but their features had been sandblasted away to nothingness.

She opened it, the delicate plastic cracking and threatening to crumble.

A young couple stared back at her from the first page, he in glasses with plastic frames and lightly tinted lenses, she in jeans flared out at the bottom. They had their arms wrapped around each other, smiles plastered across their faces. Almost everyone smiled for the birdie, but with these two it looked genuine. There was just a single shot of the wedding, them clasping hands in wide lapels and lots of lace.

She turned the pages and watched the fashions morph into brighter colors, tighter pants. The man briefly sported a comb-over before succumbing to the inevitable; the woman's hairstyle changing from free-flowing locks to a swarm of black ringlets cut short at the ears. Posed shots taken at a Sears in front of pastel inkblot backgrounds. Candid shots snapped by friends, laughing, mouths open, cigarettes ubiquitous between fingers.

Then came a new house: wider spaces, more light, a bigger bed. Two photos pasted in next to each other like some kind of private joke, one of each person sleeping. There were pictures that captured tousled hair and unaffected expressions, deeply intimate moments never intended for public consumption. Looking at them induced a hum of guilt, the electric wrongness of the peeping tom.

Laura turned the page again.

The woman's stomach was swelling now. There she was splayed out on the couch, legs propped on a stack of pillows, a light cotton housedress pulled aside to display her baby's progress. Fierce pride in her eyes. The man with his face resting on her bosom, hand above her navel, an expression of frank excitement. Here came new carpet, a wooden crib, a distinctive crosshatched wallpaper added to the—

Laura stopped.

The wallpaper had a pattern of arrowhead shapes pointed every which way, and it tickled the back of her memory. It was a feeling like déjà vu, and she discounted it as a coincidence or mistake. She moved to the next page, the plastic so thin and fragile it might dissolve at any moment. The nursery was complete, and now Laura recognized the chair as well.

She closed her eyes, opened them again.

The image swam up at her through a haze, the crimson arrowhead shapes on the wallpaper suddenly sharp looking, bladelike, cutting inward toward the plump pink chair. The chair where they used to lean against each other reading books. The chair where one of them would sit with the other between her knees, braiding hair.

The album was nowhere near its end, with plenty left to be uncovered. She didn't want to see it anymore, but her fingers seemed to move on their own. They slithered out over the plastic film and found it unexpectedly greasy and slick as they turned the pages, one after the other. Every photograph was another nail in her chest. Every face was just as she remembered.

The Merritt family, in all their former glory.

A small tremble escaped the hot forge of her throat, but even that tiny sound shattered the silence in her kitchen. She stood and walked away, circled the table like it was a cage with an exotic animal trapped inside. From the sink she drew a glass of ice-cold well water, drank it down in one go, then filled the glass again.

The album lay open beneath the overhead light. She approached again but did not sit. Instead, she looked directly down on Mr. Merritt, whose default expression was a smile; on Mrs. Merritt, who had always had a kind word; on Emily, who had been her best friend. She looked down from on high and wondered: why? Why in God's name had someone decided to keep it all these years?

Then she turned another page and froze.

One last photograph winked up at her. An outdoor shot, pines in the background, the three Merritts with sun in their faces squinting and smiling. And one more man next to them, with his arm around Bob Merritt and a hand resting on Emily's shoulder.

Laura leaned closer to the face, taking in its familiar curves and ruddy features. Crow's-feet crinkled at the corners of the eyes. A wave of grief, bottled up for so long, escaped through some interior hatchway and curled in her stomach, heavy as a stone.

Her hands kept moving. How many photos could he be in? In these later pages, the answer was all of them. All of them. Here he was sharing a meal with the Merritts; there he and Bob were painting Emily's dollhouse, white paint splatted across their overalls. Another snap of the two of them out of doors. She recognized the deep interlocking greens of his flannel shirt and the pale calfskin gloves on his hands, but his face was hidden in shadow.

Laura had only ever had two pictures of him for herself. She had never seen another. To her, every page was like food placed unexpectedly before someone half-starved. She ate and ate, ravenous, until finally she could consume no more. The images began to swirl together, and she had to grab hold of the table to keep from falling over. She closed the album. She squeezed her eyes shut, willing it to go away.

That did nothing to stop it. It emerged from her inner dark, haunting her still. No matter which direction she looked, there it was—waiting for her.

The face of her father.

CHAPTER

14

IMAGINE SUMMER, THE way it used to be, perpetual daylight and nothing to fill the hours but a rumpus of bikes and sprints and unhurried talks under weeping willow trees. Imagine time, the way it lasted back then. Forever. Only later will beloved family, and friends, and even the places that burn in memory—a battered barn, a crooked house, the hill where once a wrist was broken, hot tears against the chilly air, clutching at a ruined arm—only later do they turn hollow and run dry, their power sapped by passing years.

Imagine a child of summer, eight years old, her hair like a bird's nest, her white winter face turned nut brown by days outside from dawn till dusk. Call her up in a hand-sewn dress with bare feet long calloused by the rocky earth. See her running through fields of long grass. Notice her eyes blue as morpho butterflies, her unselfconscious gap-toothed smile. Watch her throw back her head and laugh.

Imagine the knife she lifted from her father's toolshed, clean and sharp.

Picture a clearing: two gray rocks, moss covered and smooth, jutting from the earth. See the way to get there. Ahead, a row of ten-foot pines. Young trees still, each scheming against the others for its share of light. Not all can live until maturity, but for now they grow close enough that even the low branches cross and intertwine, hiding the entrance to the path.

This clearing is their clearing.

It is situated on a slight slope, but someone has taken the time to level the ground, digging out a section about the size of a campsite. Four rows of stone join at right angles to make corners. No mortar has been used, but rather the builder has relied on clever placement and the force of gravity. In the center, find a gnarled log of ancient wood, worm-eaten, twisting furrows covering its surface like indecipherable runes. It sits upright, the top flat and smooth. Here are crudely carved figurines and other totems: river rocks, raven feathers, the foot of a rabbit, all fur and bone.

It is an altar.

Watch them dart and whirl in circles around it—pointy-toothed fairies. See their flower crowns.

Emily produces the knife. This a ritual of protection. Whether it is of her friend's own invention or adapted from some dusty book, she does not know. Her friend is scared, that much she does know, because she buries her fear the same way Laura does, the way they've both been taught by hardscrabble people too poor to shield their children from the ruggedness of the world, who learned the trick of fortitude in turn from those before them.

The knife glitters through narrow beams of sunlight that dapple the mossy ground. She takes Laura firmly by the shoulder, lifts the blade toward her neck, and cuts free a lock of hair. One of her own follows. She twists them together in the blackened bowl at the altar's middle, strikes a match, and applies a flame. They look on as a part of both of them evaporates in smoke and curls up between the trees.

Next come the board and story tiles, spilled across the dirt. She shuffles the tiles back and forth, ordering and reordering. They are all identical in size, rectangular, about the length and width of a cassette tape. Each has a unique picture on its surface. They are handmade, but the intricate carving and woodburning could never have been done by a child. Laura wonders, not for the first time, why her own father decided to make them.

She sees him solitary in his barn, hunched over a workbench, a chisel grasped in both his hands. The light, a dull red, makes the beads of sweat on his forearms appear as blood. The image bursts in her head like a firework.

The tiles are the elements of fairy tales and campfire stories ripped from their context, free to tumble into new and interesting arrangements. This is their method for beginning: Laura tosses them in the air, flips them all facedown, mixes them up, and then Emily turns them over one at a time and fits them down the length of the board.

They have both heard legends about the old ways of divination. Tarot cards. Palm reading. A great-grandmother on Laura's mother's side was supposedly skilled in augury, wherein a person's fortune is culled from the flight patterns of birds.

Laura scoffs at such stories, but Emily believes she can use the tiles to tell the future. She inspects them in their order, her eyes drawn to the darker ones.

The king, imperious, his sword held in front of him point down, a dark liquid dripping off the tip.

The magician with his twisted staff and glowing orb, a malevolent smile on his face.

The hermit with a crooked back.

The hanged man, his eyes bulging.

The specter of death in a hooded robe, scythe in hand. The robe has been allowed to hang open, the flayed, unfleshed body beneath the cloak revealed.

Emily sweeps the tiles away, unsatisfied by what she sees, and tries again. She attempts to recreate one of their favorite stories: the prince and the princess each lost in the woods, in terrible danger, only to find each other, fall in love, defeat evil, and live happily ever after. The prediction of this story has always been perfectly clear to them. Bad times are a necessary precursor to good times. Everything happens for a reason.

This day, however, the story will not work. Over and over Emily rattles the tiles across the dirt, random as dice, then turns them over one by one. And again and again, she is thwarted. As the sun falls and the shadows lengthen, she is distraught.

No matter how hard the prince and princess try to get together, another tile keeps coming between them. One with claws and teeth and a grotesque tongue. One with eyes as black as pitch.

It is the wolf.

CHAPTER

15

LAURA CHAMBERS RECOGNIZED signs of life behind the curtained windows, so she went ahead and knocked. The curtain on the front porch twitched, then the dead bolt slid open. She shouldered her way through the front door in time to see Rodgers, dressed in pajama pants and a threadbare terry cloth robe tied at his waist, lope into his small kitchen. He returned carrying two beers, one stacked on top of the other, and sprawled in an easy chair. "Sit anywhere."

The clock behind him said it was not yet nine in the morning.

"You're sure it's not too much trouble?"

He frowned and popped open his can. "Don't do that. I offered to help, so I'm helping. Forget the faux southern propriety, that's not your style."

She accepted the beer and perched on a rickety stool.

"Glad you came by, actually. Would you believe you're not my first visitor today? Walking the dog down near the end of the driveway just after dawn, I got ambushed by Whitley and Bynum. I gotta say something to you now."

"Go ahead and say it."

He took a slurp of beer. "This guy Whitley, he hates your guts."

"I know."

"No, I mean he really dislikes you. I am not engaging in hyperbole right now. You reading me?"

Laura had made the mistake of showing her bruised-black wrist to Bass Herman but had mollified him by agreeing to sniff around the interstate accident and its circumstances. Only because it would have cramped her ability to investigate had he restrained himself from marching into Sheriff Fuller's office, metaphorical guns blazing. Rodgers had an equally old-fashioned sense of honor, so she was careful to not make the same mistake again.

She said, "He's made that more than clear."

"But it gets worse."

Laura sighed, opened her can, and took a drink.

"Bynum is just as pissed. Seeing Bynum angry was like catching a glimpse of a bear wearing pants. Unnatural. I worked with him, and he's a milquetoast guy most of the time. An odd duck in this line of business."

"What did they want?"

"They came to read me the riot act. They know we were there at the motel together, Laura."

She swallowed. "I don't know how—"

He held up a hand. "Someone saw my truck, I gathered that much. Their witness must not be certain, or I got the sense I'd already be in handcuffs. Now don't you look at me like that—the cuffs would've been just a negotiating tactic, you understand? We didn't do anything the law says we can't. Look, it was fun for this racehorse to go on one last ride before he gets put out to pasture permanently. But they asked about you, Laura—where you live, where else they might find you. I fibbed a bit, told 'em I had no idea. Told 'em to pound sand, as a matter of fact. You'll have to stay away awhile, because all that's moot if they see you showing up at my house, don't you think?"

"Don," she said. His name limped out of her mouth.

"I'm not finished," he continued. "They think the motel room was searched, same as you. Only difference is, Whitley and Bynum are convinced you're the one that did it. I'm sure Benny Morno squealed at the first opportunity, told 'em you're the only other person he let inside. Plus the other thing."

"What?"

"That he saw you steal something from the room."

In her mind, Laura played back the fraught moment when she had dropped out the window. She recalled the tingle on the back of her neck, her body's way of telling her to hurry up and run. She had looked left and right before dashing for the trees and had seen no one, but those had been cursory glances. Was it possible Morno had been watching her from the far end of the building?

"Don't worry," he reassured her. "I know you wouldn't be that stupid."

She pushed up from the stool. She faced Rodgers square, her weight on both feet. "When they track me down and I end up in jail, tell Bass. He'll probably decide to bail me out."

Rodgers started to chuckle before clocking the serious look on her face and sitting up straight in his chair. "Quit that, nobody's really gonna get arrested. They're just trying to rattle your cage."

She turned to the wall. Framed certificates and a picture of his late wife hung next to one another. There was a bookshelf with a glass case. Inside were a badge and a small revolver in a velvet box, the lid of the box propped open against the wall. A small plaque on the front read FOR A LIFETIME OF SERVICE.

"What's wrong with you?" he asked.

She turned around.

His eyes were the same as in the truck the previous night, hard blue pebbles. "You never get this quiet. It's starting to scare me a little bit."

"There's no easy way to say this."

"Never will be, for some things."

"I figured out her name."

"Whose? Our Jane Doe?"

Laura nodded. "It's Emily Merritt."

She registered the surprise on his face, and in nearly the same instant watched as his inner tumblers dropped into place. The rough-hewn lines that stretched between his nose and the corners of his mouth collapsed into the deep valleys of a glower. In an instant, his experienced cop intuition had leapt from A to B to C. There was no logical way Laura Chambers could be presenting the woman's identity to him, not unless she had concealed an essential fact.

"Tell me," he said quietly, two simple words that seemed to vibrate with intensity in the morning air.

"I'm not sure what you're asking."

He slammed a palm down on the coffee table so hard it made his beer can rattle. A small portion sloshed out and ran down the side, pooling around the base. "Don't lie to me again."

She curled in on herself, the fingers of one hand wrapped like wire around the opposite wrist. Rodgers was a loud man, fond of casual profanity and mock aggression, but never had she seen such naked anger writ across his face. She tried to look him in the eye but found that she could not, her gaze sliding down to the tabletop, her shoulders folding in on themselves, making her smaller. Growing up she'd experienced her father's temper, unpredictable in what would set it off; when he screamed, she had shrunk just the same way.

When Rodgers spoke next, the cold hush in his voice was more disturbing than if he'd continued yelling. "You did take something."

She turned her face away.

He caught sight of the blush spreading across her cheeks and closed his eyes. "Goddamn it, Laura."

"The room had already been tossed when I got there, I swear it. But I did find one thing they overlooked." Quickly she told him about her discovery of the photo album in its hiding place. By the time she was done, Rodgers looked apoplectic. His face was as red as if he'd been running, and veins throbbed at his temples.

"You stole evidence from a homicide investigation," he hissed at her.

"And you drove the getaway car," she fired back, regretting the words before they even finished leaving her mouth.

He threw up his hands. "I was an idiot then, a doddering old fool. All this time we've been playing cops and robbers together, it was just a harmless diversion. You get a few little stories, I get out of the house, everybody wins. But this is different, Laura. If you're right and Jane Doe . . . Emily Merritt, whoever she is—if someone shot her and then ran her out in front of that truck, what have you done? Corrupted evidence, obstructed the investigation, the list goes on. Whitley's out for blood, and I can't say I blame him."

"You want me to apologize to you?"

Rodgers didn't answer.

"I apologize."

He let out a breath. "This is not the straight and narrow."

"I'm aware."

"You're sticking your neck out."

"I know it."

"You're sticking *my* neck out."

"And what a nice neck it is."

He almost smiled then. "Call Whitley, tell him what you've got."

"He'll throw the book at me."

"Do it now, and it'll be a pretty small book. Fib a little; you know I'd be all right with that. Say it was a mistake. He might try to bring you up on charges, but a judge won't be very interested. On the other hand, if you conceal a piece of evidence that would prevent the investigating officers from identifying a murder victim . . ." He shook his head. "I'll do what I have to do, you know I will."

"I'll call him, okay?"

"You must." There was a pleading look in his eyes. "It's the right thing to do. What about her people, Laura? Someone out there is missing her."

"I'll go see Bynum, I promise. As soon as I get in my car, I'm headed straight there."

For a long moment Rodgers drummed his fingers on the tabletop, then finally he sat back in his chair. "You got it with you?"

Laura hesitated, then pulled the album from her bag and clapped it down on the table.

"Christ," Rodgers said, and snatched up his beer. He went to the kitchen and came back with a towel to sop up the spillage and a pair of brand-new dishwashing gloves, still in their package. "Stop touching it, for God's sake. There could be fingerprints."

"From the person who shot her? They never found this."

"For the identification."

"We already know who she is."

"Don't get overconfident." He pulled on the gloves and started turning pages. "I'll be damned. That's them all right."

"Family photo albums are kept in folks' homes. My question is, what happens to the evidence in a case like the Merritts'. Do they ever release it?"

"Not for a death penalty case. They had to run a gauntlet of appeals, so I guarantee that even now it's all kept under lock and key. Maybe when Barrow's in the ground the authorities release it, but legally there's nothing stopping them from keeping evidence indefinitely."

"I see," Laura said.

"But I'm sure most of the stuff in the house wasn't classified as such. They secured it as part of the crime scene but only tagged items deemed relevant. I can't imagine they're storing a whole house's worth of furniture, for example."

"And what about those items? The nonrelevant ones."

"Next of kin," Rodgers said.

"Can you think of anyone else who would be carting this around Hillsborough two decades later?"

He didn't answer.

"So it was her, it was Emily Merritt. It's the only explanation that makes any kind of sense. Next of kin, you said it yourself. She heard Simon Barrow's due to settle up and came to see me."

"For what purpose?"

Laura set her jaw. "Still working on that."

"Who shot her? What about their purpose?"

"Don't know that either."

"Don't know much," he muttered. "This is thin as tissue paper."

"It's an idea," Laura said. "I'll run it down. I'll check up on Emily Merritt, and if no one's seen her since this past Sunday, that will pretty much settle whether this idea is right or wrong, wouldn't you say?"

Rodgers kept turning the pages with his gloved hands. In the second half of the album, almost all the pictures were missing. Blank, empty spaces stared back at him. For a long time there had been photographs there—he could see the tacky outlines of the glue that had secured them and patches of paste, yellow with age, and in a few cases ragged corners that had torn off and been left behind—but they were no longer in place.

Someone had ripped them out.

"What happened here, do you think?"

Laura ignored the question. "Where did Emily Merritt go back in '96, after it happened?"

It took a second for him to turn back to her, absent-minded. "Orphans aren't Sheriff's Office business—Social Services handles that. But there's someone over there who still owes me a favor."

"Appreciate it. One more thing." She told him about the business card that had been tucked inside the album. "Not sure a corporate lawyer will be much help, but if Emily was a client, maybe she'll be willing to confirm that for me."

Rodgers placed the album gingerly in a paper grocery bag and handed it to her. "Look, I got another bit of news for you—they found a bullet casing. Went with the dogs out to the motel this morning and found it twenty yards back from that window you went out of."

"Whitley told you this?" she said, skeptical.

"Naw, this is straight from someone I trust at OCSO. News is out I was there last night, so I got a call. This is real."

A brief flash of Emily Merritt at a dead run toward the woods crossed her vision—a shadowy figure dropping to one knee, shouldering the rifle, and just before she vanished from view, squeezing the trigger. Laura shook it off.

"They'll send it to the state crime lab, and I don't know anyone over there," she said.

Rodgers stroked his chin. "I was thinking the same, until I remembered they had a fire at the state lab."

"That was almost a year ago. It opened again."

"Not firearms identification. That's where the fire started. Heard some mishandled black powder was the culprit. Anyhow, that one section took the majority of the damage. It's still closed."

"So who will do the analysis?"

"They've been outsourcing the work to the F–B–I." He drew out each letter. "You know that fella over there. What's his name?"

Rodgers knew his name perfectly well but liked to pretend he'd forgotten whenever it came up. "Timinski," she said.

"You and him were thick as thieves, I recall."

"And he got in serious trouble for it. He was supposed to get some big job in DC, but when the Bureau caught on to the fact he was feeding information to a journalist, he became persona non grata. The Office of the Inspector General came a hair's width from canning him. He won't talk to me."

He held the door open for her. "Only one way to find out."

"Plus he was supposed to be with me the night you and Cooper pulled me out of the fire. He's an asshole."

"Nice to hear the two of you got something in common." There was a twinkle in his eye.

"Where's the dog? At least the dog likes me."

He snorted, flaring his nostrils and sending a quiver through the droopy white mustache he'd affected over the last eight months. She appreciated again just how much healthier he looked. He still drank more than he should, but his consumption was down and his weight was up to the point that his once-sallow complexion verged on ruddy.

"You can say hello when you walk out. You owe him that much."

"Because he saved my skin?"

"Couldn't have done it without him."

"Tell Cooper I say it's going to be real tough to even us out on that score."

"Oh, he's not looking for reciprocity," Rodgers said. "Just a little appreciation."

"Well, if he were here, I'd say thanks." She met his eyes. "Thanks for everything."

He looked away. "Don't go soft on me now, Chambers."

She managed a small smile. "Wouldn't dream of it."

CHAPTER

16

LAURA CALLED THE lawyer again from outside the house.

The line trilled twice before it opened. "Beth Bancroft's office."

Three words and Laura could already picture the kind of place she'd called. A distant murmur of voices, dulled by yards of thick carpeting, suggested an imperial separation between the workers and their bosses. She could almost feel the icy chill of the air conditioning, set low to accommodate the men in suits.

"May I speak to Ms. Bancroft?"

"Hold, please."

Inoffensive music began to play in her ear, mixing with the low throb of the Dart's engines. She glanced out the driver's side window over a vista of scrub pine and red earth, and it seemed about as far from a Raleigh high-rise as it was possible to get.

The music snapped off; the cool, efficient voice returned. "Ms. Bancroft is not available at this time. May I ask what this is regarding?"

"It's an emergency," Laura said, and took some pleasure in the small fumbling sounds coming down the line. In a few more minutes she managed to wheedle home and mobile numbers out of the assistant. Neither were answered. She left a message on Beth Bancroft's cell phone, but the home number just rang and rang.

* * *

She was being followed.

From Rodgers's place, she'd driven south toward downtown Hillsborough and passed a muddy brown sedan parked on the opposite side of the two-lane highway. Dust and grime clung to its glass surfaces and obscured the interior. An oil-stained white T-shirt hung like a flag from the rear passenger window, indicating a breakdown, but there were no signs of life.

Strange, Laura thought.

Strange because she had spoken with Rodgers for fewer than thirty minutes, and the car hadn't been in that spot when she drove past it the first time. The breakdown must have just occurred.

She pulled around a sharp curve and accelerated, the wind whipping the canvas top. The Dart came over the top of a small rise, and as it dropped down into the flats next to a creek, Laura caught the barest glimmer of movement in her rearview mirror.

Behind her, a dirty brown sedan crested the hill. From its rear window hung a greasy white T-shirt, flapping in the breeze.

"Son of a bitch," she muttered.

Rodgers's warning rang in her ears. Whitley wanted very much to speak with her, so much so that he'd gotten up early to lurk near the end of Rodgers's driveway this morning. Was he eager enough to requisition an undercover from the impound lot? She remembered the fire in his eyes when he'd grabbed hold of her and decided that settled the question.

Behind her, the brown car grew larger in the mirror.

Laura shifted into third and hit the gas. The Dart's V-8 engine gave a throaty roar, and she whipped through a series of turns. The last one was sharper than the others and she almost lost control, her tires slipping across wet asphalt, the Dart drifting toward a very solid looking oak tree.

She turned into the skid and punched the accelerator.

The tires caught and gained traction beneath her, the engine screaming as the car shot forward again.

Heart hammering in her chest, Laura checked the mirror.

The brown sedan slid into view.

"Son of a bitch," she said again. Whoever it was, they could drive. Momentarily she wondered why Whitley didn't just pull her over. Laura had intended to give him the slip before he could get behind her, but so far he had managed to keep pace. Now all he had to do was turn on the flashing lights. That would be the end of their little cat-and-mouse game. If she kept running, he could charge her with evading arrest too, another felony. She would have no choice but to pull over.

Laura made a final turn and sprint. Buildings—a gas station, a pharmacy—sprang up on either side of the road as she neared the north side of downtown. The intersection of Highways 86 and 70 saw enough traffic to warrant a left turn lane. The arrow was already red as Laura approached, but she pulled into the turn lane anyway and came to a stop, the Dart's engine burbling in anticipation.

People were up and headed to work now, their cars stacking up across the intersection. Behind her the brown sedan came to a stop three feet off her rear bumper. She stared into the mirror, expecting to see Whitley climb out, walk up, and rap on her window.

But the car simply waited. No movement at all was visible behind the dingy windshield. Its patience was unnerving.

What was he waiting for?

Laura didn't particularly want to find out. This traffic light was the usual three circles stacked one on top of another. There were no arrows, so when the light turned green, vehicles headed straight in both directions would have the right of way. She would pull into the middle of the intersection and wait as the long line of approaching cars blocked her path. When the last of these finally trickled past, she would be able to complete the left turn. And the brown car would follow along behind, stuck on her tail as surely as dog shit on a shoe.

The light turned green.

Laura punched the gas and the Dart leapt forward, careening into the intersection.

Traveling in the opposite direction, the first vehicle in line was a lifted pickup on huge all-terrain tires, a chrome push bar bolted to the grille. It belched exhaust as it picked up speed, barreling ahead.

Laura cut the wheel to the left, tires squealing.

For a moment, collision seemed inevitable. Then the truck rocked forward as the driver hit the brakes, and Laura slid past with inches to spare. Behind her she could hear the drone of the truck driver laying on his horn. She checked the mirror, but the line of oncoming cars had formed a wall between her and the other side of the intersection.

She pushed her speed back up, made a left onto a smaller side street, and threaded her way through a few different neighborhoods. Twice she pulled over and waited.

But the brown sedan was nowhere to be seen.

C H A P T E R

17

"YOU'RE ALL JITTERY. How many cups of coffee did you drink?" Laura went to the front window and pushed aside the curtain.

Outside the Chambers farmhouse, the Dart glinted back at her. Next to it was the mouth of the dirt drive, which ran a quarter mile to the highway through corn planted on either side. This time of year the cornstalks stood more than head high, concealing whatever lay behind them. Still, though, an approaching car would throw up a distinctive cloud of dust in its wake, a cloud that would become visible long before an engine could be heard.

This morning the sky was a deep and faultless blue.

"What the hell are you looking at?"

Walking into her mother's house, she often thought of laying one hand in a vise and using the other to spin the handle.

"You listening to me?" This last question was punctuated by a dirty sneaker thrown into the wall next to Laura's head.

Laura pushed the curtain back into place. "You get your oxygen delivery?"

"It's coming later today."

"What did the doctor say?"

"He's been calling. I haven't had time to get back to him just yet."

Diane Chambers sat in her special oversized armchair, the place she spent twelve or sixteen hours a day. On bad days, the days she slept in the chair, Laura thought her mother might go twenty-four hours at a stretch without standing up except to use the bathroom. She had her TV remote and her small cooler of Cokes within arm's reach and the phone next to her on an end table.

"Just call him back. Someone over there can help get the concentrator fixed. The bottles were only supposed to be for emergencies."

Diane shook her head, the doughy jowls beneath her chin swinging back and forth like the pendulum of a grandfather clock. "That man they sent out to fix it was some kind of pervert."

"Diane, I'm sure—"

"You should have seen the look in his eye when he shook my hand! Lord, I thought he was going to have his way with me right here in this chair. No, I like the stuff out the bottle anyway." She sniffed. "The air in here has never been pure enough for my taste. Your father's family stunk this house up for a century, and it never did air out."

"It's fine."

"They had the right idea with the first house."

"What first house?"

"This is the second house, built after the first one burned in 1895. People say lightning strike, but family legend tells some great-great-uncle or other passed out in front of the fire so drunk he didn't wake up, not when a log rolled out, not even before the whole house was a conflagration. Drunks, the lot of them."

Her mother delighted in deriding the Chambers family whenever she had the chance, and this, Laura suspected, was borne of her mother's sharp interest in the local social strata. The Chambers clan had been relegated to poverty for a generation by the time Diane married into it, but they had been prosperous farmers and landowners for the generations before that, and their name still carried weight in the surrounding area. Her mother, on the other hand, had grown up in a trailer with no name to speak of. The Chambers family may have been dirt poor, but they weren't trash. An increase in station was the reason Diane had picked Bruce Chambers to marry—she had said as much herself on several occasions.

"I never saw the foundation."

"That old tobacco-drying barn is built on top of it. Back in that corner on the other side of the train tracks, right up against the Merritts' farm. It's the spot we told you not to go."

Laura remembered now. “Old ghosts, you used to say.”

“Did you believe me? Well, you’re a big girl now. The real reason was the root cellar and the old cistern. The floor above is rotten. It’s a death trap.”

“The Merritt place—who owns it now?”

“I knew it!” her mother crowed. “You’re going to write another story about those unlucky bastards. But an unlucky bastard is still a bastard, Laura. Nobody owns it.”

“It gets planted, doesn’t it?”

“Rented out, same as ours.”

“So who does the renting?”

Her mother shrugged. “No one lives there. Have you been over to see?”

Laura shook her head.

“You’re not alone. No one wanted to spend much time in the house afterward, I reckon. Heard it’s in total disrepair now, all falling apart. People call it haunted. Maybe they’re right.”

“Where did Emily go? Afterward, I mean.”

“They shipped her off.”

“They?”

“The government, I guess.”

“You weren’t curious?”

“Is that what this is about? Your little friend, the one you begged to come stay with us?”

Laura leaned back an inch. When she had been small and without defense, the worst parts of her mother had been greatly magnified. Laura had been timid as a church mouse, unable even to ask for seconds at the dinner table, so the idea that she had asked her mother to take in Emily Merritt struck her as patently absurd.

“I never asked.”

“Better you don’t remember. All that blubbering was embarrassing. You prostrated yourself right there on that rug you’re standing on. You must have cried for a damn hour.”

Laura glanced down at the rug. It was well worn, with fringe around the outside.

“’Course I had to say no,” her mother continued. “One of you was plenty. Then they came and took her, I guess.”

“So it’s possible Emily still owns the land, either outright or some kind of trust?”

"Doubt it. That Linda Merritt always liked to spend. She didn't have a thrifty bone in her body, not like me. I'm always saving, aren't I? Do I ever even take myself out for a nice meal?"

Laura said nothing.

"The Merritts were broke. A few years before . . . before they . . . he . . ." Diane pressed her face into one fleshy elbow joint and let loose a cough. It sounded like an ungreased ball bearing grinding and rattling deep in her chest.

"Get a good breath."

Her mother held up a finger, cleared her throat, and said, "Bob Merritt took out a mortgage."

It was a short sentence that spoke volumes about the seriousness of the Merritts' financial situation. In the era of Big Agriculture, neither the Chambers nor the Merritt farm had encompassed enough acreage to make its owners rich. The margins were so thin, in fact, and the variables affecting crops—weather, commodity prices, trade relations—so capricious that only one factor made it possible to eke out a living: the land was owned outright. After generations of fighting tooth and nail and decades spent coaxing the earth to give up her bounty, the only money owed each year was the property taxes. All her life Laura had been told how lucky they were to be free and clear of banks and bankers, that the man who mortgaged his heritage was more than desperate—he was a fool.

"He wouldn't have gone spreading that around."

Her mother bristled at the implication that her gossip was anything less than accurate.

"Hattie Daniel works at First National. She and I used to go to church together, back before she decided she was better than me. Humble yourself under God's mighty hand, that's what the Bible says. Hattie never read it, let me tell you."

"They must have been near bankrupt."

"He wouldn't have done it otherwise," her mother agreed. "But Bob Merritt wasn't the sharpest tool in the shed."

"Did you know him well?"

"Didn't much care to."

"What about Daddy? He and Mr. Merritt were about the same age. The Merritt farm's been there almost as long as the Chambers one, so they grew up next to each other, just like Emily and I did. They must have been friends."

Her mother pressed the mask over her mouth. Above the clear plastic, her beady eyes fixed on Laura's face as if she were waiting for something. "Nope, they never spoke much that I can recall."

"They didn't much speak," Laura repeated.

"Frankly, your father never liked the man. I never got the details, but you know how a grudge can linger."

Laura reached into her pocket and extracted one of the photographs of Bruce Chambers standing among the Merritts, everyone aglow with summer tans, faces bright with smiles. Based on Emily's age in the picture, it couldn't have been taken too long before tragedy struck. Laura held it out at arm's length, right in front of her mother's face.

"What about this?" she said.

Her mother ripped the mask away from her face. "I ain't saying they never talked!" she barked. "They didn't associate is what I mean. They weren't friends."

"I found this pasted inside a photo album that belonged to the Merritts. There are lots more like it. Do you want to see?"

Diane gave a wet wheeze.

"After the Merritts died—right after—that's when Daddy said he had to go away."

If there'd been dry wood in Diane Chambers's line of sight, it would have burst into flame. She grabbed for the oxygen mask again, welding it over her mouth and nose and taking great gasping breaths.

Laura kept talking. "He left. He left, and he didn't come back until—"

"Until he needed us again," her mother coughed.

Laura waited until her mother's breaths shrank to reedy, suckling sips of air. Then she asked the question she'd come to ask.

"Did his leaving have something to do with the Merritts dying?"

Her mother dissolved into a fit, her head shaking back and forth, seismic waves rolling across the flab of her arms. Laura scooted forward on her chair, alarmed. It took her a moment to realize her mother wasn't coughing or gasping—she was laughing. Diane Chambers clapped her hands. She threw back her head, and a dry cackle clawed its way up out of her throat.

After a few steady breaths, she said, "What makes you say so?"

A glimmer in her mind's eye, another buried fragment of memory unearthed: gray veins in the back of her father's hand as he took her roughly by the arm. He shook a finger in her face. His mouth was open in a shout, but the memory was silent. She knew, without knowing how, that he was telling her to quit bringing up Emily Merritt's name at school.

She was never your friend, don't tell people that. Do you understand?

She tapped a finger on the photograph. "It seems like there's this whole history you both decided to erase. Why was it important to do that?"

"So there's a few pictures of them together—what does it matter?"

"I don't much believe in coincidence."

"Do you believe in cowardice? Because it was cowardice that made him leave, plain and simple, and it was cowardice that brought him back. Seemed for a while there he was the sort of man who took responsibility for his family, but of course that sort doesn't cut and run just because he's tired of his little girl following him round like a well-trained dog, asking her stupid little questions, always badgering him for a pat on the head. Your father got fed up with you is all."

"That's not true," Laura said.

But this answer was the awful one, the worst one she could imagine. In the nights after her father had left, no one had come when Laura called. The lonely hours stretched out like molasses, providing her with nothing but the dark and her own thoughts for company. Sometimes she would imagine he hadn't come home because he was dead in a ditch somewhere; other times she was sure he'd made a choice to stay far, far away, so disappointed in his daughter he never wanted to see her again. Laura had never been able to decide which answer would be worse.

"Oh yes," her mother said. "Yes, yes, yes. He hated it here, you must have sensed that. Why do you think he drank to excess, why was it he could never get himself on the straight-and-narrow path of righteousness? Because he was trapped, Laura. First by his name and the legacy of this land and the responsibility he felt to honor that legacy. Then later, once I got pregnant, by you."

Laura said, "It wasn't like that."

Her mother didn't seem to hear. "But everyone has their limit," she continued. "Shovel shit long enough, eventually the handle breaks off."

"He was sick."

Her mother scoffed. “Not then he wasn’t. And by the time he came back, cancer had eaten him halfway up inside. Can I ask you a question?”

Laura said nothing.

“When he came crawling back, you think that was because he wanted to spend his last good month with me and you? Or do you think he came back for the very simple reason that he had nowhere else to go?”

CHAPTER

18

An exhaustion settled over Laura, and she wanted to rest. The prospect of Whitley kicking in the door of her apartment occurred to her, and she decided to spend the night in her mother's house. She would call Bynum in the morning, explain what she had taken, and ask for his consideration.

But bad dreams followed her, and the long hours before dawn found her awake wrapped in damp sheets. She pushed aside the crumpled Minnie Mouse bedspread and searched the bedside table, and when she didn't find what she was looking for, she moved downstairs to the kitchen cabinets. In the junk drawer among the old keys and loose screws and the stacks of mail of medium importance, the kind neither essential enough to address nor trivial enough to throw away, she located a soft pack with four stale cigarettes and a lighter secreted inside.

Her top bedsheet served as a crude shawl, and she let herself out onto the small back porch, lit a cigarette, and inhaled. She held the smoke, feeling it slide through the walls of her lungs and inject itself into her bloodstream. The punch of nicotine was as intense and familiar as the embrace of an old lover.

Back in her room, the laptop was where she'd left it the night before, and when she opened the lid, the video of Emily Merritt's death still haunted the screen. Laura had watched it over and over again. There was a limit, she had decided, to the amount of information that could be extracted from a finite amount of footage. What could possibly be gained from watching it again?

She pressed play.

The same events unspooled again, the rain, the lashing wind, the squelch of wipers on glass, the unnerving calm inside the truck's cab. Tick, tick, tick, the seconds clicking by, and all the while the inevitable approaching through the dark.

She caught herself balling her fists, fingernails embedding themselves into her palms, and made herself relax.

At the correct time stamp she paused the video and moved forward frame by frame. The portion of the incident captured by Kevin Romano's dash cam lasted just seven-tenths of a second. At thirty frames per second, that meant there were only twenty-one frames in which Emily Merritt appeared. Impact occurred on frame twelve. After that came images of the bumper cutting her off at the knees, rolling her up and over the hood, then a brief moment when her back pressed against the edge of the windshield. Kevin Romano had jerked the wheel by this point, and in such extreme slow motion the truck behaved like a living thing. It twisted away from her, as if she were a hot coal and it were afraid to be burned. Too late, though, as the immutable physics of the encounter had already been set in motion, clockwork spinning on toward its inexorable conclusion. Emily's body glanced off the driver's side pillar, then spun away out the left side of the screen.

Frame ten, just two frames before impact, was the worst.

It was the clearest picture of Emily, and in it she had skidded to a stop in the passing lane. She tilted to the rear, as if she were just about to shift her weight in the other direction and backpedal.

But she would never get the chance.

Flat-footed on the asphalt, she turned her upper body. Arms raised. Hands out in front of her to ward off the impending collision. Wet and stringy hair plastered across the opening of her mouth, but her eyes were visible and in focus.

The eyebrows arched in surprise.

The pupils wide and black as the mouth of a well.

Laura studied the face. Emily had changed as the years passed. Time had been rough on her, the kind of hard mileage that announced itself on the skin. The Emily she had known had been smooth faced, naïve and sure of herself in equal measure. Of course, that Emily had also been eight years old and yet to experience the trauma of her parents' death.

Laura had imagined long, lean years as the cause of her friend's transformation, but now she examined another possibility. Perhaps the change had happened in an instant. All that youth, vitality, and hope drained out of her by two blasts of a shotgun.

She wound the video back again to frame number one.

Here just the barest hint of beige skin broke through the brush, Emily's leading edge as she careened toward the gap between two sections of guardrail. Another few frames and she was fully in view, arms in front of her, legs akimbo. If the truck hadn't hit her, she might have fallen.

Laura returned to the first frame and located the object of her interest.

There it was: an anomaly in the upper left corner. She reached out and touched it, a smudge of color shining in the dark.

It could be just an artifact of the recording. The composition of the shot and Emily's position made it possible this was just some rear part of her body peeking out through a thin patch of undergrowth. But the image was blurred, the depth of field unclear. Each time she stared at it, Laura felt more certain she was looking at something farther back in the frame, *behind* Emily.

Another person closing in, so close they could almost reach out with two arms and catch great handfuls of her thin and soaking slip.

So near. In another moment they would have had her.

* * *

Laura could have walked, but instead she parked the Dart as close as possible to the Merritt house. The entrance to the drive was easy to miss. It her headlights, it looked like just another turnoff for tractors between the rows.

The cornstalks were shadows still on a backdrop colored charcoal in the predawn light. Soon they gave way to tall grass that swarmed the road from either side. Ahead, a tree had fallen, blocking the way forward. Laura turned the key and cut the engine.

Night sounds flooded in through the windows. Insects quavered and keened, the wind a feeble hand through the trees. Hot September humidity hugged the world like a duvet cover. Her headlights splashed a cone of yellow light against thick, dead branches. Moths glided back and forth across the glare, circling, rising, raptors riding thermals.

She got out and passed to the cone's side, stayed to the darkness.

After twenty-three years, the driveway had eroded away to nothing. Where it cut level through a small rise, erosion had caused a miniature landslide and cast down stones and boulders. Her footsteps clicked on the rocky ground, but the moisture in the air sucked greedily at the sound, whittling it away to nothing. She reached an impenetrable wall of brush and paused.

Laura's eyes adjusted to the night.

Thick undergrowth surrounded her, but straight ahead was a splash of reddish-brown among the green. It was the color of soil, ground worn down to the clay by passing feet. A slight gap between the boughs hinted at a path.

She pushed through the thicket and discovered it fell away under the trees. She found herself on a rutted track though scrub pine.

Behind her, a rustling and the snap of a twig.

She went rigid, tried to force her breathing to a stop.

A light skitter across the pine needles, the peculiar sound of a small mammal.

She breathed out again, kept moving.

The path was a tunnel, enclosed on all sides by vines of kudzu dripping down from the branches above. The scent of summer lilac, thick and sweet, throbbed purple in the night air.

The vines rippled in a tepid breeze, and Laura felt a familiar prickle on the back of her neck: the feeling of being watched. For a beat she thought she could sense eyes between the trees, taking her measure, waiting for their moment.

She steadied herself against a tree, used the back of her sleeve to wipe the sheen of sweat from her brow. It seemed warmer now than it had during daylight, as if the world were feverish.

Abruptly, the trees ended. Ahead the forest had been cut clear, and the Merritt house rose spindly in the moonlight.

It had been grand once, a Federal-style brick box, two stories, a porch now half-collapsed. A large central chimney rose out of the roof, but the mortar had cracked, and it leaned precariously to one side. Shingles were missing, and a thick green moss crept up the walls. Old oaks surrounded the house, several decades overdue for a trim. Hundred-pound dead branches hung like guillotines.

The bars on the windows hadn't been there when she was a child. Probably the bank had added them later as protection against vandalism.

Laura tried the front door and found it unlatched.

She took a step inside and stopped, reaching out with all her senses for the subtle electricity of a space with a person inside it, but the foyer was still. The house smelled of a tomb. She hurried up stairs that groaned under her weight, slipped down the hallway, and entered the bedroom that once had belonged to Emily Merritt.

The room was curiously bare. The pink chair and the toys and the bed were gone. She'd expected no furniture but found the lack of graffiti puzzling. An abandoned murder house is the sort of place adolescents are drawn to, and she had been prepared to find bottles and cigarettes and spray-painted rude phrases.

Instead, the floor was clean, almost as if it had been recently swept. The wallpaper pattern seemed strangely crisp and unfaded. Its arrowheads were pointed teeth, the room a gaping maw about to snap shut.

Under the window stood a radiator cover built of scarred, varnished wood and shaped as a bench. Emily had never seen the radiator underneath, she'd told Laura. Neither had her father; it predated them both. This very bedroom had belonged to Bob Merritt when he was a boy, and when his only child had been old enough to inherit the family secret, he had shown her a special place to press a beveled edge and spring open a compartment.

Eight-year-olds, it turns out, aren't much for keeping secrets from their best friend.

Laura hurried to the bench and pressed the hidden button. *Click*—the little door swung open. She reached her hand inside and found countless spiderwebs and, at the back, a flat wooden box and a musty drawstring sack made of red velvet. She drew them out and set them on the floorboards.

The wooden box she recognized as a catchall for her friend's art supplies. These were hidden because they were precious. Emily had wanted to be a painter, or failing that a stage magician, and had spent all her rainy days sketching and doodling. Inside the box were hard tubes of old paint, brushes, colored pencils, a small knife for sharpening. The rear portion of the box folded up to become a modest-sized easel. Laura erected it now and found several drawings and paintings clipped to it. Mostly they were dogs and crude landscapes, but two at the back were arresting.

Human faces with big eyes over shadowy bodies. Tears on cheeks. The delirious cotton-candy colors of a Kandinsky. Looking at them made her feel disoriented, even a little sick. They were all women's faces, Laura noticed. Long hair, red lips. The second painting had black vertical lines that ran top to bottom. She turned the picture on its side, and the figures appeared to be lying down as viewed through a window blind.

Laura rolled them all up, stuck them in her back pocket. The velvet bag's drawstring loosened with ease, and she tipped the contents onto the floor.

Out spilled a rectangular board, followed by a shower of carved wooden tiles. Three on top of the pile were turned upright, revealing the illustrations burned onto their faces. One was a castle tower rising to a turret, ivy twisting around the outside. Another portrayed a child among trees, mouth shaped into an O, hands raised above the head—either in celebration or distress, it wasn't clear which.

The last depicted a wolf, oversized, monstrous, all claws and teeth, with a tongue that slithered out the mouth and drooped down between the paws. The eyes were deeper than the other features, ragged black holes burned into the pine.

CHAPTER

19

SHE WAS BEING followed again.

Early that morning, Laura had called the Orange County Sheriff's Office and asked to speak to Bynum, and when they wouldn't give her a direct phone number, she'd driven into town, made a quick stop at the *Gazette* office, and then tried to see him in person. But the best she'd been able to do was leave a message, and the deputy at the duty desk had betrayed no sign of recognition when she told him her name. Quite the opposite, he'd looked annoyed at the interruption of his crossword. He tapped his foot impatiently as she filled out a slip of paper, then shooed her out the door.

Laura backed out of a parking spot on Court Street and turned west on King, passed a bar and a bookstore, and headed out of town. Behind her, a dirty white Charger made the same turn. It matched her speed and fell in behind her, its windshield winking with the reflected late-afternoon sun.

The Dodge Charger has been the most common police vehicle for more than a decade, but the Chrysler company also sells almost a hundred thousand a year to regular consumers. Like the Ford Crown Victoria before it, the car is ubiquitous, on every road and in every parking lot. If the Charger in question is unmarked, without an obvious paint job, light bar, or cattle pusher mounted to the front, a person can never quite decide whether to worry when they see it in the rearview mirror.

The one behind Laura betrayed no ill intent. It lurked patiently behind her as their little procession put more and more distance between itself and the courthouse. Two-story buildings gave way to low-slung houses that in turn yielded to fields of rough grass. Trees sprang up at the edges of the road, growing and thickening in direct proportion to their distance from civilization. The stream of cars passing in the opposite direction weakened to a trickle, and soon the two vehicles were alone.

The growl of an engine, coaxing two thousand pounds of metal to move faster.

Laura maintained her speed, glanced up at the mirror.

The Charger jumped closer, crowding her rear bumper. Red and blue lights concealed behind the grille strobed and flashed. The siren kicked on.

She didn't change her speed.

Two deafening chirps exploded behind her, like the blasts of a foghorn. Ahead, a narrow dirt road cut away into the trees.

She pulled over onto the mouth of the driveway and turned off the engine, watching the mirror.

Whitley climbed out from behind the wheel, crossed the space between the cars, and came up to the Dart's driver's side. He looked both ways down the road, noted the empty expanse of asphalt, and nodded to himself, then hunkered down with his hands on his knees and examined her through the window, as if he were on a leisurely visit to the zoo.

He wore a dark-blue suit so rumpled he might have slept in it; the tie was loose around his throat. He lifted one meaty fist and rapped his knuckles on the glass.

Laura rolled the window down in fits and jerks with the crank handle.

"Miss Laura Chambers."

"Yes, Officer?" she asked, saccharine sweet.

He reached out and ran a hand down the Dart's lines. "She's a beauty," he said. "'70?"

She didn't like it when he touched her car but tried not to let it show in her face. "It's a '69. Was I speeding?"

"Maybe five over."

"You're writing me a ticket for five over?"

"I could if I wanted to. I'm the law." He smiled at her. He was enjoying himself.

She waited.

"We been looking for you," he continued.

The wind shifted, and the odor of alcohol wafted in through the open window, unmistakable. She scrutinized him. There was a slightly unfocused cast to his eyes. He was still bent over, hands on knees, a stable position if there ever was one. But if a person paid attention, they could notice him tilting side to side ever so slightly, this way and that, compensating and then overcompensating.

His nostrils flared, and she could hear the air wheezing in and out of him. His breath smelled of onions and, she thought, vodka.

"You like to play hide-and-seek?"

"Lieutenant, I understand—"

"You're a hard woman to find. We tried that dump of an apartment, and we went to your office twice. You don't go to work anymore?"

"I was visiting my mother. She's ill."

"I see."

"Lieutenant Whitley, this may be hard to believe, but I just came from *your* office."

"So you knew we were looking for you." It wasn't a question.

Laura gave a vigorous nod. Quickly, she said, "Don Rodgers passed along your message. I know why you've been looking for me, and you're right to do it. We can talk this out, though. We got off on the wrong foot, but I can help you. Let me help you."

"We found where she was staying—Jane Doe, I mean. That motel south of town. Funny thing is, we weren't the first ones there."

"I understand."

"Owner over there, he says you paid him to let you in."

Laura said nothing.

"Place was searched pretty damn good, almost nothing left."

She kept her mouth shut.

"He says you were stealing from the room."

"Benny Morno will say whatever you tell him to, I'm sure."

"You calling me a liar?"

"No, sir."

Whitley canvassed her up and down.

She waited, fingers still tight around the steering wheel, hating herself. This was the worst kind of obsequiousness. To act servile to Whitley, of all people, who'd said abhorrent things, who'd had the audacity to lay his hands on her. It grated against every fiber of her being.

But buried behind that unfocused stare was cold danger.

A flash of the wolf tile, its eyes so dark and deep a person could fall into them and never be seen again.

Laura had a creeping sense of the situation getting away from her, of things spinning out of control.

"I have information that will help with the identification," she said.

Whitley leaned a little closer. "So you did recognize her after all?"

"Not then, not on the road, but it turns out we used to know each other . . ." She tried to gather herself.

At this he squinted and made a face, as if he had sniffed this particular type of bullshit before and it always stung his eyes. "So you *do* know her—even though you told us you didn't—and you *didn't* recognize her, but now after, what? Thinking about it real hard? You've decided to change your mind. I got that about right?"

It sounded like a weak brand of truth even to Laura's ears. Whatever plans she'd had to come clean and hand over the photo album, the chances of doing it in this moment plummeted to zero. Whitley's body language suggested a barely repressed rage, and an admission of that kind of guilt felt like the match that might light his fuse.

But the photo album, in the end, was incidental to the information of real importance: the name. She could give him the name.

"I can identify your Jane Doe."

"A day late and a dollar short, but let's have it."

"Emily Merritt," she said.

It took him a moment to process the words, and when he was done, Whitley pushed off his knees to standing. He scratched at the almost invisible patch of reddish stubble on the chin of his baby face. He shook his head in surprise. "Don't do this."

"The injuries were so grave, I didn't recognize her at first."

He made a *tsk-tsk* sound, his white worm of a tongue against his thin, bloodless lips.

"We were friends, you know. Childhood friends. But it's been a long time since I've seen her. Since . . ."

She didn't finish.

"Disgusting," he said. "A woman is dead, and here you are trying to make money off it. You're a damn vulture."

"No, that's not—"

He cut her off straightaway. "I read your paper, I know the sort of stuff you write about. And boy howdy, I can imagine it would sell a lot of papers if Emily Merritt turned up in Hillsborough and got herself murdered on the eve of Simon Barrow's execution. Wouldn't that be a story?"

"It was her," Laura said lamely.

"A fact to which only you can attest. How convenient."

"It's the truth."

"I'm not gonna let you get away with it." He bent down into the open window again; she could feel the heat of his breath. "You may be a fine-looking woman, but you're rotten to the core. Go ahead and get out of the car."

A minor panic swirled in her, the way a fish looks for a way out from the net. She twisted and looked behind her at the Charger. Its engine was off, but the red and blue lights still flashed from behind the grille. "Is your partner with you?"

"Who now?"

"Is Captain Bynum here?"

"He's not my partner, just offered to fill in that night." Whitley tugged at his belt. "We're all alone. No one's gonna interrupt us."

She became keenly aware that in all the time they had been speaking, not a single car had passed them on the road.

"I'll talk to Bynum, not you."

His face tightened. "Step out of the car, please."

"We can talk right here."

Whitley brushed back the hem of his greasy blazer and rested his palm on the butt of the revolver clipped to his belt. "Step out of the car, please, ma'am."

Laura got out.

"Walk down here to the front of my car and place your hands on the hood."

She complied.

He twitched his head in the direction of the windshield. "Don't move," he said, and went into the car and did something to the camera on the dash. Then he walked around and came up behind her and used his foot to spread her legs wide.

He ran his hands from her wrists to her shoulders, down across her chest, then up from her ankles to the very top of her thighs.

"Can we get a female officer out here?" Laura asked.

"None available right now."

"Can you check?"

"No law saying I can't frisk you. It's for my safety." His mouth split open into a yellow-toothed grin.

He pulled a set of handcuffs off his belt and bent her arms behind her back. Cold metal kissed the bruise on her wrist, and she bucked.

"Don't resist," he said.

The other cuff snapped closed, and he got hold of her by the chain between them. He pulled her backward, a vicious yank that made her shoulders ache, and the length of his body pressed up against her. She struggled to twist away.

He gave the chain another yank and said, "Whoa there. Whoa now, girl. Take it easy." He put his face in her hair.

She had as much leverage as a horse with a bridle, Laura realized. Her eyes rolled side to side, and the minor panic fluttering inside her shifted toward frenzy.

Just then, an antique-looking farm truck puttered down the highway. Whitley took a step back, his hand still firmly on the chain. The truck slowed as it passed, and the man in a ball cap behind the wheel raised one hand in greeting. Whitley waved back.

"Laura Chambers, I'm placing you under arrest for obstruction of justice and tampering with evidence," he said, and then read her her rights. Finished, he turned her around and sat her down roughly in the dirt at the side of the road.

"I'm gonna search your car now."

"I'm not giving you permission to search."

Whitley gave a low chuckle. "Now that's rich. You talked your way inside that motel room, tossed the place, cleaned it out top to bottom. Tell me: exactly what kind of permission did you get?"

"The owner let me in."

"That's a secondary crime scene, Chambers, something you well knew. Our witness will swear it was you."

"Swear to who?"

"How about a judge?" He fished a roll of papers from his pocket, smoothed them on the Charger's hood, held them up in front of her face. "Here's the arrest warrant. Here's the warrant for your car and your apartment. And here's the one for your phone records. The judge found all those phone calls in conjunction with your half-truths up to this point very compelling. Did you know service providers have access to your voice mails?"

From another pocket came his phone. He tapped and scrolled, hit play. Emily's message—wind whipping, rain slapping, heavy breathing—played at high volume right there at the side of the road.

"There you go," Laura said. "She didn't say anything."

"So why hide it?"

"I told you there was a blackout. Did you follow up?"

He nodded. "You weren't lying about that much at least."

"The calls, the message—they all happened while I didn't have service. The voice mail didn't even register until after we finished talking."

"You should have reported it."

"Reported what? Dead air?"

"Tell me what you took."

"I don't know what you're talking about."

The lines of his face deepened. "Even the judge doesn't believe that. This isn't just an accident investigation anymore, Chambers. This is serious. This is murder, and from where I'm sitting, you're up to your neck in it. What did you take from that motel room?"

"Think I'll take you up on that offer to remain silent."

He squatted down in front of her. "Tell me now and this will go a lot easier for you."

"You're arresting me, right?"

"You're damn right I am."

"So get it over with."

Whitley shrugged and stood. "I'll put you in the back and call for a tow on the car."

He opened the back of his cruiser, got a good handful of hair, and forced her head down so it didn't hit the roof.

Just before he slammed the door closed, she got his attention.

"Whitley."

He glanced up from his phone.

"It's rear-wheel drive. Make sure you tell them or they'll destroy the transmission."

CHAPTER

20

"CHAMBERS," THE FEMALE sheriff's deputy said. "Bail's posted."

They gave back her notebook, her pen, her rings, her watch, her belt, and her shoelaces. At a desk she collected her paperwork: discharge forms and an order to appear. In four days' time a twenty something ADA would be haranguing her in front a judge. Hopefully she could convince whoever was sitting on the bench that her actions hadn't amounted to a felony.

Another deputy escorted her the last few yards, held open a door, and then she was out on the concrete steps. Less than twenty-four hours inside and already sunlight seemed a foreign concept. She shielded her eyes against the glare and took in a lungful of clean-smelling air.

"Ever spent a night in jail before?"

Bass Herman stood from the small stone bench where he'd been waiting.

"Once," she said. "When I was twenty, I was in school just north of Chicago. The cops shot someone. A kid, just twelve years old. A liquor store got robbed, the cops pulled up, the suspect ran. One of the responding officers drew and fired, and the bullet missed by a mile. It flew almost a block until it hit this kid just sitting on his stoop reading. He stopped it with his head."

"Bad luck."

"And then some. Stray bullets in Chicago are nothing new, but from a cop's gun . . . back then stories like that didn't get traction.

The cops closed ranks, no one could get a straight answer out of them."

"So it tends to go," Bass said.

"Common knowledge now, but back then it felt new, like we'd turned over a rock and found all these creepy-crawlies we'd never guessed were there. Some students organized a protest and I went. Emotions were very . . ."

"Raw."

"Right. The police came out with riot shields. Someone threw a rock, so everyone started throwing rocks. They arrested the lot of us. Of course, we were just a bunch of college kids. They put us in a special holding cell without any other prisoners in it, and in the morning they kicked most of us loose without even a ticket."

"Ah, to be young."

"Did Whitley search the *Gazette* office?"

Bass shook his head. "He knocked, I answered, he asked to look around. No warrant, though. He's picked a judge who is, shall we say, predisposed to the perspectives of law enforcement. However, there are limits to even his one-sided jurisprudence. An open-ended fishing expedition into the office of a newspaper pretty much blows a hole in the First Amendment."

"So he just left," Laura said.

"I made enough noise about the violation of our rights to scare him off. For now." He paused. "What have you done, Ms. Chambers?"

She glanced over and caught the look of repudiation stamped across his generous features.

"I just followed the story you asked me to follow."

"They tell me you robbed a dead woman."

"It wasn't like that."

He shook his head, disappointed. "I can't condone thieving," he said quietly.

That last word rocked her like a punch to the gut. Laura knew she had a habit of bending the truth. Never in print—there facts were sacrosanct. But there was plenty of gray area in the *pursuit* of truth, times when a small lie served her greater purpose. She would pretend to be someone other than a reporter to cajole information from those who would otherwise be reticent to speak with her. Or she would lean hard on sources, imply that their name could be left out of a story or not at her discretion. Laura was willing to do what was necessary to get the job done, and that was something to be proud of—at least that's what she told herself.

But she was not a thief.

"Yes, I took something."

"This is a serious ethical violation."

"I was . . . overzealous."

Bass guffawed, but then his face was serious again. "Make this right."

"I tried, goddamn it!" Her voice came out louder than she'd planned, and two lawyer-looking types with briefcases looked up at them from the opposing bench. "I tried," she said again, her voice down near a whisper. "I went looking for Bynum, but Whitley found me first."

Bass darkened. "He of the strong hands," he said slowly.

"That's the one."

"Then we'll go see Sheriff Fuller together."

"But Bass, this thing I took, it's not going to help them find who killed her. I can promise you that. All it told me was her name, and I already gave that to Whitley."

He studied her for a moment. "What are you proposing?"

"Before we get started on rectifying my ethical lapses—"

"Go on."

"You've at least got to let me show it to you."

* * *

The *Gazette* office was just a block away. A few other reporters were in the newsroom, and they hailed Bass as he entered, but when they caught sight of her, there was suddenly a renewed interest in desktops.

Bass took her into his office and shut the door.

The room looked like a bomb had gone off inside. Every wall was covered with file cabinets, and many of the drawers stood open. Issues of the *Gazette* and other papers covered the top of a walnut desk big enough to serve as the deck of an aircraft carrier, and stacked high on the couch were manila folders marked with cryptic labels.

"Sit, ah . . . anywhere." Bass gave a sweeping gesture before collapsing in his own richly padded desk chair.

Laura removed a pile of what looked like printed emails from one of the other chairs and then sat across the desk from him.

"They kept your phone. Can they get in there?"

"No," Laura said.

"They can compel you. Once they try and fail, they'll get that judge to sign another order."

"I know. I'll get another one for now."

"So what's worth all this trouble?"

She came around to his side the desk. "Excuse me." She opened the pencil drawer and found a small silver key. Then she leaned down and unlocked the bottom drawer and from inside it produced the photo album, still wrapped in a paper grocery bag.

Bass sat leaned back in his chair. "Miss Chambers, I am in shock. This is my private desk, goddamn it. That's a locked drawer."

"I know it."

"Then explain yourself!" he thundered.

Laura shrugged. "That's where you keep the good whiskey."

Bass opened his mouth, then closed it again. After a beat, he started to laugh. "I knew I wasn't going through single malt that fast."

She took the album out of the bag and placed it in front of him.

Bass Herman sighed, then centered the album on his ink blotter. He opened it and carefully examined the photographs, turned to the next page, and began again. Laura had already gone over the album enough times to recognize the pictures upside down, and she began narrating the images as they went past. "There they are when they got married. There they are when she got pregnant. There they are moving into the farmhouse. I checked the property records this morning; it belonged to his side of the family. They inherited the property when his father passed away."

"Whose father?" Bass asked. An expression of disinterest had settled over his face.

"Bob Merritt's," Laura answered.

She gave no special weight to the name, and it took Bass a moment to understand what she was saying. Then his face took on a whitish hue, and his hand jerked back from the album as if it had turned hot. "This is the Merritt family?"

She nodded.

He cleaned his glasses before pushing them high onto his nose, then plucked a tissue from its box and used it to handle the pages as he flipped through them again.

"It won't bite you."

"All the same," he said. Then, almost to himself, "It *is* them."

"You knew each other?"

"Just well enough to say hello at a church picnic. They had a daughter too; she used to smile and shake my hand. What was her name?"

"Emily."

He snapped his fingers. "That's the one."

"She was eight when it happened. Rodgers tells me an item from the house like this, not relevant to the prosecution, would have been released to the next of kin."

"Meaning Emily Merritt." He sat back from the desk and shook his head, as if trying to clear the cobwebs. "You believe she and Jane Doe are one and the same."

"The piece about Simon Barrow's execution was in last Friday's edition, exactly a week ago, and it got picked up by the *Observer* and the *News & Observer*," she said, referring to the dailies in Charlotte and Raleigh respectively, the state's two largest newspapers by circulation.

"They ran their own stories too."

"Political coverage," she said, waving a hand. "Articles about the governor's law-and-order agenda, legal history of the injunctions against capital punishment, interviews with victims' families, quotes from the lawyers. Their stories are about the state's new policy on the death penalty, not about any one specific execution. Simon Barrow's spot at the head of the line is an arbitrary detail."

"Not around here it isn't."

"And not to most readers," Laura agreed. "All that legalese makes for a dry appetizer. People are hungry for the more lurid details. Hence why they decided to pick up my story."

Bass fixed her with a look. "That's a tabloid way of thinking, Ms. Chambers."

"Whatever sells papers, right?"

He didn't bother to respond.

"Do you think the timing here—my article about Barrow, getting a phone call from the person in possession of the Merritts' photo album—do you really think all that could be a coincidence?"

"Anything is possible." He tented his fingers and looked at her. "No," he said finally.

"Emily saw the article and decided to contact me. Only I never got the chance to hear what was so important that she had to come to Hillsborough to talk to me in person. A few hours after she shows up, she's dead, shot and then chased into traffic."

"Anything else?"

"Yeah. Whoever did it came back and searched her room."

"You don't have any evidence to back that up."

"I've searched rooms before, Bass. Take my word for it."

Bass shoved himself up from behind the desk and navigated over to the window. His back to the room, he said, "All right, but there's no way to say *what* they were looking for."

"This was the only thing stuffed in a heating vent."

"And it hardly seems worth the trouble. Why bother trying to take it from her?"

Laura crossed her arms over her chest. "You're asking the wrong question, Bass. The right question is, what about it was worth dying over?"

"You tell me."

"I don't know, but I sure want to find out. Don't you?"

He slumped back into his chair. "Interesting. Keep talking."

"There always were a lot of unanswered questions surrounding Simon Barrow. No real history of violent crime, and one day he decides to conceal himself in a closet, wait for the Merritts to come home, and blow them to kingdom come. Then they catch him sleeping in his car less than a mile down the road, the shotgun still warm in the back seat. Never spoke to the police, never uttered a word at his own trial. Just sat there like the hooded specter of death and took his lumps."

"That's old news," he said.

But his complaint was all bluster. Bass was hooked; she could see the gleam in his eyes. If there was even the smallest bit of new information about the Merritt murders to be found, it would make big waves in the weeks leading up to Barrow's execution. The crime was local legend, and the *Gazette* would run articles about it no matter what. But Laura was offering him a slim chance to do something bigger.

"Emily Merritt also never spoke about her parents' murder after it happened," Bass said.

"*Catatonic* was the word used in the police reports."

"But she decided to call you now."

Laura raised her eyebrows suggestively.

"Can you get access to Barrow?" he asked.

"He doesn't talk to anyone. Not police, not reporters."

"Is there a way to get a look at the original investigation files?"

"The Sheriff's Office doesn't allow it."

"I can understand that response for an open case, but this one has been closed for twenty-three years," Bass said. "Barrow ran out of appeals a long time ago. Can't you find someone who will make an exception?"

Laura paused.

She understood the real question Bass wanted to ask. The best of her stories in 2017 had been made possible as a direct result of her relationship with Frank Stuart. He'd been willing to feed her general information about Sheriff's Office priorities, enough to direct her inquires without giving up anything that could be traced back to him. Once he was gone, though, the door had slammed shut on her special access.

"Don Rodgers and I do keep in touch," she said, underplaying the frequency of their communication. "He was a lieutenant back in '96, just a few years before he ran for sheriff."

"He work the case?"

She shook her head. "No, I asked him when I was writing the original article. He was on the outs with the acting sheriff that year, some kind of office politics. He was holed up in a back room, assigned to administrative duties."

"Probably no one's going to answer the big questions, even if he's the one asking," Bass said. "The rumor around town is that Sheriff Fuller is big on loyalty. Who else have you got?"

She said nothing.

"What about Timinski? I heard he's back in Raleigh."

"We don't keep in touch."

"Time to pick up the phone, seems like."

She turned and glanced out the window. The office's one small window looked down on Churton Street, the main drag through the center of downtown. This time on Friday morning she could see empty tables outside the pub and, around the corner, full ones in front of the coffee shop. People sipped and laughed together, the day's coming heat still only a promise in the air. She wondered how many of them had moments in their lives they would give anything to forget.

Sensing her hesitation, Bass said, “He’s a source. Don’t make it personal.”

Laura looked back over at him. “If nothing else pans out, I’ll think about it. But will you hold on to the album instead of turning it over to Fuller?”

“No, we’ve got to do right by the victim.”

“I couldn’t agree more,” she said. “But Whitley thinks I’m the one who searched that motel room, and turning in something as pedestrian as a family photo album isn’t going to mollify him. He’s going to say, all right, you did take evidence, now where’s the rest? And when I’m empty-handed, he’s going to slap the cuffs on me again.”

“Whitley has a vendetta against you, I’m not arguing that point. But Fuller will be more receptive.”

Laura held up a hand. “Fuller’s a climber. And Simon Barrow’s execution is a coup for him, so he’ll err on the side of whatever doesn’t fuck up his ascent.”

Bass didn’t seem convinced.

“Look, you’re the one who told me I owed the victim an accounting. Well, I’ve got news for you: I’m the best chance she’s got. In four days, I have to go back in front of a judge. Just give me until then.”

His face was unreadable, but he had yet to say no.

“But if Whitley comes knocking again,” Laura continued, “you’ll need to tell him to come back with a subpoena.”

Bass closed his eyes for a moment, then opened them again. He gave her a curt nod, his mind made up. “All right, I can stall. But work fast, and don’t be here in case he shows up.”

“Understood,” she said.

“Ms. Chambers?”

Laura was already halfway out the door. “Yes?”

“Don’t come back empty-handed.”

CHAPTER

21

SHE BOUGHT A cheap phone in a drugstore, and Bass loaned her one of his cars, a stately vintage Cadillac with bench seats and lap belts. At a stoplight on Churton she glanced in the mirror, and for the briefest moment she thought she saw a familiar follower.

Not this shit again.

A dirty brown sedan had jerked to the side and pulled into a parking space along the side of the street about two cars back.

The light turned green, and she drove. She kept her eyes glued to the passenger's side mirror.

No movement.

Now there were three or four cars between them, and still no action from the spot she had marked. The car didn't move, but neither did the door open. In another second, the road would curve, and she would lose sight of it.

It's just nerves. You'd jump at your own shadow right now.

A horn blasted, and she did leap up in her seat a little. Ahead a jaywalker who had stepped out from between two cars broke into a jog with an apologetic wave to the vehicle coming from the opposite direction. Laura made herself take a breath, then glanced at the side mirror again. The spot was out of sight.

She checked the rearview.

The car behind her made a quick right turn, and there, twenty car lengths back, was the dirty brown sedan.

"Son of a bitch," she said aloud.

The filthy white T-shirt no longer hung from the window, but she was certain it was the same car. Whitley had stupidly used the same undercover car a second time, or maybe he just thought she was too stupid to notice. Either way, this had his fingerprints all over it. He would keep following her, keep harassing her, until he got the answer he was looking for.

This arrangement of predator and prey resonated with the memory of the last time Whitley had caught up to her. Faint rage crackled in her chest, a china cabinet tipped over at the end of a long hallway. Laura Chambers had just about had her fill of being followed.

She kept her speed steady and waited.

Large semitrucks entered downtown from time to time to service the restaurants and other stores there. One was headed there now. It lumbered down the two-lane road faster than it should have. Late, perhaps, for a delivery.

Laura put her foot on the gas, tried to get the timing just so.

As the truck passed, the road also curved, and for a moment the big tractor trailer shielded her from view. She jerked the wheel and punched the brake, then the gas, and the Cadillac twisted like a leaf on the wind. By the end of the skid, she had turned 180 degrees and was now puttering along behind the truck.

And here came the dirty brown sedan trundling along in the opposite lane. She tried to get a look inside, but to no avail. The layer of grime on every glass surface was so thick, she wondered how the driver could see.

Laura couldn't help herself. As she and the sedan passed each other, she gave a little wave.

Then hurriedly she parked, snatched the keys from the ignition, and ducked into a storefront. She asked to use the bathroom, and when the clerk wasn't looking, she slipped into the alley out back. Laura spent the rest of the morning peering around corners, waiting in the hidden nooks of the town she knew so well. By the time the sun was high in the sky, though, she was played out. Whitley or his goons could be set up to watch the car, of course. But there was only one way to find out.

She got back in the Cadillac and made four lefts in a row, then four rights. She drove under the rail bridge and wove through quiet neighborhoods, but there was no sign of the brown sedan.

She pulled over on a mostly empty street and told her heart to quit hammering in her chest, and when it had listened, she broke open the new phone and dialed into her voice mail.

One message. It was from Don Rodgers earlier in the day.

"Laura, call me back as soon as you get this, please."

There was a strained urgency in his voice. She messaged him with her new number and told him where she wanted to meet.

* * *

Late-night storms had blown away all the clouds, leaving behind a fresh-faced blue sky. The Chambers farmhouse squatted in front of her, ten years overdue for a coat of paint. Corn surrounded it, stretching out in all directions, row after row of it. Each stalk stood more than seven feet high, and the cobs hung heavy, overdue for harvest in the September heat. Too much precipitation meant that, even from inside her car, she could see the blackened corn silks hanging from the ears, a sure sign of rot.

She got out and looked toward the highway, searching for a dust plume. Rodgers should be here any moment. Her father had taught her to look for signs like that: to spot footprints, keep track of wind direction, notice when the birds stopped chirping. He had been an intensely private man, constantly measuring himself and those around him against an internal set of principles he never bothered to share.

Most people had been found wanting.

At seven, she'd been just precocious enough to ask him a wandering question about church and God and what exactly he thought about religion, and his answer was the closest she'd ever heard him get to a description of his inner life. Even then, it had been another man's words.

He'd quoted Lincoln, though of course she hadn't known it then.

"When I do good, I feel good. When I do bad, I feel bad. That's my religion."

"Don't some people feel good when they do bad things?" she could remember asking.

"Only if they aren't raised right," he'd said.

She doubted now that it could ever be that simple, but the lesson had made a lasting impression on her—her gut was just about the only thing she trusted.

Inside, her mother was hacking into the plastic mask.

"When I was here last, they still hadn't delivered your oxygen."

Diane coughed out a wad of stringy phlegm. "They called. They're running behind. They said Thursday."

Today was Friday. "And you still haven't heard anything?"

"Oh, someone was pounding on the door yesterday, now that you mention it. I figured it was those Jehovah's Witnesses. The gall of them to pretend I'm going to hell. Used to be I tried to be polite about it, but I no longer answer the door when they come preaching."

Laura checked the closet. All the tanks were spent.

"Don't you look at me like that," Diane wheezed. "I'm the mother; you're the daughter. Don't you forget it."

"What if something happens to you? The concentrator's broke, your little canisters are empty. One touch of asthma and we'll have to get the ambulance out here."

Her mother used a chubby hand to swat the words away as if they were an annoying fly.

Outside, tires crunched on gravel.

"Don't worry, it's someone to see me," Laura said.

"A *guest*? A guest with no *notice*? Why would you do this to me?" Diane tried to push up out of her recliner but fell back, gasping.

"I said don't worry. Stay put. He's not coming inside."

"*He?*" Laura heard her mother squeal just before she pulled the front door shut behind her.

Don Rodgers was parked a respectful distance from the bottom of the steps, his F-150 looking positively spit-shined. He climbed out slowly and took a second to adjust his jeans and the grubby cowboy hat on his head. Cooper was a different story: he shot a tremulous bay toward the heavens, raced across the packed-dirt drive, and jumped up to give Laura a lick.

"Good boy," she said, and scratched him behind the ears. "Lead the way."

She and the dog walked back over to the truck. He nuzzled her hand and then took off on one of his adventures.

"Not today, my man," Rodgers said, and pointed meaningfully at the open truck door. Cooper's ears drooped, but he listened to the command. Rodgers closed the door but left the windows cracked.

"Trouble in paradise?"

He swept off the cowboy hat and scratched the top of his head. "He was out all last night tracking a skunk or a raccoon. Who knows? Wouldn't come when I called. He smells terrible. He's in the doghouse, and he knows it."

"You don't have a doghouse."

"Naw, that's just a figure of speech. He's always been an inside dog."

"You ever been out here before?" she asked, meaning the Chambers farm.

He shook his head. "Never had the opportunity."

She filled him in on the events of the two days since they'd last seen each other, and when she was done, Rodgers said, "Here I thought Bass Herman had a stick up his ass so big—"

She swatted him. "I told him we're the only ones who can do right by Emily. Which is true—Whitley sure doesn't seem interested."

"So he's gonna bend the rules for once. He must think you're pretty special."

"Bass has got an old-fashioned ethos. It's all white hats and black hats with him. Usually he thinks we're all playing for the same team."

"Naïve for such an old guy."

Laura did her best Bass Herman impression: "It's an honorable profession, Chambers; it's our duty to assist."

"You don't think it's an honorable profession?" Rodgers asked.

The question caught her flat-footed. Laura had always been ambitious, but her years as a reporter had given rise to an ambivalence about that ambition. The purpose of journalism, she believed, was to fill in the cracks in society's foundation, that the fourth estate picked up where the other three left off. Her job was to counterbalance powerful people and institutions, to take the side of the downtrodden, to empathize with the less fortunate.

But it's dangerously easy to imbue yourself with noble purpose, alarmingly effortless to forget that all people are equally afflicted by the human condition. She was not immune to greed or pride or the pursuit of fame. Her job was to choose the important stories, but these days she often wondered exactly how much of her interest was self-interest.

"Sometimes I do," she said. "What about being a cop? Is that an honorable profession?"

Rodgers answered unequivocally and without hesitation. "Yes."

"Certainty—must be nice."

"Like a warm blanket."

"Why'd you need to talk to me?"

He turned serious again. "Figured something real weird, Laura."

"Tell me."

"You know that card that was inside the album? That lady lawyer?"

"They're just called lawyers. Yes, Beth Bancroft."

"I picked up the baton when you went in the clink, made some calls of my own. Annoyed them enough to finally get a partner on the phone. I asked what she did, and he was happy to tell me in general terms. Dreadful boring stuff, even he's about to fall asleep just explaining it. No connection that I can see, none whatsoever. Then almost as an afterthought, he mentions her pro bono work."

"Who for?"

Rodgers gave a dramatic pause. "The Innocence Project. You know what that is, don't you?"

Of course she did. Laura was gobsmacked. The Innocence Project worked to exonerate those wrongfully convicted, and it had chapters in almost every state. She'd even worked on a sister project during her time in undergrad.

"Now you tell me," Rodgers said. "What is Emily Merritt of all people doing talking to a lawyer who works on the Innocence Project?"

"It's hard to imagine."

"And here's where we veer into Twilight Zone territory, so brace yourself. Beth Bancroft is dead."

"Dead?" Laura heard herself say.

"Not just dead. Murdered. Last night while you were locked up in the county jail, someone broke into her house in Raleigh and strangled her with the cord of her vacuum cleaner."

Laura was speechless.

In the truck, Cooper began to bark.

"Quiet there," Rodgers said.

But Cooper was having none of it. He began to snarl and growl, then to throw himself against the window. The window, rolled partway down and without support at the top or side, bowed outward under the force of the dog's blows. It threatened to break.

"Jesus Christ, what now?" Rodgers muttered. To Cooper: "Shut your trap!"

Just as abruptly as he'd begun to snap and howl, Cooper went still.

"I tell you, I've never seen him like that. I . . ."

Rodgers trailed off.

Because the dog wasn't the only one who had gone silent. The birds were gone, Laura noticed suddenly. Even the wind seemed to have stopped. A strange electric stillness settled over the house and the surrounding crops.

Rodgers realized it too. For a moment it looked like he was going to crack a smile, but then a shadow passed over his face. He stood up straight and looked around. The lines between his nose and the corners of his mouth, already deep, now stretched and thickened into canyons that turned him near grotesque. His face suddenly reminded Laura of a gargoyle leering from above a medieval church door.

Without warning, there came a sound like a high-pitched whine, and right on its heels the distinctive crack and echo of a gunshot.

"Down!" hollered Rodgers, and he tackled her to the ground.

CHAPTER

22

RODGERS TORE WITH his fingertips at the sleeve of his shirt, and when they found no purchase, he went to work on the buckle of his belt. The clasp snapped undone, and he wound the warm leather tight around her upper arm.

"You're bleeding, Laura," he said.

Another zip, another echoing report that boomed out over the corn.

He had her shoved up against the truck's front tire. She looked down at her arm and noticed for the first time the stream of blood escaping her outer bicep. Rodgers yanked hard on the belt, and she screamed, and the flow of blood slowed to a trickle.

"He just winged you."

"Winged me," she repeated.

"The bullet took a slice out of you. A pretty near thing, but you'll be all right."

Zip.

CRACK.

BOOOOOM.

"Big sucker," Rodgers said, almost to himself.

"Three-oh-eight," Laura responded.

He glanced over at her, raised an eyebrow.

"Like in the autopsy report."

He gave a brisk nod. "Right you are. Big, just not big enough to poke through an engine block. But he's got us pinned down good. Where's he at?"

"Is this what you did in the Army?" she murmured. Her vision fuzzed. Pulsating black fingers squeezed her view of the world down into a rapidly shrinking circle at the end of a long pipe. Even Rodgers's voice, when it came, echoed down the umbilical from awfully far away.

"Ah shit, the belt slipped," he said, and yanked on it again.

The blackness retreated; the world jumped close again. "Fuck! Stop fucking doing that!" she bellowed.

"Good to have you back, you were drifting. You're practically in shock. Put your hand here. No, right *here*. And don't let go." He moved to a crouch, took a peek over the hood, and dropped back down. "Can't see anything but corn."

Cooper started barking again.

CRACK CRACK CRACK—three rounds pounded the truck in quick succession. The front tire on the far side let go with a hiss, and the truck slumped sideways.

Another clap like thunder, and above their heads the windshield exploded into a million shards of glass. Cooper gave a pathetic yip, then went silent.

"Oh God. Down, boy! Just stay down!" To Laura: "Where is he?"

"He sounds close."

Rodgers cocked his head to one side. "No, that's not right. He's an okay shot, the rounds are getting close enough to hear them pass. But notice the little separation between that sound and the sound of the rifle?" He was talking fast now; he didn't wait for any kind of answer. "He's pretty far, he's out at the tree line. Tell me where."

"I have no idea."

"Think, Laura. I can't see shit 'cause of all this corn, but that's a two-way street. He's got to have a line of sight on us, but the corn should be blocking him. Where can you see the house from?"

"Maybe he's up in a tree."

"Naw, that wouldn't work. He's got to be laid out."

Her ears throbbed. Her arm was oddly painless, which worried her even more. An idea floated by and she tried to get hold of it, but it drifted away. There it was again, and this time she latched on for dear life.

"I've got it: the railroad track. It's running on a gravel hump across the back of the property, it's about twenty feet high. He's there."

"Any chance a train is coming?

She turned to see if he was serious. "The Norfolk Southern comes by a couple times a week. Don't count on it."

"What's the range?"

She understood he was asking for the distance to the tracks. "Three fifty, maybe four hundred yards."

He nodded, calculating.

"What if we run? Can he hit us from there?"

"If he knows what he's doing, putting lead on target at four hundred yards is about as easy as throwing a wad of paper in the wastepaper basket."

"Sometimes I miss the wastepaper basket," Laura said.

"Sure, sometimes," Rodgers said. "But you wouldn't bet your life on it. He hit you in your arm with a cold bore shot, and that ain't nothing."

Laura held the end of the belt in her teeth and fished her phone out of her pocket. She dialed 911, then juggled the phone up between her ear and shoulder and got her hand firmly back on the belt. When the operator came on the line, she explained that someone was outside her house shooting at her with a rifle and gave the address.

The front door of the house opened.

"Get back inside, Momma," she yelled.

Diane Chambers trundled out onto the front porch. She wore bunny slippers and a floral-print housedress that hung off her like a shampoo cape, and she had rollers in her hair. "What are you doing out here, Laura?"

Alarmed, Laura moved to a low crouch and patted the air in front of her with her free hand, as if she could shove her mother back inside from a distance. "You gotta go back inside right now."

Another crack from the rifle.

This bullet didn't hit near the truck, and Laura wondered if this shot had been aimed at her mother.

"Now!"

But Diane seemed to find nothing disquieting about her daughter plastered down in the dirt with blood leaking out her arm. In a tone as placid as *Pass the potato salad, please*, she called out, "Knock it off, you two. Now you've set fire to something behind the house. I can smell it." As if to punctuate her point, thick gray tendrils of smoke began to slither out the open doorway behind her.

"Somebody is shooting at us. You have to go out the back door." Laura waved and pointed, hoping her mother would get the message.

"Fine, but don't think it's because of all this rude screaming. I don't want that man to see me dressed like this," Diane said primly. With that, she turned and went back inside and slammed the front door behind her.

"The smoke is coming from the back," Rodgers said. "She's not getting out that way."

Laura looked over the roof.

Smoke boiled up from behind the house; a black crown of soot wreathed the chimney.

"Well, shit." To the 911 operator, Laura said, "You still there? The house is on fire. Yes, the same place. Send the fire department." To her mother: "Diane, come back here!"

No response.

"Momma?" she yelled, and heard the sharp quavering edge in her voice.

No movement at the door or the windows. Smoke began pouring out from under the eaves.

Double shit. She turned to Rodgers. "The house is on fire."

"Uh, I noticed."

"My mother has problems with her lungs. She can't breathe right."

He understood straightaway what she was asking. "The tricky part is to track left and right with the scope. I'll scoot down to the tailgate and stick my head up—"

"Don—"

"Just for a microsecond, you understand. He'll catch the movement and pan over. That's when you go." His jaw was set, his mouth a hard slash across the bottom of his face. "Ready?"

She got hold of the belt and nodded.

"Three . . . two . . . one . . . now."

Her feet didn't move.

"Goddamn it," Rodgers said. Almost immediately, he softened. "It happens plenty, believe me. Don't think about it."

But it was all she could think about. Her imagination was tumbling, totally out of control. It conjured up what it would feel like when the bullet penetrated her. Like fire, she thought. Like being run through with a red-hot bayonet. Then would come the ice. Her body would turn cold—that would be the result of a gaping, fist-sized hole in her chest, what blood remained inside her draining into the already red mud. And then all she would see was blue, blue sky, blue sky fading into white.

They tried it again. "Now!" Rodgers grunted.

She flinched, but that was all. She was frozen in place.

Laura knew the exact place where the bullet would go in. It burned, as if someone had heated up a quarter in the flame of a blowtorch and then pressed it to her skin.

"I can try it," Rodgers said. "I'm a bit older than you, of course."

An understatement. He had arthritic knees, and some days he could barely walk the dog. She had seen it herself. The distance between the truck and the house was almost a hundred feet.

She didn't answer him, just prepared herself again.

"Last chance, otherwise he'll figure what's happening. Three, two, one. Now," Rodgers said softly.

Laura ran. She accelerated hard and got up on her toes, legs pumping. At the foot of the stairs, she slipped and went down, the wooden corners taking her in the ribs, but she pushed herself back up with her injured arm. All the while her feet churned like the two whisks in an electric mixer. Driving her forward, come hell or high water.

She hit the flat top of the porch at a dead sprint, slammed her shoulder into the door and turned the knob at the same time, and burst into the foyer of the farmhouse.

A wall of smoke greeted her. It poured past her toward the open door, and Laura moved against the tide. It was so thick she couldn't see. Her eyes watered. She took a deep breath, winded from her run, and hacked it back up again.

She found her mother in the recliner, head thrown back, motionless. She wasn't breathing, Laura thought, but she put her ear near Diane's mouth and heard a sound like a death rattle. Still alive. Laura took her by the shoulder and shook, but all she got in response was the quiver of unconscious flesh, a pressure-wave sensation like sitting on a water bed. She tried pulling her mother up from the chair, but it was no good, she would never make it.

In the end, Laura rotated the recliner until it faced backward into the house, then ratcheted down the back until it would go no farther. She tilted the chair all the way back until it made a little ramp, and her mother slid into an unceremonious clump on the floor. Laura got her under the arms and began to drag her across the hardwood floor toward the door.

She'd forgotten about the belt around her arm, but her arm reminded her now. Pain arced into her shoulder. Her ulnar nerve started to jump and tingle under the pressure, like an electric shock was shooting up her bones. Under her armpit, the fabric of her shirt felt sticky.

She pulled, and it was like towing ten bags of sand stacked on a tarp. Her mother's heavy body slid a few inches.

She dug in her heels and pulled.

Gray whorls swarmed the edges of her vision.

"Wake up, wake up, wakeupwakeupwakeup," she heard herself saying.

She pulled again, and her feet went out from under her.

From the ground, Laura looked back toward the door. It was just a few more pulls away, if only she could manage to stand. Through the opening she could peek at the world outside, bright and free, trapped between the edges of the frame. She could see the distant trees. And she could see Rodgers, hat crumpled in his fist, as he locked eyes with her.

"No," she said, but her voice weak.

Rodgers half stood, half rolled himself to his right. He threw his weight forward and started to run. His hand stretched out in front of him, searching for the banister of the stairs.

The distant crack of the rifle.

His momentum carried him like a rag doll down onto the gravel. Wind-tossed, unintelligible yelling. An animal cry. He'd been shot high on the leg, Laura could see. It must surely have shattered his pelvis. Somehow, though, he got to his knees. Blood streamed down his face from a cut near his eye. He screamed, and with a terrific effort came to his feet and started a limping jog toward the house.

He didn't make it far.

Blood had slicked the dirt under his feet. He clutched for the stairs. His left boot lost its purchase and slid out from under him. He went down hard. His head bounced once off the ground, he tried to push himself back up—

—and the second shot caught him in the center of his chest.

Laura didn't remember crawling to the door, but the next moment she was there, on her knees at the threshold, her head clasped between her hands. He was close, so close. He was just at the bottom of the stairs. She could get him. He was almost near enough to reach out and touch.

As she watched, an enormous shiver ran from his head down to the tips of his toes.

"Don't," he said, and she heard it clear as day.

Then his eyes rolled back in his head, and he spoke no more.

In the distance, the rising wail of sirens.

Laura blacked out.

CHAPTER

23

LAURA'S FATHER ABANDONED her twice: once when she was eight years old, when he vanished for a year, and then again when he came home to die.

The first time, in late August 1996, he woke Laura before dawn, let her take a sip of his coffee, and told her she wouldn't be going to school. It was the first day of bowhunting season, but Bruce Chambers had never been big on following rules. She watched as he cleaned the .30-30 lever-action carbine that had belonged to his own father. He buffed the walnut stock until it gleamed, his den filling with the musk of gun oil, then showed her how to sling the rifle across her shoulders.

He led her outside, across the back acreage of the Chambers farm, and up onto the gravel hump of the train tracks slashed across the rear property line. She hopped from one railroad tie to the next, and when they came to a trestle across a draw, when the ground between the ties turned to empty air, she reached for him.

"Hold my hand, Daddy," she said.

It was a mistake. Of all the things her father wanted for her, helplessness was the least of them.

He batted her arm away. "Don't need me for that anymore."

They finished crossing, then turned perpendicular to the tracks and marched down the berm, into the longleaf pines. Their path traced a bone-dry creek bed blown full of fallen leaves. Her father's boots stayed silent even as hers crackled.

"Quiet now," he said. He was a soft-spoken man ordinarily, and the barnacled whisper of his voice in the trees was the same as ever. He had a voice made for hunting. One gloved finger came to his lips, the supple calfskin grating across his week-old stubble, then pointed toward higher ground.

Two pines rotted on their sides. The thinner, weaker one had been the victim of a summer storm, and when it fell the tree had acted as a massive lever, prizing not only its own roots out of the ground but the roots of its brother. The trees had grown too close to each other, and when one fell, it dragged the other down with it.

They rested behind the tangled, dirt-clumped root ball. Laura offered her father the rifle, and he took it, resting the stock along the top of the tree trunk. They waited while the shadows shortened, and all Laura could hear was the rustle of wind and her own breathing and eventually the grumble of her stomach, and when late morning arrived without any sign, her father flipped the rifle up onto his shoulder and stood.

"Maybe this evening," he said. "We'll come out here again, try our luck."

She followed him to their special hiding place. Her father had told her the story many times, and it went like this: The day after she was born had come a storm to end all storms, a fury of ice and fire. Central North Carolina was famous for its ice storms, when in the winter months humidity seemed to crystallize right out of the air and coat everything in sight, the weight of it dragging down gutters, power lines, and full-grown trees. This storm had been one of those frozen cataclysms, but with a twist.

"Lightning," her father would say. "Lightning shooting through the inside of the clouds so as you could see the ice crystals whirling inside. I never saw another storm like that." Then, after a beat: "You got one hell of a welcome party."

The next morning he had walked the Chambers property, throwing out salt and clearing downed tree limbs, stopping only when he reached the train tracks to lift his head and sniff the air.

An unmistakable smell: woodsmoke.

"It was still burning when I got there. Surrounded by a thousand trees sheathed in ice, and this old oak engulfed in flame."

When she was old enough, her father showed Laura the tree. Even for a child it was easy to pick out, a landmark, the charred and hulking corpse a deeper black than anything else in their woods. A knot had popped and exploded in the heat, leaving behind a cavity where her father would store cigarettes, matches, and extra ammunition, all sealed up together in a plastic bag. That morning he had crouched at the base of their special tree, a filterless Lucky Strike welded into the corner of his mouth, and patted the ground next to him.

"Out here where you meet your friend?"

"Yes."

"This side of the bridge?"

She shook her head. "Over the tracks, into the woods."

"You tell her your secrets?"

Laura pressed her lips together. "Momma doesn't like me talking about her."

Her father knelt down and pressed one calfskinned finger under her chin until she looked up at him. He had eyes like dark water, the same eyes she saw in the mirror. "It's not her fault. Your momma never had a childhood, so she doesn't understand children."

"She doesn't like me."

"I like you enough for both of us."

The sun rose a bit more, cresting the high branches and spilling down onto their resting place.

"What do you know?" he asked. "What have you heard?"

He meant the terrible thing that had happened to Emily's parents. "Mr. and Mrs. Merritt are dead," she said.

"That's right."

"But Emily's okay."

"She survived," he allowed. "They took her to live with relatives."

"Could she stay with us?"

"She's already gone, Laura. You won't see her again."

Laura chewed on that.

"Your momma doesn't want you telling people how good of a friend Emily Merritt was, and neither do I. Do you understand? We don't want people knowing about that. We don't want them associating us with something so . . ." He paused, as if searching for the word, but he did not finish.

"I don't want to forget her, Daddy."

His eyes were no longer with her, they were out among the trees, and when he spoke again, his voice seemed distant. "I'm leaving tomorrow morning. I've got to go away for a while."

Laura didn't hesitate. "Because of Momma?"

"It's complicated."

"Don't leave me with her."

"Take care of your momma on her bad days. She's family, and you can't turn your back on that." He pressed his hand to her chest. "You've got a good heart in there. I know, because I put it there."

"I'll hate you if you leave me with her," she said. "Take me with you."

Even across a gulf of decades, she could still picture the expression on his face: dismay overlaid with anger. She caught only a glimpse of it before he turned crisply on his heel, as though he couldn't bear to look at her, and gave his answer to the pines.

He said, "I can't."

Even at eight years old, Laura already knew that the fear of something was usually worse than the thing itself; singing the first few notes of the church musical had elevated anxiety into giddiness. But now the opposite happened: dread at her father's answer blossomed from the pit of her stomach down into her legs, gnarled vines of despair threading between the muscle and the bone. She could feel them constricting, locking her in place. Another instant and she would be frozen.

She forced herself to turn, and then to run for home, pumping her arms, breath catching on dry lips as she climbed the hill toward the train tracks. Her eyes stayed glued to the worn tips of her boots, her feet danced between the wooden strips, and she never stopped moving, even when her heart started to hammer against the inside of her threadbare flannel jacket, even when she reached the trestle and the red clay soil yielded to chasm and the slitted breaks between the ties winked up visions of the void.

She crossed the trestle without her father's help.

She didn't need him anymore.

CHAPTER 24

A DOCTOR ENTERED THE room, distinguished looking, with a neatly trimmed beard that matched his white coat. He was polite enough to avert his eyes. She had been to the restroom for the first time since waking up, and the damn paper gown was bunching up around her waist.

She got herself settled back on the bed and covered up.

"Someone has spoken to you about your mother?" he asked, after turning back around.

"Yes."

"And what about you? How do you feel?"

"What do they say?" she asked in return, and pointed to the collection of machines at the bedside, monitors flashing with ever-shifting numbers and ticker-tape lines of information in a language she couldn't speak.

The doctor was blunt, which she appreciated.

"They say you're well. I examined you myself when you first arrived. Do you remember that?"

She shook her head.

"Well, I agree with the machines, as it happens. That arm was a nasty business indeed, but the wound narrowly avoided the brachial artery. Still, we had to give you five units of blood. That's why you passed out—hypotension, low blood pressure. The damage to the muscle of your upper arm will take time to heal, months perhaps. With physical therapy, however, you should make a full recovery."

"There was a man with me. His name is Don Rodgers."

"I can't talk to you about patients to whom you aren't related. Confidentiality, you understand."

It was the same answer she'd gotten from the nurse earlier, but the nurse hadn't known the name Don Rodgers. The doctor, though, knew exactly who she was talking about. He might not be willing to give her an answer, but it didn't matter: the answer was written all over his face.

She closed her eyes.

"There are two police officers here who want to speak with you."

"What time is it?"

He checked his wristwatch. "Almost four in the morning. They've been milling around the floor all day, and I'm afraid they're quite insistent. Do you think you're up to it?"

A splash of color across her vision: the cut above his eye, weeping.

She blinked it away. "Send them in," she said.

Whitley and Bynum shuffled into the room, Whitley in a clean suit but with the tie still loose around his neck, Bynum in a sport coat, his horseshoe of gray hair combed back, the Coke-bottle lenses glinting in the overhead lights, insectile as he studied her.

"We'd like to take a statement," Whitley said respectfully. He appeared much chastened compared to their previous meeting.

"If you can remember," Bynum added.

"Rodgers?" she asked him.

Bynum turned his head to examine the monitors. Surprisingly, it was Whitley who looked her square in the eye and gave his head a definite shake.

No.

No more Rodgers.

She wasn't surprised he was gone—she had seen enough to guess. But she was shocked by the paucity of her emotion. In the place where it should have been was only a grief-shaped hole, black and empty.

"All right," she said.

Whitley said, "Before we begin, I want to inform you that the Orange County Sheriff's Office is treating the homicide of our Jane Doe from the interstate—"

"Emily Merritt," she interjected.

Bynum said, "We're looking into that. We're having someone track her down."

"We're treating that homicide and the subsequent murder of Don Rodgers as related incidents," Whitley continued. "We know he assisted you. Our witness puts him at the motel. That plus the method in both cases . . ."

"Hunted like a deer." She was perplexed to hear the coldness in her voice.

"That's correct," Whitley said.

There was an empty beat, then Bynum said, "We'll get him."

He's trying to reassure me.

Bynum produced a voice recorder and put it next to her on the bed. She recounted the events as best she could. She told them about the dirty brown sedan that had been following her the past few days. When she was finished, she said, "I think there were two of them."

"Explain that."

"The shooter was up on the railroad tracks."

Whitley and Bynum exchanged a glance.

"What?" she asked.

"Your mother's house is a crime scene, all cordoned off," Bynum answered. "We were out there all afternoon with forensics. There were plenty of holes in the truck, more than enough to reverse-engineer trajectories. Best we can figure, the shooter was right where you say he was. But—"

"No brass," Whitley said. "Not a single shell casing. Very neat and tidy."

"But someone also had to start the fire," Laura continued. "I think they expected us to be inside the house. The plan was to use the fire to drive us outside so the shooter up on the berm could get a clean look at us."

"The perp probably set the fire, then circled around to the tracks and took his shot."

"No, the fire and the first shot happened too close together. He would have had to set the blaze, then hoof it almost a quarter mile though the corn to get set up. Impossible to make it in time. I think we surprised them, threw a wrench into their plan. My mother was annoying the shit out of me, so we went and stood in the driveway of our own accord. The shooter sees us, goes ahead and makes his move." Laura held up her two index fingers and then moved them apart. "Two people. About the time Rodgers and I are headed out the front door, someone's out back with a book of matches. It's the only thing that makes sense."

Neither Whitley nor Bynum offered their opinion of her theory. Instead, Whitley said, "We also visited your apartment again, and this time we found the door kicked in. Forensics is taking a look as we speak. Is there a reason we shouldn't tie it in with the events of this morning? Any angry ex-boyfriends we should know about?"

Laura crossed her arms and stared at him.

"That's enough for now," Bynum said. He collected his recorder and left the room.

But Whitley stayed behind a moment.

"What else?" Laura snapped. She wanted to be alone now.

"Who were they really trying to ace, I wonder? You or Don Rodgers?"

She opened her mouth to answer, but no words came out.

"I think Don Rodgers was collateral damage. Another person unlucky enough to be your friend. You were the one they wanted, Chambers. Explains why the first shot was aimed in your direction. So, here's my question: Are you finally going to tell me what you took from that motel room?"

Laura said nothing.

"Because the killer wants it real bad, seems to me." He reached out and put a hand on her bandaged upper arm. "Tell me now, and I can protect you."

"Ahem." In the doorway, the doctor clearing his throat.

Whitley took back his hand, and for a moment he put his thumb to his ear and his pinkie to his mouth. Then he left.

Call me.

Call me when you're scared enough, and maybe I'll decide to answer.

"Another gentleman to see you," the doctor said. "Another one with a badge—but this one says he knows you personally."

* * *

A gentle knock on the door.

"Come in," she said.

The first time she'd seen FBI special agent Timinski had been though the barrel of a zoom lens. She'd been spying on him from a high ridgeline as he processed an outdoor crime scene. Other than the lack of rubber boots on his feet, his appearance was identical to what she'd noticed at their first encounter: government-issue suit and tie, head shaved clean, thick eyebrows that made his face seem more expressive than it was. And beneath them, eyes that would detect all lies. That's how it had always seemed to Laura, at least—that nothing ever got past him.

"Let me guess," she said. "You're here to convince me to go to Whitley with open arms. Well, in that case you might as well crawl back under whatever rock you came from, because I won't do it. He makes me sick. And let me tell you another thing: he doesn't give a good goddamn about me, or Rodgers for that matter. I'm laying here in this bed in these stupid open-backed pajamas, and it makes me look weak and vulnerable. I'm not. I'm *not.* I seem that way, so Whitley comes in here to twist the knife a bit. It's sport to him."

The whole time she'd been speaking, Timinski's caterpillar eyebrows had been creeping up and up his forehead. When she was finished, he said, "Nice to see you again too, Laura."

It had been more than eighteen months since they'd spoken.

"Sorry."

"But some sort of protective custody wouldn't be the worst idea."

"Using the Orange County Sheriff's Office to protect me makes about as much sense as sending a fox to guard the henhouse. At this point, we're natural enemies."

"It's worth considering."

She pointed at the door. "Mention it again, and you can get out."

He raised his arms at his sides, palms out. "Okay, okay. Whatever you want. I didn't mean to upset you."

There was something about Timinski she couldn't put her finger on. The way he seemed to read her with those watery blue eyes, or the way he phrased his sentences—something about him always seemed to get her goat.

"Upset me. *Upset* me, like I'm a tea service that got knocked on the ground. I'm not upset, Tim . . . I'm mad."

"I gather you're working on a story."

"They say what about?"

He shook his head. "No, we mostly talked about the events of this morning."

"Are they going to catch whoever shot him?"

"I can't know that, Laura," he said.

But for once she was the lie detector. As clearly as she'd read the confirmation of Rodgers's death in the doctor's face, now she saw a glimmer in Timinski's eyes, like gold panned from the bottom of a stream.

"You know something, though. Give it to me."

He sighed. "You know the FBI lab is still doing the ballistics work for the OCSO? Okay, so I know someone over there. Word is they recovered the bullet. The one that . . ."

"From Don Rodgers," she finished for him.

"That's right. It wasn't a through-and-through, and it was in reasonably good shape. They matched it."

Laura's mind pulled up short. "No, that's not right. The Jane Doe from I-40 was shot with a rifle too, but they never found the bullet or anything else."

Here she was careful to call her Jane Doe—if Timinski didn't already know she was Emily Merritt, Laura wasn't sure she wanted to tell him.

"No, not with the Jane Doe. It matched a bullet from a different victim."

Now her mind was spinning. "Who?"

"Jacob Radford."

"Never heard of him."

"No reason you should have. It happened out east, near Wilmington, about a week ago. It was a hunting accident. Radford was in the woods wearing orange blaze with a rifle of his own, only he was the one that ended up shot. The incident wasn't even classified as foul play until now. They thought it was another hunter who shot him on accident, panicked, and took off. Or who didn't even know his target was a person. That happens sometimes, you know—hunter takes a shot at something moving, never bothers to check up on it. Now the cops out there are treating it differently, of course."

"Can you find out more?"

"I'm not here in any official capacity. Besides, right now I think you need to rest."

She closed her eyes again. It was all too much: Emily Merritt, Don Rodgers, and before either of them, this man Jacob Radford. All of them connected by the rifle. It had drawn a bright shining line between the three of them as it zipped from place to place on its deadly mission. But the rifle was just an inanimate object. She was much more interested in the finger on the trigger, a finger connected to a hand, a hand on the end of an arm, which led to a face.

She couldn't see the face.

Suddenly, a thought hit her with all the force of a .308. Her eyes snapped open, and she shot up in her bed. "Jesus, Cooper!"

"Excuse me?

"The dog, Rodgers's dog. What happened to the dog?"

"I . . . I don't—"

"He was in the truck." Her eyes darted toward the door. "Are there any deputies still around? Just check, please."

Timinski left and was gone for a long five minutes. When he came back into the room, he shrugged. "No dog."

"Oh no."

"Wait, wait, poor choice of words on my part. I'm not saying he was hurt, just that they didn't find him. In all the confusion, he must have run off."

Laura let out a trembling breath. Oh God, the dog would have been one thing too many. It would have been more than she could take. But Cooper had always had a habit of wandering off, often for days at a time. He could fend for himself, at least in the short term.

"Promise me when you leave here, you'll go back and look for him."

He promised.

"I have to go see my mother," she said, and tried to stand.

Timinski looked alarmed and stepped forward. "Can I help you?"

She waved him off. "Just look behind you."

"What am I supposed to be looking at?"

"Anything but me—I'm getting dressed."

CHAPTER

25

TIMINSKI RODE WITH her on the elevator and walked next to her down the hall to the intensive care unit.

"Was she talking at the house?"

Laura pressed her lips together. "She was slumped in that chair of hers, eyes screwed shut, pale as a white sheet. I thought she was dead already."

"Any change in her condition?"

"No. I can't get a straight answer out of the doctors on when she'll wake up, or even if she'll wake up."

"That means they don't know. Nobody likes to say that, though, because doctors rely on their authority to keep the wheels turning. One admission of uncertainty and the whole house of cards starts crumbling. It was like that when my dad passed—plenty of hiding behind the jargon, not a lot of straight answers."

The hallway was very long and quiet. Most of the patients were sleeping, and the lights had been dimmed.

"With my father too," she said. "This is the same hospital, actually. What happened to yours?"

Timinski didn't hesitate. She admired that part of him. "Killed in the line of duty."

"Was he FBI as well?"

"Oh, he'd be stricken to even hear you suggest that. No, he was a motor officer. The galling thing about it, before it happened he used to work task forces, go door-knocking with the ATF, stuff like that.

Up in the Tennessee hills, that was serious, dangerous work. Later he went into the motor unit, my mother thought it would be safer."

"What happened?"

"He was directing traffic, and someone ran him down. Yours?"

"It was cancer. GBM."

"I don't know that one."

"Glioblastoma multiforme. It's a brain tumor. It has survival rates down near five percent. I'll always remember the way one doctor described it. He said, imagine you've opened up a patient's skull, and you find someone has thrown a handful of sand inside."

Timinski stopped walking. "Sand?"

"Sand everywhere. And you, being the talented neurosurgeon that you are, get to work cleaning up. You get out your tweezers and start picking out the grains, one by one. But there's a problem."

"What?"

"Sand is impossible to get rid of. Wear your shoes on the beach just that one time, and you're dumping it out for weeks. That's GBM. All spread out, and it's nearly impossible to get rid of it all during surgery. Which means it just comes back."

"I'm sorry," Timinski said.

The way he spoke the two simple words, there was weight sewn inside them. Laura wasn't sure if he meant he was sorry about her father or about Don Rodgers.

"It was a long time ago, and he had ample warning of what was coming down the pike. We got to spend some nice moments together even after he'd checked in here for the last time. Here's what I remember: doctors speak one way to people's faces and a very different way behind their backs. It's the same in law enforcement, I'm sure."

"No comment."

"But doctors don't notice a nine-year-old underfoot; no one does. I caught them talking about my father's diagnosis in the hall, and they said the abbreviation really meant something else. I ran back to his room and whispered it in his ear, and it made him laugh and laugh."

Laura grinned at the memory.

"What did they say?"

"GBM," Laura said. "It really stands for *Good-bye, motherfucker.*"

But Timinski didn't smile back. "Dark stuff for a kid."

Laura felt her face close up. Without her noticing, the events of the past twelve hours had excavated the soil of her soul, the dirt she kept packed tight over the top of the things she wanted buried. She never spoke of those later moments with her father. Now she wished she could claw them back, keep them just for her.

"He didn't hide anything from me," she said.

They reached the end of the hall. A door opened, and another doctor came out. This one was young, without much in the way of a bedside manner.

"You're the daughter?"

"That's right."

"She's stable for now. I understand the first responders found you both on the front porch, just outside the door of the house."

Last she could remember, they'd still been in the foyer. Laura said as much.

"Well, if you managed to get her outside, you probably saved her life. The damage is still very serious, however. Smoke inhalation caused her to stop breathing, and her brain was oxygen deprived for a significant period of time. Her lungs were already damaged before this. She's been using supplemental oxygen?"

"For about six months."

"I'll consult with her pulmonologist, but during intake we discovered an abscess in her left lung that was infected. It had been there for some time but was greatly exacerbated by the smoke inhalation. We had to perform a thoracoscopic lobectomy."

"I know some of those words," Timinski said.

"We removed the most damaged part of the lung without opening the chest, which will improve her chances of recovery. She's still on a ventilator, so for now we're keeping her sedated. Can you give us a complete medical history?"

Laura said, "My mother fought against every doctor's appointment I ever made her. Your guess is as good as mine. Ask the pulmonologist."

"I want to prepare you for the fact that we may have to operate again. One lobe of her right lung is in nearly as bad a shape. During this last surgery we encountered considerable scar tissue, probably the result of her hysterectomy. The scarring looks like it's been there about thirty years. Techniques have changed since then, so I'd like to see the records if possible."

"I didn't know she'd had a hysterectomy," Laura said.

"How old are you?"

"Born in 1988."

He nodded thoughtfully. "She must have had it done just after. Lucky she had you in time."

Some luck, Laura thought but did not say.

"I have some forms for you to sign over at the nurses' station."

Timinski touched her good shoulder. "I'll leave you alone now. You need anything else before I get out of your hair?"

She told him she didn't.

"If you think of something," he said, "don't hesitate to call."

* * *

The second time her father left, it had happened in a room identical to the one she was sitting in now.

Laura checked her watch, then rose from her chair and stretched her back. She flipped up the light switch and waited while the overhead fluorescent tubes hummed and guttered to life.

Her mother sprawled across the full surface of the hospital bed, tubes in her nose and in her arm and a rainbow of wires snaking from her chest to a wheeled cart stuffed with electronics. Her jowls hung to the sides, pulling the flesh of her face as smooth and taut as drum skin. Under the harsh lights, she had the color of used candle wax. Only the crumpling of her paper gown as she breathed and the steady, confident throb of the machines hinted at the fact that she was still alive.

She flipped the switch down again. She stood in the dim half-light of the window and let the overchilled hospital air play across her bare forearms. She studied the unmoving body on the bed and waited. For hours she'd patiently anticipated some emotion bubbling to the surface, the moment when she would have more of a reaction to Rodgers's death and Diane's coma than to, say, rain without an umbrella.

But all Laura Chambers felt was smooth as a river stone. A damaged lung had finally plugged the endless morass of distortion spewing from her mother's mouth, and she'd expected to experience at least some sense of relief. Once she'd seen a video about ferromagnetic fluids, black oily liquids juiced with particles of iron, then twisted by magnetic fields into nightmarish, spike-laden sculptures. That was how she often imagined herself: an object with a jagged surface. Some spikes pointed outward, impaling the people she was supposed to love. Most pointed inward, lancing down through all her soft spots, stalactites of anger and depression and self-doubt.

At the moment she'd learned her mother might never wake up, Laura had prepared herself to become more serrated still. Instead, her thoughts gave way to water made sleek by the dawn. Her insides turned to glass taking its first breath outside the kiln, cooling rapidly, the molecules arranging themselves into something polished and hard and clear.

Someone smart would quit now, she thought. It was the sensible choice. Whoever had killed Emily, now they wanted Laura dead too. Whatever information Emily had possessed, the killers thought she had passed it along. Laura had never received it, but somehow she doubted she'd get a chance to explain that to the people who had gunned down Don Rodgers in cold blood. And without Emily's secret as an arrow in her quiver, the coming struggle would be a one-sided fight of epic proportions.

She had been in the room a long time, but outside it was still dark. She pulled the chair in front of the window and sat and rocked and hugged herself against the chill.

Emily Merritt's deft fingers in her hair, weaving her first French braid.

All of it part of the same picture, just out of focus.

Laura's mother in the picture from her bedroom, strawberry blond, already angry, but young, with her whole life left to change.

Would they try to kill her again?

Laura's father home during planting season, bone-tired, the pearl snaps on his shirt open at the throat.

By the time Laura had decided what she would do, the sky had turned the colors of a peach.

CHAPTER

26

Her apartment looked like it had been hit by a tornado.

The quality solid-wood front door hung off its hinges, and the doorjamb appeared to have exploded, showering the entryway with splinters. Inside, water on the floor. Probably it had rained last night, as it did almost every evening in these parts at this time of year, and wind had blown the raindrops straight through the gap.

Shards of smashed plates littered the kitchen floor.

The couch cushions lay sliced open, all the stuffing pulled out.

In the bedroom, her bed had been flipped up onto the wall. All the dresser drawers had been dumped out onto the ground. She pictured one of them pawing through the pile of her underwear, and just the thought of it made her shudder.

They had found nothing, Laura knew, because there was nothing to find. Part of her wished she could have seen the look on their faces when they were forced to finally give up. Such a personal violation should have enraged her, but the coldness she had acquired at the hospital lingered in her still. She stepped carefully from room to room in the apartment, waded through knee-high destruction, but didn't see any of it as an expression of power over her. It did not strike fear into her heart.

Instead, she noticed the signs of hurry: a few bottles left unmolested in the medicine cabinet; a closet no one had bothered to open.

They had been pressed for time, she realized. They were only human beings, after all. When she looked around, what she saw was desperation.

In her pocket, her new cell phone started ringing.

* * *

Alma Fuentes, the director of Social Services for Orange County, sat straight backed behind a scarred metal desk painted an institutional green. She was a severe-looking woman, with a dress shirt buttoned to the top and streaks of iron gray running through thick black hair tied up in a bun.

Laura told her what she wanted, and for a long moment the woman behind the desk just stared at her. Then she said, "Close the door, please."

Laura leaned back and gave the office door a push. It swung shut, the latch clicking into place.

"Access to files involving minors, even minors who have since crossed the line into adulthood, is strictly controlled. No one is permitted to look willy-nilly through their contents, not even law enforcement. It requires a court order, and even then, most identifying information is redacted."

"I don't have a court order," Laura said.

"What you're asking for is illegal."

"Yes."

"I could lose my job."

"I understand."

"I could even be arrested."

"You'd be well within your rights to throw me out of here right now, Ms. Fuentes."

"Call me Alma."

"Alma, you asked me to close the door."

The woman tapped the pen in her hand against the metal desktop. "Yes, I did."

"Can I take that to mean you're not going to call security?"

"That depends."

"On?"

"Why do you want to know these things?"

"A person reached out to me recently. I think it was Emily Merritt."

Alma's eyes widened in surprise. "I've tried to get in touch with her a few times, but she never responded. She's doing well, then?"

"You were close?" Laura asked, taking note of the interest.

Alma shook her head. "No, not really. We spent less than a week together more than twenty years ago. But some cases stick with you, don't they?"

"To be honest, I'm not sure if she's doing well or not. In fact, there's some evidence to suggest she was killed earlier this week. She left me, ah, a message, and the cell phone she called from was found with the body of the woman who was struck on the freeway Sunday night."

Alma's hand went to her mouth. "My God, that was Emily?"

Laura took a breath. "The accident was very severe. They're having some trouble making an identification."

"Surely this is a matter for the police."

"Surely," Laura said. "In fact, a charming lieutenant by the name of Whitley will probably be down here with one of those court orders you mentioned just as soon as I can get him to listen to me."

"But she could be alive."

"I don't want to give false hope."

"No, you just want a head start on the Sheriff's Office."

"If possible."

Alma Fuentes dropped the pen in her hand, reached down into a desk drawer, and extracted a yellowed file folder. She placed it on the desk between them. When Laura didn't take it, she picked it up and thrust it out.

"Alma, can you clarify something for me?"

"Certainly."

"Why are you doing this?"

The hint of a smile quirked the corner of her mouth. "There's only one reason: because before he died, Don Rodgers called and asked me to."

"You two kept in touch?"

"Hadn't spoken in years."

Laura met her eyes. "And yet you're willing to go out on a limb like this, an *I could be arrested* limb, to honor his request?"

"Did you know I started my career here right out of school as a social worker for the county? A tough job. Plenty of people are born with the deck stacked against them, but everyday folks don't much care to attribute others' circumstances to factors like the house they were born into, or the language they speak, or the health—or lack thereof—God gave them. 'Personal responsibility' and 'work ethic' get bandied about a lot, leastwise until bad fortune finds its way to their own front door."

"Temporarily embarrassed millionaires."

Alma frowned. "Who's that?"

"People say Steinbeck."

"Sounds like him, doesn't it?"

Laura nodded.

"I'm not passing judgment, you understand. A person being firmly in control of their circumstances, that's a more comforting story than the alternative. That way the world has a measure of justice in it. The poor are the lazy lying in the beds they made; the sick are sinners reaping their reward. Because if that's not how things work . . ."

"Then it's random. It's chaos."

"No one likes to imagine they were born into a cosmic game of Russian roulette. Police officers, I find, are particularly susceptible to the notion that life is essentially fair. Goes with the job description."

"And what about a social worker?"

She snorted. "The opposite. We think the game is rigged. Always has been, always will be. All we can do is put our thumb on the scale, try to even the odds a little."

"Don Rodgers called you a formidable woman."

Now she did smile. Her mouth cracked open, revealing very white teeth between the bookends of her red lipstick. "He did, did he? Don always had a soft spot for me."

"That's why you're helping me."

"No," Alma said. "Don Rodgers rates a favor because of the countless kids I personally watched him help over the years. Back when we met each other, the term *community policing* hadn't been invented yet, but that's exactly what he was doing. Most officers back then wouldn't have bothered to get involved with a child that had criminals for parents, or even just the wrong color skin. Don wasn't like that. He bent the rules when they needed bending, broke the rules he thought were broken. Changed the course of a lot of lives, I think—although he would never admit that himself."

"Just doing my job," said Laura, in a half-decent imitation of Rodgers's voice.

"That's him. Both of our jobs were pretty thankless. We helped each other when we could."

"Can I ask about Emily? What was your time with her like?"

Alma's gaze drifted off to the side, and her eyes lost focus. "It was a few days before I could locate her next of kin, and a couple more days after that for them to make arrangements to come get her. She stayed with me in the meantime."

"Who was it, her next of kin?"

"A distant uncle. He was older than we'd hoped. Children are time- and energy-consuming, and Emily needed another ten years of guardianship. But beggars can't be choosers, and he was her only living family."

"Can I contact him?"

Alma nodded. "Although I'd prefer you left my name out of it. His name is Ernest Sparks. The phone number stopped working some years back, but I'll write down the address." She flipped to a page in the file, jotted down the relevant information on a scrap of paper, and handed it across the desk.

"Is it usual for a child to stay with you personally?"

"Never happened before or since," said Alma. "If we can't find a family to house them, off to the group home they go. But Emily was a special case. My supervisor at the time asked if I'd be willing to take her in, and I said yes."

"A special case," Laura repeated.

"It didn't seem right to put her with the other children. Not after what happened, you understand. I asked a few experienced foster families if they could house her temporarily, but they all declined."

"Because of her . . ." Laura searched for the right word.

"Notoriety?"

"That's one way to put it."

"How about this—they treated her like she was cursed. As if the misfortune that had befallen her family was a contagious disease and she was infected."

Laura took a breath and asked the question she'd been putting off. "How was she?"

Alma caught her eyes and held them. "You knew her, isn't that right? Don mentioned it to me. Thought it would melt my heart on the issue. You didn't stay in touch? She was your friend."

A small hitch caught at the back of Laura's throat. The two of them had spent almost every day that summer together in the woods, right up until the day it happened. After that, though, Emily Merritt had vanished and Laura hadn't tried very hard to find her. She could have asked after her with the other children at school, or asked a teacher, or she could have tried to write her a letter.

But she had done none of those things.

She was no better than those foster families who had turned her away, poisoned by association. Looking back now, it shocked Laura how quickly she had traded worry for a kind of intentional forgetting, at how easy it had been to rake all those shared memories into a box and seal the lid shut. They had known each other, yes, spent countless hours together, certainly—but what kind of *friend* would do that?

"We were neighbors," Laura answered, hating the indifference of the word even as it passed her lips.

"I see," Alma said. "Then I don't mind telling you she was not well. She probably should have been taken to a hospital, in fact, but protocols were different back then. I gave her clothes, which she wore. I fed her meals, which she ate. I spoke to her. I didn't go to work that week. We were together all the time, and I talked endlessly." She opened her mouth, closed it again.

"What?"

"She never spoke, not one word. Then her uncle came, and my part in it was over. I only wish I could have done more."

Laura stood. "Thank you for your help."

"You're welcome. I wish I got to tell Don Rodgers he owes me one."

The same hitch at the back of her throat. "Me too."

"And your father, is he still with us? Give him my best."

Laura had already packed her phone and notebook and the scrap of paper into her bag, closed the top, and slung it over her shoulder. Her thoughts were already on her next move, and so for a long moment she didn't fully comprehend the words.

Without thinking, she said, "He died a long time ago."

"Ah, I'm sorry to hear that."

Laura turned back. "You knew him?"

"We met once. We spoke. That's why I assumed you and Emily were friends."

"When?"

A moment of confusion passed behind Alma Fuentes's eyes.

"When Emily was staying with me," she answered. "Your father was the only one who came to visit her."

CHAPTER

27

Ernest Sparks lived in Colerain, North Carolina, a three-hour drive from Hillsborough, on River Street. The name of the street was accurate, as a half mile past his house the road dead-ended on the bank of the Chowan. Laura missed the address on her first pass and found herself penned against the water. The river stretched nearly a mile wide, dark and still, churning silently southward the final miles to the Albemarle Sound and, beyond that, the Atlantic.

She turned around, hunted left and right, and found the numbers she was looking for attached to the mailbox in front of a one-story bungalow. It had chipped blue paint and purple shutters and one crooked chimney poking through a sheet-metal roof. The state of the front lawn and the gaping holes rotted through the floor of the porch suggested no one lived there, but Ernest Sparks answered promptly.

Inside, to her surprise, the house was neat as a pin. In no time at all Laura found herself in the front sitting room ensconced in an ancient but well-built wingback chair, listening to her host puttering around the kitchen as he made tea.

Laura's knee jumped up and down. She tapped her toes. This was not, she told herself, a death notification. That wasn't her place. Her every instinct, every fiber of her being, told her that Emily Merritt had died in Hillsborough six days ago. But Laura had been wrong before, and fast approaching was the moment when she would find out for certain. In the meantime, her main concern was to conceal the purpose of her visit from Mr. Sparks.

"Miss, what was your name again?" he called.

Ernest Sparks appeared to be more than eighty years old, and his voice had weakened through the years. The words drifted into the front room barely audible, and Laura made sure to speak clearly and loudly when she answered.

"Laura Chambers," she said.

"Lana Cambers."

"Laura. Chambers."

"Chambers, Chambers," he said. His volume was even lower than before, as if he was speaking to himself, trying to commit the name to memory. In another moment he emerged from the kitchen pushing a walker with one hand and carrying a sterling-silver tea service in the other. The porcelain cups and saucers tinkled against each other as he shuffled across the long stretch of floor.

"Can I help you with that?"

"Sit down, sit down," he barked at her. "You're the guest, don't you know?" He sat across from her, poured the tea, and added a small bit of milk.

Laura accepted the cup and sipped. "It's very good."

"My wife's," he said, indicating the tea service. "She was big on manners. Wouldn't have cared much for the world today. Better that she's dead."

He brought his own cup to his lips, and his hands shook so badly the liquid threatened to spill into his lap.

"Was she here when you took Emily in?"

"No, my wife passed very young. I'd been a widower for decades by the time little Emily arrived."

"And Emily spent the rest of her childhood with you," Laura said. "She grew up here with her uncle."

"I'm her first cousin twice removed—my grandparents were her mother's great-grandparents. But that doesn't exactly roll off the tongue, does it?" He gave a small chuckle. "We settled on Uncle Ernie in the end."

"I'm sorry about what happened to her family."

"Terrible thing."

"Did you know the Merritts? Her parents, I mean."

"Knew of them. The Sparks clan lore held that a branch of our people moved to the Piedmont a few generations back, but we lost touch. It had been many lonely years for me when Emily arrived. She was loved. I can't tell you how happy I was to find out I had a family again."

Laura nearly told him then but caught herself just in time. She wanted to be certain. Ernest Sparks seemed frail enough that the wrong kind of news might cause him real, physical harm. She should wait until someone else was present.

"We were neighbors when we were children," she said instead. "We were friends."

"I see," he said.

"And I always wanted to reconnect with her. I thought this might be my best shot."

Ernest Sparks placed the teacup back in its saucer and considered his guest. "You two lived next door to each other."

"Yes."

"Must be a hard thing to have happen to your friend. How old were you when it happened?"

"I was the same age as Emily," Laura said. "I was eight."

"How long has it been now?"

"The, ah . . . the anniversary was a few weeks ago. It's been twenty-three years."

He patted his own hand, as if he were trying to reassure himself. "A long time, then," he mumbled, and his gaze drifted off toward the mantel. On it sat a picture of him and Emily together. She looked to be nine or ten, and both were smiling, fishing rods in their hands. Behind them, Laura recognized the same sluggish expanse of river.

"Don't let the picture fool you," Ernest said. "I always loved to fish, but I could never get Emily to take to it. I tried, believe me. When she was young, not too long after she came to live here, I'd make her get in the boat with me and we'd putter up and down the banks. She'd tell me to take her back. I could almost never hear her. My ears were better then, but she could only whisper. Me, I'd just"—he mimed casting a fishing rod—"drop my line, reel it in, try again."

"Some people find it a bit boring."

He cast her an appraising look. "Some people, huh?"

"So I've heard."

"You sit in a boat doing nothing—of course it's boring. That's the point. Fishing is an exercise in patience. I wanted to teach her how to do that."

"Not much of a student, I take it."

He gave the same low chuckle. "That's the problem with young people: no tolerance for the quiet moments. She hated it at the beginning, but over time she grew to accept it, and by the time she graduated high school it had become our tradition. The Chowan is a blackwater river, did you know that?"

Laura shook her head.

"Most all the blackwater rivers on earth are only two places: the Amazon and here. Dark and deep and still—she liked that part. Later, around the time she moved out, we would still fish. We'd find a spot and just sit together in the boat. Not talking, you understand? Some things can't be talked about."

Laura shifted back and forth in her seat. "Have you spoken with her recently?"

"I visit her often."

"In the last few days?" Laura asked, trying to keep the tone of her voice under control.

"Just yesterday, as a matter of fact."

Laura's heart leapt in her chest. Her head spun.

Emily as she knelt before the woodland altar, their hair twisted together and turned to ash.

Hot tears on her cheek. She had to steady herself against an antique sideboard.

"Are you all right?" Ernest Sparks was looking at her, concerned.

"Do you have a number I can call?"

"Don't own a phone myself. Never liked them much."

"An address, then," she barked.

He gave a short nod. "I can tell you where to find her: the old Sparks place on the far side of town. The big house out front is falling to pieces, you have to go around back."

Laura set her teacup back on the tray.

"She's not always there, mind," Ernest Sparks said, "but you might catch her if the timing's right."

* * *

The old Sparks property no longer had an entrance fit for vehicles. Once there had been a driveway leading to a narrow bridge that spanned a creek. Their remnants were still visible, but the sandy soil of the drive was pitted and run through with little streams. The wooden timbers of the bridge had folded down into the water, and green moss crept skyward along their length.

Off to one side, a deer trail wound its way down the bank and back up the other side, disappearing into a grove of young trees.

Laura scrambled down and hopped across. In the soft mud there she could see footprints of different sizes, so she followed the path as it meandered between the saplings and kept to it even when it dove into long grass.

She topped a small rise, and the house came into view, huge and decrepit. It listed to one side like a sinking ship, with most of the second floor collapsed all the way down into the basement. One gabled roof still stood, and on top of it perched a weather vane that creaked and twirled in a sudden breeze.

Laura buttoned another button on her shirt, chilled despite the late-summer heat.

The path continued up to the place where the house's front door had once been, then darted sideways and curved around the back. Probably it led to something like a carriage house, Laura imagined. A modest structure that had once been a stable or a summer kitchen, renovated with new windows and modern insulation, equipped with electricity and running water and a new concrete driveway that connected to the road at some other place.

Just as quickly as the image had sprung up in her mind, though, it faded to nothingness. There were no power lines here, and without power there could be no well pump. A camp, then—a tent and a fire and a hundred-year-old hand pump that still drew up cold, clean water.

She turned the corner of the house.

More grass, longer still, tall as her shoulder and stretching into the distance. It rippled and waved in the breeze, crests chasing each other quick as sparrows toward the horizon. There were no other structures, just an ancient-looking live oak dripping with Spanish moss, and at its base a rectangular area enclosed by an iron fence.

She picked her way to a narrow gate and freed the latch.

It swung open under its own weight. Metal shrieked against metal, and the gate's bottom drove itself into the earth. Beyond, someone had tended to the landscape. Flowers had been planted. The grass had been cut and trimmed around the headstones.

They were white limestone, stained and cracked, the overall impression a mouthful of rotten teeth. The earliest dates were in the middle of the nineteenth century, and all the later dates clustered in the 1950s.

All except one.

It matched the headstones of the other children. The sculpture on top was of a small lamb, lying down, curled in on itself, eternally asleep. But this stone was paler, cleaner, newer than the others. It stood out like a neon sign, glowing in the dark.

Laura knelt, brushed away grass clippings that clung to the face, and read an inscription three lines long.

EMILY MARIE MERRITT
1988–2016
"With the angels now"

PART TWO

CHAPTER

28

All this time, she had been chasing a ghost.

Laura's cold resolve shattered and broke open, just as Emily had against the pavement—

No, stop. As the *victim* had. The *victim*. Old habits die hard, and for a long time now Laura had been pasting an image of her friend over the torn and swollen face she'd seen in the back of that ambulance. But she'd been wrong. At the moment Jane Doe ran out onto the interstate, Emily Merritt had been dead three years.

The walk back around the ruined house, through the grass, across the creek, the drive in the car, all of it passed like a blur. Then she was back on the porch that belonged to Ernest Sparks, pounding on his door. She was going to give him a piece of her mind. How could he have been so obtuse as to let her believe? How could he have been so cruel as to encourage hope to take root in her heart? A final chance to set right the wrong she had done to her friend so long ago—he had given that to her, and when she was properly off-balance, he had ripped it from beneath her.

When he opened the door, she would slap him across the face.

He opened the door.

Laura wore her pain and regret like a crown of thorns. It telegraphed across the space between them and reached Ernest Sparks far faster than an open hand or even words could hope to. He looked upon her, and his wrinkled lip began to tremble. He opened his arms.

She went to him, buried her face in his moth-eaten cardigan.

He embraced her.

* * *

"Why didn't you tell me?"

They were drinking more tea. Ernest Sparks had insisted on it.

"I lose the thread sometimes. Or perhaps I just didn't want to say it out loud." His eyes were shining. "Having you here . . . for a brief moment she was back, you understand?"

For a brief moment, she was back. Laura understood perfectly well.

"How did she pass?"

At this, a grave and wooden stillness passed into him.

"It's important to me, Mr. Sparks. I need to know."

He answered with great resistance; when he spoke, the words were heavy stones in his mouth. "She took her own life, you see."

"I see."

"There were addictions before that."

"More than one?"

"She wasn't very particular. Would you be, if it had happened to you?"

It did happen to me, she almost said. That wasn't quite true, though, was it? It had been awful, yes. It had affected her deeply. But when it came to the tragedy of the Merritt family, Laura Chambers had held tickets for the balcony—and it was Emily who had gotten stuck with a front-row seat.

Laura explained the mysterious phone call from a woman who had been killed soon after and her discovery of the photo album in the woman's motel room. "That's why I came," she said. "I thought it was Emily."

Ernest Sparks hung his head. "A terrible thing. I'm sorry, my dear."

"But Emily is still the only person I can come up with who makes sense. These were intensely personal pictures to keep for so many years. Did you ever see any like it?"

He puzzled over it. "No, we never had anything like that around."

"This album, it was probably sitting on a shelf or in a box somewhere in the house. Eventually everything inside the house would have gone to Emily, isn't that right?"

"Oh, you mean the estate. Let me see here." He pushed himself up shakily to standing, then tottered over to an old rolltop desk. "I have it here somewhere. There was no money, the bank got the land. The house, well . . . as you can imagine, no one was interested in the house."

"No one ever came asking about the contents?"

"No one," he said firmly. "Frankly, I wasn't interested either. Or Emily, for that matter—too painful. Most of it went into storage. And we hired a man out there, a dealer. Some of the furniture was quite old and valuable. He's sold it piece by piece over the years, and we get a bit of money from him time to time. Here we are."

With a flourish, he handed over a business card.

"Does he send you updated inventory lists?"

"Nothing like that, I'm afraid. It's just cash in the mail."

She looked at the brittle, aged card.

In a cursive script, it read:

JAMESON PELT
FINE ANTIQUES
Sales—Appraisals—Estates

And beneath that, on its own line: *Trustworthy!*

* * *

The phone number was still in service, and the business to which it belonged was still an antiques dealer. After twenty-three years, Laura hadn't been confident either would be true. The person on the other end of the line was even eager to answer her questions. But when she mentioned the name Jameson Pelt, the conversation hit a dead end. No one there by that name, thank you very much.

"Perhaps you should speak to the owner, Mrs. Richards."

"Perhaps I should."

She could hear the sound of papers being crumpled and slid against each other. She was put on hold. There was no music. The wait was very long, but it didn't bother Laura one bit. She was driving back from Colerain on Highway 64, and for the next two hours she had nothing but time.

"You, there."

"Yes, ma'am. Is this Mrs. Richards?"

"You're the girl who called asking after Mr. Pelt." Mrs. Richards sounded positively ancient. "What is your interest in speaking with him, may I ask?"

"Professional."

"I'm very sorry to hear that. Amelia passed along your questions, so let me get straight to the point. Yes, he worked for me, until the fall of 1998. No, he doesn't work here any longer. We have no association with Mr. Pelt. He was caught stealing from the petty cash, and I fired him straightaway."

"Does he still live in Hillsborough? Is he still in the same line of work?"

Mrs. Richards harrumphed.

"Sorry, I didn't quite catch that."

"I said, young lady, that my business is well respected and has been in continuous operation for more than fifty years. And that a thief who sells overpriced tchotchkes over the internet from a ginned-up storage unit doesn't deserve to be mentioned in the same breath, let alone considered to be in *my* line of work."

"Did you say a storage unit?" Laura asked.

* * *

Some of the self-storage facilities that had sprung up in Hillsborough over the past decade had a certain self-effacing charm: appropriately bright colors, clean lines and clean parking lots, climate controlled, fireproofed, well tended and well guarded.

U-Lock Self-Storage was none of these things.

It predated the current storage boom, and the facility showed its age. Plenty of rust coated the roll-up doors, and color-matched piles of orange pine needles mounded in front of the ones that looked as if they hadn't been opened in a very long time. The gate was unlocked and open, as was the door to a small Quonset hut with a hand-lettered sign over the door. It said OFFICE. There was no one behind the desk. Laura rang the bell and waited, tried a second time, and finally gave up.

Row followed identical row of metal garages, and in the very last row she found the place Mrs. Richards had told her about. Unit 18-C did appear to have a bit of spit and polish to it, at least in comparison to its cousins. No accumulation of pine needles, no rust on the door. The same couldn't be said of the Crown Victoria parked outside, which looked as if it had been purchased at a police auction a decade earlier and was now more parts corrosion than car.

But just the presence of the vehicle here was suggestive. Even better, most of the units were secured by padlocks, but the lock on unit 18-C was notably absent.

Laura made a fist and pounded on the sheet-metal door.

It rolled up with a squeal, letting out the hot air inside. The air smelled of body odor and cologne and marijuana, and underneath was a sharp note of sulfur, like rotten eggs, which Laura knew was the aroma of smoked meth.

Jameson Pelt greeted her. He was a man who had once been fat but was now rail thin. He had too much of everything: too much skin for his scrawny neck, too much fabric in his clothes for them to fit his scarecrow body. He wore a jacket despite the heat, and when he gestured—which he did often, and with great enthusiasm—the sides flapped behind him like a cape.

He slicked back his stringy hair with both hands, then stuck one hand out to shake.

Laura shook.

"Name of Jameson Pelt. Lemme guess, you're here about the statuettes, am I right? Statuettes for a statuesque lady, that makes sense. No? The Louis Vuitton then, it must be. I can't let it go for less than five hundred, I told your husband the same over the phone. Don't bother me with how far you drove to get here, it doesn't matter. Sob stories wear thin in this business, let me tell you."

Behind him, the large storage unit was a Tetris screen of overstuffed couches and flimsy-looking vanities. Two roaches skittered out the open door.

"Mr. Pelt, do you know the name Simon Barrow?"

That stalled him for a second. He squinted into the air. Then he had it. "'Course I know who he is, I keep up with the news. He's the Shotgun Slayer. Now what do I win? Say, do you like beer? I might have a cold one in the bottom of the cooler somewhere. Maybe there's two. If not, we can share."

"What about Emily Merritt—do you recognize that name?"

He smoothed his hair back again. "Sure, sure. That poor girl."

"Mr. Pelt, I am an attorney representing Ms. Merritt. Ms. Merritt is in the process of suing both the executrix of her parents' estate and the state of North Carolina for misappropriation of funds and the mishandling of certain property. Our records indicate that in 1996, Ms. Merritt's guardian"—here Laura pretended to consult her notebook—"one Mr. Ernest Sparks, retained your services, to include the appraisal and sale of antique furniture from the Merritt household, and that other personal items were delivered to you as well. Is that all correct?"

"Execu-trucks?" He scratched his head. "You said you're some kind of lawyer?"

"That's right, Mr. Pelt. I'm the lawyer that's suing you."

Suddenly he was literally backpedaling away from her. "Naw, naw, that's all right. None for me, thanks."

"This isn't someone trying to sell you something, Mr. Pelt," she said with a smile. "I'm here to tell you we're going to take you for everything you're worth."

"She . . . he . . . I never—" He stumbled over his tongue, stuttering the words out.

"And that there's nothing you can do to stop it. I'm a good lawyer, I should know."

Jameson Pelt looked as if his hair were about to light on fire.

"You were hired by Mr. Sparks, isn't that right?"

"Yes . . ."

"Speak up, please."

"Yes!"

"To sell the antique furniture from the house?"

"Yes."

"And other personal items were delivered to you as well?"

"They delivered it all to me, down to the clothes from the closets. And I sold what I could, but that's just what Mr. Sparks asked me to do! I even gave him a good deal on the commission."

"A *good* deal?" She scoffed. "Mr. Sparks was trusting enough to accept cash in envelopes without any other accounting or receipts, but you'll need to do better when we subpoena the documents. We have an excellent idea of what was in the house and its approximate value, and Mr. Sparks wrote down exactly what you sent him, every red cent. I'm here to tell you, Mr. Pelt, the numbers do . . . not . . . match."

Jameson Pelt jingled the keys in his pocket, and he kept eyeballing the Crown Victoria. He was thinking of just jumping behind the wheel and peeling out for parts unknown, and if she pushed him any harder, Laura thought, he might actually do it.

She'd set his house on fire; now it was time to show him the fire exit.

"Of course, there's a slim possibility we can work this out just between us."

"Yes! Anything. I don't have much."

"I've worked closely with Ms. Merritt, and I can tell you that financial renumeration is the furthest thing from her mind."

"Renumer what now?"

"She doesn't want money."

"Oh . . . oh! That's great, then."

"Ms. Merritt is interested in recovering some personal keepsakes. Specifically, the family photo album."

"And if I can get you this photo album, you'll lay off me?"

She nodded.

"Huh."

"What's the problem?"

"I don't want to say. I'm afraid you'll be mad at me."

"I . . . I'm a professional, Mr. Pelt. There's nothing you can say that will make me angry with you or even get me to care one way or another. Just give me the album, please."

"I can't. I sold it."

It was so unexpected it that it brought her up short. "You *sold* a family photo album. To whom?"

"Like I said, you'll be mad."

"It's this or the other thing."

He hung his head. "The lawsuit, you mean."

"That's right, Mr. Pelt." She clapped her hands together twice. "Chop-chop."

CHAPTER 29

INSIDE THE STORAGE unit, Jameson Pelt had a desk hidden from view behind a water-stained mattress. There was a computer, and the computer had internet access. How he was receiving cable service, or even electric for that matter, inside the storage unit was a bit of a mystery, one Laura wasn't particularly keen to solve.

Pelt rolled down the roller door halfway. "For privacy."

"Is that necessary?"

"These are trade secrets I'm sharing here, lady."

"Confidential, I promise."

"Guess I'll have to trust you." He adjusted his too-big jacket. "So eBay, you heard of it?"

She stared at him. "Yep."

"Okay, so I sell most of the stuff on eBay. All you have to do is take a few pictures and write up a little description, and it's like an auction, you just—"

She cut him off. "I know what eBay is. That's where you sold the album?"

"Remember, you promised not to get mad."

He was like a little boy caught by the teacher. She'd used the truncheon enough. Time to offer him something sweet.

She put a hand on his shoulder. "Don't worry so much. I can tell you did something baaaaad. Did you do something bad, Jameson?"

He looked up at her, eyes wide. "Maybe. Do you ever do anything bad?"

"Get me that beer, why don't you."

"Yes, ma'am!" he said, groped in a stained ice chest, and came out with a light domestic. She opened hers and slurped and tried not to think of his hand touching the mouth of the can.

"So you've got a little something on the side. We all do that." She put her finger to her lips. "Shhhh."

"Right on," he said, in a stage whisper.

"Show me yours."

"It's mostly eBay, I swear. But there are these other websites." He put his hand on the mouse, started to navigate. "Places where hobbyists can meet and talk and even trade."

"What kind of hobby?"

He turned in his swivel chair before speaking. He wanted to be able to study her face at the moment he said the words. "True crime."

Laura kept her face carefully neutral.

"Sounds weird, I know."

"Not to me, it doesn't."

"Right? *Right?* It's pretty mainstream, actually. A lot of girls think it's hot. Bundy, Dahmer, all those guys got letters like you wouldn't believe. Bundy even married one, he got her pregnant from behind bars. How wild is that?"

She touched his shoulder again. "Just show me, Jameson."

He licked his lips. "Right."

He brought up a page with a black background spattered with crimson blood.

At the top it read *MURDER MEMORABILIA.*

And under that: *USDA Prime.*

"Classy," Laura said.

But sarcasm was lost on him. "I know, right? Look at some of this stuff, it takes your breath away." He turned to face her again. "I have some items of my own. A modest collection. Would you like me to show them to you? Would you enjoy that? We'll have to roll the door the rest of the way down."

There was a flatness in his eyes, like two blank sheets of paper, and Laura didn't like it one bit. She'd misread Jameson Pelt. She'd pegged him as a sleazeball and nothing more, but now she found herself wishing she had her father's rifle.

"Just tell me who you sold it to."

"We'll have a good time together, I just know we will."

Laura pulled out her phone and held it against her thigh. "Do it now, or I call the cops."

He narrowed his eyes. "I have rights. You need a subpoena . . . you said so yourself."

She unlocked the phone.

He stood and stepped toward her. "Now that I think about it, you never even told me your name."

"Three, two, one—"

"It's fine, it's fine," he said, backing off. "I'll get the records. I keep excellent records. I'm a businessman, after all."

Laura said, "I'll wait outside for them."

She ducked under the door. Gorge rose in the back of her throat, but she fought it down. She sucked in deep breaths of unpolluted air.

In a few minutes Jameson Pelt came out with a dusty ledger, which he laid on the hood of his Crown Victoria. He opened it and ran his finger down various columns. "Here," he said, and tapped the page. "From the Merritt estate, I sold two photo albums. I ship everything myself, so I'll have a name and address to go with each."

Laura got out her notebook. "I'm ready."

"Both albums were purchased in December of 1996 by the same person."

"Give it to me."

"Huh, that's weird. It's someone right here in Hillsborough."

"Give me the name, Pelt!"

He ran a yellow fingernail across the row. "Name is Chambers, Diane Chambers. That mean anything to you?"

* * *

Laura went home.

Two orange cones barricaded the entrance, and a third had blown down into the ditch. The tires of Bass's Cadillac crunched and spun. Deeper ruts than she had ever seen pocked the dirt driveway, and in places it was nothing but a puddle of mud. The fire engine, she figured, all weight and water.

She had to park quite a distance from the house. Spools of bright-yellow tape had been strung across the drive. The tape was tied to two posts on the front porch, the ones that flanked the stairs, and then connected to four wrist-thick wooden stakes that had been pounded into the earth with a mallet—six vertices that marked out a roughly hexagonal area. In the center was Rodger's truck, riddled with bullet holes big enough to stick a thumb through. Between the truck and the house lay another, humbler circle of stakes inside the first.

Laura knew it was where Rodgers had died, but from a distance the patch of dirt looked no different from any other.

She cupped her hands around her mouth. "Cooper!"

No answer.

"Here, boy! They're all gone now."

A rustle through the cornstalks, but it was only a breeze.

She climbed up the side of the porch and let herself inside.

There was a terrible odor of smoke. Nothing resembling the pleasant smell of a campfire but rather a chemical stink, like burnt plastic, the result of the insulation inside the walls being incinerated. But otherwise, the foyer and living room appeared strangely undamaged. The only sign of disturbance was her mother's recliner, knocked over on its side.

She went into the kitchen.

Black fingers stretched above the stove and cabinets. The source of the fire was just on the other side, and the heat of the burning insulation inside the wall had been so intense, smoke had literally squirted through the drywall. It had left behind a picture that reminded her of a river delta, twisting tributaries of fire leading back to the source.

The fire department had responded quickly; otherwise there would have been no house left.

The sink worked, and the water that came out smelled fine. She filled a ceramic bowl with water and in another mixed a bit of water with oatmeal and put both out on the front porch.

A thought flapped at the edges of her mind like a bird that had flown in a window. Why? Her mother hated the Merritts, hated them enough that she'd never spoken of them in all the years since they'd been killed. Diane had deleted them from her and Laura's lives . . . and yet had then taken the time to track down their family heirlooms.

To what end?

Laura's insides were a frothing mixture of excitement and dread. The former because the list of people in her mother's life was so very short. One way or another, she would be able track down the person to whom her mother had given the album. Whether it was Jane Doe or not didn't matter. It was a link in the chain, and the chain would lead her inexorably to the identity of the woman on the freeway.

And from there, to the people who had killed her.

The latter, the dread, because her family seemed mixed up with the Merritts in ways she had never imagined.

She began to search. All the nooks and crannies of the house were familiar to her, because this was the place she had grown up. If there was a hide-and-seek spot worth knowing about, then she was familiar with it.

Two albums had sold, according to Jameson Pelt's records.

Laura had taken a picture and then examined the ledger closely. It was written in pen, and no alterations had been made. It seemed to her very authentic.

One album had been stuffed into a heating vent in a sad motel room.

Laura might not be much for math, but she could subtract.

In the hot attic, inside her mother's memory chest, she found it. A thick coating of dust sat on top of the same canvas cover. The binding creaked when it opened.

It shocked Laura worse than the first. These photos were in loose plastic sleeves and had been moved out of chronological order. There was her father and Bob Merritt growing up together. Her mother and Linda Merritt next to each other on lawn chairs, her mother glowering at the camera. It painted a picture of two families who were close friends. Nothing like what she had been told.

When it happened, she and Emily Merritt had been due to start third grade together in just a few short weeks. For the thousandth time, she racked her memory for some notable or relevant occurrence from that summer, but nothing presented itself. For Laura it had been a magical time, long days traipsing through the woods between their houses, building stick forts to act as castles, playing alternatively the dragon or the damsel in distress. Missing, however, was any recollection of her father and the Merritts being in the same room. They had never spoken, as far as she knew. Her mother would nod to Mrs. Merritt at the rare school choir event she deigned to attend, but that was the extent of the relationship.

Bruce Chambers's body language—the way he'd wrapped one arm around Bob Merritt, the fatherly hand on Emily's shoulder, the wide grin on his face—all of it stank of an intimacy she could not fathom. Why didn't she remember these moments? Why had her father visited Emily in the time between her parents' murder and when she was taken in by Ernest Sparks? No matter how she approached it, the facts wouldn't square. Some unknown element was fouling the equation, throwing it out of balance. Nothing added up.

Laura herself appeared in this set of photos, perhaps six or seven years old.

Her gap-toothed grin and wild, curly hair next to a tree.

Hugging Emily, their cheeks pressed together.

She touched the photo with a single finger. As horrible as the end had been for Emily's parents, at least it had been quick. An infinitely short moment for them had stretched forever for their daughter. A single moment that had wormed its way inside Emily and never left. Infested her, made a nest for itself. Burrowed deep, until it was impossible to leave behind.

Laura thought about all of it as she looked at the two of them. She marveled to see the face of her friend before any of it had happened.

When she was finished, she closed the cover, stood, and put her hand on the lid of the memory box to close it.

From its shadowed interior, behind a scrim of quilts and lace, came the slightest hint of beige.

The moment her fingers touched it, she knew what it was. Her hand jumped back as if bitten. She reached inside again and pulled it into the light.

In her hands was a second photo album.

CHAPTER

30

THAT WAS THE summer Laura went to sleep easy but woke up screaming. Terror came for her in the dark, seeping through the crack at the bottom of her closet door, slithering out of the blackness beneath the bed before creeping up across the sheets, smothering her feet, pressing itself into the vulnerable softness of her stomach, bubbling up past her neck, leaving time only for one last gasping breath before horror pressed its damp hand over her mouth, flooding her nostrils, worming its way down her throat, begging her to scream.

Which was how she woke up most nights: screaming.

She slept a deep and dreamless sleep until she didn't anymore, snapping awake like someone had flipped a light switch wired to her brain and finding herself crouched in the corner, sobbing, tears already dried to her face. She could never remember climbing out of the bed, wrapping the blanket around her trembling body, or beginning to cry. She knew only that she was afraid and that the fear had originated somewhere outside her body, entering her and gestating while she slept.

Most nights her mother would pound a fleshy fist on the wall, yelling for her to go back to sleep, and that would be that. Sometimes, though, her father would unlock her door and come into the room. He would leave the light off, and together they would feel their way through the darkness, down the stairs, across the front room, out onto the porch. The air keeps its warmth in the thick summer months in North Carolina, so she was not cold wearing only her pajamas and the sandals he'd put on her feet. She did not shiver when they walked away from the house, out into a fallow field to the place where he would spread the blanket on the ground. Then they would lie next to each other, staring up at the stars.

Sometimes her father said nothing.

Sometimes, he would speak.

"What scared you so damn bad it's got you yelling?"

Her skin tightened at the memory: palpable dread invading her pores. She bit down on her lip.

"A dream?"

"Not a dream. Not exactly."

"Something happened at school?"

She shook her head.

"You've got to give me something, Laura."

"It's just . . . sometimes I get scared."

"Everyone gets scared."

"Even you?"

"All the time. More than most, I suspect."

"You never seem afraid."

"I learned to hide it."

"Can I learn to hide it too?" she asked. "Can you teach me?"

He exhaled long and hard, the breath whistling between his teeth. "I'd rather you weren't scared to begin with. I'll help you if you let me."

"But Daddy?"

"Laura."

"If you can't even cure your own fear, how can you help me do it?"

He chuckled at this. "Aren't you a smart little thing?"

"Momma says no."

"Don't listen to all that. Your momma says things just to hurt, which is how her own momma talked to her."

"That's part of it," Laura said.

"Of being afraid?"

"Afraid is like a spider caught up in your hair. Once it crawls off, you're not scared anymore."

"But some fears linger." He spoke with a quiet conviction, and for the first time Laura imagined she might avoid the troublesome task of finding the words to fit her feelings. Maybe he already understood.

Her father studied the sky, scratching under his chin at the first blush of a beard. "Forget it."

"What?"

"All my talk about you never being afraid. It's a weakness for me to hope you'll never be scared, never hurt, never cry. All that and more is your debt to pay, the cost of living in this world. I love you, Laura, and it pains me to see you like this. The greater part of me wants to protect you from ever encountering worse. But the better part of me recognizes the fatal folly of that path. I do you no favors by delaying the inevitable, and if I ever seem unkind, it's only because I refuse to leave my daughter unprepared. So that when the bill comes due, the cost will not break her."

She had never heard him speak so many words at once.

"Do you understand?"

"Yes," she answered, although she didn't. Not really.

"You have to be able to take care of yourself. You have to get ready. Tell me about them." He gestured upward.

Stars spilled across a sky so dark all of them were visible, from the brightest ones like pinpricks though a thick blanket down to the dim, nameless ones, stars with such low apparent magnitude they left only the barest impression on the black, their collective glow blending into incandescent cotton fluff. As she had on all the other nights she and her father had spent on this spot of empty earth, Laura pointed heavenward and named their names.

She called out the summer triangle of Vega, Deneb, and Altair, each the brightest star of their separate constellations, dominating the very apex of the sky.

She described Ursa Major and inside it the Big Dipper, paying special attention to the two stars at the far side of its bowl that together traced a line toward the north.

She made sure to point to Cassiopeia, in all her glory.

Her father could not teach her to conquer fear, but he had taught her this.

"If you're ever lost," he said, "this will give you a sense of direction." And it had. So too had those comparatively short moments under his tutelage always shone bright in her collection of memories, the recollection of his calm guidance offering comfort during times of tumult. Laura dreamed of those nights often, her subconscious dredging them up from the depths and replaying them weeks after they happened, then months, then years. Even as an adult she would dream the dream, and most times she would wake feeling centered and complete, as if the perpetually missing part of herself had been replenished while she slept.

Most times the dream was a good dream, because that was where it ended.

But their conversation on that final night, the last time he had scooped her up in his arms and carried her out under the stars—it had not ended there. He had spoken the words she wanted to forget.

Sometimes, though, she dreamed the rest.

Her father said, "What if something happens to me?"

"Like what?"

"Something. Anything. A person's luck always runs out, it's only a question of when."

"You'll be okay," she said, wanting it to be true.

"I don't want you playing with Emily Merritt anymore."

"She's my friend."

"Never go over to her house, understand?"

She didn't.

"If something happens to me, I want you to take care of your mother. Promise me."

"I promise," she said.

The fear was back then, a wending cloak of dread wrapping itself around her head, cinching at the neck. She reached out for her father's hand, but he was already gone. The stars above glittered and danced, cold uncaring eyes surveying her suffering, eternally unmoved. They began to dim, fading toward oblivion.

And as she watched, one by one, they went out.

CHAPTER

31

THE BAR WAS called Port, and it looked like it might have been trendy at times other than noon on a Monday. The interior sported brass lanterns and knotted-rope chandeliers suspended over two-person booths; a long line of copper mugs hung from hooks over the liquor bottles. A lone bartender stayed focused on the glass he was polishing as they entered, and Laura sketched a wave in his direction before heading toward the booth at the very back.

"Are they open?" she asked, sliding in across from him.

"Not for another hour, but I called ahead. The owner owes me a couple favors. Why, you want something?"

"It's a little early for me."

"All business," Timinski said. "Same old Laura."

She'd messaged him late on Sunday, and he'd been quick to suggest the location and time. The bar was close enough to the Raleigh FBI office to be convenient but still far enough away to ensure that none of his colleagues would see them together. Now he was sitting across from her, same shaved head, same iceberg eyes. He wore a dark-red tie over a bone-white shirt, and his gray wool suit was a winter weight. It was a northern suit, not intended for a North Carolina summer, and she could see the strained thickness of the fabric where it wrapped around his broad shoulders.

"I'm glad you decided to get in touch," he said. "You look healthy."

The sling had come off her arm at a doctor's appointment this morning. Now there was a thick wrapping of gauze secured by an elastic bandage.

"I'm still not supposed to bend it."

He gestured to the bartender, who set a glass of water in front of each of them and slid a beer in a frosted mug toward Timinski.

"You're sure you don't want anything?" he asked again.

She just shook her head, and the bartender went back to polishing glasses.

"It's a shame we didn't keep in touch. But last year the Bureau was all over me. It was a major embarrassment to have a journalist find something the FBI overlooked. Any more contact between us would have been a serious setback to my career."

"I understand the concept of covering your ass," Laura said. "You don't have to explain it to me."

"Look, I'm sorry about the way—forget it."

He twisted back and forth in the narrow booth, struggling to pull his arms free from his jacket, stripping it off completely and folding it onto the seat next to him. In the wake of the quick movements, she could smell him: soap, clean sweat, a hint of sandalwood.

"In the end, none of it mattered," he continued. "DC has a long memory; they shipped me back here first chance they got."

"Nothing available in the middle of the desert?"

He gave her a tight-lipped smile. "If there was, maybe I'd be out among the geckos right now. Or not. Say what you will about the Bureau, but they're not wasteful. My background goes a long way down here."

Timinski had grown up poor in the mountains of Tennessee, just across the border from North Carolina. Years of practice meant he could suppress the accent, but it was a conscious choice, Laura knew. When he got excited or started yelling, his real voice seeped out around the edges. Most of his professional career had been spent right here in the South, and the job in DC had been a long-sought promotion.

"Sorry to hear about the job," she said.

"Oh, hell." He blew out a breath. "It's all stuffed shirts up there anyhow."

A moment of understanding passed between them. The raw, nervous energy of the encounter dropped from a boil to a simmer. There had been loss on both sides of the table, all of it now so much water under the bridge.

"This isn't just two old friends meeting for a drink, is it?"

"Well, you know I consider you a very valuable resource."

He leaned back from the table. "Stop. I don't think I can handle being showered in so much praise."

She steamrolled right over him. "You offered to help me, Tim, and if you were serious—here I am, asking for a favor."

"Ah," he said. "The other shoe drops. I'm just another source to you."

Behind him, the bar's smoked-glass door swung open to admit two more men in suits. They stepped up to the bar, and Timinski looked them over as they ordered drinks.

"Problem?" Laura asked.

"No, I don't think so," he said after a beat.

"Embarrassed to be seen with me?"

"Hell yes I am," he muttered under his breath. "I'm noon drinking with a reporter, one who's guilt-tripping me, playing me like a fiddle. It's a goddamn travesty."

"Oh, so it's working?"

"The last time we were together, you almost ruined my career, and now you're about to ask me to help you insert yourself into an active homicide investigation."

"This isn't about Don Rodgers."

He turned back around, his eyes clouded with suspicion. "Then make with your ask already."

Laura slid a manila envelope toward the center of the table, and Timinski unwound the string and pulled out a copy of the Simon Barrow article. He glanced at it, put it away.

"You're not going to read it?"

"I read it when it came out," he said.

"Now you're making me blush."

"Not sure what it has to do with me, though."

"You were around for the Merritt murders?"

"I was green, but I was here."

"Did the FBI have a file on it?"

He didn't need to consult anything but his memory—the crime was infamous enough for the details to have stuck with him. "Yes, it wasn't our jurisdiction, but the locals asked for a forensic consult. It was a real mess in there."

"So, here's the part where I ask for the favor."

"All right," he said slowly.

"The file—can I take a look?"

He blew out a breath. "That's what this is about? You know I can't let you start copying files. It'll be my ass."

"Come on, the case has been closed for twenty-three years."

"Doesn't matter."

"Deep background only," she said. "If I can't confirm the facts somewhere else, I won't use them. Nothing gets traced back to you. But I'm scrambling for a foothold here, Tim."

"No, you want the Sheriff's Office file; it'll be a lot more complete."

She stifled a laugh. "They don't talk to me much these days. Besides, like you said, the Bureau isn't wasteful. I bet they saved all kinds of interesting things."

He gave her a hard look. "It's not like you to just move on. You're the most stubborn person I know."

"I haven't forgotten about Don, believe me. But this is an important story too."

He twisted around for another look at the only other customers, the two men at the bar. "Let's get out of here," he said, and left some money on the table.

Together they pushed out the door into humidity thick and sticky as molasses. He loosened his tie, rolled back his cuffs, and pointed to a black Tahoe parked on the curb. Inside, he set the air conditioning to maximum. For a long moment he just stared out the windshield, considering. Only when the jets of air had cooled him down enough and the sweat on his brow had started to evaporate did he speak again.

"You have identification? Not a press pass, a driver's license."

"Sure."

"Use it. Don't tell them who you are."

"Of course," she said. "And if this works out, maybe you could get me a copy of the Sheriff's Office file too."

He turned to look at her, the lines in his face deeper than they had seemed a moment ago. "Jesus, Laura, you never quit."

* * *

The FBI's presence in Raleigh was what they called a resident agency, one step down the food chain from the field office in Charlotte. It slouched behind the beige walls of an unassuming office park just west of the North Carolina State campus, any signage conspicuously absent.

Timinski left the Tahoe in a parking garage designated for visitors, then flashed a badge at the security guard standing behind the front desk. It was a plain lobby fitted with gray furniture upholstered in cheap synthetic fabrics, the kind found in the waiting rooms of untalented dentists. Laura knew what to expect, and she was ready with her driver's license. The guard took her identification and ran it through a scanner. His mechanical keyboard clicked rapidly as he typed a few lines into the computer, each sharp little snap echoing off the tiled floor like the fracture of a wishbone. The printer behind him hummed, and he slid a small card into a hinged piece of plastic and sealed it at the bottom. He clipped it to a lanyard and handed it to her along with her ID.

"You're all set, Ms. Chambers," he said, and Laura hustled to catch the door as Timinski let it close behind him.

She followed him down another off-white hallway and then into an empty conference room. A modern-looking wooden table sat surrounded by an earlier generation of dented metal chairs. The walls lacked even the minimum flourish of motel art, and it smelled like low-grade disinfectant.

"You guys just move in?"

"Naw, we just spend all our money on suits. It'll take me a good while to check file inventory—just sit tight," he said, and closed the door behind him.

So far, so good. Timinski had been far more accommodating than she had expected. As far as risk tolerance went, bringing a reporter inside the FBI office earned him high marks. He was taking a real chance to help her. She mused on the depth of his feelings, both for her and over the death of Don Rodgers, and wondered how far she could push him before they ran dry.

Laura had deliberately not yet mentioned the body on the interstate, her ongoing sparring match with Whitley, or the photo albums. Timinski had agreed to help, but only because the extent of the favor was access to a case that had been in storage for more than two decades. Even the barest hint of interference in an ongoing investigation would send him running for the hills.

Once burned, twice shy, she thought.

She would feed him information one bite at a time, careful not to spook him.

The door opened, and Timinski came in with something in his hands. "Are you all right?" he asked. "You're flushed."

"It must be the heat."

His eyes lingered on her for a moment, then he pushed her bag aside and set down a bulky laptop. "The Bureau has an ongoing project to digitize old files to allow easier access, make them searchable and so on. It's not exactly top priority, but we're working backward."

"You're back farther than 1996?"

"Just barely," he said. "Listen, I did a quick perusal of the case summary, and there's something here you might find very interesting indeed."

The laptop finished booting, and he picked his way through directories labeled via an inscrutable naming convention, finally landing on a folder called *306-CE-32098 Merritt.* It was filled with audio files. He went down the screen, found the one he was looking for, and hit play.

A hiss of static filled the small conference room, followed by what sounded like a scratch of pencil on paper very near the microphone. A male voice murmured, too low and far away to be intelligible. Then a loud cough.

"That's a bold claim," a man said.

"Everyone knew about it an hour after you found them," a second voice responded. "Secrets don't keep around here, you know that."

Laura froze in place, and an envelope of warmth encircled her chest, bearing down, the pressure increasing by the second.

"Did you hear we found the daughter?" the first person asked.

The recording stopped.

Timinski clicked and traced circles on the track pad, then rapped his knuckles on the hard plastic next to the keyboard, but nothing happened. "Damn thing's frozen up," he said. "We're not allowed to keep Bureau materials anywhere but the machines they issue, but these archive computers are worthless, outdated crap. I make the requisitions, but it's radio silence from upstairs. Maybe when they finish outfitting the anti-terrorism boys with all the latest bells and whistles . . ."

Laura stared into the whiteness of the wall in front of her, not hearing a word of it.

He put a hand on her shoulder. "You okay?"

She nodded. "Is there any more?"

"Sure, I've got the originals down in my office. You recognize the voice, huh?"

In her head, the tiny snippet of recording played again and again.

Everyone knew about it an hour after you found them.

Secrets don't keep around here, you know that.

It was the way his emphasis landed on the last word that made her certain.

Of course she knew the voice. She remembered his clipped cadence, the impatience of a man perpetually frustrated by words, a man for whom time spent speaking was time wasted. She could never forget that unmistakable timbre, barbed and obstinate, like a late-summer sandbur hooked into her heel.

The voice belonged to Bruce Chambers.

It belonged to her father.

CHAPTER

32

THE FREIGHT ELEVATOR had to be operated manually by way of a metal thumb switch, its brass plating worn down to dirty pewter by years of sweaty fingers.

"This back part of the building is close to a hundred years old," Timinski explained. "It was some kind of warehouse at the turn of the century, and they added on the rest later. Lots of storage down here. I think that's why the Bureau was interested in the space."

The car lurched to a stop a few inches above the floor level, and the wooden divider slid upward to reveal a brick wall. A darkened hallway extended in either direction, the only illumination small emergency lights spaced every thirty feet. An arrow had been painted on the wall in front of them. It pointed to the right, just above a sign reading PROPERTY/EVIDENCE.

"Watch your step," Timinski said. He headed to the left instead, motion-activated lights sputtering to life in his wake.

The office, when they reached it, looked like a space hollowed out of file storage. Ceiling-high stacks of boxes lined three walls. On the fourth wall was a large desk littered with folders and legal pads, four computer towers blinking beneath it. A rough wooden workbench ran down the center of the room, an overhead light shining down on more papers and a series of large maps.

Timinski must have caught the look of surprise on her face. "Don't get many visitors down here."

"I knew you were in the doghouse, but even doghouses are usually aboveground."

He shrugged. "Nice and quiet, though."

Timinski had never done anything nice or quiet in his life, she thought. He was putting on a brave face, and she understood now that corralling her into a conference room had been his attempt to conceal just how far his star had fallen.

She pushed aside any feelings she had about his circumstances, or her part in it, and just tried to frame her next question. But the words wouldn't come. Shock at hearing her father's voice had yet to wear off. The Chambers family had never been one to take a lot of home movies, and her father in particular had shunned such activities as wasted energy. "No use reliving the past," he liked to say. There wasn't a recording of her father anywhere, not a video or even a cassette tape. He had died twenty-two years ago, and his voice had died with him.

At least she'd thought it had. An hour ago, she would have sworn to it.

"Let me hear the rest of it."

Timinski ran a finger down the row of boxes, pulled one out, and placed it on the workbench. The cardboard handles had creased and sagged under the weight of the contents, and someone had scrawled a notation across the lid with black sharpie: *306-CE-32098.*

Next, he reached down and unlatched a wide, squat cabinet. In the front were several rectangular black boxes that looked like reel-to-reel tape recorders. Each hulking machine had two round plastic tape rolls jutting out its top, and they leered up at her like the eyes of some mechanical bug.

Laura stared at them. "What is this place?"

"Storage for equipment that's turned obsolete," Timinski said.

She wondered whether he meant the items in the cabinets or the man assigned to mind them. From behind the ancient tape recorders, he extracted a slightly more recent audiocassette player, and from the file box a gray cassette tape. He put the tape in the player and hit rewind. The mechanical wheels gained traction, and the tape began to whinny and whine. It lurched to a stop, and in the close quarters of the concrete room, the sound of the STOP/EJECT button snapping back into place jolted Laura like a gunshot.

Timinski opened his mouth, as though he was about to offer some preamble.

"Just play the tape," Laura said.

The wheels began to turn, and first came an interminable silence.

Then the same hiss of static. A male voice spoke.

"It's now approximately eight forty-five PM on the twenty-second of August 1996. This is Investigator Ennis Ford of the Orange County Sheriff's Office. We're in interview room B at the courthouse, and here in the room with me are Sergeant William Bynum and Bruce Chambers. Mr. Chambers, can we get you a glass of water? Are you comfortable?"

"Plenty comfortable," her father said. "You've got air conditioning."

"We like it too, and thank you for coming in this evening. Did Sergeant Bynum explain the circumstances of this interview?"

"He didn't explain jack shit."

"I see," Ford said. "Well, the reason we asked you down here today is—"

"I know why you asked me down here."

"I thought you—"

"I said your deputy didn't explain jack shit. I doubt he even knows jack shit. That don't mean I'm confused about why you pulled me down here."

Ford's annoyance came through in the tone of his next question. Her father had tended to have that effect on people.

"Why don't you explain it to me, then?"

"This is about the Merritts getting killed," Bruce said. He coughed.

"That's a bold claim."

"Everyone knew about it an hour after you found them. Secrets don't keep around here, you know that."

"Did you hear we found the daughter?"

Ford waited for an answer, but one was not forthcoming. The static droned along, a recording of the unbroken stillness between them.

"Aren't you going to ask if she's okay?"

This last question came from a new voice, presumably a much younger version of Bynum. He sounded different. Even over audio, Laura could sense Ford bristle at the interruption. Interview techniques hadn't changed much since '96, and she felt certain he'd been waiting for Bruce Chambers to break the silence.

Good luck with that, Laura thought.

The clearest mental image of her father popped into her head: him sitting across from this OCSO investigator, arms crossed and hat tilted back, his face fixed in a perpetual scowl, the expression of a man whose distaste for the vagaries of language knew no bounds. Silence wasn't something Bruce Chambers had ever been afraid of.

"She's alive," Ford said finally.

Even across the gulf of twenty-three years, and even through the imperfect medium of a cassette tape, Laura could feel the energy in the room change. Ford had played some kind of ace, she just didn't understand what kind.

"Answer Sergeant Bynum," Ford said. "Ask if she's okay."

Her father said nothing.

"We found her out in those woods behind your house."

A curious crackling that might have been the sound of a struck match.

"Did you know her? It's okay to admit you knew her, Bruce. Your next closest neighbors after the Merritts are another mile out. What would be strange is if you sit here and tell us you didn't know her."

"I knew her," her father allowed.

"Bob and Linda Merritt?"

"Knew them too."

"You were friends?"

"Just neighbors."

"Good neighbors?"

"That thicket of woods makes a pretty good fence, so yeah, good neighbors. We saw each other every six months or so."

"And if we ask around about you and the Merritts, are we gonna hear any stories? Land disputes? You hit on his wife? Anything like that?"

Her father gave a low chuckle. "Boy, you sure are fishing, aren't you? Can't say that's comforting."

"Just answer the question, Mr. Chambers."

"I may not have been close with the Merritts, but I got a little girl of my own the same age, and she sleeps not a mile from where it happened. So tell me something: are you going to catch this guy?"

A shuffling of folders, the scratch of pencil lead on paper.

"That it?" her father asked.

"We haven't talked to Emily Merritt yet, but when we do, what's she going to tell us?"

"Who did it, I hope," her father answered.

"Me too," said Ford.

A chair scraped back on concrete.

Another silence, but this time the recording was over.

* * *

"Are you all right?"

Timinski wore a concerned expression, and Laura realized she'd been biting the lowest knuckle on her index finger.

"I'm fine," she lied. Listening to his voice had thrown off her center of gravity, affecting her deeply. After all these years, he had been alive again. Sometimes she would reach out for him in her memory. His boots and his Wranglers, his sheepskin coat, the hat he always wore—all those things would fly together into a vaguely human shape, hovering in the blackness, waiting for a face. More and more often, she found, the face wouldn't come. She'd squeeze her eyes shut and try to conjure it, but instead of her father's features, there would be only—

Void.

Most days he would just slip away.

To hear the odd halting quality of his voice had been the hardest part. Not too long after the Merritts were killed had been the final argument between her parents in the Chambers house, the blowout to end all blowouts, the apocalypse of marital strife. Her parents' union had never been a happy one, but for years the relationship had plugged along. Then one night the two of them woke her up with their screaming, and the next day her father was gone.

He didn't come back for almost a year, and only then because he'd gotten sick enough that he had nowhere else to go. One day she'd walked up the dirt driveway to find him sitting on their single ratty porch chair. She ran to him, threw her arms around his waist, and wailed. "I love you, Daddy," she'd said, sobbing the words into the dirty denim of his jeans, then wiped her eyes, waiting to hear it back.

But by then it was already too late for *I love you too*. He had lost the ability to speak.

"It's got to be a shock to hear him interviewed in connection with a crime," Timinski said.

Laura blinked the memory away. "It's not that, Tim—he *was* a criminal. He used to steal copper. One time he stole a bunch of coil from a construction site, unloaded it on some shady junkyard owner, then came back that night and stole it again." She laughed. "The junkyard man came pounding on our door, screaming that he was a thief. Daddy said, 'Guess you better call the cops.'"

"Good dad?" Timinski asked.

"He could be a real son of a bitch. We were poor, and he was stubborn."

"I thought you seemed upset. It's my mistake."

"No, I'm sure I did," Laura said. "This is the first time I've heard his voice since he died. It caught me off guard."

"You didn't take home movies when you were a kid?"

"It wasn't that kind of family."

"I see," he said.

"Do you have other recordings?"

He shook his head. "Things were different back then. Mostly they just took notes. Your dad was never really a suspect, of course. This interview happened about eighteen hours after the murders; at that point Ford was still casting a wide net."

"And then?"

"About this same time a deputy found Simon Barrow asleep in his car with the murder weapon in the back seat, and the rest is history."

"Let me see the file."

He frowned. "It's getting late. I have a meeting."

"Find me a place to read it. I won't bother anyone."

His eyes narrowed, and for a moment she thought he would show her the door. Then his expression softened. "You can read it back in the conference room, okay? But no copies."

He put two heavy boxes on a compact rolling cart, pushed them to the elevator, and led her back into another windowless conference room. At first, she thought it was the same one. It had four identical bare walls pressing in from all sides, but some of the chairs looked a little different. Maybe all the rooms in this building looked the same. Timinski assured her that no one would interrupt her and closed the door behind him on his way out, leaving her alone to read.

C H A P T E R

33

THE FILE CONTAINED no earth-shattering information. There were no dramatic reveals, no reams of secret evidence that pierced the veil of mystery surrounding Simon Barrow's motives. As far as Laura could tell, the broad strokes of the story—the legend of the Shotgun Slayer known by everyone in Hillsborough—were fully supported by the facts.

There were small differences, though. Minute changes in little details that aggregated themselves into something fresh and new.

For starters, take the discovery of Simon Barrow asleep in his car. Invariably this tidbit would be shared around the campfire whenever some half-drunk camper trotted out the real, one-hundred-percent true, cross-my-heart-and-hope-to-die story of the Merritts, and the implication was always the same: that the stuff that passed for blood in Barrow's veins must run ice cold.

Here was a man who only twenty hours earlier had reduced two innocent people to so much red mist, and they find him sleeping like a baby. Not just asleep, but asleep in a car parked on the side of the road less than three miles from the crime scene. Not just recklessly exposed to discovery but with the murder weapon lying uncovered on the back seat, visible to anyone who might look in through the window. It was a Winchester Model 97 pump-action shotgun, the so-called "trench gun" used to clean up German leftovers in the First World War. It was fitted for double-aught buckshot and lacked a trigger disconnector, so that the operator could simply hold the trigger down and pump away until it went click.

According to the legend, Barrow was a shameless, guiltless night crawler who'd slithered out from under a rock. He was a sociopathic monster whose essential nature was a mystery to the society charged with caging or killing him once he had been dragged into the light.

But there were inconsistencies, tiny variations in the truth distorted by time and retelling.

The shotgun had been in the trunk, not in the back seat. The ejected shells littering the Merritt house had no fingerprints on them, but they could be matched to the shotgun, and the shotgun in turn had Barrow's fingerprints on the barrel.

And Barrow himself had not been asleep—in fact, he hadn't been discovered inside the car at all. The FBI's records were remarkably complete, every scrap of paper photocopied, collated, and organized by some enterprising young agent. Arrest records were part of the public domain, but they were a terse recounting of events, just names, dates, and places. All the specifics, none of the flavor.

Here, though, were transcripts of the interview between the arresting officer and the case lead, Ennis Ford. As the case blossomed into screaming headlines and public terror, a slaughtered family with the perpetrator still on the loose, Ford had become especially careful about preserving evidence. He documented the investigation down to the smallest details. When an arrest was made, Ford brought in the man who made the collar, sat him down in front of a typewriter, and made him write down everything he remembered.

Deputy Tom Morehouse had been on routine patrol when he happened across Barrow's car. There had been nothing routine about that evening's patrol, of course; every law enforcement officer in four counties had heard radio chatter about a horrific discovery at a small farm in Hillsborough. The Orange County sheriff wanted nothing more than to put out an APB or a BOLO, but there were as yet no details on whom, exactly, to be on the lookout for. So far the investigation had produced no suspects, no leads, no usable witnesses.

Then they found the Merritt girl.

She was discovered half-buried in the soft mud at the bottom of a ditch, sticks and leaves dragged across her face. At first investigators assumed they were looking at a secondary crime scene: the perpetrator had kidnapped Emily Merritt from the house, dragged her into the woods, assaulted her, and left her for dead. Soon, however, it became apparent the facts did not support such a scenario. No other footprints were found at the scene. They waited an hour for a forensics team. The first tech began to clear away the debris on her face, and without warning, Emily had leapt to her feet and sprinted into the trees.

One deputy was so startled, he fired a shot into the ground.

It took them another hour to chase her down and corral her into a waiting car. Despite the horrific picture she had presented at first glance, once they cleaned her up, she appeared uninjured.

Physically, at least.

No, the girl had done it to herself. She'd fled her house into a field of corn tall enough to conceal her, run through the woods until fear or exhaustion had made her go to ground. And then, like an animal, she'd played dead. She'd pressed herself into the earth, motionless for almost half a day, enduring hunger and thirst and the endless mosquitoes that had made a feast of her flesh, a patience too terrible for any ordinary eight-year-old.

Here were pages of reports written by three different psychologists. They drew the same vague conclusion, summarized thus: the murder of her parents had damaged her mind. Exact nomenclature varied. A psychotic break. A hypersensitive fight-or-flight response. Theories about how to get her to talk. They made every effort to get answers from her, but eventually the word went out: don't hold your breath waiting for a description of the killer, because the Merritt girl is catatonic.

What kind of fear could make a child lie still like that?

Morehouse had some idea. He had been inside the house. He had breathed air thick with the smell of old pennies and felt it lodge in the back of his throat, like rotting food caught in a drain trap.

And the perpetrator, a madman capable of unspeakable transgression, had walked away clean, vanished without so much as a trace. He could be anywhere or anyone, and the very fact of his existence made the world thrum with pitched hysteria.

All that was playing through Morehouse's head as he white-knuckled the steering wheel of his police cruiser and made a so-called routine patrol through the area north of downtown. He drove north, east, south, west, circumnavigating the crime scene in an ever-widening circle, and at 10:03 in the evening came upon a vehicle pulled over at a gravel turnout.

The car, a dark-maroon 1989 Cutlass Supreme, had all windows down and no visible occupants. Morehouse had turned on his light bar and approached on the driver's side, his service revolver dangling at his thigh and a twelve-inch Maglite perched on his shoulder. Its powerful beam played across the passenger compartment, revealing mounds of fast-food wrappers piled on the floorboards and strewn across the dirty, torn upholstery. In the back seat were two blankets with something underneath, and Morehouse admitted to being so keyed up he almost fired into them before tugging on the blankets' edge, exposing the two ratty pillows underneath. The hood of the vehicle, when he reached it, was cool to the touch.

Then came a shout from the surrounding woods. Morehouse had the presence of mind—and the nerve—to shut off his radio. He backed his police cruiser a hundred feet up the road, turned off the engine and lights, and observed the parked car. It was a gamble, far from standard procedure, but he'd probably decided he would have better luck lying in wait than wandering through the forest at night. Or maybe it was the recent discovery of Emily Merritt that had given him the guts to wait there, all alone in the darkness.

If she could do it, he could do it.

More shouts, getting closer, resolving themselves now into the kind of calls through cupped hands they'd used during the search for the Merritt girl. For a brief span he wondered if the Sheriff's Office had called in civilian help for the search; maybe this was just some helpful resident who hadn't gotten the message that the girl had been found.

The hair on the back of Morehouse's neck stood straight up.

No, none of that made sense. The hour was too late, the night almost moonless. Any law-abiding citizen would have left hours ago, not parked on this godforsaken stretch of highway and hiked out among the trees, by themselves, with the killer still on the loose.

Of that much, he felt more than certain.

Then a man emerged onto the road between Morehouse and the parked car. As was documented later in the arrest report, he was white, five foot eight inches tall, with stringy black hair that fell past his shoulders and an acne-scarred complexion. He wore a white undershirt with stained armpits and a dark-inked tattoo swirled up one arm and onto his neck.

Morehouse, standing next to his cruiser, reached in through the window and popped on the headlights. Barrow froze like a deer, then uttered his first and only words to a member of law enforcement.

Barrow said, "I'm looking for—"

And stopped.

Later, once the car had been searched and the shotgun discovered in the trunk and Barrow had been booked into custody, Tom Morehouse claimed it was the strangest arrest he'd ever made—the two of them alone on that lonely stretch of road, Barrow silent as the grave.

"He looked so sad, though," Morehouse said. "More than sad. He looked . . . stricken."

Barrow had been arrested many times before, and his fingerprints led to a quick identification. All his previous crimes were of two types: drug charges or smash-and-grab burglaries committed in empty houses. Now he had graduated to something much more sinister. Curious was the lack of any sign of forced entry. Ford's first theory of the crime assumed the Merritts had accidentally left the front door or a window unlocked and thus given Barrow access to the house. Among the detritus of his car, however, they found stolen items from two other burglaries. In each case there had been no visible means of entry. Barrow had clearly learned some new skills, like lockpicking.

In the end, though, Ford's meticulous collection of all the small details hadn't really mattered—the shotgun alone was enough to earn Simon Barrow the needle.

* * *

"Almost finished?"

Laura peeled her eyes off the file and saw Timinski's head poking in through the door. Stacks of paper littered the conference table, and to a casual observer they would have looked haphazard, careless even. In reality they were carefully organized, chronological. Each pile represented a single slice of the time line. Laura had ingested every page and every word, everything except the crime scene photographs. Those she'd left in their envelope and pushed to the opposite end of the table.

She glanced at her watch. "Quitting time already?"

"You know how it is—government work." He flashed her a quick and surprising grin. It was there and gone again, his usually severe expression split open to reveal teeth very white against his lips.

"Any chance I could stay?"

He leaned back into the hallway, glanced left and right, then came inside and pulled the door shut behind him. "We've only got another few minutes—any longer and we'll have to jump through hoops to get you signed out after hours. That would draw attention."

His face had turned serious again, the frigid blue of his eyes darkened by worry, and she remembered that her very presence in this windowless room imperiled his career. A sliver of guilt worked its way loose from the back of her mind. If it ever came to light that he'd allowed her access to this file, the consequences for him could be devastating.

She said, "Remind me to thank you for the help."

He gave her a puzzled look. "Remind you?"

"Yeah. Later, if it ends up helping, I'll make sure to actually say it."

"Can't wait," he said.

They packed the file back together and descended back into the basement. Timinski returned the file to its box, the box to its stack, and asked, "Questions?"

"Anything in the crime scene photos?"

"You tell me," he said.

"I didn't look."

"I could go over them if you want, let you know if something turns up."

"I'd appreciate it."

"What am I looking for?" he asked.

"Nothing in particular. Anything out of place."

He paused. "Not like you to be squeamish."

Laura considered her answer. Her personal connection was bound to come out one way or another. Hillsborough was a small town, and all it would take would be some quick arithmetic for Timinski to realize she and Emily Merritt had been in the same class at school. It was only a question of when.

"I knew them," she answered.

"Who? The Merritts?"

Laura stepped past him and clicked on the light hanging over the large wooden table in the center of the room. Earlier she'd seen several maps spread across it, but those had been rolled up and replaced with a new one. It was a satellite image overlaid with topographical curves and road names, and most of what was on display was the homogeneous deep green of trees viewed from above. Still, she could pick out a few familiar landmarks: an unnatural cluster of right angles in the streets of downtown; a distinctive pattern of concentric loops marking a high point that had to be Occoneechee Mountain, the highest point in Orange County; and the soft silver turns of the Eno River.

It was a map of Hillsborough.

"This wasn't here before," she said.

"Part of another archiving project," he offered. "The Bureau has lots of composite maps like that, some from way back. The more recent ones are from satellites, and before that they stitched 'em together from pictures taken by planes."

"And this one?"

He tried to shrug it off, but Laura knew he was familiar with the location of her mother's house. "If you bothered to dig this out, you must have noticed how close the Merritt and Chambers farms are to one another."

The confused expression he'd been pretending at dropped away, his face closing up. "Emily Merritt was the same age as you too."

Laura found the Chambers farm on the map and touched a fingernail to it, a spot about three miles north of downtown. She could make out the house and its outbuildings, the fields, and at the back of the property, the black line of the train tracks slashing through the woods, running straight for miles.

"We were neighbors."

"Friends?" Timinski asked.

"My momma would never let me ride a bike on the highway. I had no way to get to town unless she drove me, which wasn't likely. There weren't exactly a lot of kids in the neighborhood, you know?"

"That's how making friends works when you're a kid," he said. "Surviving childhood is like going through boot camp together. Forced proximity is common ground enough."

"Circumstance may have pushed us together, but we were best friends. She was . . ." Laura searched for the right word.

"Nice?"

"I was going to say savage. Emily had the nice-girl routine down pat. It was all ponies and princesses over at her house, but then we'd go together into the woods and she'd be totally different. You never saw someone love to get dirty like that. One time she nicked a hunting knife from her daddy. We took it back into those trees, and within a few minutes she'd managed to slice her hand open. I wanted to go back, get help. But she smeared the blood on her face like war paint and started running through the brush, whooping and hollering to the treetops."

"Tough kid."

"Pain never seemed to be a problem for her."

"And after it happened?"

"She got shipped off to live with family. I never saw her again."

"She didn't show up at school or come to say good-bye?"

Laura shook her head.

"And is that a factor here?"

She looked up from the map. "What's that supposed to mean?"

"You're bullheaded most of the time, and that's when it's not even personal." He shrugged. "You're up to something, I know it. You know I know it. I'm not stupid, Laura. Your friend's story is very sad, but how the hell does it end with a sniper after you and Don Rodgers?"

Do or die time.

"Let me tell you a story," she said.

CHAPTER

34

SHE TOLD HIM everything.

When she was done, he made her go back and tell it again. Then a third time. The line between "normal hours" and "after hours" came and went, but Timinski no longer seemed worried. It could have been because he had engineered a new way to get her out of the building without being noticed, but Laura didn't think so.

She had him hooked.

The fourth time she told the story, Timinski had started jotting on note cards and pinning them to an old corkboard. He pointed to them now.

"Are you certain there were only two albums? Walk me though the chain of evidence."

"Ernest Sparks conveyed everything to Jameson Pelt. Pelt sold them both to my mother. I found both in the attic, looking like they hadn't been handled in a very long time. And now they're both sitting here under this table." She kicked the big paper bag Timinski had gone out and gotten from her car. "Sparks to Pelt to Diane to me, all their time accounted for."

"Except there's a third one in the bag."

"That's right."

"Go backward, before they were released to the estate."

The two file boxes had been opened again over the course of the past two hours, and their contents were spread across the surface of the wooden worktable. Laura turned a few more pages and found the sheet she was looking for. She ran her finger down a typed column. "Here's the inventory from the Merritt house, from the crime scene. They've got everything on here, down to the number of spoons in the utensil drawer. You know the investigator, Ennis Ford?"

"Sure."

"He's dead," Laura said. She'd been able to figure that much from a simple internet search. "Lung cancer. He was a smoker; they all were back then. You've read the file—do you think he was competent?"

Timinski scoffed. "Think they would have assigned some schmuck chasing a pension to a case like this? Ford strikes me as a thorough guy no matter the case, but the Merritts were an honest-to-goodness red ball. I'm not surprised he was going the extra mile."

Laura's finger stopped, hovering over one specific row of the crime scene inventory.

DATE: 8/23/96
INCIDENT NUMBER: 32098
SUPERVISING OFFICER: Ford, E.
ITEM #: 173
DESCRIPTION OF PROPERTY: Two (2) family photo albums located on bookshelf in foyer / living room.

She turned it around so Timinski could read it.

"So if Ford's reliable, there were only two in the house when the cops got there, and they were entered into evidence. Those two went to the estate, hence those are the two I found in the attic."

"And the other?"

"Take your own advice, Tim. You've got to go backward."

He understood her then. "Christ, you think Barrow took it?"

"Who else could have? Who else was in the house? He liked to keep little souvenirs; they found the others in the trunk. It makes a sick kind of sense."

"But no photo album, Laura. As far as anyone could tell, he never even drove the Cutlass Supreme away from the spot he parked before he did the crime. Did the album walk off on its own?"

"That's a problem," she said.

"You think?" Timinski stood and stretched. He studied the corkboard. When he turned around, there was a cold glitter behind his eyes that Laura had seen before.

"You've caught my interest, okay?"

She crossed her arm. "I know it."

"It's strange as all hell." He pointed to a few different index cards. "Let's call the ones from the estate albums one and two. The one from your Jane Doe, that's album number zero."

Patient zero. She liked that; it had a certain resonance.

"Here's a list of what we don't know." Timinski counted them off on his fingers. "First, why did your mother purchase albums number one and two?

"Second, why did Jane Doe hide album zero in that heating vent? It implies value, but we're missing something.

"Third, on the subject of value, why are our mystery men so keen to get album zero? They've murdered two people trying to lay their hands on it. What about this stupid thing is worth killing over?"

Laura didn't have any good answers to those questions.

They'd been over the albums before, but Timinski reached for the paper sack and spread them out under the bright overhead light. The last album wasn't any different from the first two. More of the Merritts, more of Emily, with the Chambers family sprinkled in—and Laura had returned the photos of her father to the first album. She didn't want to see them anymore. She wished she weren't in a basement so she could smoke a cigarette.

"I'll take a shot at the first question, for partial credit," she said. "You've seen the pictures now, so we both just listened to my father lie to Investigator Ford on that tape. My mother bought numbers one and two for the same reason I was told to never talk about the Merritts ever again. For the same reason you heard my father lie. It seems to me that, for some reason, my parents tried very, very hard to erase the past between our families."

"It's thin," said Timinski.

But the idea wouldn't leave her.

* * *

The two of them bandied about outrageous ideas, talked in circles, acted as a sounding board for each other. Toward midnight, Laura circled back to the notion that Barrow had album zero under his arm when he left the Merritt house.

"He carried it out of there. He *must* have. It didn't teleport, Tim."

Timinski was midsip from one of the cans of diet soda he'd produced. His mouth was full, and he could only shake his head. "Uh-uh, uh-uh!" He swallowed. "Don't put words in my mouth. Nobody mentioned teleportation. I said it was a bum explanation. Because where did it go after that?"

"His other trophies were in the trunk."

"Just not this time, apparently."

Laura flipped through the file and located the pages she wanted: a list of items recovered from Barrow's car pinned to the incident reports from two previous unsolved burglaries. "Barrow had a pretty long arrest record."

"A habitual reoffender, as I recall."

"Mostly drugs, mostly misdemeanors. But he served a six-month jail sentence for a probation violation, plus eighteen months in prison when they got him for breaking and entering. Then he gets out, and nothing. Almost two years go by, and nobody hears a peep from Simon Barrow until they pick him up for multiple homicide."

"Chalk one up for rehabilitation."

"He ended up killing two people, Don."

"Never said it was a perfect system."

"I mean, we're talking about a guy who was getting arrested every three or four months. Given the way things played out, I think it's fair to say he didn't clean up his act. So what happened during those two years? They found things in his car. Jewelry, a silver money clip that had been engraved, cash still in a wallet with the credit cards. And of course, they found the shotgun too."

She looked at Timinski's face and could almost hear the wheels spinning as he reached down into his voluminous memory, one that seemed capable of delivering any face, name, or date, even from cases he hadn't worked, even from incidents more than two decades in the past. When he spoke, it was with authority.

"That's correct, he stole the shotgun. The owner reported it missing a few weeks before. A Mr. Sutton."

"We knew the Suttons," Laura said. "Mr. Sutton, he sold up not too long after his gun got used on the Merritts, moved the whole family somewhere like Arizona or Utah. A desert place."

"And the jewelry and the money clip, they were stolen in a burglary reported by a Mrs. Rexrode," Timinski said. "You remember them?"

"They're still around, a good chunk of property out past Efland."

"Another farm. Nice and remote, with no one around to see. That was his MO."

"No, that's exactly my point," Laura said. "That was never his style. His MO was smash-and-grab jobs wherever he could find them. He would break the window of a house or car at midday and then sprint away on foot. One time he stole a jar of change—that's the definition of petty. Then he gets out of prison. The Sheriff's Office starts investigating this new series of thefts, but they can't make heads or tails of them. No forced entry, no sign of a disturbance. They were calling it a cat burglar. Can we really be talking about the same guy?"

"Prison is like getting a graduate degree for some people," said Timinski.

She pressed her fingers to her temples. Her head throbbed from too many hours reading too-faintly-mimeographed reports under the too-bright halogen lights. She could feel it sitting right there in front of her, just out of focus.

"I read every piece of paper in here, and this dog just doesn't seem bright enough to learn a bunch of new tricks. It doesn't make sense to me."

"When in doubt, ask all the same questions over again. Did you try calling them?"

"Who?" she asked.

"The Suttons and the Rexrodes," Timinski said. "Let's see who feels like taking a trip down memory lane."

CHAPTER

35

LAURA FOUGHT THE rush hour traffic out of Raleigh and drove west, the density of commuters falling off as the scenery outside her window changed. High-rise buildings gave way to office parks and then to subdivisions, row upon row of identical houses in one of three preapproved shades of pastel. Soon even these far-flung colonies of city life yielded to the trees and the fields, and by the time she was approaching the exit for Efland, her car seemed like the only one left.

The interstate ran right into the sun where it hung on the horizon, sinking in a blaze of glory, but Laura didn't get that far. She exited and turned north.

The Rexrode house was far north and west of town, and when Laura reached the address, she thought there had been a mistake.

There was no house here. Soybeans stretched out on either side of the road, and on one side stood a collection of farm buildings: a silver silo, a ramshackle red barn, and a bit closer to the road, a low-slung equipment shed. The fields were being farmed, but the structures here looked abandoned.

Timinski was already there, parked on the shoulder. He got out and came to her window. "The map says this is the place," he said, and put his phone back into his pocket.

"Are you getting service?"

He shrugged. "A couple bars. Let's hike over and see if anyone's home."

They climbed over a locked gate, hopped over a cattle grid, and started walking.

Soybeans are only about knee high, and these were big fields that rolled lightly into the distance. Open space in every direction, no kind of cover.

Halfway to the buildings, Laura started breathing hard.

She had a premonition of a bullet in flight. The first she knew of it would be the moment of impact. Only once she was on the ground with a hole in her gut would the sharp crack of the gunshot reverberate across the open field. She could feel the place where the bullet's tip would pierce her flesh, as if someone had heated a coin in a blowtorch and then pressed it against her skin. As she squirmed, the hot coin drifted. It burned the back of her neck, her stomach, just above her left breast. All her hackles were up. She looked back toward their vehicles, checked the barn, the silo, the shed, then back to her Cadillac, around again. Faster and faster. She was eyeballing all 360 degrees so quickly she was practically spinning. Or maybe the ground was spinning, and she was standing still. Laura found herself unsure which was right.

A flash of rifle sights, iron sights, coming into alignment. An invisible line between the black open mouth of the barrel and her center of mass. The trigger had already been pulled. The train had left the station. The bullet was already soaring though its parabolic arc, on its way to meet her. It would feel like a kiss on her neck, she thought, and then it would feel like nothing at all.

A painful tightening in her chest. The world seemed to tilt on its axis.

She fell onto her hands and knees. She started crawling back toward the cars. Her inhales of breath came in great gasps, and the exhales were wheezes that reminded her of her mother.

Laura, Laura, Laura.

Timinski had her by the shoulder. He was shaking her.

"Look at me," he said. He was down in the dirt next to her. "Look me in the eyes."

Pale blue. Glacial.

"Now breathe with me," he said.

She did.

"In and out, that's right."

He helped her to her feet, and when she tried to head for the car, he pulled her in the opposite direction. "The shed's closer."

The chipped red door hung open. As soon as walls surrounded her again, her airway opened back up. "I'm sorry. I'm so sorry."

"Quit apologizing, just breathe. That ever happen before?"

"No," she managed. "We need to get to the hospital. There's something wrong with my heart."

"Folks in the middle of a heart attack don't go skittering across the ground on all fours faster than I can run. It's going to be fine. You just had a panic attack."

"I've never had a panic attack."

"I get them," Timinski said. He offered no other details. "Keep breathing."

He was right—after another few minutes, other than a nasty throbbing in her injured arm, she was better.

"You've got a touch of agoraphobia, Chambers."

"Funny how being shot, with a rifle, by a person so far away you can't see them, tends to do that to a person. Did you try Sutton yet?"

"We agreed you would do it."

"I tried from the car, but he hung up on me. You still getting those bars?"

This structure they'd been calling an equipment shed had been a stable once. Its history was apparent from the divided stalls and a couple of horseshoes nailed up high on the wall, over the door. Timinski brushed dust off a low table that had once been used for repairing tack and put his phone on speaker. A man answered, and Timinski identified himself as a special agent with the FBI. He launched into an explanation, but Sutton cut him off.

"I know why you're calling."

"You do?"

"It's not rocket science. A federal cop from North Carolina calls me in Nevada, where I've lived for two decades . . . what else could it be about? I read the news. I know they're finally going to execute the bastard. This is some kind of final follow-up, am I right?"

Timinski didn't disabuse him of the notion.

"He could still appeal?"

"He's exhausted his legal options, Mr. Sutton. We're just crossing our *t*s. You understand."

A long exhale of air from the other end of the line. "I'm glad they're finally doing it. I hope he fries, seizes, whatever. I'll feel better when it's done. He killed them with my gun. With *my gun*. You know what it's like to live with that?"

"I can imagine it's very difficult, sir."

"No, you cannot imagine," he sputtered. Sutton was good and angry now. "My grandfather carried that gun in the trenches of the Great War. It was a priceless family heirloom. Irreplaceable."

"After he, ah, once Barrow's been executed, it's possible we can arrange for it to be returned to you."

"You think I want it back?" Sutton was incredulous.

"Priceless to the family, you said."

"Was, I said. *Was*. If they gave it back to me now, I'd have it melted down into slag. I didn't keep it safe. I have to live with that. Nothing like what that girl has to live with, but it's my piece of that business to carry. I think about it all the time. Like I said, I'll feel better when he's dead and buried."

Sutton seemed to have calmed, the way the guilty often do after their confession. Timinski sensed he wouldn't be able to keep the man on the line for much longer. He probed as quickly and gently as he could.

Sutton had nothing to add to his original statement. The break-in had occurred at night while the family was sleeping. He had woken to the sound of shattered glass, but by the time he had made himself decent and located the baseball bat in the back of the master bedroom closet and crept downstairs, all that was left to see was an open front door and the empty gun cabinet. A few other valuables were taken, but they were so minor he couldn't recall their nature and referred Timinski to the paperwork from back then.

"Whatever it says I said he stole."

"And there were no signs of forced entry?"

"No, none whatsoever."

"You're certain you locked the front door? People forget sometimes."

Another lengthy sigh. "I've asked myself that one a million times. I'd be a liar if I said I was one hundred percent sure. Anything is possible. In my heart, though, I believe I locked it. It was part of my routine every night."

"Clearly you locked the gun cabinet."

"For all the good it did. But it wasn't one of those fancy gun safes like people have now. It looked like a china cabinet, with a glass front. It was for display, you understand. The weapons in there were antiques, there wasn't even any ammunition in the house."

Mr. Sutton had painted a vivid picture. Laura caught an image of the shattered glass, the empty racks where once there had been weapons. Something about it puzzled her.

"But yes, I locked it," Sutton continued. "I could have told you that no matter what. I'm very serious about gun safety, believe it or not—that's partly why this awful thing hurt me so bad, painful irony or some such thing. Anyway, my daughter had some new friend she'd met at school sleeping over that night, so I'd been real careful to give her the whole spiel."

"The gun is always loaded, that kind of thing," Timinski said.

"More like *don't touch, very bad, hurt you*."

"Excuse me?"

"My daughter's friend was deaf. She could read lips real well, but I'd never interacted with a child like that before. That's why I can remember so clearly locking the gun cabinet but not the front door."

Laura had written a few lines in her notepad. She ripped out the page and thrust it in front of Timinski's face. He read it with a frown.

"Mr. Sutton, was that a good lock on your gun cabinet?"

"One of those twist locks. The one where you turn the little key and it turns, and you can see the metal arm go from straight up and down to sideways, and then you can't pull the door open anymore."

"The kind you can pop open with a butter knife."

"It seemed sturdy to me," Sutton said quietly.

"Meaning no disrespect, Mr. Sutton," Timinski said quickly. "That lock was never at issue anyway. What about the front door?"

"Better—a quality dead bolt, and I always locked the knob too."

"You said in your statement, I'm reading here, 'He must have picked the lock.' That sound about right?"

"There was no other explanation."

"Here's my question, Mr. Sutton: If Simon Barrow had the skill to pick two locks on your front door and sneak inside without waking anybody up, why didn't he do the same to the lock on your gun cabinet? Why break the glass?"

"Hmm," Mr. Sutton said. There was a long pause. "That is strange, now that you mention it."

* * *

Laura peered left and right out the door of the stable, then took a deep breath and forced herself not to sprint across the expanse of soybeans. Back at the highway, she waited hunkered down in the big tank of a Cadillac while Timinski flagged down a passing car. He learned theirs was a common navigation error—"Damn machines have ruined everything," she heard the man say before driving off—and that the driveway of the Rexrode residence was attached to the parallel road on the far side of the fields.

It was a brick ranch. Mrs. Rexrode answered the door promptly. Timinski's badge got a warm reaction, and she let them inside.

Laura was relieved to be off the stoop.

Mrs. Rexrode was about seventy and a recent widow. The disease of loneliness is insidious indeed, and four eager, listening ears appeared to strike her as medicinal.

Mrs. Rexrode talked without pause—about her late husband, but also her children, her other family, her friends, their friends, politics, the weather, the dos and don'ts of hosting, the must-haves for the upcoming holiday season, and her personal lord and savior, Jesus Christ. Every five minutes or so she would stop to breathe, and Timinski would get to ask her a question.

"We were out to dinner with my in-laws that night. We came home, got undressed. I put on my nightgown, if you can believe it." Here she reached out and touched Laura's arm, woman to woman. "What a shock to discover the Shotgun Slayer was hiding in my house."

"But you don't think he was in the house at that point? He'd already gone, isn't that right?" Laura asked.

"Well, yes. But he *could* have been in here, that's the important thing, isn't it? And I in my nightgown. He almost got me," Mrs. Rexrode said wistfully.

Timinski plodded on through a copy of her statement from 1996 but unearthed nothing worth mentioning.

Laura inquired, "Later, when your things—"

"My good pearl earrings and my diamond necklace—just a quarter carat, anything more is garish, don't you think? And my husband's money clip, his engraved silver money clip! I gifted it to him for our twenty-fifth anniversary. Would you like to see it?"

"No thank you," Laura said.

"Are you sure? They returned it to us after the trial. The workmanship is really quite exquisite."

"When your things were taken," Laura continued, "you reported no visible means of entry."

"That was the terrifying thing, you see? If the door had been kicked in, I never would have allowed myself to become undressed in the house, not until the police had searched it top to bottom. As it happened, though, we didn't notice until I took out the studs I'd worn to dinner and went to put them back into my jewelry box. I screamed, let me tell you."

"You were frightened," Timinski offered.

Mrs. Rexrode frowned. "Well, no, I wasn't frightened at all. You have to remember, until they found my husband's money clip in that awful man's trunk a few weeks later, we had no idea the horrible truth of who'd robbed us. Did he grope my underthings? I wonder. I washed them on hot, I can tell you that much."

"But you screamed," Laura said.

"Yes, I was angry. I was certain my older daughter had taken what was missing. She was a teenager at the time, and we had a little problem with her." Mrs. Rexrode leaned closer to Laura and in a stage whisper said, "*Sticky fingers.*" She straightened up again. "It's all fine now. She's a dental hygienist in Charlotte. Do you have children?"

"No," Laura said.

"Are you married?"

"No."

"There's still time. Don't delay, my dear."

Timinski threw himself into the gap. "You thought your daughter was stealing from you."

"My older one, yes. But my younger one confessed, tried to fall on her sword. How sweet is that? She saw her sister getting in trouble, and she took the blame. Really brave of her. She said, 'Mom, I saw my friend do it.' They're really precious at that age."

"How old was she?"

"When this happened? Eight, I think. There was a pack of girls the same age that would ride their bikes house to house, decimating pantries and trying on mothers' lipsticks, so it was a very believable story. I thought that was the truth right up until we got the call."

"That your things had been found in Simon Barrow's trunk," Tim said.

"That's right. She said she caught this low-rent little friend of hers peeking and pawing through my jewelry box. I had only met this girl one other time, and she did not come from good stock. She never even had shoes! And always with the hands, the signing. I couldn't understand a word of it. Gracie told me she'd had a fever as a baby and her parents hadn't even bothered to do anything, so she went completely deaf—"

As one, Laura and Timinski both sprang to their feet. Laura's chair tipped over and clattered to the floor behind her.

"What's happening? What's wrong?"

They let themselves out the front door.

"Was it something I said?" Mrs. Rexrode called after them.

CHAPTER

36

Polk Correctional Institution is in Granville County, North Carolina, located north but mostly east of Hillsborough; the easiest way to reach it is to cross the bridge over Falls Lake. Its original name was the Polk Youth Institution, opened in 1920, a prison for children built on the grounds of a World War I tank base. Later they began to incarcerate adults as well, and in time it became home to the state's first high-security maximum control unit.

The visitor parking lot is surrounded by two sets of twenty-foot-high fences, with a no-man's-land in between and sparkling loops of razor wire welded at the top.

They sat in Timinski's Suburban and waited for the appointed hour.

"No records I can find of Barrow having a daughter."

"Paternity's the one that doesn't always get recorded, Tim."

"Right."

"What's it like inside? I've been to plenty of jails, not so many prisons."

"Some prisons can make for a bad visit, but this won't be one of them. Maximum control means they're all in their own cells, they work out alone in the yard. No trouble."

"They told me he was at Raleigh Central."

"There's a problem with the roof right over death row. Right now they're fixing it, plus doing the necessary work to prepare to resume executions. In the meantime, they moved the death row inmates out here."

"Redecorating before the big event—how thoughtful. Will he see us?"

Timinski sucked a tooth. "That's the question, isn't it? I heard he never spoke a single word to his own defense attorney. When the jury read the verdict, when the judge sentenced him to die—not a peep. If he can stay quiet thorough all that, what are the chances he's going to talk to us now?"

"Folks do tend to get loose-lipped near the end. Deathbed confessions happen more often than you might think."

Timinski just shook his head.

"Plus I'm not here to interview him."

"No, you're here to give him news instead." He checked his watch. "Shift change coming up in five."

From the visitor lot, they had watched through the fences as traffic into the employee lot grew, reached a peak, and then slowed to a trickle. Now they watched the same process in reverse as the night shift left. Soon the very last car rolled off toward a home-cooked meal or a strip club or whatever it was prison guards did during their off hours to forget awhile about the men locked in boxes whom they were paid to secure.

"Night shift is on."

"Your friend can get it to him?"

Timinski nodded. "He can drop it in his mail. Then we wait."

Under normal circumstances, Tim's credentials would be more than sufficient for gaining them access to a prisoner. But, as he had pointed out to Laura, this wasn't the drunk tank at the county jail. Plenty of escapes had been fashioned from as little as a suit, a fake badge, and some confidence. If he attempted to visit Barrow in his official capacity as an FBI agent, checks would be run. Phone calls would be made and confirmations sought. Timinski elegantly summed up what his situation would be then.

"I'd be straight fucked," he said. "Barrow has to put us on the visitor list like anybody else. Did you finish the note?"

"Ready to go." She handed him a pale-green envelope with nothing written on the outside.

"It's sealed. They're going to open it before they give it to him, you know."

"That's fine."

"Can I read it?"

"It's about daughters and fathers. I'm not sure you'd understand."

* * *

Timinski came back to the Suburban at a brisk walk, shooting her a thumbs-up. From inside his jacket he pulled a set of loose-leaf papers, and he held them out to her.

"Barrow's visitor logs," he said, by way of explanation. "He snapped a few quick photos, then printed them out for me."

"That is one *good* friend," Laura said.

Timinski grinned. "What can I say? He owes me one."

Laura snatched the pages from his hand and began to read the most recent entry:

DATE: September 14, 2019
LAST NAME: Lucchi
FIRST NAME: Cassandra
START TIME: 08:32 AM
END TIME: 09:49 AM
VISIT TYPE: Personal

Laura flipped to the next page, and the next. "He never sees his lawyer?"

"Very tight-lipped, as advertised."

The same name featured in every single entry: Cassandra Lucchi. She'd come every month or so for at least two years. That was as far back as their log copies went.

Laura let out a satisfied sigh. "She's the only one who ever visits him."

"Suggestive, isn't it?"

She leaned over and used her good hand to punch him in the shoulder. "Quit being so goddamn understated."

* * *

They waited for visiting hours to begin, and then Laura went in alone.

It seemed a farfetched idea, getting him to talk. As a plan, it was fragile as spun sugar. If Timinski were present, the prisoner would demand an introduction. Then those three famous letters printed in fat blue type on his credentials would destroy whatever slim chance they'd had of prying loose Simon Barrow's tongue.

It was better if she went in alone, they had decided.

The guard who checked her in reminded her of one of the stone heads on Easter Island, big and impassive. She had to give him credit: when he asked who she was here to see and Laura answered with Barrow's name, his face didn't change one iota. His hand twitched on the mouse, and there was just the slightest hesitation before he spoke.

"Looks like you're on the list," he said in a deep baritone.

The guard's name tag said JOHNSON. He searched her bag while she stepped through the metal detector. Then he briefed her on procedure.

"No ballpoint pens, no paper clips. Ma'am, I'm going to have to ask you to remove your earrings and leave them here. He's in a special unit, an old cell block we opened up to house the Raleigh Central population. It doesn't have a visiting room, so we've been doing it at the picnic tables in the yard. It's one group at a time, so you'll be the only two people out there."

"Besides the guards," Laura said.

"Guards are in the towers. You might not see them, but they will most definitely see you. This is a no-contact visit, so no touching. Don't hand him anything or vice versa. You can either walk the perimeter or sit at one of the tables. They're metal, so I recommend the one under the sun shade."

"My phone?" Laura held it up. "Can I use it to take pictures or record?"

He nodded. "That's fine, just don't give it to him."

They started walking down the hall.

Laura must have looked nervous. Without prompting, Johnson said, "Don't sweat it. Simon Barrow is very well behaved."

* * *

It wasn't yet nine in the morning, but already the sun burned overhead. The sun shade was translucent but effective; it cast the metal table underneath in the kind of hard steel light Laura associated with the time just before dawn.

Beyond the fence, low hills ranged in the middle distance.

Without warning, the specter of the hot coin returned. The ghost of a bullet passed through her chest, and she felt it as viscerally as if she'd been run through with a spear. She clamped her hands onto the edge of the table, held herself in place, and tried to breathe.

At the far corner of the building, a door swung open. One person was admitted to the yard, and then the metal door slammed shut behind him with a reverberating clang.

He had on prison whites, close cousin to the scrubs worn by everyone who had taken care of Laura in the hospital. He shuffled across the asphalt yard toward her. Before sitting down, he touched the metal table to see if it was hot.

Laura recalled the description from the Merritt file of Deputy Morehouse's first encounter with Simon Barrow on a lonely stretch of road:

> **White, five foot eight inches tall, with stringy black hair that fell past his shoulders and an acne-scarred complexion. A dark-inked tattoo swirled up one arm and onto his neck.**

The man across from her looked nothing like what she had imagined.

Acne scars still marked his cheeks, but his hair was neatly barbered. He wore thin-framed glasses and sat with his hands folded. The tattoo was still there. She could see now that it was a snake. It slithered from between the knuckles of his right hand up his arm, out the loose V neck of the prison uniform, and wrapped around his throat. Over the years, its scales had faded to bottle green.

"Simon Barrow?"

He didn't answer, just studied her. He had soft brown eyes, fawn-like, and behind the glasses they appeared clear and intelligent.

"Mr. Barrow, I'm a reporter for the *Hillsborough Gazette*."

"I know who you are, Laura Chambers." He had a measured voice. His enunciation was precise.

"I wrote a recent article about your upcoming, ah . . ."

"It doesn't upset me to mention my execution. I read the article."

"I wasn't sure you got the newspaper."

He nodded sagely. "We get them all, and the library here is quite excellent, better than at my last posting. And of course, I have the time to read everything. Books are one of the only things that have kept me sane. 'Be thine own palace, or the world's thy jail.'"

"The Bible?"

He pursed his lips. "John Donne. But I've read that one too."

"What else has kept you sane, Mr. Barrow?"

A shadow passed over his face. The hand with the snake's tail reached into one of his loose pockets and came back with the envelope she had given to Timinski, now crumpled nearly into a ball. He smoothed it on the tabletop. "This says you want to talk to me about my daughter."

"That's right, Mr. Barrow."

"I don't have a daughter."

"No, you don't, at least not in any record system that I could think of."

He paused. "There's been some mistake."

"That's what I'm here to ascertain."

"I don't speak on the record with reporters. I was given to understand that was common knowledge on the outside."

"I'm not here to interview you, Mr. Barrow."

Now she had really piqued his interest. "Then why?"

Laura shared her discovery: a description of the same eight-year-old girl, deaf, at both houses burgled by Simon Barrow in the weeks leading up to his final crime.

Barrow pressed his lips together and refused to comment.

"I do have a question, actually," Laura said. "Did she let you into the Merritt house too? Is that how you got inside?"

The color seemed to drain from Barrow's already pale face, but still he did not reply.

"I had a woman contact me. She didn't tell me her name, but she was about my age and build." With a grimace at the electric pain that crackled in her bicep, Laura lifted her elbow and pointed to a spot on her rib cage. "She had a tattoo here. Little circles with a zigzag around them, connected to each other by dotted lines in a W shape. They're supposed to be stars, aren't they? The constellation Cassiopeia, I thought."

His face underwent a remarkable transformation. First a renewed recalcitrance. Then shock, his eyebrows so far up his forehead she thought they might never come back down. Finally there came a growing sense of horror as his mind leapt forward across inferences as smoothly as a skipping stone.

"You can't possibly know that. How can you know that?" he muttered, almost to himself.

"I saw it," Laura said carefully, "when they showed me her body."

The face went blank.

"Mr. Barrow, I'm sorry to have to tell you this. The woman I just described to you—she's dead."

"Prove it to me," he said, disbelieving.

Laura had brought along a few select pictures taken during the autopsy, ones that showed both the tattoo and the less damaged hemisphere of the face. She retrieved them but held them close to her chest. "I'm not supposed to hand you anything."

"Put them on the table, then." Desperation in his voice now, thin and reedy.

"I brought the ones I thought were best. Mr. Barrow, I want to warn you . . . these will be difficult to look at."

He said nothing.

She turned the over the photographs and slid them in front of him, one by one, their glossy surfaces like mirrors in the light.

For the longest time he did not move. Then an animal wail, like the scream of a fox, clawed its way from his mouth. He beat his fists on the table. He began to drive his own temple down into the metal table—*thump, thump, thump*—and soon there was blood, the unexpected volume of blood that accompanies all head wounds.

Twenty-two years under a sentence of death hadn't broken him, but these pictures threatened to do the job.

A klaxon sounded. The door banged open, and guards came out. Johnson's thick baton was out of its holster, pointed at Simon Barrow's head, and he was shouting, but Barrow didn't know he was there. It took three guards to subdue him.

"You'll have to come back another time, ma'am," Johnson grunted.

That seemed to snap him out of his reverie. "No!" Barrow screamed. "No, please, I'm fine now. I'm fine, look. Just a few more minutes, I'm begging you."

The guards looked at each other, and Johnson shrugged. To Barrow: "No more trouble?"

"I swear it."

The wound was superficial. They brought a clean towel, told him to keep pressure on it, and left the two of them alone again.

Barrow's eyes were red from tears; the pupils were black and wide-mouthed wells, holes without bottom. In the symphony of our emotions, the delicate piccolos of melody are love and grace and hope, and fear is the cello's constant, scraping thrum. But percussive, omnipresent anger underpins them all.

Now anger drowned out all of Barrow's other instruments. His face was a drumbeat of rage.

"You're a reporter. You have something to record?"

"Yes."

"Get it out," he barked.

She set her phone between them.

"It's on?" he asked.

She nodded.

"I'm innocent," he shouted, cold fire between the words. "You hear me? I'm innocent. I didn't kill that family."

CHAPTER

37

THEY LET HER give him a cigarette.

In the designated smoking area, his hands had to be cuffed; they rose and fell together, coming to his lips and dropping back down again.

"I haven't smoked since about five years after they locked me up."

"Why'd you quit?"

"Health reasons," he said. "That probably seems like the height of irony, but I was . . . a man on death row with something to live for."

"Your daughter."

"She asked me to stop, so I did. Her name is Cassandra, but to me she was always Cassie. The constellation, that was an inside joke of ours."

"You two were close."

"Don't think I haven't meditated long and hard on the irony of *that* fact as well. How close can people be when one of them is locked away?" He let two streams of smoke escape his nostrils. "Yes, we were very close."

"And the Merritt murders?"

"We had a deal: I keep my mouth shut, and they wouldn't hurt my daughter. All these years, I held up my end of the bargain, and still they . . ."

"What deal? Who with?" she sputtered.

But grief caught him from an unexpected angle, and he began to sob.

Laura had so many questions she felt as if she might burst. The second-hardest part of her job was to poke and prod and strong-arm where necessary, trying to wrench free by force of will the answers she needed. The hardest part was to recognize the moment when a floodgate was about to open, and then listen and be still.

In his own time, in his own way, Simon Barrow told her the story.

* * *

"The first thing you have to understand is that I was a heroin addict. I was a piece of shit, and a two-bit thief, and a liar, and a bad father too. But mostly I was a heroin addict. You read my record?"

She nodded.

"Then you understand. When I got out the last time, though, Cassie's mother had passed away. Overdose. Her mother and I didn't get along, so the two of us never spent much time together—me and Cassie, I mean. God, I never knew what I was missing. Being inside forced me to get clean, but I can tell you, all I was thinking about was my first high once I hit the streets.

"The day I got out, she found me. She ran away from some youth home and tracked me down. She was so smart, Laura, you should have seen her. She could have been a senator or an astronaut. I'm not just saying that—Cassie could have done anything if she'd had better luck than to get me as a daddy. When she was a baby, me and her mom were so out of it, we left her screaming in her crib for days. She had scarlet fever, it turned out, and we didn't get her the medicine in time."

"She lost her hearing," Laura said.

"That's right, and she was mute as well. The doctors weren't so sure how to explain it. Physically there was nothing preventing it, but she never made a peep. When I got out after her mom passed, she could read lips, she tried to teach me sign language, although I was never very good at it. By all rights she should have hated my guts, but for some reason I'll never understand, she loved me and kept me instead. I tried to quit the drugs, but it wasn't going so hot. Couldn't keep a job. Couldn't get enough to eat. She was so thin." There were tears on his cheeks.

"You started to steal again."

"Yes, but she wanted to help me. It was her idea. I'm not saying that to lay off my share of the blame, you understand. She was a child, my share is one hundred percent. The responsibility to do right and to provide was mine and mine alone. But I failed at those things . . . and she was smart as a whip.

"She'd blend into a crowd, make a friend, and then case the house. Sometimes she'd unlock a basement window or the cellar door, a place where no one would notice right away. Sometimes she managed to get an invitation to sleep over."

"What about August twenty-second, 1996?"

The joy of the memory of his daughter faded, and his face closed up.

"A man approached me, and he knew exactly what we had been doing. He knew we'd been pulling jobs in all the counties around here, and he had all the details, you understand? I thought he was a cop at first. I almost stuck out my wrists for the cuffs. But it wasn't an arrest, it was a job offer. He would pay us, and we could take whatever else we found. The Merritts weren't just another burglary—someone hired us to hit their house specifically."

"For what purpose?"

"They had a safe, he told me. Now I've got no idea how to crack a safe, but he knew where it was in the house, and he had the combination too. He wanted me to get something from it and then deliver it back to him."

"What was it?"

"A tape," Simon Barrow said. "He told me it was a videotape.

"That afternoon, I sneaked up to the house and stole the starter relay from their truck. Then about sunset, I sent Cassie through the woods, climbed up the telephone pole, and snipped the line running to their house. This was all pretty standard operating procedure for us by then. It was a strange house, though—bars on all the windows, newly installed, like they were expecting someone to try to get in. That sort of thing usually works, but they never saw my daughter coming."

"She let you in later that night," Laura said.

"Are you listening to me? I'm innocent, I didn't kill anyone. I waited at the spot where I'd parked the car, and the guy met me there. He was supposed to bring the rest of the money, and we'd give him the tape. Then . . ."

Another sob escaped his lips.

"Please, Mr. Barrow. It's important."

"He asked about the exact details of the plan, if Cassie was already inside, when she was supposed to unlock the front door, stuff like that. It was very casual, just making conversation. Then I made the stupidest mistake of my life: I answered every question.

"He did something to me then, I can't remember. I think he hit me over the head with something heavy. When I came back to my senses, I had the worst headache of my life and he'd handcuffed me to the steering wheel.

"I begged him to just be allowed to finish the job, but he said, and this is burned into my memory: 'There's no turning back from what they've done.'"

"Who's they? The Merritts?"

Barrow shrugged. "Your guess is as good as mine. He told me to remember that if I ever told anyone about him, he would track us down, and he would kill my daughter.

"Then he shot me up with junk . . . a lot of junk. He cooked it on a spoon and put it in my arm. I woke up in the back of my car, and I knew that a lot of time had passed. It was real dark. I needed to find Cassie. We were still at the place I parked when I sent her through the woods, so I started looking. That's what I was doing—wandering around, calling out her name—when that cop found me."

"Who was the man who hired you?"

Barrow took a breath.

"I don't have the slightest idea. I talked to him exactly twice before the night he killed that family: once in a diner, the day he approached me, and the second time in a parking lot to collect half the money up front. That's when he told me what I was after. It's been almost twenty-five years, and I was more than half in the bag during those meetings. I can't come up with anything useful. Believe me, I've had plenty of time to try."

Laura didn't speak, let him try again for moment.

"Cassie could have told you," said Barrow finally. "She was always with me back then, even during those meetings, and she never forgot a face. No one cared because she was just some little deaf girl."

"Is there anything you could think of that could identify him?"

Barrow leaned closer. In a half whisper, he said, "He knew people, I can tell you that. The very first night I was in jail after they arrested me for the Merritts, I got a note. It was in my damn food, rolled up in this little tube. It told me what would happen to Cass if

I said anything. I mean, it went into explicit detail. It said he would flay her skin off piece by piece. And after what happened to that family, I damn well believed it."

He gave Laura a pleading look. "I was locked up, so how could I protect her? What choice did I have?"

Laura reached out and put her hand on top of his. "No choice at all, Mr. Barrow."

He nodded to himself, reassured. "None at all. Me in here, the two of them out there—it was like he had her hostage.

"And I've gotten other notes over the years. Reminders to keep my mouth shut or else." He leaned in close again. "Some of them got passed to me by prison guards."

"Why was Cassie trying to get in touch with me now?"

He leaned back, and again his face held a look of fatherly pride. "Like I said, she was smart. My girl had it all figured out. She came in here all excited two weeks ago—"

"Saturday, September fourteenth," Laura said, consulting the log.

"That's right, the day after you published that story about me. I remember because we talked about it. She was practically jumping up and down. She said she knew, and that she had a plan."

"What does that mean?"

"You have to understand, they read our letters, they listen to our phone calls. Even this table probably has a listening device nearby—that's why this one has the sun shade over it."

Laura glanced around, paranoid.

"See, that's how it was around here all the time. We were even afraid someone who knew ASL might be watching, so we were careful what we said. But Cassie and I were close, so I can tell you exactly what she meant. She knew: that meant she knew who did this to us. She had a plan: that meant a plan to get me out. She told me to trust her, and I did. What possible help could I have been from inside these walls?" His eyes welled up. "She promised to be careful. She promised."

Simon Barrow started to cry again.

"After all this time, we were finally supposed to be together."

CHAPTER

38

SHE SET A meeting with Timinski at a bar in downtown Hillsborough, a new place on King Street. She and Frank Stuart used to frequent it back when it had a different name, and the patrons hadn't changed much. Entering, Laura caught a few dirty looks from a group of men in the back.

She didn't care—all she wanted was a drink.

When Timinski sat down next to her, there was already two fingers of neat bourbon in front of his stool. Asking whether it had been a tough day seemed unnecessary, as the answer was pretty much a foregone conclusion, so he just gave her his full attention while she related the events at the prison. When she was done, he picked up his glass and finished the bourbon in one swallow.

"Your turn," she said.

"Good news, bad news," he said. "Good news is I finally got a call back about Jake Radford."

"He of the quote-unquote hunting accident."

"That's right." He signaled the bartender for another round. "Nothing more from forensics, no witnesses, still no suspects. But it turns out our boy has a record. Listen to this: Jacob Radford was arrested on human trafficking charges."

"Recently? Maybe he was killed by a coconspirator so he couldn't be a witness."

He shook his head. "Naw, this was in 1995. That's the bad news: it's a dead end, Laura. All I got from my man in records out there was a bunch of long-winded backstory. It's got nothing to do with Don Rodgers getting shot or Cassandra Lucchi getting pancaked on the freeway."

She glared at him.

"Sorry, didn't mean to be glib about it. Anyway, back in 1995, Radford owned a boat, a truck, and a shop. The boat was a commercial fishing boat. Monday through Thursday he would go way out past Frying Pan Shoals to net sea bass or red drum, or he would trawl the coast working crab traps. Whatever he couldn't catch, he bought off the docks. Then he'd load it all into his refrigerated truck, drive the catch to his shop, and sell it all during the weekend. A very neat little operation."

"Except?" Laura said.

"Except really he was rendezvousing with freighters bound for the East Coast before they reached customs. Out there on the Gulf Stream, they'd crack open a shipping container or two and pass the contents over."

"Women, you mean."

"That's right—Eastern European, mostly. Or Turkish or Greek. This was starting back in the mid-eighties. He'd stow them in a secret compartment in the truck; they found it during the raid."

"Where was he taking them?"

Timinski shrugged.

"And if this is all public record, how was he walking around hunting last week?"

"First of all, he was poaching. Gun season isn't until October."

"Don't you think I know that? I grew up hunting, and let me tell you, we didn't always wait for fall."

"Why isn't he rotting in a cell, you mean? He got convicted, but they threw it out on appeal. Technicality in the warrant."

"It's been a rough one," Laura said. "Thanks for cheering me up."

"Anytime," Timinski said. "Your family ever go there back in the day?"

"Where do you mean?"

"The little fish market. It was called Radford Seafood."

She cocked her head, confused. "It was around here?"

"Oh yes, just about twenty minutes from this very spot."

She got a sudden twirl of movement and color, like a fly buzzing at the edge of her peripheral vision.

A quick mental image of Emily's easel: deforming, stretching until it popped like a balloon.

Big eyes, red lips.

Faces through a window blind.

Laura downed the tumbler of bourbon, held up a finger, and ran out to her car. When she came back, she had the items she'd discovered in Emily's old room.

Timinski looked down as the story tiles sprawled across the bar. "Good God, what are those?"

Laura explained their purpose, and he examined them, twisting them left and right, rearranging them into different combinations. He held up one that depicted a human skeleton with cloven feet and the head of a horse. "Your father made these for you when you were *eight*?"

"Of course not. I'd had them for years by that point," Laura said. "There was a trick to them too. They were supposed to fit together like a big puzzle, but I could never figure it out. Hold on, I wanted to show you something else."

She found what she was looking for. "Here," she said, and spread out the series of paintings Emily had made and then hidden away next to the radiator for all those years: misshapen faces always frowning, eyelashes crooked like the legs of a spider. All of it rendered in nausea-inducing pastels.

As Timinski looked at them, the smile on his face fell away.

"And this one." She pointed to the worst of the lot.

It was a woman reaching her arms up in the air, head turned to look at the viewer, her anguish apparent even though it had been captured by Emily's crude brushstrokes. Thick black lines ran side to side as if to conceal parts of her body from view.

"I thought she was recreating something she saw through a window, you understand? I thought these were window blinds. But look."

Laura turned the painting ninety degrees. Now the figure was standing, reaching out for something. And the lines no longer appeared to be window blinds.

Instead, they bore a striking resemblance to the bars of a cage.

"Where could she have possibly seen something like that?" Timinski wanted to know.

"We were never far from home back then, and we knew every inch of the property. Except the one place they told us never to go."

Laura checked her watch.

There were still a few good hours of daylight left.

CHAPTER

39

LAURA FOUND THE food and water bowls upended on the front porch. She let herself inside, filled them again, then placed them at the foot of the stairs. She cupped her hands around her mouth and called a few times for Cooper.

"No luck?"

"Don't ask stupid questions," Laura said, and then she led Timinski toward the woods.

The corn rose as high as eight feet, with main stalks the diameter of a baseball and leaves the size of dinner plates. Each stalk stood ten inches from the next, and the rows were three feet apart, all of them running toward a vanishing point in the distance.

An unchanging, featureless wall of green in every direction.

Now they were out in the corn, bending and twisting, moving between the rows. The stalks offered no shade despite their height, and the sun was out in force. It shone down blithely, an alarming juxtaposition of raw power and indifference.

The temperature ticked up into the nineties, unusually warm for mid-September. A bead of sweat trickled its way between Laura's shoulder blades, and she could feel moisture working itself down into the waistband of her pants.

Timinski stumbled crossing a row, went down on one knee, pushed himself back up. "Did you really come out here as a kid?"

"All the time," Laura said. "It was just like this that summer in '96, too. We rotate the crops, but it was corn that year as well. Corn gets planted in April, harvested in October. In the heat of the summer, it was high. High as an elephant's eye."

"Seems difficult to find the way back."

She understood his concern. Late-season corn is like a perfectly uniform forest: no landmarks. "That always made me uncomfortable."

"If it scared you, why come out here at all?"

Laura noticed the way Timinski had traded in *uncomfortable* for *scared*. What she had felt all those years ago was not fear, and she had tasted enough terror in her time to know the difference. Her memories from that summer were some of the most vivid of her life. She conjured them instantly, without effort. No, the feeling in corn had been an ephemeral uneasiness, a creeping quiver up the back of her neck. It was the sensation of being watched, of undetectable shapes hidden behind the rows, of eyes she could not see.

"I wanted to explore. One of the first adult conversations I can remember having with my father was about coming out here alone. He said it was dangerous to play in the corn. He said the corn would take me."

"Take you?"

"He meant that it would turn me around until I was lost. Can you point toward the house?"

Timinski scratched his head and turned in circles, looking for some kind of hint.

But in the corn, there were no hints.

Finally he gave up and just pointed behind them.

Laura shook her head. "He taught me the position of the sun, how it moved, how to use it to navigate. He made sure I always had a mental map updating in the back of my head—where I was, where I'd been, how to get back."

The cornstalks thinned, then gave way to a tractor-wide cleared area marking the edge of the field. In front of them rose a gravel berm with the train tracks running across the top.

Laura scrambled up the loose stone. "Not much traffic on this line. Even when I was a kid, it had fallen off to a couple trains a day. Now there's a single train three or four days a week, the Norfolk Southern freight line. Every year they talk about shutting it down."

They slid down the opposite slope and moved into a stand of longleaf pine. The song of the cicadas faded to nothing, leaving behind an eerie quiet. It made Laura feel like an intruder, reminded her of going into a church without being a believer. These pines were a place she didn't belong. For the first time, she thought about turning back.

Ahead of them, a dry creek bed blocked the path. The sides sloped inward at a steep angle, cracked red clay threatening to crumble under the slightest pressure. A wooden two-by-four spanned the five-foot gap.

"It's still here," Laura said.

"Whose property is this?"

"Chambers, Merritt, no one was ever sure. The soil was no good for farming, so no one cared much either. Some of it could belong to the railroad, maybe to the county or the state."

They balanced across the plank, and in a minute or two the trees opened up into flat space. Two gray rocks, moss covered and smooth, jutted from the earth, and a worm-eaten log stood upended in the center.

"You hunted out here?"

"Mostly we'd walk up the tracks and cross the trestle. There was a ravine, a natural funnel for animals, and my father favored it."

"Which way?"

"That way," Laura said, and pointed—deeper into the pines.

They walked. The shadows grew long, and the light turned to amber. A low, trembling thud boomed to the south, and the air was suddenly imbued with a charged stillness, the harbinger of an electrical storm.

Ahead, the trees opened up into a natural clearing. On a small rise was a decrepit one-story house that looked like it might have started off its life as a sharecropper's cabin or a tobacco barn. It had a tin roof and a skinny front porch, and the walls were made of chinked logs.

A set of wheel ruts ran from the barn out the other side of the clearing.

"Where do those go?" Timinski asked.

"Toward the Merritt house, more or less. It probably intersects one of the other farm tracks. Those pop out onto the highway in a few different locations."

"They're eroded now, but you could have got a truck up here twenty years ago, don't you think?"

Laura headed for the barn, and he hurried to catch up with her.

Burlap sacks had been tacked up over the windows from the inside. A light buzzing filled the air. They moved closer, and she caught the smell—spoiled chicken in a dumpster on a hot day.

Laura's eyes narrowed. She set her jaw, walked across the dirt, and pulled on the door.

It was locked.

"What now?" he asked. The distant rumble of thunder. "We could go back."

In answer, she located a softball-sized rock and tossed it through one of the windows.

"Or that," Timinski said.

Laura used a branch to clear the glass out of the frame, then stepped through. Tim had difficulty getting his leg high enough. The fabric of his pants caught on a shard of broken glass. Laura held out her hand, and he took it. He tried again to pull himself free. This time, when he was almost in, Laura gave his arm a final tug.

He tumbled through the window, landing on top of her, and they went down in a heap. Tim yelped and grabbed at his leg.

"Ah shit," he said. "It's my trick knee."

Laura raised an eyebrow. "I thought that was a joke with you old guys."

"No, the patella slides out of place," he groaned. His jaw was clenched, his nostrils whistling as they sucked air. He was in real pain. "I'll have to see a doctor."

"Is this an emergency room situation, or are we talking urgent care?"

"Same old Laura," he said. But he smiled.

"Hang tight." She stood and for the first time took in her surroundings.

The buzzing was much louder. Flies crawled on the walls, the ceiling, the burlap on the windows. Millipedes squirmed across the floor.

"Maybe there's some standing water around and they're breeding," he said.

"You're thinking of mosquitoes."

The inside of the cabin was otherwise surprisingly neat but an odd mismatch with the log cabin aesthetic. The interior had been renovated the way one might build out a DIY garage apartment. There were unpainted kitchen cabinets along one wall, and a sink.

One corner had been walled off, and inside was a chemical toilet. The floor was covered in broad, ceramic floor tiles, and there were a few kitchen chairs but no table. Still the odor of rotting meat persisted. As Laura explored the space, she found it seemed to linger in the corners.

The cabin was only one room plus the small bathroom. A thorough search took only five minutes, and the only evidence of past habitation was a few cans of food in one cabinet.

"Find anything?" Timinski asked hopefully.

She shook her head.

"Think anyone's been out here recently?"

"I don't think so. The air seems stale."

"What about the food? Are there expiration dates?"

She opened the pantry and started sorting through cans of carrots and baked beans and Vienna sausages, reading off the dates. Most of them had expired around the year 2000.

"It's going to be different intervals depending on the type of food and the company," he said. "Take pictures of them. We can track down the lot number later, figure out when they were put there."

"Okay," she said, and turned to get the phone out of her pocket. One of the cans slipped off the shelf and rolled across the smooth tile floor. It clicked over the grouted junctions like a train moving between sections of track.

Click-click, click-click, click-click.

It rolled over the last tile near the wall.

Click-clunk.

They looked at each other. Timinski scooted along the floor and tapped his way down the same path. When he got to the wall and rapped hard with his knuckles, the ceramic tile there sounded hollow.

"I don't think there's anything supporting it underneath."

The edges were all grouted, so he sent Laura back for her tree branch. She handed it to him, and he brought it down like an ax. The tile shattered into fang-shaped pieces, and Laura cleared them out, revealing what was underneath.

A crude wooden hatch.

"It's a tornado shelter," she said.

The hatch weighed at least a hundred pounds, but together they managed to pull it up.

The smell washed over them.

Timinski said, "Oh Jesus."

Laura dug into her bag and located her flashlight. It was small enough to fit in the palm of her hand, but the LEDs packed a wallop. She shined it down into the earth.

A crude wooden ladder descended into the dark. All she could see was a dirt floor.

"Are you ready?" she asked.

Tim didn't answer. Sweat soaked his brow; the collar at the back of his neck was drenched. The air was humid again today, but this was something else. "I'm hurting," he said.

"The smell could be anything," she said, trying to convince herself. "There's probably just a dead raccoon down there. We have to look."

His teeth were gritted together. "I'll never make it back up the ladder."

He was still holding up the heavy door, and his arms were starting to shake. She got one of the kitchen chairs wedged underneath and turned to climb down the ladder.

"Be careful," he said.

"You just hold down the fort."

The ladder proved quite stable, and she clambered down to the dirt floor in no time. One quick scan with the flashlight revealed she'd been wrong about the hole's origins. It wasn't a tornado shelter at all—it was a root cellar.

It was low ceilinged but large, the size of the house. Little tunnels ran sideways into the earth in all directions, as if a giant mole or spider had nested in the clay. One of the tunnels seemed larger than the rest but still not large enough for a person. She played the flashlight inside and saw mounds covered in more burlap.

Holding her breath, she reached out, picked one up, and turned it over.

It was a rotted sack of potatoes.

"Anything?" Timinski called down.

"Nothing yet."

The house above was supported by an old-fashioned pier-and-beam foundation. Thick brick pillars were scattered around the space, holding up the floor above. She moved around and between them, scanning the walls with the light. Ahead was a place where there should have been a wall, but her light dipped into blackness instead.

An alcove, with a brick arch supporting the entryway.

Laura moved closed. She lifted her arm, and the light shone thought the archway.

Her arms and legs locked in place. She willed them to move, but her limbs would no longer respond. Her tongue flicked out to lick her lips, but her mouth had gone bone dry.

On the ground in front of her was a semicircle of chains bolted to a concrete floor. At the end of the chains, leg irons and metal collars glinted in the light.

Against the far wall was a welded steel cage.

I'm in a dungeon.

And in the small and pathetic corner of the alcove, a pile of bones.

This is no dungeon. This is a charnel house.

A squeak and a crunch came from behind her, and then something fell down through the hole, into the cellar with her.

A shot of adrenaline put her into sudden motion, and she spun around.

In the pool of light at the base of the ladder was the kitchen chair.

"I'm losing it!" came the shout.

She shot across the dirt floor, grabbed hold of the first rung, and looked up.

Timinski was fumbling and clawing at the trapdoor, desperate for purchase. Without the use of his leg, he couldn't get any leverage. "The chair legs slipped on the tile. I can't hold it, Laura. You have to hurry."

She started to climb.

"Faster," he grunted.

Then one of his hands slipped.

The trapdoor slammed shut, and Laura was plunged into blackness.

Behind her, in the dark, something moved.

CHAPTER

40

"A BAT?"

"It was the biggest bat you ever saw," Laura said. "It was the size of a dachshund. It came snuffling out of the dark, and I turned on my light, and I just screamed."

"That part I heard," Timinski said. "I thought you were getting attacked down there. I almost had a heart attack."

She ran her fingers through her hair for the hundredth time. "Keep this between you and me, okay?" she said. "I don't like to advertise it, but I hate bats. I can't stand their wings made of skin, and I despise those long-fingered, almost-human hands. I hate 'em."

Timinski had eventually managed to pry up the trapdoor, and with his arm draped over Laura's shoulder, they had been able to hobble back to the Chambers farmhouse. Laura had driven his Suburban, him in the back with his leg propped up.

She parked in front of the *Gazette* office, came around to the rear door, and helped him down onto the sidewalk. "I'm parked around back. You can drive yourself home?"

He put his foot on the ground gingerly, testing it with his weight. "Yeah, she'll do."

From the shadows behind a streetlight stepped a man in a gray suit. "Special Agent Timinski?"

Timinski straightened. "That's right.

The man in the gray suit produced a small black leather folio and flipped it open. "I'm Special Agent Duncan. You need to come with me, please."

"What's this about?" Laura asked.

Timinski reached out and took her by the arm. "This one's not your fight."

"Agent Timinski, I'd rather not do this on the street. You've been recalled by the Office of the Inspector General."

"On what grounds?"

"Giving a civilian access to restricted files."

"What civilian?"

Duncan smirked. "I was told you'd be with the reporter."

Timinski didn't move.

"The special agent in charge doesn't want to make waves," Duncan said. "But if you refuse to come with me, I've been ordered to put you on the ground and cuff you."

To Laura, Timinski said, "It's been fun. We should do it again some time."

Duncan took him roughly by the arm, shoved him into the back of his own Suburban, and slammed the door. He held out his hand to her. "Keys?"

She handed them over.

"Twice now," Duncan said. "I'm not sure what he sees in you."

Laura bared her teeth. "You're a toad."

"We all have our part to play. They're waiting for you upstairs, by the way," he said.

As the Suburban drove off down the road, Laura turned and looked up at the windows of Bass Herman's office.

Four silhouettes stared back at her.

* * *

Waiting for her inside were Bass and Whitley and Bynum, and also Sheriff Michael Fuller in one of his pinstriped politician's suits. He'd been a lawyer before he was a lawman, and it showed in the quality of his tailor and the cost of his haircut.

She pointed at Whitley. "I'm not talking to anyone with *him* here. Either he goes or I do."

"Sheriff, this woman is—"

Fuller held up a hand, and Whitley's mouth snapped shut like a bear trap. "Mr. Herman tells me there's been some friction."

Laura looked to Bass, but his face betrayed nothing.

"And I'm looking for a clean slate between you two."

"We have a duty to arrest her right now," Whitley said.

"You already tried that once," Laura shot back.

"Sheriff, we're dealing with a—"

The hand went up again. Fuller's voice was resonant and smooth, the voice of a stage actor. "Now the lieutenant does have a point. You missed your meeting with the judge this afternoon."

Laura slapped a palm to her forehead. Caught up in the whirlwind of events since discovering the truth about Barrow's daughter, she had managed to completely forget her court date.

"The judge is pissed, pardon my French. But we're good colleagues, and he listens when I offer my opinion. This afternoon at your hearing, I asked him to hold off on the warrant for failure to appear. I told him I would talk to you personally and get this resolved. Because I don't think you searched that motel room."

Tiny flecks of white froth appeared at the corners of Whitley's mouth. "We have an eyewitness who says she stole evidence from the room. I want to know what she took."

Fuller, half seated on one of the newsroom desks, didn't even take the time to acknowledge his subordinate. The seat of his expensive pants slid on the wood as he pivoted to Herman. "Bass, can we use your office?"

"Of course, Michael."

"Hope I'm not putting you out."

"Not at all."

"Captain, Lieutenant, just hold tight and let me talk to these two a minute."

Whitley seethed; cords stood out on his neck.

Laura cleared a stack of papers off a chair in front of Bass's desk. Fuller did the same without comment, and when they were both seated, Bass shut the door to the office.

"I'll start," Fuller said. "I'm interested in a peaceful resolution of this dispute between the Sheriff's Office and your paper. I can set the dogs on you, and you can write nasty stories about us in response, and back and forth we'll go. Nobody wins. But Whitley's got you dead to rights, Laura. Can I call you Laura?"

She nodded.

"He could frog-march you back to jail, and the judge would have you stay awhile. Mind you, this is all just on the failure to appear. The tampering with evidence, the obstruction of justice—the hammer is yet to fall on those issues. Do I have to tell you how serious a felony is?"

Laura sat up straight and put her hands in her lap. "No, you don't."

"Here's what I came to say: I'm willing to makc it go away. Whitley insists you were the one who searched that motel room top to bottom, but I don't believe it. You didn't search your own apartment while you were in the hospital, and you certainly didn't shoot Don Rodgers with a rifle. Setting aside for a moment your lack of motive to do those things, you simply didn't have the opportunity. There was a third party at play in that motel room. Are we on the same frequency in thinking it's the person who shot our Jane Doe and in turn Don Rodgers?"

"Absolutely, we are."

"Good. But I also think it's possible—just possible, mind you—that an eagle-eyed reporter such as yourself might have located something the killer did not. Certainly that's what the manager at the motel is willing to testify to: that he saw you flee out the window of the room and into the woods behind the motel with something under your arm."

"Did he say what I supposedly took?" Laura asked. "Is he sure? It was dark and rainy that night in Hillsborough."

Fuller raised the hand again. "Now that's exactly the sort of adversarial path I don't want us to wander down. Hypothetically, even if this were true, I'd want you to know that you could share it with me now without consequence."

"Why would you do that?"

"You're the least of my problems, Laura. I'm already investigating two homicides, and now we have to coordinate with New Hanover County on the connection to this Radford fellow."

"Not to mention Beth Bancroft," Laura said.

"Excuse me?"

"The lawyer from the business card that was in the motel room. It's okay, I already saw the card, Sheriff."

Fuller frowned. "I'm not aware of any business card that was discovered. Believe me, if we knew of someone who'd spoken to our Jane Doe, we would have been extremely interested."

This threw Laura for a loop. She was certain the Sheriff's Office had followed up and discovered the same information as Rodgers: that Beth Bancroft had been strangled with the cord a day after all of this had started.

She told Fuller now, and he seemed troubled. He looked through the glass wall at Whitley and Bynum. "Heads will roll if it's still stuck behind the toilet tank."

"That's why Don was with me that morning. He told me just before—"

She choked back a sob.

Fuller had an extremely prominent nose in the middle of an otherwise classically handsome face. He scratched the side of it and sighed.

"The other reason I'm willing to help is that Don Rodgers thought the world of you. I knew the man a very long time. He and I didn't always see eye to eye, but neither of us would want to see you hurt. It's very clear to me Lieutenant Whitley is not the only one who thinks you took something of value. These people tried to kill you to get it, and Rodgers died in the process. This has all gone too far. I'm not here to arrest you, Laura—I'm here to beg for your help."

He had an expression of such genuine pain when he mentioned Don Rodgers that Laura found herself moved. And Fuller had never been her enemy. A bit too political for her tastes—he was a climber—but he of all the folks at the Sheriff's Office had always treated her as a professional.

She turned to Bass Herman. "How about a drink, Bass?"

Bass's eyebrows crept up his forehead. "You certain about that, Miss Chambers?"

"I'm quite thirsty," she said.

Bass shrugged, then located the small silver key and opened the locked drawer in the bottom of his desk. He came out with a bag, one that by the look on his face was much heavier than expected. From inside he produced three photo albums, all with the same beige canvas covers.

Laura pointed. "This one I took from the motel room. The other two I recovered from the estate."

Fuller was puzzled. "What estate?"

"The Merritt estate."

From a back pocket, Fuller produced a pair of white cotton gloves and began turning the pages of the unlisted album.

Laura gave him a few minutes to absorb the contents before saying, "I found it stuffed into a heating vent."

"And this is *all* you found?" he asked, a sudden sharpness in his voice. He looked up at her for her answer.

"Yes, that was all, I swear it."

"It makes no sense to me. Why hide it in a vent? Why kill to take it? I'm at sea here, Laura. Throw me a lifeline. Explain to me what's going on."

"I can tell you why I hid it from Whitley. These pictures were in the second half." From her own bag, Laura pulled out an envelope and spread the pictures over the desktop. Out of the corner of her eye, she caught the look of betrayal on Bass's face. She pushed it away, ignored it for now.

"What am I looking at?"

"This is my father, and this is my mother. Here's me as a kid."

"They were family friends? I didn't know that."

"That's just it, Sheriff—we were not. I can recall my friendship with Emily in fits and starts, but after Bob and Linda Merritt were killed, I was told never to mention them again. My own parents went to an awful lot of trouble to conceal the fact that there had ever been a connection between our families."

Quickly she explained the provenance of the two albums from her mother's attic.

"Here," she said, and showed Fuller a copy of the inventory list from the OCSO's own original Merritt investigation. "Two albums accounted for."

Fuller said, "And yet you have three."

"That's right—this one was carried out of the Merritt house the night they were killed, so it never ended up on the inventory list."

"Barrow carried it out?"

"No," Laura said carefully. "His daughter did."

It dropped like a bombshell in the office. She could almost hear whistling as the two men processed what she had said, growing louder as they understood her meaning, and then exploding in a flurry of questions. She calmed them down and explained Barrow's true method for casing and burglarizing houses in the area, concluding with the news that his daughter was the woman who had died in the left lane of the interstate.

"Her name was Cassandra Lucchi, and she kept the album all these years. She came to Hillsborough to talk to the reporter at the *Gazette* who'd been writing about her father's upcoming execution so she could tell her father's real story, and she brought along the album so she'd have evidence beyond just her word that the story was true." Laura pointed to its open pages. "I wouldn't have believed her at first, but this would have been enough to get me to start tugging at loose threads. It was a chance, the only chance she had."

"Her father's real story—what's that supposed to mean?"

Laura took a breath. "Simon Barrow is innocent."

If the revelation of Barrow's daughter had been a bombshell, this was a nuclear warhead. Both Fuller and Bass were on their feet, peppering her with questions.

Bass was the louder of the two. "You actually spoke with Barrow? He agreed to be interviewed? He said this on tape?"

Laura told Bass that he had.

Bass sat down hard in his chair. She could already see the wheels turning in his head and the dollar signs in his eyes. If Laura was correct, it would rock the very foundation of the town and upend what everyone thought they knew about their collective past.

Now they were both shouting over each other again.

"Gentlemen, gentlemen, listen to me." In broad strokes, she recounted Barrow's tale: that he was hired to get a videotape from the Merritts and that the man who'd hired him to steal it was the real Shotgun Slayer. "Barrow was just the fall guy," she finished. "All of it—the Merritts, Cassandra Lucchi, Don Rodgers—are part of the same ongoing cover-up."

"To cover up what?" Fuller demanded to know.

Laura took another breath, and this time she told them of the horrors she had discovered in the earth. She described the chains and collars and the pile of what might be human remains. And to her great shame, she had to include her own father in the story.

Fuller squinted at the opposite wall, thinking hard. "You're suggesting Jacob Radford's ultimate destination with his human cargo back in the eighties and nineties was this secret underground depot right here in Hillsborough. And you're accusing your *own parents* of being party to this, to this . . ."

Fuller couldn't finish the sentence.

"That's right, and the Merritts too." Laura said. "No way it could have been happening on their land without them knowing about it. But I want to be clear: I don't think either family was in charge. My father wasn't a criminal mastermind, he was a drunk. And the Merritts were in a lot of financial trouble back then; they were about to lose the farm altogether. These were not the folks at the top of the food chain."

"And the tape?" Fuller barked. "Why did the so-called real Shotgun Slayer want it so badly?"

Laura shrugged. "We slipped over the line into speculation a while ago, but I think Bob Merritt had evidence on that tape, either as an insurance policy or maybe he was trying to dig his family out of the hole they were in."

"Blackmail, you mean," Fuller said. "And Barrow's daughter, she must have carried it away as well that night."

"I don't know," Laura said.

Fuller studied her. "This feels like a very familiar discussion. I know we're trying to be civil to each other, Laura, so I'll only ask this once: did you find this videotape in the motel room? Do you have it? These are deeply troubling, *disturbing* allegations. If you have proof, I need to see it right away."

"I never saw any tape, Sheriff Fuller. I only know about it because Simon Barrow told me about it."

"The word of a convicted murderer."

"Respectfully, sir, he's not the one who put that dungeon behind my childhood home."

"A fair point," Fuller said, and stood. "Laura, this has to be one of the most outrageous, craziest stories I've ever heard. But if it's true, there's an easy way to prove it."

"We'll have to walk through the woods. It's dark now."

"At first light then. Take Whitley and Bynum out to your family's farm and show them the evidence you just described."

Laura shook her head. "Whitley and I—"

Once again Fuller held up a well-proportioned, well-manicured hand. "I'll talk to the lieutenant, and I promise he'll behave himself."

CHAPTER

41

LAURA SLEPT ON the couch in Bass's office, and early the next morning she pulled his Cadillac up to the yellow tape in front of the Chambers farmhouse. Whitley and Bynum were already waiting for her. As she approached, Whitley squinted into the sun, his eyes bloodshot, his face haggard. Bynum kept watch on him the way a boxing referee watches a fighter guilty of throwing low blows.

"I never thought you'd sink this low," Whitley said as she got close. "Cooking up some story to keep that ass out of jail. Actually, I take it back, I did think you would. You'll go lower, I bet."

Laura had rehearsed what she would say to him on the drive over. "Lieutenant Whitley, I—"

He took a quick step closer to her. "Look down at your feet."

"Excuse me?"

His jaw was clamped so tight she thought his teeth would snap. "Your feet, look at them. You recognize this spot? This is where Don Rodgers bled out into the dirt. Did you thank him? He did that for you, you little bitch."

"Hey now," Bynum said.

"Because he was aiming for you, we know that." His breath smelled of vodka again. His voice was lower now, a grating kind of whisper. "Maybe he's out here again this morning. Could be he has a bead on you right now, you ever think of that?"

"Knock it off," Bynum said.

Whitley threw open his arms, a wild look in his eyes. "Are you out there?" he yelled. "Can you hear me?"

His voice echoed off the side of the house.

"I said stop," Bynum said.

But Whitley wouldn't listen. "If you're out there, take the shot! Pull the trigger! Pull it!"

"I said that's enough," Bynum said, and grabbed him by the arm. Whitley tried to shrug him off, and the two men struggled with each other. Then, from behind them, came a distinct rustling sound.

All three of them froze. Whitley turned his head, listening. There it was again.

It was coming from inside the corn.

Bynum and Whitley both drew their sidearms and pointed them forward. Whitley called, "Come out with your hands up!"

There it was again: the unmistakable sound of footsteps.

"Come out now!"

The corn silk at the tops of the stalks oscillated in sequence as someone passed beneath them. It was like a wave rolling toward the shore, headed straight for them.

But between the stalks, they could see nothing.

Another second and it would reach them.

"Last chance!" Whitley shouted.

The movement stopped, and she saw Whitley and Bynum relax just a hair.

Then, without warning, a dark shape burst from the wall of green and charged.

The guns came up again.

"Don't shoot!" Laura screamed. "Don't shoot, dontshootdont-shoot." Then she was down on her knees with her arms wrapped around him, hugging him for all she was worth. He gave her face a great lick, then threw back his head and howled.

Whitley was breathing hard. "What the hell, Chambers?"

"It's Cooper, it's Rodgers's dog. He's been lost since the shooting."

This was the sweetest dog Laura had ever known, so it was a shock when he put himself between her and the two police officers, planted his front paws in the dirt, and pulled his lips back from his teeth. From somewhere deep inside, Cooper started to growl.

Laura put her hand on his collar just in time. Cooper leapt at the two men, snapping and snarling, and it was all Laura could do to hold him back.

"Control the dog, please," Bynum said. There was a note of alarm in his voice.

"Cooper, calm down. Calm down! It's okay, it's just me."

But her words had no effect on him. Cooper tried for another leap, and this time it appeared he wanted to bite Whitley in the throat.

"Christ," Whitley said. "Get him under control or I'll shoot him myself."

"No! No, just let me get him inside. It's not in great shape, but we can keep him in there."

She had to drag him across the dirt and up the stairs into the house. The other two followed her into the foyer and watched as she put Cooper into the living room and closed the French doors to keep him inside.

He kept growling. The doors rattled as he jumped against them.

The smell of the house washed over them, like sour milk slathered on burnt toast.

Timinski pinched his nose. "You weren't kidding."

"The fire department cut the power. No air conditioning, and the place has been closed up since Friday. No one's been here to empty out the fridge or take out the trash."

"Not to mention the, ah, everything else," said Bynum. He meant the stacks of old pizza boxes and other garbage pushed into the corners. Her mother had been doing that for so long, Laura didn't even notice anymore.

"Just hold your breath and help me get the windows open," she said.

Cooper wouldn't stop barking, and Laura's head started to throb. The throaty yips and wails pummeled her ears. She pressed her palms to the sides of her head and closed her eyes tight. Unbidden, uncontrollable memories started flashing though her head, not a movie but a slide show. It was like the bright light of a projector shining directly into an eye she could not close.

The eerie silence that descended on the land before the first bullet struck.

The dog throwing himself at the window of Rodgers's truck, frothing at the mouth, desperate to warn them.

Rodgers on the ground, reaching for the stairs, reaching for her. She was so close.

She tried to shake the images away, but they proved resilient, and Cooper barked and barked and barked.

Cooper desperate to warn them . . .

To Laura, everything around her seemed to slow down. Her senses sharpened until the world was painful to behold.

Beams of light slithered in through the hopper windows, and dust motes rippled in their wake. She registered the stained wooden writing desk that stood against one wall, and on top of it a coffee can that had been her father's, filled with old spent casings. The smell of ancient coffee and old gunpowder. The creak of the floorboards as Whitley shifted his weight.

The world sped up again.

Laura took her hands away from her head. "Cooper, shush," she said, and even from behind the doors, Cooper listened. The room was filled with a sudden silence.

When Laura spoke, her own voice surprised her. To Whitley she said, "You were the first on scene at the Merritt house, isn't that right?"

Whitley put his hands on his hips. "That's right."

"And you found them what, early the morning after?"

"Morbid curiosity doesn't suit you." When she didn't respond, he said, "Yes, I was first on scene."

"I poured over the file from back then. Linda Merritt's best friend popped over when she called, and the line was out of service. She drove back toward town, stopped at another friend's house when she passed it, and used the phone there to call 911. According to the report you wrote back then, you reached the house less than five minutes later."

"What's your point?"

"Quite a response time," she said. She trailed her fingertips along the surface of the writing desk. "Did Sheriff Fuller pass along all the details I shared with him?"

Bynum said that he had.

Whitley crossed his arms over his chest. "I don't believe a word of it."

"Don't you think it's strange that Cassandra Lucchi tried to get in touch with me instead of the police?"

Whitley let out a breath of hot, stinking air. "I'll say."

But Laura wasn't really listening to him. Almost as if she were talking to herself, she said, "Even in her last moments, shot and being chased to her death, she called me instead."

Whitley just stared at her, open disgust on his face.

"And the notes that Simon Barrow has been getting passed to him for all these years, some of them by prison guards. It makes sense, of course. It must be nearly impossible to keep a person quiet for twenty-three years. The only way to achieve that is to hold a guillotine suspended over his family's neck and to never let him forget it. Threaten his daughter, and if a man really loves her, he'll walk himself onto death row.

"But if enough time goes by, how can he be sure his daughter is still in danger? You have to do a little maintenance from time to time, remind him what he has to lose. That's the purpose of the notes. They could have been letters, but anyone can send a letter. Simon Barrow got them from the *guards themselves*.

"The medium is the message, you understand? It says, 'If we can get to you here, then we can get to your daughter out there. We have eyes everywhere. We're powerful,' it says."

Whitley chuckled. "You must be losing your goddamn mind."

"Let me tell you something else," Laura said. "There were three of us here when Rodgers died. It was me, it was Rodgers, and it was Cooper. The dog tried to warn us, Whitley. Even before the first shot, he knew someone was here. Do you know how? Ask me how he knew."

Whatever Whitley saw in her face at that moment, he didn't like it. He looked almost afraid. "Fine, tell me how."

"He fucking *smelled* him, Whitley. He sniffed out the worm in the apple."

"That's nuts. You're crazy, Chambers."

"A bloodhound can follow a trail more than a hundred miles. They can smell cancer. What, you think Cooper can't detect a body odor and cologne? Bloodhounds have got great memories too. If they've ever smelled you before, they know it. Cooper might as well be walking around with a close-up picture of the perp."

"That shooter was three hundred and fifty yards away, easy," Whitley said. "The dog didn't follow a trail; he was in the truck. Is he supposed to be psychic?"

Laura spun to face him. "I didn't mean the shooter, Whitley. Did you forget there were two of them? I'm talking about the one who set the fire. The one who was just around the corner."

Whitley said nothing.

Laura turned to look at Cooper through the glass panes of the doors. "The prison guards are going to be a big problem for whoever paid them to deliver those notes. That's what I would do next—put the fear of Jesus into the guards and see who starts talking."

From behind her, nothing but silence.

"Who could possibly have done all the things we talked about?" she mused. "Do you know who it sounds like to me? It sounds like a cop."

Laura wheeled back around, hoping to catch Whitley unaware, and studied him. All she could see on his face, however, was a look of total surprise and confusion.

Just at the edge of her vision, she saw Bynum move.

Quick as a wink, he drew a black automatic pistol from behind his back, raised his arm, and shot Lieutenant Whitley through the side of his head.

CHAPTER

42

LAURA FROZE.

Terror bloomed in her then, a dank moonflower, a Venus flytrap clamped shut around her lungs. Behind her, Cooper going berserk—baying, howling, backing up to charge the glass, throwing himself against the panes without the slightest regard for his own well-being. Doing it again.

Genteel, aging Bynum, on the verge of retirement. Bynum the milquetoast. Bynum in his fishing vest and bucket hat the day they met. Concealed behind his Coke-bottle lenses, insectile Bynum studied her coldly from across the room.

He appraised her as if she were a fish with a hook through its cheek.

Laura forced herself to meet his eyes.

No emotion lived in the flat gray of his irises; the pupils were twin black holes boring into emptiness. He considered her as one would a menu at a restaurant, or a choice of jelly bean. Under the weight of his gaze, she was made an arbitrary thing, of slight interest but ultimately insignificant. She sensed from him a mild curiosity about what clockwork lurked inside her head.

A sudden calmness, a clarity, descended on her.

"Secrets, secrets, are no fun," she heard herself say.

Where had that come from?

The gray eyes didn't blink. "Secrets, secrets, hurt someone."

"What now?"

"Now I make it look like you killed him, and that I killed you in turn."

Laura stared at him. "And why did I do that?"

Bynum made a vague gesture with the gun in his hand. "Who cares? You hated Whitley, or you were despondent over Don Rodgers. It doesn't matter. People will make up their own story, they always do. I'll say that's what happened, and they'll believe me."

Almost more terrifying than the gun was the fact that he was right.

"It was a good deal, you know."

"What was?" she asked.

Keep him talking, keep him talking.

"The depot. You saw it, you must have seen that it had a kind of genius to it. It was a whole new distribution model. Imagine an Amazon warehouse but for women—that was us. Radford would meet the boats off the coast, bring them in his truck, the items would be stored for a few days, and then they'd be shipped off."

"On different trucks," Laura said.

"You wouldn't believe how many, going all different places. Don't look at me like that—we didn't create the demand, just offered some supply. It was a triumph of economics, of logistics. None of it stayed local, that's the beauty part. Clean hands . . . and you get rich in the process."

"But nothing lasts forever."

Cooper sacrificing his body against the door, howling, yelping, whimpering.

"Just so," Bynum said. "Radford got sloppy and it all fell apart. But that was fine: easy come, easy go. It was all fine until Bob Merritt decided he could soak us for our hard-earned cash."

"He told you he had a videotape."

"Sneaked down underneath and got it somehow. Not sure how he managed it. It was real enough, though—he sent us a copy. Ungrateful of him. We paid Bob Merritt and Bruce Chambers a fair rent to use that land, and we paid them a hundred times that amount to not ask questions. They were never supposed to know what we were doing."

"But they found out."

"Secrets, secrets, are no fun," Bynum intoned.

"Bob Merritt blackmailed you."

"And that dog don't hunt. You pay a blackmailer once and you'll be paying forever. You know what we had to do."

"I don't know, what?"

"You want me to lay it all out for you? Fine, it doesn't matter anymore. Barrow's daughter opened the front door for me and almost puked her guts out. She was still expecting daddy, of course, and I must have been a sight in a ski mask with a shotgun in my hand. Her mouth opened like she was going to scream, so I grabbed her by the neck and tossed her out of the house."

"She had the album in her hand."

"That's right," Bynum said. "Then I shot them. It was quick. They barely knew what happened. The daughter slipped away before I could get her, but that was fine."

"But the safe was empty."

He nodded. "The tape had never been there. The combination I gave Barrow was bogus, so I know his daughter didn't get it that way. I never even knew the combination. I took the whole thing with me and cut it open later."

She imagined the fear and rage he must have felt at cutting the safe open only to find it empty. At that moment, Laura had to suppress a flash of glee.

"It was all fine until Barrow's daughter contacted us all these years later, saying she had the tape after all, making demands."

"She had to go too," said Laura slowly.

Bynum's eyes had been lost in thought, and now they fixed on her again. To him, she was meat on a scale.

"If you hadn't published that facile little article, the Barrow girl would still be alive," he said. "All this is your doing. You won't believe me, but I've been on the straight and narrow since the night the Merritts died. I worked hard to put all this behind me. The man who did those things is long gone."

Agree to disagree, Laura thought but did not say.

"Since then, I've gotten married, had children. They love me. They can never know what happened."

Bynum had fast hands, much faster than Laura had expected—she remembered well the speed with which he'd killed Whitley. Now the hands blurred again. In a span of time too short for her to even think of moving, Bynum dropped the small black automatic into the pocket of his jacket, then unholstered his service weapon. He pulled the slide part way back and peered inside, making sure there was a bullet in the chamber, then let it drop down next to his thigh.

"Shut that damn dog up right now."

From across the room, she raised her hands and patted the air. "Shush, Cooper. Shush now. It's going to be all right."

Cooper watched her and listened to her, and on the other side of the doors he went still.

"Now tell me where you hid the tape," Bynum said.

Laura started to move to her left, slow steps, no sudden movements.

Bynum frowned. "Stay still, please."

Laura tried not to make a habit of taking advice from her enemy, so she didn't listen. She started circling, stepping one way and then another, looking for some advantage. Now she stopped with the French doors at her back.

"Cassandra never gave me the tape," Laura said.

"You found it in that motel room. You must have."

"No," Laura said. She started slowly circling the edge of the room again.

Bynum circled in the same direction, careful to always stay directly opposite her. He was beginning to look frustrated. "Stop moving, please," he said.

"I don't have the slightest fucking idea what happened to it," Laura said.

Near to her now was the entrance to the hallway. It headed away to the left, leading to the stairs. She moved toward it. In a few more feet, Bynum would be blocked by the edge of the doorway, and she would have a chance.

"I'll give you this much," Bynum said. "You're a very stubborn young woman."

"I'm my father's daughter," Laura said.

For the first and only time during their interaction, Bynum smiled. "Is that what you've been telling yourself all these years?"

Laura took a step, and that was apparently one too far for Bynum's taste. "Fine, have it your way," he said, raised the gun, and pointed it at her.

Now Laura felt fear. Momentarily deferred, it seemed to have accumulated interest. It was a running, jumping, galloping fear, a living creature that beat on the inside of her chest, that squirmed in her groin. The world became nothing but a collection of still frames, soundless, spooled out one after the other.

Motes of dust hovering in a sunbeam.

Bynum's tongue touched to the tip of his incisors.

The gun, gray and cold, seeking her with its one black eye.

Her vision collapsed into a tunnel, and at the end of the tunnel was the gun. Degree by degree it twisted toward her, a nightmarish geometry problem. Or perhaps it was algebra: if Laura jumps toward the hallway at X feet per second, with the barrel of the gun turning toward her at Y degrees per millisecond, at what speed must she travel to stay alive? How fast must she go to avoid the bullet?

The bullet.

She had laid eyes on it just a few minutes before when Bynum had pulled back the slide. Back then, at the height of her detachment, the bullet had seemed to her an insignificant cylinder, inert, unremarkable as it slumbered in its chamber. Now it was transformed: it was a beast, a tiger straining at the end of a rusty chain, hungry for her blood.

Panic threatened to dismantle her entirely.

Lucky for Laura, she had a secret.

"Secrets, secrets, hurt someone," she muttered.

Bynum quirked his mouth, confused, and lowered the gun just a touch. They had gone through half a revolution, and now he was protecting both the front door and the doors into the living room. Laura Chambers, meanwhile, had literally backed herself into a corner.

With all the volume and intensity she could muster, Laura screamed. "Now, Cooper!"

Cooper threw himself into the French doors with all his might, and because Laura had twisted the small knob to unlock them when she'd passed the first time, this time the doors exploded inward in a hail of ragged splinters and razored glass and furious, snapping bloodhound. The dog bit into Bynum's leg. He pulled the trigger on his gun, but the shot went wide, through the decorative plate hanging on the wall next to Laura's head.

It might as well have been a starting pistol.

She darted down the hallway, past the stairs, into the kitchen, and toward the back door she knew was standing open. The screen door had been latched to keep it from blowing in the wind, but she didn't slow down for an instant. She blew right through it onto the small back porch, all the while her mind whirring like a computer, calculating angles, ranking options.

The Cadillac was parked around the front, and the keys were in her pocket, but it would be trivial for Bynum to simply step through the front door and beat her to the punch. If she went around the side of the house, he would already be there to meet her. It was too big a risk to try for the car.

Which left only one option.

Laura ran into the corn.

CHAPTER

43

LAURA RAN.

She raced, she sprinted, she bolted. She kept on and on, until her throat turned raw from gasping and the stitch in her side became a paper bag of jagged glass crushed against her ribs. All around her the thrum and whine of cicadas continued without pause, but in those fleeting moments when she stopped, she could hear him chasing her. Then she would ignore the clamoring pain and run faster still.

She was in the corn. Skinny, ear-laden stalks rose at well-spaced intervals, none more than a few inches in diameter. There was plenty of room for a person to run down the rows, but the rows themselves had meshed like gears. She crashed her way through them, jumping from row to row and attempting to obscure any clear path to follow her.

And once she was deep enough in, she stopped. She listened.

No sound out of place.

From her pocket she removed her phone. She never lowered her eyes, just held down the lock button, hit EMERGENCY CALL, and held the phone to her ear.

"Nine-one-one, what's the nature of your emergency?"

Speaking in a low whisper, Laura gave her name and the address and explained that a man was pursuing her through the cornfield behind the house. She told the operator to send the police as fast as humanly possible. The last thing she said was for the benefit of the recorders, for whoever might be listening to the tape of this call at a future date.

"The name of the man chasing me is Captain William Bynum. I just watched him murder Lieutenant David Whitley in cold blood, after which he confessed to killing Bob and Linda Merritt in 1996. There, that was in case he gets me first."

"Ma'am, is there a place you can hide? Can you try to—"

"Just send them," said Laura, and ended the call.

It was the sweltering heat of high summer, and beads of sweat ran into her eyes. She tried to wipe them away, but her hands were covered in dust.

She listened.

Nothing but the lazy hum of sun-drunk insects and a humid breeze that slouched in from the west, plucking the sweat from her back and leaving behind a pleasant chill.

With a crash, Bynum burst into her row perhaps thirty feet away. He spotted her, and then the barrel of the gun was rising, rising.

Laura plunged sideways into the green maze. She never stopped pumping her legs. Her muscles screamed in protest, but she pushed the pain to the back of her mind and just kept moving. Then the sliver-of-glass sensation in her side morphed into outright agony, and she skittered to a stop.

They were far out into the middle of the field now.

She closed her eyes and listened.

Laura had played enough hide-and-seek to understand the rules of this game: it was impossible to move in the corn without making noise, but the rustling was so loud that it was also impossible to hear your quarry's noise so long as you were moving. They were like two submarines hunting each other on the bottom of the North Atlantic. You could run the screws and give chase, but you would be blind. Or you could stop and listen, but you could not move. Those were the only choices.

The very environment demanded a kind of détente between the pursuer and the pursued, a cold war of move and countermove. Laura had stopped to listen closely, and she could hear him coming up behind her.

Knowing Bynum wouldn't be able to detect her as long as he was walking, she started moving perpendicular to her original path, and after a minute, she'd lost him again.

The drone of the cicadas vanished as abruptly as if someone had slammed a window shut. A creeping sensation wriggled across Laura's neck, the familiar sensation of being watched. She whirled around, but there was no one behind her. Fear made her legs tremble.

Where is he?

A thought occurred to her: in her wallet she still had Bynum's card, the one he had given her the first time they met. Quickly she dug it out and dialed the number.

From fifty feet to her left: *ring, ring, ring.* Bynum's ringer, the old-fashioned variety.

She heard him curse and used the distraction to turn back toward the house. With any luck, a few sheriff's deputies would be there waiting for her.

To Laura's horror, her own phone began ringing in her hand. To make sure she would wake up if someone called at night, it was the impossible-to-miss, deafening bleat of a foghorn.

She stared at the screen: Bynum, returning her call.

He crashed through the corn behind her. In another moment he would be upon her.

Bynum's strategy, she realized, had been to prevent her from ever getting out of this field and back to civilization. He wanted to be the catcher in the rye, the victor in the most serious game of red rover either of them had ever played. Now that he thought she was between him and the house, headed for the goal line, he would be panicked.

So Laura did the only thing she could think of. She pulled back her arm and launched the still-ringing cell phone as hard as she could in the direction of the house, and then she ran in the opposite direction.

It didn't work.

Bynum seemed inhuman. He flew toward her and she took off at a sprint, and in her panic she forgot her father's lesson: Laura let herself get turned around, and she no longer knew which direction through the field was the way out.

She stopped.

Nearby, a rustle in the leaves.

She dropped, crouched low, and held her breath.

She could see the color of his shirt shifting between the rows, perhaps twenty feet away. As long as she stayed low and didn't move, he would go past her.

Bynum was moving around, but he couldn't find her. He started ranting and raving, but she couldn't make out the words. Her legs gave out under her. She didn't think she could make another run, so she sat down between two rows and did her level best to pull her knees up to her ears, like when she was a little girl. She just sat there, silent and unmoving, and for the first time she noticed that she was covered in Whitley's blood.

It was working. He was moving away.

And then he changed direction. He came back toward her, getting closer and closer and closer. If she stayed, she was dead. If she moved, she was dead.

In the distance, growing closer, she could hear the warbling shriek of the coming sirens.

But it was already too late. She could see him now. It was over. She only hoped it would be quick.

The timbre of the noise changed. A slight rumble, a high-pitched squeal. Then the conductor sounded his horn—

And she knew.

The train.

It was the train, the train, my God, the train. The Norfolk Southern freight line conducting its biweekly flyby of the Chambers farm. The train that someone upstairs had sent her, the train that had come to save her life.

It blew by on the high gravel berm, horn blaring, and it obliterated every other sound in the world.

Laura gathered the last of her strength and she ran. She sprinted away directly away from the train, and under cover of its massive roar, Bynum never heard a thing.

She burst out of the corn a hundred yards from the house. The flashing lights of two police cruisers were already outside. She limped over the last piece of open ground to reach them and toppled into a waiting deputy's arms.

"The corn," she said weakly. "He's in the corn."

The Orange County Sheriff's Office surrounded the field on all sides. Dogs patrolled the border. A man in a suit stood on top of his car with a bullhorn and issued an ultimatum.

And from deep in the corn, Bynum answered with the sound of a single gunshot.

CHAPTER

44

Laura's father left her for the last time in 1997. That year the summer had been mild instead of hot, with gentle rains instead of thunderstorms. That year they had planted soybeans instead of corn.

His voice had been taken from him by then, so it was Laura who would speak for him. At nine years old, she made her daddy's phone calls. She managed his doctor's appointments, and when he needed medicine, she got in touch with the pharmacy.

So it was no surprise to Laura when her father left for the hospital on a one-way trip. In fact, she had been the one to call and inform the hospice staff that the time had come and to ask politely if they could send someone to collect him.

Her mother was hidden somewhere inside the house when they arrived. Two orderlies in white jackets were about to lift his wheelchair and carry him down the stairs when he gestured for them to wait. He found his chalkboard and wrote to her in the big capital letters he had always favored. He chalked the words and held them up for her to see.

IF YOU MISS ME, *he said,* LEAVE ME A MESSAGE

He erased the board and chalked again.

OUR SPECIAL PLACE

YOU CAN FIND ME THERE

CHAPTER

45

IF YOU MISS me . . .

Laura Chambers was sitting up, alert and already more than a little bored, when Timinski pushed through the door into her hospital room, a huge grin splitting his face.

She shot to her feet. "Good news?"

"Great news. They found Cooper shut up in the house, and he's fine. He's shaken up, but he's fine."

She glanced over at the door, then back to Tim. "Well, where is he, then?"

He let out a chuckle. "You think they'd let a dog into a hospital? Not an animal exactly known for being sterile. He's at my place. You can see him when you get out of here."

Laura let out a shaky breath, her relief palpable. "Okay," she said. "All right. Did you bring the rest?"

Timinski slung a gym bag up onto the room's small table. "Wasn't sure what you'd want, so I just packed everything from the trunk in here."

She sorted through and found a pair of jeans, a T-shirt, underwear, and socks that all smelled better than awful. The clothes she'd had on when Bynum shot Whitley had been bagged as evidence because they were soaked in his blood. But if they had been the only option, Laura would have pulled them back on.

Anything was better than this paper gown.

"All the evidence in your mother's foyer supports the story you told the Sheriff's Office. And if that hadn't convinced them, Bynum's suicide would probably have done the trick."

"Don't start celebrating yet. We're not done."

"You can rest a minute, Laura. And you're alive. You might not have gotten all the answers, but that *is* worth a celebration."

"Maybe a little one," she allowed.

She poked around in the bag and found a rolled-up, crumpled section of the *Gazette.* Inside were the board and the velvet bag of story tiles. Absent-mindedly, she tugged loose the drawstring and dumped the tiles on the table.

"Here's my question," Timinski said. "Why not just turn the videotape in? I know Bynum was a cop, so it would have been terrifying to go the police but . . . what about taking it to the State Bureau of Investigation? Or the FBI? With her witness statement, it would have made a real impact."

"She never had the tape," Laura said.

Timinski frowned. "Explain yourself."

"She set this whole thing in motion, but everyone's forgetting: she was eight years old back then. It was supposed to be locked in a safe. Even Bynum couldn't find it, and he was a full-grown man."

"So what then?"

Laura gave a shrug. "She bluffed. She knew the tape existed, and she gambled that they'd never managed to get their hands on it. And when the state of North Carolina finally decided to take her father away from her, she leveraged that knowledge to try and get him out."

"In the end, it got her killed."

"That's a fierce kind of love," Laura said.

As they spoke, she was turning the story tiles, lining them up.

"Here's one for you," Laura said. "After all this time, how did she figure out it was Bynum? She met the man who hired her father, but she never had a name to go with the face."

Timinski shook his head, stumped.

"Trick question. She didn't recognize *Bynum* at all. There were two of them, remember? It had to have been Bynum who set the fire, because that's how Cooper recognized his smell. That means the other one was behind the rifle."

"I'm not following."

"At the prison, Barrow said she came to see him the day after my story about his execution came out. She had read it and she was *excited* by it. She was jumping up and down, he said."

"Still not catching on."

"And at my mother's house, Bynum said—I'll try to quote him here as best I can—'If you hadn't published that article, the Barrow girl would still be alive.'"

A light of realization went on behind Timinski's eyes. "It was the article that started it. Cassandra Lucchi went to read about her father, and right there in the story was a picture of the man who put him on death row. She finally had a name to go with the face. There's something karmic about that," he said, awe in his voice.

"You're close," Laura said. "But Bynum's photo isn't the one in the article."

From one of her folders, she produced a copy of it and slid it across the table in front of Timinski. Two men were pictured. One was Lieutenant David Whitley, whose relative innocence had been more or less established by virtue of his taking a bullet in the head. And the other—

"I don't believe it," Timinski muttered.

"I remember when he ran for sheriff, people were kind of lukewarm on him as a lawman because he's a lawyer and he dresses in those fancy suits. Didn't seem tough, you know? So his campaign started running ads touting his military service. I can still remember the tag line: *From Soldier to Sheriff.* Isn't that nice?"

"Laura—"

"Bet me."

"I don't know what—"

"Come on, bet me. How much do you want to bet that if we check Sheriff Fuller's military service record, we'll see he was rated an expert marksman?"

Timinski let out his breath in a long whistle. "That's not proof of anything. We'll *never* prove it now, not unless we can find that tape. If it wasn't in the safe, where would Bob Merritt have thought was a safe place to put it? Who would he have trusted enough to give it to?"

She reached into her wallet and pulled out one of the photographs from the album, the one where Bruce Chambers had his arm wrapped around Bob Merritt's shoulders and they were both grinning. She handed it to him. "They grew up in those woods together, just like me and Emily."

"Where would he have put it, your dad?"

Laura set in place the rest of her tiles. The forest. The all-seeing eye. The knight with his sword. She twisted and fit together the prince, the treasure, the moon, and the sun. There were other tiles, ones with more disturbing imagery, but she fit them into the larger picture just the same.

Like an optical illusion, each one was now part of a larger picture: an image of a large tree split by lightning.

"I've got exactly one guess," Laura said.

* * *

They drove, and then she led him past the house, through the cornfield, across the back acreage of the Chambers farm, and up onto the gravel hump of the train tracks. They hopped from one railroad tie to the next and crossed a trestle over a draw.

Then they were in the longleaf pines, tracing a path through a bone-dry creek bed.

They passed two pines rotting on their sides. The trees had grown too close to each other, and when one fell, it dragged the other down with it.

Laura said, "When I was old enough, we would hunt deer at two different tree stands about a half mile apart. Right in the middle between them is a tree you couldn't miss. Even for a child, it was easy to pick out because it had been struck by lightning. It had a cavity, and we would use it to leave each other messages so neither had to walk the entire mile back and forth. It was a private game between us."

"A secret," Timinski said.

"That's right, it was our special place."

They reached the tree. Laura, who once had to stand up on her tiptoes to reach inside the cavity, now found she had to bend over to get the correct angle. Her father's things were still inside, and she came out bearing cigarettes, matches, and extra ammunition, all sealed up together in a plastic bag.

And from deep inside the tree, she pulled something else.

It was tightly wrapped in many layers of plastic, but the plastic was clear, and she could see that it was a videotape.

She handed it to Timinski.

He turned it in his hands. "Some mail for you here. You want to read it now?" He held it out so she could see.

"Later," she said. "I'll read it later."

Between two of the layers of plastic was an envelope. It had been addressed, the name written in the big capital letters her father had always favored.

It said FOR LAURA.

ORANGE COUNTY SHERIFF ARRESTED;
BARROW EXECUTION DELAYED

By Laura Chambers

September 29, 2019

HILLSBOROUGH, N.C. — Orange County Sheriff Michael Fuller was arrested yesterday on suspicion of murder, allegedly responsible for the shooting death of former Orange County Sheriff Donald Rodgers.

While serving a search warrant at Fuller's home, the North Carolina State Bureau of Investigation discovered a rifle concealed underground at the rear of the property. The FBI ballistics laboratory in Raleigh has subsequently confirmed it to be the murder weapon.

Fuller's attorney, Henry McCraven, made a statement critical of the SBI's tactics. "Sheriff Fuller is entitled to due process just as much as the next citizen, but the government seems determined to try him in the court of public opinion," McCraven said. "The sheriff has not even considered resigning. Expect a plea of not guilty."

This arrest is the latest in a series of developments stemming from the murder of the Sheriff's Office's own Lt. David Whitley by a fellow law enforcement officer, Capt. Raymond Bynum. Bynum took his own life before he could be questioned, but the investigation into these circumstances uncovered a human trafficking scheme that operated in Hillsborough between 1985 and 1996. Evidence suggests both Bynum and Fuller were participants, both in the trafficking itself and in the wide-ranging cover-up that followed.

The North Carolina Department of Justice yesterday issued a statement that the execution of Simon Barrow has been delayed. Barrow, convicted of the murder of Bob and Linda Merritt in 1996 and sentenced to death, spoke publicly for the first time this week. He declared his innocence, and claims to have been silenced during the intervening decades by threats against his family by members of law enforcement.

Sources close to the investigation say the NC DOJ's decision to delay is closely related to the investigation into Sheriff Fuller.

Sheriff Michael Fuller did not respond to a request for comment.

CHAPTER

46

THE MODIFICATIONS MADE to us as children are difficult to alter.

Laura felt that truth acutely as she looked at her mother, draped across the hospital bed, tubes coming out of her, connected to a forest of beeping machines. There was a certain way a daughter was supposed to feel in this situation, but for the life of her, all Laura could summon was the faintest sense of ennui.

Diane blinked at her. "I said, quit staring at me."

The doctor popped his head up from the chart and looked at her. Laura realized he'd asked her a question, but she hadn't been listening.

"Excuse me?"

"You must be pleased, I said. Your mother is awake, and despite her, ah, other health problems, she should make a full recovery. If you have any questions, I would be happy—"

"We're done with you now, young man," said Diane.

The doctor looked at his patient to see if she was serious, then checked in with Laura. Laura gave a little shrug. The doctor closed his mouth and took his leave.

"I talked a while with that doctor out in the hall," Laura said. "He told me you have an autoimmune disorder. That's what's wrong with your lungs, among other things. He said that the disorder is also probably why you had to have a hysterectomy way back when, that your uterine tissue was trying to claw its way into your abdominal cavity."

She pulled the bedsheet up to her chin. "What a disgusting little man. My female parts are none of his business—or yours."

"I looked it up, Diane—it says women with this autoimmune condition can't get pregnant."

"That's not true, it's possible."

"It says the chances are about one in two hundred thousand."

"Miracles happen, Laura!"

"Are you saying I'm a miracle?"

Diane's plump cheeks jiggled in silent laughter. "Your words, not mine."

"Where did I come from?" she asked quietly.

"The stork, my child. You came from the stork."

"You didn't adopt me. I've seen my birth certificate, and you and Daddy are both on there."

"Why, that's the easy part. Anyone can do it," Diane said. "You just stay at home where no one can see you for three or four months to make it believable. Then at the first pediatrician appointment, you just tell them it was a home birth. That's how it worked back then, at least."

"No, Diane, I mean, where did you get a baby?"

"A lady never tells, my dear. Who planted this rotten seed in your head?"

"It was something Captain Bynum said, the way he looked at me when he said it—I knew then."

"Horrible man," said Diane.

"So you knew him?"

"You know I did. I've been reading all your little stories." She stretched the vowels of the last word, mocking it, making her feelings on the matter clear. "Everything you've been writing is true. About the Merritts, about us. How could you do it to me, Laura?"

Laura didn't reply.

"I gobbled up those photo albums from the estate because I wanted to make sure what happened to the Merritts never happened to us."

"You didn't want to get caught, you mean. You erased the connection so no one would ever know what you did."

"For all the good it did. Now our dirty laundry is flapping in the breeze thanks to little Laura."

"There were women?" Laura wanted to know.

"Keep your voice down. Yes, all right? We knew they were using that old root cellar for something illegal, but they told us it was guns. You know your father was 2A all the way. We had money troubles, and it seemed like an acceptable risk for an acceptable reward. By the time we found out what was really going on . . . it was too late."

"You could have gone to the police."

"We would have gone to prison, all of us. When we finally figured it out, Linda Merritt had just had Emily. She was petrified to leave that baby alone in this world. She begged us to keep our mouths shut. Well, she didn't have to ask me twice, I didn't want to go to jail. It was fine for a while."

"And then?"

"A few months after Emily was born, that horrible man, Bynum, he came out of the woods one night and knocked on our door. He was drunk. He said he had a problem, one that needed a woman's touch. He offered big money, so me and your daddy and Bob went out there while Linda stayed back with the baby. Anyway, what we found in that root cellar was not guns."

"Women," Laura said. "Sex trafficking victims."

"I said keep your voice down!"

Laura waited.

"Here's what we walked into: one of the women is dead on the ground with a chain around her neck, and there's a baby screaming, and Bynum, he starts crying, telling us he didn't mean to do it, and that he doesn't know what to do with the kid. He had called Fuller, and Fuller had told him to get rid of it, but Bynum says he can't do it."

Laura felt like she might throw up.

"Bynum's the criminal, not us. But he looks at me like a little boy, all doe-eyed, and he says, 'Ma'am, what should I do?'"

The roomed seemed to shrink, the walls closing in.

"Your doctor friend out there is right; I could never have children. But your father wanted them badly. He took one look at you screaming on that concrete floor and said: we'll take her. Just like that."

Laura felt as if she were about to burst.

"Your daddy convinced them it would bind us even further. Now we could never talk, he said, for fear of losing our child. And he was right. Bob Merritt was a greedy little rube, always had a hand out, so I'm not surprised it ended in tears for the Merritts. When they got killed, Fuller and Bynum told your daddy to make himself scarce until they said otherwise. He was to stay clear of Hillsborough under penalty of . . . well, you can guess, I suppose. They only let him come back because he was about to die anyway."

A crystal shard of understanding skewered Laura in her frontal lobe. "What about you?" she asked. "What did you say, Diane, when I was down there on the ground screaming?"

There was no hesitation in her mother's answer. She didn't even flinch. "I said let bygones be bygones."

* * *

In the hospital lobby, Laura saw a man reading a copy of the *Hillsborough Gazette.* ORANGE COUNTY SHERIFF ARRESTED; BARROW EXECUTION DELAYED blared the headline in hundred-point type. The story was under her byline.

She got in the Dart and drove, drove anywhere, tried to forget. Without meaning to, she drove home.

Up the dirt drive, to the front of the house where she'd grown up.

The Chambers family had maintained a cemetery on its land for generations, but Laura had refused to visit since the day she had to put him in the ground. She walked the unfamiliar path, and under an oak tree, she found her father's grave. Her eyes closed, she thought about the lives lost, the relationships between fathers and daughters haunted by secrets. She breathed deeply.

Laura opened her eyes.

When she was calm, when she was ready, she opened her father's letter.

ACKNOWLEDGMENTS

MY THANKS TO everyone who made this book possible. Thank you to my editor, Melissa Rechter, for her keen insight, and to every member the talented team at Crooked Lane. Thanks to Jenny Chen, who worked on an earlier version of this book. Thank you to my agent, Alice Martell, for her support. A debt is owed to fellow writers who suffered through various early incarnations of this story, and who were always gentle with their feedback: Eryk Pruitt, Russell W. Johnson, Scott Blackburn, and J.M. Rasinske, with a very special thanks to Philip Kimbrough. Thanks and love to my parents, Scott Hetherton and Daisy Gallagher-Hetherton, and my brother, Tait Hetherton. My deepest appreciation for Alice Lamson, Nancy Lamson, Bob Hollister, Brooke Lamson, and Tom Pollard. And the lion's share of gratitude goes, as always, to my wife, Alice, and our children, Ellie and Annie—I couldn't have done it without you.